Valaida

Valaida

Candace Allen

Virago

A *Virago* Book

First published in Great Britain by Virago Press 2004

Copyright © Candace Allen 2004
Acknowledgements on p. 505 form part of this copyright page.

The moral right of the author has been asserted

A CIP catalogue record for this book
is available from the British Library

ISBN 1 86049 944 9

Typeset in Caslon by M Rules
Printed and bound in Great Britain by Clays Ltd, St Ives plc

Virago Press
An imprint of
Time Warner Books UK
Brettenham House
Lancaster Place
London WC2E 7EN

www.virago.co.uk

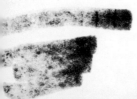

To Simon,
without whose love and support, nothing

And to Billie,
without whose love and example, nothing

I Prelude

Chapter one

Brooklyn, New York, May 1956

Shake it to the east, Sally
Shake it to the west . . .

Little girl giggles riffle through the window on warm spring breezes as the woman in the bedroom dresses to go out. She's small, not more than five foot tall, and lushly fleshed, zipping up a cotton sateen dress, its ivory lustre pleasing contrast to the yellow-brown of her leg, the figure of its print playing subtle background riff to the deep chestnut of her hair. She moves her arms, crooked together, side to side, up, down, and grunts with disgust. The arms are fine; but goddam, she hates a girdle, instrument of the devil sent to reduce the most steadfast woman to a whimpering, low-count slave; only you can't be playing without your underclothes, Miss Valaida, no matter what your dreams . . .

'Ooh, sweet little mama my gift, satin moving one way, caramel cakes moving another! I'm starvin', darlin'! 'Bout to 'spire here for hunger! Come on home to Papa, and let me feast awhile!' And we'd sashay down to shake again and watch them weep.

Them days are long gone, sister. Too much comfort on the rear, too much playground to pull up and in *and* blow a decent tone. Sweat congregating between the rolls, clammy as all get out and unaesthetic, my dear. Fabric getting those telltale lines across it, getting stuck in all the wrong places for all the wrong reasons. Never had that problem when you were still shaking Miss Lucy, but showbiz has changed. It ain't about the grab-'em-grab-'em-love-me wows, as though the knees could handle that any way. They'd be flipping out their sockets on the first stop time. So, deal with it, sugar. Thumbs up and under to adjust those rolls, wrestle that elastic, straighten those stays. Welcome to the world of being almost fifty- . . . well, who's to know, and who's to say? On a good day, Time's a righteous trouper and telling no tales.

A moment in the glass: eyes only red from the inside tip. Eyedrops working wonders on those faint filigrees of strain. A few splashes of Arpege, then the bottle into the case. A necessity, the scent, basic as cake mascara and a questioning eye, needed to rise up from between breasts and defuse surrounding funks of excitation and desperation. Valaida loves her Arpege, and how nice of nephew Charles to spend so many scarce dollars just to please his auntie. He's a good boy, is Charles, doing fine down at Fisk, even if he makes his daddy crazy skipping school to drive the boycotters in Montgomery. Not a bad-looking young man that Reverend Martin Luther King. He's got a soft baby face, must have been coddled by his mama, but there's a smoulder in his eyes. Charles's daddy Marshall practically foaming at the mouth on how he *ain't* paying out his hard-earned cash sending Charles to college so's the boy can chauffeur a bunch of nappy-headed niggers that ain't got dust for brains. Don't need a college education to drive no damn automobile, those days are gone, until

Yolanda said, hush, it's about freedom after all, your freedom, too; and Valaida's Earle threw an arm around his brother's shoulder, took him outside for a stroll and a cigar. It's always about freedom, always has been, always will be. Earle understands this, reflects Valaida with a smile. Maybe that's why this one has lasted.

The doorbell downstairs, followed by voices.

There are three evening dresses hanging on the closet door; two are shades of yellow and one is envy green. Well, the green's not in the spirit of the function, and last time they'd stepped out, she'd strained the gussets hard, been gasping for breath when its hooks were undone, had another one of her spells. It just might be the end of the line for Miss Envy. But the stagehands had wolf-whistled for real, young ones too. We may have to give the green another day.

A child's footsteps running up the stairs.

So, the topaz satin or the daffodil chiffon? It's been warm for early May, gonna be hotter than Hades under those lights.

A light knock on the door.

'Auntie Vee?'

So many names she's had. First Valada, then Valaida. Fru Snowberry, Mrs Edwards. Ladishka, Miss Vee, Val, Auntie Vee. A different aspect for every one of them, and more besides, but Auntie Vee she's finding especially sweet.

'Come on in, honey.'

The girl's nearly taller than Valaida already. Darker-complected with a halo of chin-to-nape-length braids fastened with blue, yellow, and white plastic bow barrettes to match her shirt and shorts, mahogany cat's eyes shining curious and respectful. 'There's a white man downstairs. Says he's here to take you to the the-atre.'

Valaida's standing in front of the mirror, holding up one yellow then another. We were always partial to yellow, not obvious drop-'em-dead maybe, but showing up the tones in our skin . . . *'Enhancing it,' didn't he say? 'A hot-house jungle flower, searing my heart with your dusky heat.' He was a sweet one, that boy, but without a clue. Saved him from himself, or maybe not.*

'Oh, the satin, definitely.'

'It's more than eighty degrees already. Your aunt'll die of heat prostration.'

'Yes, but the way it folds in front makes you look much taller and when you lift Eugene into the lights you'll be a shimmering column of gold!'

'A column laid out on a stretcher, and where'd you learn to say "shimmering"? You're ten years old, Miss Cheryl. Ten-year-olds say "shiny".'

'Miss Piedmont says I know the most words of anyone in my class, but she doesn't know the half of it. Yesterday I heard Granddad talking with Mr Fowler about that lady 'cross the street—'

'Not here, not now, missy. I've got no time to be washing out your mouth. Find the shoes that go with the satin while I check on Eugene. What's the white man's name?'

'Mr Goldman.'

Valaida leans out the door. 'Five minutes, Mr Goldman. Sorry to keep you waiting.'

'No trouble, Miss Snow. We've got plenty of time.' A light, young voice. Early twenties more than like, educated, no knocks, and lying politely. Valaida's pushing it as usual, cutting time to its edge, and she knows it.

Cheryl bags dress and shoes with the practice of a pro, turns to find her aunt tending to Eugene, running caressing fingers over his loops and curves, rubbing the shadow out of his occasional scratch.

'Can I hold him up, Auntie? Just for a sec? I've been lookin' and lookin' at the case since we moved here, but Mama said if I touched it without permission you'd have my hide.'

'Your mama was absolutely right. Would you like to hold him now?'

'But what about the white man?'

6

'The white man's fine,' informs Valaida. 'Don't be turning down chances that may never come again. Come on over here.'

Cheryl leans into her auntie's bosom while wrapping her hand carefully around the trumpet's valves, stretching her left fingers to flutter over its pistons, then steps forward grandly to catch herself in the glass.

'Ladies and gentlemen, *mesdames et messieurs*, *mine damer og herrer*, Cheryl Edwards, Queen of the Trumpet!'

Down comes Eugene. 'Not me, Auntie Vee. I'm gonna be a nurse.'

'Make it a doctor, and I'll let you have your way. No clever girl-kin of mine's going to be slopping chamberpots.'

'But Mama says that doctor schools don't like to take girls.'

'That may be true, but if we only did what folks wanted us to do we'd still be picking cotton with rags on our backs. You liked the red and green flowered dress we got at Altman's yesterday?'

'Yes, but—'

'No but. If we only did what folks said we should, it would have been made out of a feed bag and handed down from your sister Lila.'

Cheryl's never seen a feed bag, but the idea makes her giggle. 'You're so funny, Auntie Vee! Mama says you're Something Else.'

'She's not the first one. Now hand me back Eugene before the young man gets too jumpy.' The trumpet slides back comfortably into its blue plush womb. There was a time the womb was red, but it's been blue now for quite a while. Cool blue. Cooler styles, cooler thoughts, cooler notes, cooler times. Softer, mellower. Cool. But hot too, staccato heat. Focused, intense, like a blowtorch flame. What we're looking for anyhow.

'He sure looks pretty, Auntie.'

'That he does, sweetheart.'

'Did you ever think anything else looked this good?'

'You're way out ahead of yourself today, missy. Some mysteries a girl has to figure on her own.'

'Did you?'

'I certainly tried, but we better get downstairs before the young man pees himself. These charity concert white folks have a tendency towards nerves.'

Riding smooth in this long quiet car. She always did like a long, quiet car. The orchid Mercedes. When was that? 1930 . . . something. Now she was a sweet one. Inside, room for crystal drinks service and a game of rummy, while outside, heads turned, lips whistled, children chased, and their mamas tut-tutted . . . Is this an Oldsmobile? Earl Hines had had an Oldsmobile. How come she'd had so many Earls in her life? Some women had their Williams and Lord knows a pack have had their Johns. Valaida's speciality has been Earls and not one of them worth good goddam until this last with the 'e' on the end. Radio rumouring on trouble in Hungary. How did she manage not to play Hungary? There'd been times to be had in Budapest, so she'd been told, all that gypsy fire, boat rides down the Danube at dawn . . .

The driver's brow is high and clear. He's got a sensitive jaw that could learn to be strong, a slender neck moving to the knot in his tie, abundant black hair not wanting to know its place. A lock of it has worked itself free, flipped forward to skirt above the eyes. Shoulders not wide, but straight and held back. Dancers' shoulders, but no way he's a dancer. Might have run track, but how good could he have been unless he was running from something or fixing to get somewhere? Has that high, clear brow ever known need? The sun's suddenly stronger, blindingly strong, jumping off the dashboard like a half-mad gorilla. The topaz satin? She's going to melt tonight, going to ooze down the floor in a pretty, pride-full puddle, which will serve her right, entrusting her health to a child. But a wonderful child, smart, direct; Cheryl could shake her world. Valaida digs in her bag and pulls out her darker shades. Not as fashionable as the ones she has been wearing; she'll be sure to switch back to snazzy before her Palace entrée. The young man is tense. Valaida turns to him and smiles.

8

'This is a nice car, Mr Goldman. You keep it well.'

'Please, call me Paul, and it's my father's car.'

'Well then, Paul. You handle it well.'

Paul's fingers relax their grip of the wheel. He glances quickly over to the dusky woman by his side, now casually massaging her right hand with her left. The fingernails are short and polished. Their colour would match the necklaces brought back from Florida by almost every woman he knows, the ones with all those branchy things. Co . . . co . . . cobalt? No, cobalt's blue. Coral? Yeah. Coral. The fingers look strong going through their bend and flex. Flashing glamour. Paul clears his throat and decides to take the plunge.

'My father's a big fan of yours, Miss Snow. He used to catch you all the time at the Apollo and the Lafayette. He said he wished you hadn't spent so many years away.'

Heavy-framed dark lenses turn directly onto him. 'How nice of him to say so, but what was your father doing at the Apollo and the Lafayette?'

Damn it's hot, like the dog days of August at the beginning of May. Paul's wondering why he didn't save the tie for later. He could have worn that open-necked shirt he'd bought last year with Hannah, the one she thought looked cool, but then Paul isn't very good at cool. It is the core of Paul's deepest longings that the burgeoning battle for Negro rights will bring more justice to America, and that the advent of integration will also teach him cool.

'My father grew up in Harlem, so they were his neighbourhood nightspots. He was wondering if you might remember Goldman's Variety? On the corner of One Hundred-Thirty-Third and Seventh Avenue? He said lots of show people bought their trunk supplies there, bottles and hangers, things like that. He thinks he remembers you coming in once or twice.'

It's hard to know what she's thinking behind the very dark shades, but the heat has raised a dewy mist on her cheeks, which a light finger could erase . . .

Valaida smiles. 'I probably did.'

'He'd love an autographed picture if it wasn't too much trouble.'

'He won't be at the benefit tonight?'

'Well, he will actually, but he wanted me . . . He won't be coming backstage . . .'

Valaida waits.

'I've got a jealous step-mother.'

Valaida laughs, her contralto taking the young man by surprise. 'Should she be?'

Now he's blushing. Always attractive unless the skin's cratered or scarred, which this boy's is not, naturally. No scars in his world, no blades, no poxes. 'Of course not!' he says.

'How do you know? Are you your father's keeper?'

'Well, no, I'm not . . .' Paul laughs, flustered. And delighted. He could have been driving Henny Youngman. Great jokes maybe, but nowhere near the ride.

A light's turned green with the boy just staring front, lips fighting the grin that wants to lope across his face. Yes, the chin could be made real strong by a knowledgeable woman with time on her hands, which Valaida knows not to be an apt description of who she's been. 'Come on back, Mr Goldman. Drive this car and don't be letting total strangers into your family business. What's your father's name?'

'Emanuel. Manny. Manny Goldman.'

'Come backstage any time this evening, and you'll have a signed autographed picture with all best wishes from Valaida through Paul to Manny.'

'I'd like one for myself, if it wouldn't be too much trouble.'

'If I've brought enough along, it would be no trouble at all.'

Too hot sunlight shuttering through the trees, some stiffness in her fingers, and lies all around. Jewish shopkeeper from Harlem grabs fast onto the New York dream, has a business in the West Thirties now, a homestead out in New Rochelle, a second wife strutting out in knock-off Pauline Trigere, and an unabated hunger for the old dark rhythms; making hand-over-fist dollars but riffing on the time when lithe-limbered hoofers in cock-of-the-walk threads slouched into Goldman's Variety for their Herkert & Meisel Theatrical Trunks' supplies, juggled verbal plates and torches while the Owner's Son, behind the counter, could hardly wrap up the chamois, sponges, and sterno pots for fascination and the hope that maybe some of the girls would come strutting in as well, silk crêpes slipping around red or violet-silked knees, cloche hats pinned to ebony marcels, fingers glittering with brilliants, some of them real. And when the Variety finally pulls down its shade at an hour convenient to late-rising clientele, he's grabbing his hat, the Owner's Son, and rushing into the street, maybe to a theatre or maybe to the Savoy, where, with dimes he's hoarded away all week long, he can dance with girls that just might be strutting in silk one day, feel the rhythm flow from them, truck a bit or fly, and maybe, just maybe, get to more than that, get to wrap himself in burnt-yellow/bronze/coffee-coloured arms, fingers searching the thrilling rough of kinking hair, nose, lips nuzzling a different form of musk. Dusky musk. Sepia lust. Groin twitching with the memory that can't be touched upon around the Second Wife, who acts as though she's only known the civility of New Rochelle (she lies) and prefers her serenades by the strings of Mantovani rather than the soul-thumping stomps of Lunceford, Basie, or Eckstine. So, Manny's got this drawer in his office, the one secured with the key even his secretary doesn't have, and in it piles his trove from the life that never was. Valaida's picture will go there. He'll take it out sometimes, when the office is totally deserted and he's tossing back the double scotch that sets him up for home and the evening's *Woman's Day* delight. He lies and she lies about pasts that did and didn't happen, and why the hell not? Just who the hell made history a god?

'I'm sorry about the traffic, Miss Snow. Maybe I should stop and give the theatre a call.'

'Relax, Mr Goldman—'

'Paul, please, Paul.'

'Paul. Relax. It's rehearsal. They'll figure it out.'

Paul can't relax. Traffic has come to a standstill; the temperature's going up. His task is to deliver this woman to the theatre by one-thirty and it's past one-thirty. Paul's out of the car, to learn the cause of the commotion, chart another course to the Palace, or maybe just for air as Dinah Washington's husky tears willow-weep through the afternoon haze from a record store across the way. There are Negroes all around – '*Verdammte Schwarzes*,' his Great-Uncle Herbie would say. '*You can't trust them, Paulie. They're a primitive people, a primitive people. You don't blame them, no, because they ain't made like us. But trust them? You never trust them.*' If Paul asked for a shortcut, would he be told the truth? Is it true what they say about time and coloured people? It's melting towards two, and the dark-glassed dark woman in his father's front seat looks as calm as she could be.

Unflustered, unfazed, and taking in the sights. Valaida's been making it to gigs for some forty-odd years. You get there. One way or another. There's a light-skinned man of maybe twenty-two halfway out the door of Dinah Washington's record shop, ribbed-knit shirt sliding across well-built chest, casual stance advertising a host of attributes, almost-good hair slicked into layback by the power of Congolene, hunting gaze taking in a clutch of drivers moving towards frustrated push-out in the street and two young honeys, waiting for a bus, pigmeat, shirtwaisted schoolgirl prey. Conked hair glistens orange in the sun as Slick slides close up on the women, seeps into their space, conjuring sweetness to the purr of Dinah's vanished summer dreams. The girls are young enough to listen and old enough to know better; at eight years old they already knew better; posing, like he's getting nowhere, but obeahed by the lies. Stances adjusting, leaning into the lies, shifting away. Their bus has appeared, three blocks down the way. Will he cop before it comes? This stretch belongs to him; this concrete's his domain, sidewalk courtship his art form, this moment his mastery. A particular angle on a cheekbone and Valaida has to smile. John Snow. It could be Papa John Snow, stalking new territories and poaching Etta Mae. Papa Too Good. Too bad. It was too easy. She was a Christian.

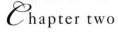

Chapter two

Washington, DC, 1898

'Etta Mae! Etta Mae!'

In a centre dress circle box of her city's Academy of Music, Etta Mae Washington is only minimally aware of the nudgings and silvery giggles of the companion by her side. Despite the large numbers in attendance at this performance of John W. Isham's famous *Octoroons*, Etta Mae Washington is in a dream world of her own. She has never been to a real theatricale, and she would not be savouring the glorious gowns of the beauteous Octoroon chorus, appreciating their graceful movements to music pulsing from the orchestra pit, wouldn't be here at all in fact, if it weren't for her dear friend Allegretta Simpson.

Etta Mae's people don't hold with music that's not for the glory of God, but they, like most everyone who comes across her path, are as nothing before the charms of Allegretta. Daughter of a

13

former Congressman, with three generations of culture behind her, Allegretta is the pixie angel of Washington's coloured elite. The alabaster pearl of her complexion is appreciated by one and all as the essence of her soul; the copper fire of her hair, the radiant warmth of a democratic heart. Allegretta is not a snob. Despite being at least four shades darker than accepted desirability, with a hard-working but barely literate coachman father and a mother who caters wonderful pies, pies commissioned by the households of the city's most discriminating Caucasians, but pies nonetheless, Etta Mae Washington is Allegretta's best friend. The girls' fellowship began in the music rooms of Howard University, for Allegretta's angelic nature extends to her voice as well, and in Etta Mae, ignored by many for the humbleness of her background and near complete self-effacement, but amazingly gifted with all the womanly instruments, piano, harp, mandolin, cello, Allegretta found an accompanist of exquisite sensitivity, whose modest exterior veiled a core of such inordinate depth and wonder.

'It's in your eyes, Etta Mae,' Allegretta often declared. 'If you would only lift up your eyes, all the world could see what I know.'

It's generally accepted among coloured Washington's Upper Tens that Allegretta will marry an appropriate young man, a Syphax or a Grimke, Henry Shadd or Cyrus Bell, to name but two of the number hovering ceaselessly about her flame. She will establish an exemplary home, and nurture two or three children to further propel and Represent the Race. She will be a 'parlour lady', who will chair women's clubs devoted to culture and good works, who might lecture on occasion to organizations for less fortunate but worthy women seeking self-improvement. But Allegretta sees another future for herself. She has no intentions of closeting up with coloured Washington's bourgeoisie, whose ever vigilant insulations cannot obscure the fact that the Race has been heading relentlessly back instead of forward. There are no longer any Negro senators, and the few congressmen remaining have not the slightest exercise of power. Jim Crow has not been introduced onto capital streetcars yet, but it will come. It will come. Even the strongest optimists know this truth deep down in their souls, and Allegretta has resolved not to simply sit and wait for this unpleasantness within the comforts of her cocoon. She dreams a world of beauty and delight, of music and adventure. She intends to tour the world's concert stages singing wondrous songs attesting to the magnificence of her birthright. Mozart, Schubert, Coleridge-Taylor, Donizetti, with sorrow songs as a balancing American touch and sometimes, when she's feeling particularly spritely, a bit of James Bland. *Oh! Dem Golden Slippers! The Negro voice is not all sadness after all.*

And Etta Mae is part of Allegretta's dream. Etta Mae will accompany and perhaps – with Allegretta's encouragement and that of enlightened, unprejudiced individuals they're bound to find beyond their own benighted shores, who will marvel at Etta's art – finally, finally, dare to compose.

Allegretta is not alone in her assessment of Etta's virtues. Struck by Etta's talents, the professor in charge of piano study at Howard had gently expanded Etta's perceptions of where the sacred was found in music and made his own fine instrument available to her for practise. No, there was no questioning Etta's gifts. What she lacked was self-confidence and even the smallest sense of entitlement to joy. Her people are so serious! Allegretta wonders if Mr Washington has ever cracked a smile. No dancing, no singing outside the church, no playing cards, no ribbons, for goodness' sake! Only work and Trust in the Coming Reward. It is amazing to think that Mrs Washington's craft is pies, for isn't sugar a frivolity after all? Doesn't sugar make your taste buds want to dance? Allegretta has been raised to venerate the truth, and she can't imagine lying to achieve a purely selfish end; but her dear friend Etta Mae *needed* to see the *Octoroons*. She *had* to experience the fizzle of music as social and secular fun because if Etta Mae remains outside the realm of joy, she'll never be open to Allegretta's plans; and Allegretta needs Etta Mae. Only Etta Mae's playing has coaxed Allegretta's voice so surely into the worlds it seeks to conquer. And so, late this morning, Allegretta had sat up in Mrs Washington's kitchen and sworn, as though butter would be hard pressed to melt in her mouth, that the afternoon's entertainment to which she was inviting Etta Mae was the performance of a visiting Methodist choir, to be followed by a simple soirée at the Simpson home (the latter part at least was true), and wouldn't Mrs Washington like to come as well (knowing full well that with near a dozen pies cooling on racks and up to her elbows in flour for near a dozen more, there was nary a chance Mrs Washington could venture out the door)? Etta Mae did her best not to gag while her mother pondered then finally agreed that it would be most edifying for Etta Mae to hear how other believers sang the Lord's blessings. Did Allegretta feel guilty manipulating love of the Lord to a cause as lapsed as John Isham's *Octoroons*? Well, yes she had for a bit, but then the show had begun, and the music and the comedians and the look on Etta's face . . .

Such an orgy of delight it was being here, part of which had to be watching the audience embrace the show, which was not all that different from being in church, if you looked at things creatively. Well, maybe not her own St Luke's Episcopal, where diamonds, lace, and refinement were the order of the day, but the shouting, rolling churches so abhorred by the Upper Tens, which Allegretta attended upon occasion with her thrill-seeking cousin Roscoe? There the congregation could put on a show; and who was to say that the sister rolling in the aisles, dimity petticoats flying and arms stretched over head, wasn't directing her spirits to a good-looking reverend as much as that hussy third from the left in the Octoroon chorus line, with the project-her-bosoms back and the fake beauty spot just to the right of her eye, was casting her net for any moneyed man she could find; and who was swimming closer to that net than Lemuel Tyler, whose fiancée, Amanda Gilliard, would simply die of embarrassment if she could see her betrothed carrying on in this way, except it would probably do her good, since everybody knows Lemuel Tyler to be the first and last reprobate, trawling bawdy houses for pleasure with exceedingly more diligence than he ever displays in his studies for the law.

16

'Etta Mae, have you seen Lemuel Tyler? Why he's drooling over himself! All the time posing as the suave sophisticate when he's really just as common as a barnyard dog! Did you see him over there?'

'Lemuel? Well no, actually, I didn't. Should I have?' Etta's voice is so soft and hesitant that Allegretta just has to wrap her friend in a hug.

'Are you enjoying it, Etta Mae? Are you glad we've come?'

'Glad' goes nowhere near describing the emotions of Etta Mae (though she herself couldn't find a better word, for Etta Mae is as modest with words as she is with everything else). As the Octoroon Chorus sashays into the wings and the comic team of Tom McIntosh and his wife Hattie bigfoots and harrumphs before the curtain for the next olio, Etta Mae smooths the fabric of her russet wool skirt, feels its reassuring, familiar texture along the palms of her hands, runs a finger under tucks secured by the precise, tiny stitches she learned at her mother's side. Easier to contemplate these known things, which represent the best that she is, has come from, than consider the meanings of this day out with Allegretta. Burnt-corked Tom chides his partner, using the name of the Lord in vain. He is blasphemous; he is funny. Etta pulls a delicate lace handkerchief from her sleeve. Her upper lip is moist. Would blotting it bring too much attention to the confusion she feels?

The handkerchief, a gift from her mother upon entering Howard's Minor Normal School, is the one true luxury Etta has ever owned; but even in the face of Allegretta's vast array of pretties, Etta has never felt a twinge of envy, never once felt she had reason to complain, for had not her own parents, both hailing from the most degraded of circumstances, starting with nothing more than their fire to survive, supplied her with all the nurture there was to give and supported her love of music beyond their own imaginations? Etta could never be grateful enough to a father who, upon seeing his child's fascination with sounds she produced plucking stretched yarn from her mother's darning basket, had gathered wood and catgut to fashion a mandolin with his own hands; and she will never forget the day her father brought the spinet home. The instrument had been in a desperately sorry state, but Henry Washington, with his wife Cora's blessings, had taken it as payment for a two-week hauling job, rather than money for fuel and food, rather than lumber to repair the outhouse wall, and, again, sacrificed precious hours of rest, gluing, re-stringing, laboriously replacing felts until the piano produced sounds vaguely within the boundaries of music.

Etta is the child of the Washingtons' later life, their Freedom life. She is the God-granted miracle of a love formed in the chaos that followed the emancipating war, when roads and countrysides teemed with the chalk to charcoal rainbow of former slaves seeking new beginnings. She was neither her mother's first nor only child. Three of the slave Cora's children had been wrenched from her side, sold as a job lot at ages thirteen, ten, and six, when their master/father's rice came up a cropper two years in a row. The babies left, Violet and Caleb, ages three years and ten months, died in the fever that fouled the Carolinas in the summer of 1863. Isolated by grief and the machinations of the McGintys, Cora didn't hear of Emancipation till more than a year after the deed, till after the war had finally ended; but the very next night, all that night, she was down in the copse by the graves of her little ones, telling them how much she loved and missed them, begging their forgiveness for leaving their plots to nature, but saying that she had to leave this blighted place, for their sweet souls as much as for her own. Then, at first light, she scooped a handful of earth from each of the mounds, sewed them into a pocket, and hit the road, taking nothing else with her, not a bowl, not a blanket, not a single ear of corn. After thirty-one years dedicated to the support and comfort of the Broadlands Plantation, with its raping, child-stealing master blind and raving helpless in the last stages of disease, with his wife offering bribes of silk and silver if only Cora would stay just a few short months – *'But we're your only family, Cora! How can you leave us now?'* – Cora had wanted nothing from the only place she'd ever known but distance.

Cora met Henry Washington in the rainbow. He never would speak much of the past, only that he had come from down Alabama way and left early to fight with the Union. An acquaintance told tales of valiant spy missions and leading wavering slaves to the righteous cause, proclaiming Henry a hero of the race; but Henry would neither say yes or no, just stand there impassive, waiting for the man to change the subject or get tired and walk away. Cora respected Henry's ways, and from the day that they met, he always made sure that she had fresh game to eat and watched over her in sleep. For the first time in her life, Cora felt protection. It was bewildering, to tell the truth, near as dizzying as freedom.

Arriving in their nation's capital, Cora and Henry joined many other freed couples in formalizing their union in the eyes of church and state, and had not been parted since. Both the Washingtons bear masters' blood in their veins; she is the colour of cured tobacco, he café au lait; but unlike so many members of the District's coloured elite, they had derived no benefits from their Caucasian kith and kin. There had been no manumissions in their tangled family trees, no land grants, no reading, but they worked hard in freedom – Henry hauling freight and then passengers, Cora taking in laundry and sewing, then purveying coveted confections to the town's rich households, both coloured and Caucasian – and they prospered. Etta Mae was born a dozen years into the Washingtons' peace together, years after they knew such a gift could never be. She was their faith's reward.

Though he can barely write his name, Henry has always treasured books and the power they possess. The Good Book soothed souls and directed nations. A Northern white woman's novel had prodded consciences toward the right of abolition. There was never any question that Etta should stop or slow her schooling to earn. Her acceptance to Howard's preparatory school was the day of her father's greatest pride. He, who had been confined to stud cabins to impregnate field women and never more than held a baby in his arms, who had been whipped senseless at age nine for merely picking up a book, had raised up a lived-with, learned daughter. Both Henry and Cora pray that Etta will become a teacher, a profession they endow with near-religious significance, and perhaps later find the protection of an upright Christian man. The Washingtons wouldn't mind a life of chastity for their child, would prefer it to her living the degradations they have known; and Etta has been at home within her parents' wishes.

Etta dearly loves her mother and father, has always done her best to live as they'd approve; yet she is here at this performance of Isham's *Octoroons*, reeling from the enormity of her transgression while embracing the excitement of this vertigo as well. Her dear friend Allegretta has a luminous soul and a big heart. Etta celebrates the union their music represents – it and love of the Lord lift her spirits to the sky – but Allegretta is a flighty-minded girl. Whatever does hearing 'No Coon Can Come Too Black For Me' have to do with singing Schubert in Berlin? Not that Etta can really conceive of playing Schubert in Berlin or London or St Petersburg or any of the other far-flung cities that Allegretta has described in such detail and could be Brobdingnag or Atlantis as far as Etta is concerned. If Etta Mae could ever contemplate the mere idea of ruse, she might consider that Allegretta had other reasons for attending the show, like displaying her delicate pastel beauty against Etta Mae's sombre earth for the appreciation and, yes, titillation of one Winfield Hannibal Gardner, a young man so disreputable that even the extraordinarily broad-minded Simpsons have barred him from their door. Allegretta is happy for her parents' protection, has no intentions of encumbering her future plans with men; but Winfield is so shockingly wicked, and what a triumph to slip a ring through his well-shaped nose! But Etta's mind does not function that way, so she is without distractions and defenceless against the *Octoroon* assault. Against every precept she's been trained to, Etta is enthralled by the company's harmonies and sass, by the struts from bodies not studying on the wrath of a vengeful God. Enjoying themselves. Not serving, not praying. Enjoying themselves.

20

The theatre aches with laughter at the McIntoshes parting jibes. The music changes. The curtains part.

Young women in mantillas wave their fans from a properly demure distance as their swains, the Spanish Serenaders, commence to plead their troth in song. Swain Number One is funny, a long, tall drink of chocolate mirth. His señorita, feigning embarrassed annoyance, raps her fan on his outstretched palm, returns him hang-dog morose to the Serenader line; and then comes the turn of Swain Number Two, a shorter, lighter, classically beautiful man, with a high, brooding brow and vermilion, voluptuous lips. He steps forward, Number Two, fixes his intended with ardent regard, then lets slip a voice of such ethereal tenor sweetness that the women of the audience swoon immediately into his web. Their collective bosoms sigh, their collective hearts a-flutter with pulse of Cupid wings. Etta's perspiring hand tightens on her no longer dainty bit of lace. A persimmon flush surges through her burnt-sugar cheeks.

In the company of any self-respecting 1890s travelling theatricale, the Tenor's job is to seduce the ladies, bring tears to their eyes, throbbing to their loins, their silver poised and ready for the next return engagement, and Swain Number Two knows his job. There is such tenderness in his entreaties, so many avenues inviting entry into the heart of a Sensitive Soul. Etta imagines herself rushing headlong down such a road, deep into the dominion of such eyes, such a heart, washing away this unaccustomed heat she's feeling in the cool, clear waters of his nature's lush Eden . . .

After the performance, Allegretta had insisted upon a flirtation with Winfield Gardner in front of the theatre, happy in the certainty that news of the encounter would be speeded to her parents, who in turn would try to distract her from the scoundrel with yet another gown. Etta had stood silently on the side for the entirety of the exchange, the teasing idiom of such courtship indecipherable as Arabic to her ears. It would not have been her choice to spend so much time directly beside a playbill advertising

Isham's *Octoroons*. Was it her feelings of guilt, or had the woman in the brown straw hat boarding the streetcar across the way not been Sister Hunter of her church's Women's Auxiliary? Had not the woman in the brown hat turned to look across the street after boarding as though to get a better look? If it had been Sister Hunter, Etta's certain future would involve Sister Hunter going direct to Sister Washington before returning to her own Christian home to report the aberration of a member of their congregation, namely the Washingtons' only daughter treading anywhere near such an example of the Devil's own work. How could Etta face her parents if confronted with her lie? She'd never even thought of bearing false witness before or acting so contrary to her parents', no her own, religious beliefs, but would she really have wanted to miss the *Octoroons*' performance? Was it really so sinful to witness what really seemed to be such innocent exuberance and experience such fun? Yes, it had been fun! But was it right to be thinking this way? Should she even be asking such questions? Should she instead be praying for guidance and forgiveness?

'You don't approve of me, Etta,' said her friend, as they hurried across M Street. 'I can see it in your eyes.' It seemed that every cab willing to service coloured had been snapped up by more diligent *Octoroon* patrons, and another streetcar just had not come.

'Disapprove? Not exactly, no, not ever . . . I just don't understand you is all. If Winfield is so worthless, and you don't like him at all, why do you spend the time?'

'Oh Etta, because it's fun! Because when he wants to touch my hand, and I know I'll never let him, I get a stirring at the back of my neck . . .' Her friend's expression is both troubled and bewildered, and Allegretta's laughter is a tumble of silver bells. 'Dearest, Etta, you really don't know what I mean! Aren't you ever even curious? I mean, what about Edgar Johnson? Am I mistaken or have I not seen him with the moon eyes whenever you walk into class?'

'Edgar Johnson? Edgar Johnson? But he's only fifteen! He's still throwing spit-balls!'

'You've got to start somewhere!'

'But with Edgar Johnson? Edgar Johnson?' Even Etta has to laugh at this. 'You're going to take that back!'

The friends are breathless as they hurry up the grand Simpson walkway with its well-trimmed shrubs and opulent hydrangeas, straightening their skirts, securing their hairpins, fanning their cheeks. Etta's recent gaiety has passed. She is nervous now. She has been to the Simpson home a few times before, has marvelled at its glistening wood floors overlaid with subtly figured carpets, its opulently heavy drapes, the framed diplomas and free papers, the antebellum silver, its gilded harp that no one can play, its piano from Germany, but she's never been to one of Viola Simpson's renowned and coveted 'at homes'.

The door is answered by a uniformed buxom blonde, eyes dutifully cast to the floor, broad-faced and square-handed.

'Hello, Maria. Have many of the guests arrived?'

'Quite a number, Miss Allegretta. Your mother already pours.' Maria's words are thick with the stolid burr of her Rhenish homeland and do nothing towards setting Etta's heart at ease. There is eeriness to a household where white will work for coloured, like a shiny toy stuck upside-down, but liable to right itself at any moment. Maria boards in, but on her few days off meets girls like herself, hard-working peasant stock, slowly deciphering the ways of this New World. When will she learn to use the cursed word? The Simpsons know that the day will come when Maria will at least be thinking that word, when her eyes will lift and her lips will smirk, and Mrs Simpson will do the cleaning until someone else is found. For all the elegant trappings, Etta sees no blessings in living this way. She moves her skirts out of Maria's path, and follows Allegretta into the parlour.

'Stay close to me, Etta. You have such a good effect on Mother.'

The parlour sparkles more than normal, with heavy bouquets in crystal vases alongside silver trays laden with delicate treats. Laces and silks are swishing, jewels are sparkling, ladies are laughing, but not too loudly. Some guests, while smiling and waving at Allegretta, wonder at the identity of her darker, subdued shadow, and Etta is wondering why she agreed to come. She has transgressed by attending *The Octoroons*. Will her payment be two-fold, shunning here among the coloured community's aristocracy, and only the Lord knows what at home? Across the room, Allegretta's mother, Viola, sits at her Meissen tea service, which was transported from Europe three voyages ago and remains the envy of all of her set. Mrs Simpson is a formidable woman, able to pour with elegance, conduct polite conversation, and silently interrogate her approaching daughter at the self-same time. Her current companion is a distinguished-looking man of the cloth, the only hint to whose ancestry is the slightest shadow about the eyes.

'You surprise me, Viola,' he is saying. 'Whenever I see a notice for yet another cakewalk contest with its promise of over-dressing, over-prancing, gutter-bound buffoonery, I pray to our Lord for patience. The dominant race will never take our better classes seriously while we suffer these jamborees in silence!'

'I don't suffer them in silence, Reverend. I tap my foot. But we won't take this any further at the moment, for my wayward daughter has arrived at last; and she's about to take my seat so that I may better attend my guests, including you, Reverend Wilson. I must introduce you to Euphonia Hickock. She agrees with you completely.' Viola offers her cheek to her daughter to be kissed.

'Hello, Mother. There were no cabs again. It's getting worse and worse.'

Viola puts a finger to her daughter's lips. 'I know why you were late and the reason behind it, which has nothing to do with Jim Crow cabs, and it's not going to work. You've had more than your share of gowns this season, young lady, and I will instruct your father accordingly. Welcome, Etta Mae. I must say I'm disappointed. You usually manage to keep my daughter closer to the

24

path of good sense, but I trust your playing later on will convince me to forgive you.'

Reverend Wilson is aghast. 'Not ragtime!'

'Oh, of course not, Samuel. Meyerbeer. Come along.'

'Oh well,' said Allegretta, settling into her chair, 'it could have been worse, I guess. She could have forbidden me hats as well. Would you like a cup of tea?'

Etta shakes her head. The last thing she wants to do is juggle one of those irreplaceable cups with this entire room wondering how she came to be here. She'd rather some lemonade. The gaslights have been lit, the atmosphere has become closer, and Etta's one good dress is heavy for the District in late spring. Perhaps she should take up Allegretta's offer of a hand-me-down dress. She'd have to change it, of course, remove the ever-present bows and fripperies; but if she altered one for her mother as well, maybe her father would not disapprove. For all his severity, Henry Washington dearly loved seeing his Cora smile, and would his Cora not smile at having Allegretta's dark blue cotton? Etta's mother worked so hard. What a wonderful gift a new dress would be, or was just being in this room a corrupting influence? Was Etta thinking far too much of unimportant, worldly things? Did she not indeed have all that she needed? Had not last Tuesday evening's lesson been that to covet was a sure step down into the belly of the Beast? Why had she agreed to come to this suffocating parlour? She didn't even like Meyerbeer! What she really should do was make her excuses.

Having left Reverend Wilson in the sympathetic company of Euphonia Hickock, Viola has moved through her guests to receive her last two arrivals, two young men, both well-dressed, though one flashier than the other. Viola embraces the less flamboyant and accepts introduction to his companion with an expression at once bemused and noncommittal. Allegretta is tugging at Etta's skirt.

'Etta Mae, do you know who that is, who just came in with my cousin Roscoe? There! There! Look! Don't you recognize him?

He's from *The Octoroons*, one of the Spanish Serenaders! Don't you remember him? The one with the voice, that glorious tenor? Didn't you just want to fall right into a lover's arms when you heard him sing? I can't believe he's here! However did Roscoe get to know him? That Roscoe! He does go such places. But bringing him here! His mother would just die if she knew. Etta, don't you see? Over there in the grey!'

Etta doesn't need her friend's prodding. She recognizes the man in grey, and once again her handkerchief has been brought into service. The heat radiating from Etta's bosom is beyond what her dainty can handle, all the more disturbing for its unexpected onslaught, and Etta is overtaken by the certainty that it is time to quit this place. Had Mrs Simpson not raised her hand that very instant, summoning the girls to play, Etta would have made her excuses. No matter what the Simpsons' disappointment, no matter what the smirks of their guests, Etta would have excused herself, stammering probably, stumbling perhaps, but instead she takes her place at the piano, where, while Mrs Simpson introduces the coming musical offering, Etta's flushes gently recede; for Allegretta is wrong about her friend. Etta is familiar with joy. It is here within the ivory, ebony, and steel of this piano, in the brass of its pedals, in the timbre of its chords, elusive, yes, but there for the having with application. Allegretta assumes her posture, moving her head slightly into profile. This is Etta's cue. She inhales and applies fingertips to ivories.

The last notes of the Meyerbeer are greeted by enthusiastic applause. Allegretta has bowed her head in the manner of an accomplished réciteuse, then, unable to contain her excitement, quickly looks up with a captivating grin. She might not have the range of Anna Madah Hyers or the soaring majesty of Sissieretta Jones, but she is beautiful, musical, and lovable anywhere you might find her, but particularly here in her parents' parlour. Etta knows the applause is not for her, but she does not mind. It has been enough to play this magnificent instrument, and it will be easier to take her leave with attentions elsewhere. Having fulfilled her promise, she will thank her hostess and make the long trip home to whatever awaits her. She slides to the end of the piano's bench, with one last, light caress of immaculate keys, wondering if she will ever play its like again.

'I thought somebody ought to compliment the accompanist.' It is a male voice. 'I thought you were very good.'

'I would have liked to practise more.' Etta's eyes are down. She is embarrassed by compliments and wishes only to slip away. 'I made mistakes.'

'If so, you made it seem as if nothing had happened. That takes a skill of its own.' Home training demands that Etta look up, and her world reverses its spin.

'Have you been studying long?' asks the man in grey.

'A good long time,' Etta says. 'I have been blessed.'

'No, we have,' replies the man. He is not as tall as he appeared on stage. The ripples of his pomaded, dark chestnut hair glisten in the gaslight. The hair is wavy good and parted to the left, his eyes light, hazel cat's eyes flecked with emerald green and gold. Etta's never been so close to a man's light eyes. How well they complement his golden complexion. He wears a richly brocaded waistcoat beneath the dove-grey jacket. There's a diamond stickpin in his foulard tie. Etta's eyes have dropped again. His buttoned kid shoes match his suit.

'John Snow,' says the man, extending his hand.

Home training coming into play once more. 'Etta Washington,' she murmurs, taking the hand. It feels cool and strong.

'This *is* a hand that could play with such grace.' Etta pulls away, and John Snow smiles. 'I don't mean to offend you.'

'You didn't. It's just that it's time for me to leave.'

His smile brings out the slight crinkles by his eyes. Is it years or what he's seen? 'But we've only just met.'

Etta has no idea what to say to this. Her ears are throbbing. She needs to go home. 'Excuse me, but I really have to go,' she says.

'Are you going far?'

'Georgetown.'

After she has made her apologies, she finds him waiting, hat in hand, in the foyer. 'Georgetown is too far for you to venture all alone. If you will allow me . . .'

'But you've only just arrived.' *What does one do?* Can that noise be her heart?

'And we've only just met, but I can assure you that I'd trust me before I'd allow myself to walk along Florida Avenue at this hour unescorted.' He sees her glancing furtively into the parlour, hoping to catch Allegretta's eye, but Allegretta is settling into a game of whist. She thinks Etta already gone. John Snow smiles.

'Your friend doesn't know me any better than you do, and no self-respecting lady would take Roscoe's recommendation. You will have to trust your instincts.'

What is in that smile? It is not innocent. It knows more than that of any man to have stepped so far into her space. From outside saloons, of course, passing in the street, naturally, along with the whistles and the comments; but a lady averted her eyes and kept her own counsel, and there was never the feeling that any of it was personal. It was more a way of passing the time for the men, a game like many others, with rules all its own; but John Snow's smile is personal. He is looking at her, seeing her in a way she's never been seen. Nor perhaps has ever even wanted to be seen. And yet Etta does not want to walk alone, for John Snow is right. White men, not all of them drunk, have been known to accost women of her race without shame or provocation, particularly at the borders of white and coloured neighborhoods.

'You may walk me to the streetcar. I shall be happy to be on my own from there.'

'As you wish,' he says. 'It will be my pleasure.'

Maria has appeared to open the door. How long has she been there? Etta wonders if Maria has heard her heart pound. John Snow has put on his hat, offered Etta his arm after, without a touch, moving her into his space and out of the door.

Brooklyn, New York, May 1956

The sidewalk Slick has not bagged his prey. Valaida, still marooned in the Oldsmobile that cannot turn left, smiles as the ripe-for-plucking schoolgirls sway hips onto their bus. The bus can't go far in this traffic, and rather than roast his passengers, not to mention himself, the bus driver has obligingly left open his doors. Slick could climb on if he wanted to, take another road to the poach, but the rules of cool demand that he not leave his turf, no matter that the girls have regressed to maybe half their age, nudging and pointing out the window, with 'He's so cute!' giggles, 'Girl, he was lookin' at you! He had your number! What you doin' on this bus?!'

Paul Goldman bangs the steering wheel in frustration. 'I must have been insane to take Fulton at this time of day! Mel Blumberg's gonna kill me! I'll be back with the Hadassah girls licking stamps.'

Valaida hands the young man a handkerchief. 'Wipe your brow, Mr Goldman. The traffic will move. It's got no choice, and neither do we. Now, let's see if we can find some sounds that will help to ease the pain.' Coral-painted fingers twirl the radio dial. A plush saxophone fills the air. 'Ah, that's nice. The Hawk in flight. Will Coleman do?'

'He'll do.' Valaida's handkerchief smells faintly of perfume. Paul feels cooler, but no less dizzy. The dark-glassed lady beside him is serene, discreetly nodding her head to that beat he can never find. Cool. Paul wishing for the key, as Valaida spins on what the schoolgirls missed and Etta Mae gained.

*C*hapter three

Washington, DC, 1898

She did not take her streetcar alone. There'd been a group of three white men on the car, amusing themselves loudly with coon jokes, declaring how they planned to celebrate when the District finally Jim Crowed niggers into their rightful places once and for all. The men were young and well-dressed, university students, as like as not, with stiff, snowy collars and languid hands, strong only in their whiteness, which has always been enough. On her own, Etta would not have stayed on the streetcar long, but John Snow's hand was firm on her arm as he guided her to their seats. He ignored the young men but did not avert his eyes. He did not fear them, and his lack of fear sapped their bravado. They mumbled, fell silent, shuffled their feet. Etta felt proud and safe and something completely unfamiliar. She quickened, and, despite a certainty that this feeling was just what she had been nurtured to resist, Etta knew she belonged to John Snow.

Henry and Cora had indeed been alerted by their Sister in Jesus, Eloise Hunter, who had travelled from outside the Academy of Music direct to the Washingtons' door. Their daughter, Etta, had sinned, had held court with the Devil's Disciples, but what was far worse, what was near impossible to fathom, she had lied. The disappointment in her parents' eyes and spirits was almost more than Etta could bear. That they should forbid her further intimate contact with Allegretta seemed only appropriate punishment, that she should no longer linger on campus to practise on her professor's grand piano did not produce the expected twinge. Allegretta needn't have bothered seeking to apologize to Etta for having found another accompanist for the final school recital. Priscilla Jackson would now be ear to Allegretta's fantasies about St Petersburg and Berlin. Etta knew her destiny lay elsewhere, in a place that would only pain her parents more. She completed her course that term knowing that there never would be a degree. She dutifully helped her mother with the baking, taught the junior Bible class, mended clothing for the destitute, aware that it was only a matter of time.

Praise God that the rain had waited until she had delivered the pies; for the order had come late, the musicale was that evening, and Mrs Carlisle too good a customer to upset despite her unreasonable ways. It was a tropical downpour, rain coming down so thick and hard that it was skewing hats and you could hardly see.

Perhaps a hurricane's heading up from the Carolinas, thinks Etta as she struggles up the sidewalk. Her streetcar is approaching its stop some two hundred yards away, but she won't be able to make it. Horses and their vehicles are slipping unpredictably in the road, and her weather-sodden skirts have greatly handicapped her speed. The storm is a blessing of sorts. The heat has been oppressive these last two weeks, the air foul with rotting garbage, animal urine, and sweaty bodies in too-heavy clothes. A group of

31

street children has stripped down to their underwear and dances in the street to the rain's percussion, aping the scandalized citizens who think them uncouth, spinning joyfully in the shower, palms and faces to the sky. Etta watches them with envy as her streetcar pulls away.

'So, who doesn't have sense to come in out the rain?'

He is standing in the doorway of what appears a rooming house, wearing a green waistcoat, no jacket. There's a flashing ring on the hand that holds the cheroot.

'I thought you would have left with *The Octoroons*.' She wonders at the surprising steadiness of her voice.

'What?'

'I thought you would have left—'

'I can't hear you over this racket. Would you please step into some shelter before you get washed away?'

His landlady's cheeks carry colour that the Lord never intended, but she doesn't flinch when Etta is escorted into her parlour soaking wet and tracking mud. She clucks protectively, wraps a shawl about the young woman's shoulders, bustles out to make some tea as John indicates two seats before a well-swept hearth. He does not seem surprised to see her. His hazel eyes appear greener with the vest.

'So what was it you were trying to say?'

His gaze is direct. Etta bids her shivering stop, and it does. '*The Octoroons* left weeks ago. I thought you had moved on with them.'

'Their regular tenor came back. I was only a substitute.' His voice is calm. There is no regret, and Etta is confused.

'But surely with your voice . . .' she says. 'I would have thought they'd have wanted . . .'

More of a smile now in the gaze. 'I had business to attend to here. The singing is something I do when need and opportunity arise at the same time.'

'But you shouldn't squander God's gifts! Your voice is a blessing!'

Etta is herself surprised by the force of her words. Heat now, indeed again that rising flush, and John Snow laughs outright.

'Am I so ridiculous?'

'No,' John replies. 'You're wonderful, Etta Mae Washington.' The landlady delivers the tea then discreetly withdraws. Although she has no experience with such things, Etta knows that now is the time for her to leave as well; but she does not. She is surprised she can taste the tea. It is overly sweet. John's eyes have drifted to her shoulders before he starts to speak.

'I heard your friend again in recital. I'd thought to see you there.' But he hadn't, not really.

'Things have changed,' replies Etta. As he knew that they would. He had seen Henry Washington's eyes when Etta's father opened the door on the *Octoroon* evening to his innocent daughter and the fancy-dressed man. John had offered the appropriate words, made the appropriate greetings, but known that the father had taken his measure and found him wanting. Henry had recognized in John Snow a sensation-seeking renegade completely lost to God, which did not bother John at all. It is true. He likes it that way; it is what he strives for.

'Do you regret it?' he asks.

'I respect my parents' wishes,' she replies. Her eyes are down.

John has discarded his cheroot to hold Etta's hand. She does not pull it away.

'Do you regret it?'

'I'm not sure I know what you mean.'

With the first finger of his other hand, John moves an errant lock of hair away from Etta's brow. He looks about her face then into her eyes. 'Do you regret losing your music, Etta Washington, because I accompanied you home?'

'Music is never lost, but sometimes it hides for a while and comes out another way.'

John's thumb is caressing the flesh between Etta's fingers, then passing along the lifeline on her palm. It is an arresting sensation. Her heart is all percussion. She grasps his hand tight.

33

The Palace Theatre, New York, May 1956

Emerging from the Oldsmobile, Valaida accepts Paul Goldman's hand with grace, but she reclaims Eugene from the back seat of the car herself. The young man's nerves have been tested by the traffic to Manhattan. With each taxi horn blast and directed curse, a cheek muscle pops and his eyelashes flicker. *They could be longer, those lashes, but they do not mar the whole. A pretty, vulnerable, not-quite man.* She'd rather he didn't drop her Good Man.

'Shouldn't I, Miss Snow? It's not too—'

'That's OK. Baby stays with his Mama. Why don't you grab the dress?' She has changed back to the star shades, the ones bought in Los Angeles back in 1944, with the grey-green lenses and the light tortoise frames, a luxury when she'd barely had two dimes for castanets. They're classics, these shades. They always make her look good, but they're not as dark as they might be. She's glad that the shadows are side-street long because there's still that tell-tale throb behind her eyes. Her name is not to be seen on this side of the marquee, the one the artists check as they hit the stage door, and she knows it's not out front. There was a time when she wouldn't have been consigned to the blind side, not even downtown; but that's not why you're here, Valaida. Shall we go inside and shake a leg?

The first step through the door brings a welcome moment of cool. Valaida relishes the instant because she knows it's not going to last. An off-key piano thumping a number downstairs, laid over by the screams of a dance director with no time, less co-operation, and a triple bypass in his next six months. Last year's hot comedian moving in on a groupie courting next year's star. He'll be regretting that move a few years down the pike when bookings are rare on the ground, and he wonders how it all fell apart so soon.

'Miss Snow, at last! We were beginning to get worried.' Unctuous, belligerent. Has to be Blumberg. 'Everything all right? Can you believe this weather? Like the long, hot summer at the beginning of May, but don't worry; we're bringing in plenty of ice. Lucy, show Miss Snow to her dressing room. Goldman, I want a word.'

A flounce of dancers huddles around the food table, wolfing down pastrami on rye and danish, their hair upswept into neat little buns. Pulled-up posture, turned-out toes, tucked-under behinds declaring ballet training. Even the coloured girl among them has tamed her behind. *And they call what they sell jazz, as if any one of them could find a beat if it stepped right up and called them Sister. What Will Marion Cook would have done to their nature! He'd have scared them past crying, but if they ended up standing, they would have been stomping.* One girl stands apart, eyes steady as she sips her seltzer, searching for quarry, studying the terrain. Valaida knows she's the one to watch, and God protect the minnows in her wake. Paul Goldman's being primed for crucifixion as Valaida climbs the stairs. She leans over the railing with a smile, lifts her shades.

'I hope you know what you've got in this young man, Mel. We'd have been another half hour if he hadn't known his streets.'

'If you say so, Miss Snow.' Blumberg's disappointed. The executive-producers have just trod his ass, and he was needing a taste of fresh blood to keep tight on his game. Lucy's no fun. She doesn't give a damn. 'We've had to go on with the order, I'm afraid. Figure half hour, forty-five.'

'Gives me some time to settle in.' Valaida turns before catching Paul's sigh of relief followed by grateful and captivated look. She doesn't need to pause; she knows it's there as she swings her hip just a bit more prettily to the side.

Lucy's the daughter of the theatre-owner's niece, been around the business since she was wearing Mary Janes, has a partner, writes songs. She won't be working this gig this time next year, but she'll miss the buzz. She walked out of Vassar because she's one who likes it raw. 'We're tight as usual, Miss Snow. You're sharing with Liz LaFontaine, an "interpretive dancer" on her way up, up, and up.'

'No more G-strings?'

'A college boy chorus and one of those Cyd Charisse skirts. You girls decent?'

From inside: 'Like it matters to you?'

Lucy opens the door. 'At least I ask. Tori and Teri, the Chapman Twins, Acrobatic Jugglers Extraordinaire, Liz LaFontaine, Valaida Snow.'

'I saw your name in the releases. The trumpet player, right?'

Valaida just smiles. The dancer's not a beauty, but she's got lips as pert as her shapely legs, lips that make men dream. Aside from her table, all surfaces are covered with hairpieces, fishnet stockings, spangled juggling rings; and there are no moves to make space for Valaida.

'You might clear those drowned rats from the table,' says Lucy. 'Be hospitable. Give a gal some room.'

'You're all heart, Lucy. Who we got coming in next? The Trapp Family Singers? We've still got room to twitch.' The Chapmans are short, blonde, more than likely ten years older than the eighteen they look, each now stretching a leg up and over their heads.

'If you don't have room, swing on the chandelier. Twenty minutes.'

'Or forty-five. We've been waiting around since ten.'

In a practised sweep of arm, Lucy effects space for Valaida and moves back into the hall. 'Door opened or closed?'

'Open,' says Valaida, 'if you ladies don't mind. Keep the air moving at least for a while.' The twins shrug and straddle-split a wall while the dancer steals a curious look as Valaida opens up Eugene.

'What's wrong, Brenda?' says one of the twins, now arching into a backbend. 'Never seen a trumpet before?'

'Of course I've seen a trumpet, and I already warned you about calling me Brenda.'

'You were Brenda when we met you. You were Brenda in Poughkepsie, and you'll always be Sweet Brenda to us.'

The dancer sighs and decides on a higher road. Her career will, after all, be lasting far longer than the twins'. 'So what brings you into this snake pit, Miss Snow? Did Irv ask you, too?'

'We all love Irv here,' chimes in a hand-standing Twin.

'Yes,' says her sister/partner. 'If it weren't for Irving, we'd still be tumbling for peanuts in Brattleboro, Vermont. So when Irv Rosen calls—'

'We're *happy* to come running.'

'More than happy. Delighted!'

'No, I'm not on Irv Rosen's list,' replies Valaida, sorting through her music. 'My husband handles all my business.'

'So what in the world you doing here?' asks a Twin, genuinely intrigued.

Another backbend into handstand, barely missing a wig form. 'As if you don't know,' counters her sister. 'Acts would pay their own money to get on this stage tonight. Do you know who'll be out front?'

'I support the Appeal.' Valaida gives these silly girls more patience than she would have once upon a time. Her Earle would give her points.

'Don't we all?' remarks the dancer. 'Hey, aren't you the one—'

A Twin's cascading leg has connected with Paul Goldman, who is holding Valaida's garment bag. 'Whoops,' she giggles, eyeing Paul as she rights herself. 'Sorry about that.'

'Like hell you are,' says her sister. 'She thinks you're cute, and she's right. You're very, very cute. What can we do for you, very cute boy?'

'Where should I hang this, Miss Snow?' Paul finds these women unsettling. He is not attracted by the dancer's lips, now pouting in his direction. They look like they've fed on too much raw flesh.

'There on the wall will be fine.' Valaida continues shifting through her music as Paul stretches to the wall behind her.

'Look! He's blushing! Isn't that sweet!'

'Give it a rest, Theresa. Sit down, shut up, or go and find a grip to *schtump*.'

'And just who the hell made you Queen for a day?' growls Twin Number One. 'And who's known up and down this street for *sch-tumping* every pair of pants that points?'

'Every pants that points! That's rich!' crows Twin Two. 'Where'd you get that line?'

'She didn't make it up,' sniffs the dancer. 'That much we know.'

Paul again wonders at the calm of Valaida now among these bickering harpies. Her sheath dress fresh despite the long, sweltering drive, chestnut hair in and out of the back of her stand-up collar, better than if it all were calmly on the outside. When she moves her head, the hair shifts sides, but not silkily like that of the women he's more accustomed to being around. With more body, holding on. He wonders how it feels. It looks thicker, stronger. 'I wanted to thank you. I mean with Blumberg. He gets so—'

'No need.' Valaida wishes the throbbing would stop. It would be fun to play just a little with this young boy, but maybe the throbbing is God's way of telling her to behave. She smiles at this. She might even listen. 'But why don't you go down to the table and get us a Coca-Cola?'

Chapter four

Chattanooga, Tennessee, 1906

The floor is shiny and smooth, and if you spread out flat, shoes off, hands down, face to the side and very, very still, you can feel the buzz-thump through the wood and hear the joy even more. When the joy stops, you look up, and Mama's always there. Sometimes she's sitting. Sometimes she's standing. Sometimes she says, 'Let's try that again.' Other times she says, 'That was nice. I can see you worked hard.' Until it's all over, and he would say, 'Thank you, Mrs Snow'; or she would say, 'Thank you, Mrs Snow'; and they hand Mama some coins. Then Mama walks him or her to the door, and they'd say, 'See you next week'; and you're sitting up now, and you're watching, because then Mama would close the door; and after she closed the door, sometimes she'd sigh. If Mama has sighed, you scramble to your feet, try not to trip on your dress, and slip-slide run to meet her at the piano. Mama would sit on the bench; and you would sit with your back against the piano; and Mama would play. When Mama played, the joy ripples all over and through your insides and outsides. Your fingers tingle and your feet want to jump. It feels like rain sounds on the windows at night. You never want it to stop. You always say, 'Again, Mama, please!' And most times she says, 'You come and help me, Valada,' which is the best part of all because then you climb into Mama's lap, and you make joy yourself. Your fingers push the white teeth down and sometimes the black stairs too. The sounds *ping pang pong* or *pong pang pang bam ping pong* or whatever joy you like; there are so many different ways; and most times you laugh and clap your hands together because it feels so good. Mama hugs you and kisses your hair, and after your fingers get tired, you just sit in her lap, rubbing the shiny flat egg that hangs from around her neck, remembering all the joy until the baby starts to cry. Then Mama gets up and says, 'Put your shoes on, Valada,' and if your sister's not close by, she'll call out, 'Alvada, come and help your sister with her shoes. I have to feed the baby.' Just what is it that's so special about a baby?

As Etta Washington, now Snow, moves to tend to her newest child, she wonders that she ever could have lived another life. Once she lived in a city; Washington was a city, with brick or concrete sidewalks radiating out from government buildings that had precious little to do with most coloured folks but still gave a tone to the place. Chattanooga was not a grown-up city. It was a railroad town with the energy, noise, and mess of a young boy just discovering what the organ between his legs could do. Folks didn't worry about tone in Chattanooga. They tried to prosper, but even if they didn't they were going to have a good time in whatever way they could. God was in Chattanooga, but His gaze was not severe.

Unfastening her shirtwaist, Etta carefully twists her locket's chain around a button and out of the baby's way. This baby, like her long-departed, grieved-for brother, is hesitant at the breast, and Etta wonders if she too will be gathered up to God. Etta hopes not, she prays not, but she would be ready this time. She would know that there was life and even gladness after loss, with now other children to care for along with the continuing mystery of her love for John Vincent Snow. She had not been prepared for the death of her John Henry Patrick.

He had been named for all the men about his life, his father, the grandfather he might have known, and the grandfather who was unknowable, but whose blood he obviously bore. He'd been a golden baby, almost the colour of yellow pine, his head a-tumble with curling ringlets of silken ginger-cake brown. He'd smelled of sweet clotted cream, and his beauty was so bright Etta had truly believed that, though her mother and father had never forgiven her for leaving home and church for love of John, the Lord Above, in all His infinite wisdom, had recognized their rapture and deemed to bless their union. The birth had not been easy. She had laboured for hours, much of it on her own. John's sister had been sickly, and his mother had travelled to her. John had been away in town, as he was sometimes for days at a time, which had been something for her to adjust to at first, but what she'd come to understand to be part of the man he was.

John Snow does not choose to live by his voice. His time with *The Octoroons* was a brief nod to a recent past, when he'd travelled the country with his school's jubilee singers. The jubileers had provided him a way to move, see the back of the books and boredom of his small Mississippi campus; but John was not a man of God, and soon his fascination with the Devil's works had forced his comrades to show him the door. He'd borne them no ill will and happily gone on to sample the life of various travelling secular shows – one or two minstrel troupes, cakewalking operettas, miscellaneous Smart Sets. What he learned in this time was that he was far more restless than most. He enjoyed the spotlights of show business, but he disliked its teams. John Snow was without the patience for teamwork. Life was too precarious and brief to wait for groups to reach a meeting of the minds, especially for a southern-born coloured man. He preferred going his own way, living by his own wits, less at the mercy of the white man's whims, and therefore chose to be a gambler. *The Octoroons'* need of a temporary tenor had found him in town and

41

between possibilities. As the miracle of his voice had somehow withstood abuses of late nights and raw liquor, he'd said, 'Why not?' and Etta Washington had met her man.

On the afternoon that John invited Etta out of the rain, the intertwine of fingers had led, as natural, to other things. John's boarding house was not among the number in which passion was a furtive affair. With his painted landlady discreetly in her kitchen, John had had no need to tiptoe Etta up the stairs. He had escorted her as a gentleman would, the arm around her waist supportive but not overly familiar, kissing her gently on the lips as one hand quietly closed his room's door. As she moved into his embrace, Etta Mae had wondered if God's true house was not here in John's arms. Indeed she'd thought it so.

Perhaps that blasphemy could not go unpunished. It had not been punishment to be turned out of her parents' house. That their daughter had succumbed to temptation was not beyond the boundaries of their forgiveness; but that she felt no shame, harboured no senses of guilt or waste, defied them time and time again to lay with a sporting man who offered her nothing but lust, was finally more than they could bear. It was neither indignant neighbours nor the frowns of the church that finally forced their hands, but memories of their own sordid lives in captivity. Etta's parents demanded that John Snow marry their daughter; but John Snow would not, could not in fact, for he already had a wife, a wife of his early youth whom he would never see again, or so he said; but the banns had been legal, and there were children besides. Etta didn't care. John was leaving the District, and she would be by his side, with or without assorted High or human blessings. She was not a fallen woman. She had not shortened her skirts or applied rouge to her cheeks. She never entered the saloons where her man plied his trade, had never shuffled cards or even handled dice. Aside from the traces she sometimes found on her lover's lips, Etta had not tasted spirits and knew she never would. She still prayed, read scripture, and sewed; but she belonged to John Snow. For her there would be no one else, and she did not mean to live without him.

So she left Washington, followed John to St Louis and then to Mississippi. Sometimes they were short on food and forced to board in the most seedy of hovels; but this was not punishment, for when John was there, there was the comfort of his arms. She knew that John had amazed himself with the choice of her. Her beauty, like her presence, was of the quiet sort. She was never tempted to flashy taffetas and fringes. Her hats were sombre, her outer rhythm demure, but she was his princess, the sole purity about his life; and, though he left her solitary for days on end, often returning penniless and reeking of cheap perfume, he cherished her in his fashion and fulfilled all her needs. John's not living by rules and his constant courtship of danger were things about her man that she loved most of all. She demanded only that he love her when he came home, and this he did without fail.

The puzzle had been that it took so long for her to miss a monthly. She had taken to wonder if punishment was to be a barren womb, but the sign came at last. She swelled, and John took her home, to a small neat wooden house in the woods outside Eupora, to the care of his mother. Hattie Snow was kind, but distracted by twenty-five years of waiting for the unscheduled visits of the local plantation owner's son who had fathered her children. Etta longed for her own mother but knew there was no hope in it. A letter to Cora and Henry Washington would be to no avail. They could not read and would surely not take a letter of hers to be read them by a friend for fear of the shame and pain it might reveal. So Etta prayed, hoping that somehow her fervour would communicate to her parents the imminent joy that would soon be theirs to share.

John, too, seemed happy with the coming baby, but was increasingly away as Etta's confinement neared its end. They would be needing more money after all, or so he said. Etta would have preferred his not bothering to lie.

When Hattie Snow returned from tending her own daughter in Columbus, she found Etta labouring in pain in a bed drenched with blood. There was no time to fetch a midwife. Hattie delivered her grandson herself and tended his mother the best that she could. John Henry Patrick was a good-sized child, so it seemed certain he would survive. Etta's fate was less sure. When John finally arrived four days after the fact, bearing a mandolin and a locket for his princess and first shoes for his boy, Etta still could not speak for fever. The baby was farmed out to a neighbour, for Etta lay that way for weeks; and, when she finally improved and John Henry Patrick came home to nurse, the baby glowed but did not prosper. He did not engage. No manner of coaxing or sweetening of nipples could convince him to suck for long. Small drops of milk placed in his mouth dribbled out more times than not. So he withered. So he died.

As the body of her little angel was being placed in his elm wood coffin, Etta snipped off a curl of his ginger-cake hair and slipped it into the locket that now hung about her neck. Here indeed was punishment at last.

It was music that finally brought Etta back to life. John continued to travel, but with each return brought an additional instrument for the house. After the mandolin came a guitar, then a cello, and a violin. John would place the offering in Etta's hands, only to see her stroke it and put it quietly aside. Until the occasion of Hattie's fortieth birthday (or at least the date Hattie thought it to be). At his mother's request, John broke a long-standing policy to sing her a simple song. Delighted, his mother pleaded for another verse. Her son's glorious a capella seemed to still the birds and clouds. John obliged, but this time found himself accompanied by mandolin. Etta was back with life.

Without benefit of state or clergy, Etta became a Snow. Baby Lawrence was born, and the Snows moved to Tennessee. The town of Chattanooga, with its river traffic and mountain people, had an open embrace for a man of John Snow's talents. His winnings brought them this house on E Street, with an indoor toilet and a piano in the parlour. Another baby came and another.

Etta hears the front door open and close, the sound of little shod feet scurrying quickly across the floor, then squeals of delighted laughter.

'How's my girl?' his voice asks. 'How's my big, beautiful girl?'

'Higher, Daddy!' squeals Valada. 'Higher and higher!'

'As high as the trees?' says her father.

'Yes!'

'As high as the sky?'

'Yes!' In Valada's world there is no feeling like it. The room goes up and down so fast that it's just colours running together. Your skirts and curls flop all around, and your feet can kick in every direction. Sometimes you flap your arms like a bird. Sometimes you sing the notes you played on the piano. No matter how high you go up, Daddy's hands always catch you when you fall; but sometimes he plays like he's going to drop you, and that's when you laugh the most.

'Do me, Daddy! Do me! Do me!' Alvada's tugging at Daddy's leg, wanting to have a turn, but Daddy doesn't fly Alvada any more because she always cries. After you fly, Daddy will sit on a chair, and Alvada will just ride on his knee.

'John, be careful. You'll scare her.' Mama always gets worried.

'Valada? Not on your life. There's no scaring this girl. She's as strong as a boy. Aren't you, sweetheart? You're Daddy's second little boy.' You've been laughing so hard that there's no breath for words. You just bury your head in his neck and hug Daddy tight. Everything seems to sparkle whenever Daddy comes home.

But this night has been quieter than most nights when Daddy was home. Usually he would tell funny stories at dinner, and Mama would play like she was upset and say, 'John, you shouldn't tell such tales. The children won't know what to believe'; and Daddy would say, 'Oh Etta, relax. We're just having some fun is all. Don't you like my stories?' And you'd all cry out, 'Yes!' After dinner, you would jump around with Alvada and Lawrence to music that Mama would play, and Daddy would laugh and clap his hands, and there'd be lots of hugs and kisses before everyone went to bed. But this night has been different. Daddy didn't tell funny stories. His mouth didn't smile, and his eyes didn't shine. After dinner, Mama wouldn't play. She and Daddy held all of you

45

in their arms and talked about Them. Mama said that They could do what They wanted. There was no stopping Them; but Daddy said They only did what we let them do. We had to stop Them ourselves. You were trying to figure who They were. They sounded as big and strong as monsters, who shook the ground when they walked and ate little girls and boys for breakfast; but even though Daddy told tall tales, he always said that really, really there were no such things as monsters, and that there was nothing to fear in moonless nights or old hollow trees. But if They weren't monsters, what were They then? They didn't sound like folks, like neighbours you knew or even strangers in the street. They made everyone angry or sad.

You heard rumbles and shouts. There was some flickering light, then the most terrible scream that just went on and on. You weren't afraid of much, not big dogs or big storms or falling down the porch steps, but that noise made you want to hide in the smallest hole, quick like a mouse into the ground, never coming out ever again, not even for green barley sugar sticks. Mama was crying, and Daddy's eyes were shiny now. He grabbed his gun and wanted to run out the door, but Mama pulled on his jacket and screamed at him to stay. You all slept together that night, wrapped up in covers on the parlour floor. When you woke up, Mama's eyes were tired, and Daddy was gone. All day the streets outside were quiet. No one came for lessons, and you went without fresh milk.

The Palace Theatre, New York, May 1956

Valaida savours the cool crispness of her Coca-Cola. That night way back when had been the closest she'd ever come to a lynching; three short blocks and a benevolent destiny away . . . How many coloured were burned and slaughtered that year by hate-crazed white folk running amok? Or the year after that, and the year after that? And still going on, the horror always there, lurking around your freedom, breaking up bodies, crunching on souls. Last year, that poor young boy Emmett Till. If you held on it too long . . . Well, you didn't, not if you wanted to live and love and play.

Alvada had always enjoyed relating tales of Valada's nightmares that haunted their house for weeks after the lynching, but here Valaida's memory is blank. What she did know was after that night, John Snow was changed. He became wilder, and harder, though he still loved his girls.

The juggling blondes continue to bend and flex their bodies all over the dressing room's confined space, their scent and hair marking the area like dog piss.

'You don't mind, do you?' Twin Two finally asks. 'We always perform better if we work out in small spaces. Gets our antenna going. It's a twin thing, I guess.'

'Be my guests,' says Valaida. 'Just mind the horn.'

Liz LaFontaine is not blessed with so open a mind. When a Twin's foot flicks too close to her costume, the dancer is on her feet cursing like a sailor just as stage manager Lucy sticks her head in the door. 'Now, now, what have we here? Not disagreement, I hope? Tori and Teri, shake legs. You're up. Let me help you with your stuff. Liz, you could give the floor a sweep with that broom you've got hidden around here somewhere. Miss Snow, I congratulate you on your goodwill. They're talking twenty, thirty minutes, but I wouldn't hold my breath.'

'I'll be here,' says Valaida, running over various fingerings in her head. Over the clatter of gathered juggling rings, dancers' feet on rickety stairs, a vocalizing tenor, and the barks of small dogs float strains of virtuoso violin, the notes flawless, the tone fleet. A child, more than like. A girl in crinolined skirts, frilly socks in shiny shoes, or a boy in a Peter Pan collar with naked knees, either one sporting a serious expression and a harridan mom. So much skill; so little play. How lucky we were not to come from that.

hapter five

Chattanooga, Tennessee, 1910

Mama never called it a 'fiddle'; she called it a 'violin', and that's
what Valada called it too. 'Violin' sounded more like the smooth
brown wood felt when you pulled the bow across its strings, and
the tingling went through your fingers and up to your elbow, from
under your chin into your head and down your neck. She'd always
loved the shape of it, with its ridged waist and the yellow strings
and the fancy scroll on top, like a doll baby, but better because it
could speak and sing. When you were still just a little thing, not
even three years old, Mama would stand the violin in her lap sometimes and let you stroke the shapes, put your fingers in the curvy
holes, even touch the standy-up wood thing under the strings; but
most times you couldn't hold it on your own. Mama said you had
to be more gentle with the violin. You couldn't pound it like the
piano. You'd have to be much more patient if you were going to

unlock its secrets. You always answered, 'I'll be patient, Mama. I promise,' and you thought your mama believed you because your words would always make her smile; but still you'd had to wait. Your arms were too short, and too short, until finally that changed. Now you were six, and you had been playing for a year.

When you'd first started trying to play, brother Lawrence used to laugh and say your arms were still too short, that you looked like you was trying to choke yourself, and anyway you sounded like a hungry old alley cat. But he'd stopped talking that way after you'd tripped him out back in the yard and mushed his face with rotten peaches. Sometimes big brothers just had to have a whupping. Otherwise, they'd think they could sass you any time they wanted.

It was funny that Lawrence never wanted to play instruments any more. He could sing really well, and he could dance; but he didn't want to sit still and learn any notes or hold onto anything he had to worry about breaking. He just wanted to run the streets, and he almost never came to school. Lawrence was eleven, and most of his friends had already left school to shine shoes or run errands or work the fields with their folks. Lawrence hated having to sit in that schoolroom with all the little kids, with the teacher spending so much time with the ABCs and counting and never getting to him. He could read as well as he needed, he said, and what was the point anyway? Coloured folk couldn't get work that needed schooling. White folks wouldn't let them. Lawrence was always going on about white folks this, and peckerwoods that. Valada didn't think that much about white folks. She didn't see them very much, and most she saw were no lighter than Lydia Dobson or Aurelia Sue Jackson or even Lawrence, to tell the truth, so really, why were white folks such a great big deal?

Lawrence said he planned to be like Daddy. Gamblers just needed to know how to count, and he could count real good. But Daddy didn't agree. He came home and heard that Lawrence had been giving Mama lip and hadn't been going to school, and he'd whipped him from noon till Sunday up and down the yard. Only Daddy wasn't home all that much, and so Lawrence stayed in those streets. You had to be careful about Daddy. Sometimes when he came home he'd be all laughs and kisses, pulling pretty ribbons out of his pockets and wooden toys or earbobs for Mama. He'd tell funny stories and throw his girls in the air, except for Alvada, whom he called his China Princess because she was always acting like she was gonna break. He'd ask everyone to do their music, and he'd clap his hands and sometimes he'd sing. But sometimes he'd come home with his eyes looking all hollow and red. There'd be no stories, even if everyone begged. Sometimes he'd even be cross with Mama. He'd talk to her quiet and mean, and sometimes he grabbed her arm in a way that made all the kids scared – Lawrence's eyes would start kind of clicking – but Mama never got cross with Daddy. She'd take him into their room and close the door, and things would get mostly quiet.

'Valada! Stop! You always do that!'

'Do what?'

'Play notes that aren't there! It makes me lose my place!' Alvada has pushed away from the piano and flounced her hands into her lap.

'But Mama says the music's not just the notes on the paper. She says the joy's in the notes you hear inside your heart, so I'm just trying to find the other—'

'You're not Mama, and you mess me up. If you don't follow the notes, I'm not going to play.'

'I won't do it any more. I promise.'

Valada sighs. She and her sister have this argument all the time. On the floor by the piano, their sister Lavada has stopped playing with Baby Hattie. Lavada always watches when her sisters argue because if they argue too much, then Mama will take over and play music they can dance to, music that rocked back and forth and spun all around. Alvada and Valada never argued when they danced. They would make up things and try them together, and they always liked Lavada to join in. Somewhere along the line, someone would always bump into somebody else, and they'd all end up on the floor in a tangle of muslin dresses and laced-up shoes, hugging and kissing and laughing, until someone rolled onto Baby Hattie, who started to cry. Dancing was always so much fun, sashaying and wiggling and kicking up your legs so the air went rushing all the way round the insides of your skirts; but this time Valada wants to keep playing the violin.

'OK.' Alvada starts the introduction again. No matter how hard she tries, the joy never comes to her with the ease it comes to Mama and Valada. Sometimes she thinks that she would like to stop playing, but if she did, there'd be more time for chores. Struggling with the piano was much better than having to make soap. Mama didn't want her girls making soap because it would make it harder for their hands to feel what the instruments were saying. Alvada had already stopped with the mandolin. If there was no more piano, it would be hello to soda flakes and lye; so Alvada concentrated hard.

Bow at the ready, waiting for her cue to play, Valada looks over to Lavada on the floor. Lavada's eyes are down, and she's playing dancing fingers. 'Don't worry, Louie. We've got the picnic tonight, and we'll all be dancing there.' She begins to play, concentrating on the notes, willing herself to do what they say and not upset her sister, but when she gets to that part where the notes go up with a lot of space between them, just going 'dee-dee-dee', she can't help herself. She goes down and adds some more besides.

Ezekiel saw the wheel, way up in the middle of the air . . .

Come time to leave for the picnic, Lawrence was nowhere to be found. Mama had been worried and wanted to wait, but Valada and her sisters were in such a fever to go that they finally convinced their mama to leave without him. Everyone knew they'd find him at the picnic because Lawrence was never gonna miss him a lot of good food. Not having Lawrence meant that everyone had to carry more, but better having to carry than miss the torchlight parade. The parades were always fun. Everyone who could play an instrument joined in as choirs marched through the streets singing praises to the Lord. The torches smelled of pitch and moss and threw shadows on the street that danced like the goblins Valada knew didn't exist but suited her fancy anyhow. As the procession moved towards the campground, everyone danced some way to the music's rhythm. Even if they were only walking, they were walking on a beat, and when you were carrying things, like blankets and baskets, the rhythm made carrying easier. Everyone would be smiling and nodding their heads, and the darkness under Mama's eyes would seem to disappear.

Once the parade reached the campground, the ladies would start laying out food on the tables, fried chicken, hog maws, coconut cake, collard greens, roasted corn, lemonade. The dishes went on for ever, with everyone bringing their best. The torches would be stood up in stones or dirt; and the goblins would take to the trees. Usually Valada liked to chase and dance with the goblins. She'd run in and out of the trees, up and down the clearing, trying to grab hold of their hands and touch toes with their feet – even if there was no music, they had a rhythm of their own – until Mama would say to stop acting so crazy and come over here and help; but there'd be no goblin-dancing this evening.

The sky had been nothing but clouds all day, like the oldest grey coverlet with little white feathers poking out, and smudges of black like it had been walked on all over by dirty boots. Valada had been afraid that it might start raining again and wash out the streets and the picnic too, but it didn't rain; a fresh breeze started to blow, and Mama had started packing up the baskets. Once they'd quit waiting for Lawrence, they'd hurried down E Street to Eighth Street as quick as Lavada's legs could go, past the corner shop where Mama let them buy candy sometimes and if you were lucky a few of the sugar balls were purple; past Mouf Mary's house, with the falling down porch and yard running up and down with cats.

There must have been two hundred cats in Mary's yard this evening, but they weren't making any noise. They were just sitting there looking, or licking their legs and backs, like they were waiting for humans to learn the secrets they already knew. Valada liked cats because they always did what they wanted and they only stayed where they wanted to be, which seemed a good way to live from what Valada could see. Daddy lived that way, and his smiles seemed happier than Mama's. Mama's smiles were beautiful and warm, and you felt safer in her smiles than you did in Daddy's; but there always seemed like there was something sad in them, like she'd lost something special that she wasn't going to find again. It made you love her harder and hug her more, but Valada thought when she grew up that she wanted her own smiles to be like Daddy's.

Ninth Street was a great big party of romping sounds and flickering lights. There were many more folks in the parade than Valada could ever remember, with musicians playing ways she had never heard before. The stepping was livelier, and laughter like bells of all different kinds of sizes, men like the white folks' church bells, women like the bell Miss Fiske the schoolteacher used to call her students into class, kids like the harness bells on Sam the iceman's horse. All around, folks were asking, 'Do ya think we'll see it?' 'You think it's gonna be there?' 'What ya think it looks like?' Miz Lewis said she'd heard tell that a man in Texas had gotten so hot and bothered about it all that he'd upped and crucified himself just like Jesus. Old Mr Johnson laughed so hard you could see his back tooth (you didn't see it often, and it was the only one he had), saying, 'Why, the man's a damn fool!'

Valada tugs on her sister's sleeve, trying to talk in between the beats. 'What they talking about, Alva? What all they fixing to see?'

'The star,' said Alvada, who is concentrating on keeping a basket on her head and ballin' the jack at the same time.

'What's so special about a star? There's stars all over the place.'

'This one's got a tail. Didn't you listen in school this week? Miss Fiske talked about it most every day.'

Valada is hardly going to admit that she hasn't listened to Miss Fiske. It would give Alvada power that she certainly didn't need, but big sisters came in handy once in a while. They sometimes knew more things than you did, a few things anyway. 'So a man

53

wants to Jesus hisself just because a star has a tail? That must be some kind of star.'

The basket has refused to stay on Alvada's bouncing curls, so now she's hugging it in both arms and trying her luck with the Georgia Hunch. 'Some folks say that if the tail touches the ground, the whole earth will just explode.'

This sounds so serious that Valada almost loses her beat. 'If folks are thinking that, then how come they're dancing?'

'I don't know. You better ask Mama.' Alvada's really good at the Georgia Hunch. She's got a little half-step in her shuffle that Valada thinks is really sweet, but even while she's trying hard to copy her big sister and finally not doing so bad at all, Valada can't help wondering why folks are laughing and dancing if they think the world might end. And she's not sure that asking Mama is such a good idea because Mama's not dancing like everyone else; she never dances in fact. She's just walking with the music, with her kind-of-sad smile, a big basket over one arm and Baby Hattie in the other. Lawrence said that Mama was sanctified once, which is why she doesn't dance, because Sanctifies think that dancing's the Devil's work, which is confusing to Valada because if God's in charge, why should the Devil have so much fun? Would she rather dance with the Devil or fly on angel wings, be one of Jesus' blessed lambs or learn to shimmy like a champ? Duquesne Mantee starts laying into his big bass drum. The drum's twice as big as he is, but he's booming and bamming till Valada's ribs are shaking like twigs in a thunderstorm wind and her heart feels as though it's bouncing on a bed. The crowd's yelling, 'Yah! Uh-huh!' 'Take it to the alley, Duquesne!' All that can manage are talk-clapping to the drum, and everyone does the Strut on the way to the star.

Ezekiel saw the wheel, way up in the middle of the air . . .

They hadn't had to wait too long. Almost as soon as the parade arrived at the campground, just as the ladies were fixing to lay out the tables, and the men were steadying the lights, Deacon

54

Williams looked up at the sky and cried out, 'Clouds partin'! Clouds partin'!' Everyone stopped what they were doing to look up at the sky. Mothers called for their children, wanting to wrap them in their arms, and most of the kids came running, except for the older boys, who stayed together. They sure weren't gonna be seen running to their mamas, but they were looking nervous, kicking up dirt and pushing and pulling among themselves. Valada imagined that Lawrence was over there in the shadows, but she didn't have time to check because she was holding on to Lavada. Lavada was too young to know what was happening, and all she wanted to do was chase after fireflies.

They saw the crescent moon first, laying lazy on its side with one big, bright spot of light just an arm's length away. 'Is that it?' cried Tucker Haywood, who was only three years old.

'No, son,' said his granddad, who'd hauled freight on the Mississippi and knew all sorts of things about the night. 'That there's the planet Venus, named for the Goddess of Love. See, she shines yellow so's you remember how love can warm your heart.'

'And the Lord said, thou shalt have no other gods before me,' called out Deacon Williams, and the church said, 'Amen.'

A strong wind had come up, and now the clouds were moving fast. Stars were sprinkling all over the sky like sugar crystals spilling over a big-skirted black velvet dress; and then suddenly, there it was. It was the biggest star in the sky, a great white fuzz of a star, and its tail didn't trail it like a fox but spread all out behind like the most beautiful white lace fan.

'Praise God!' cried Sister Green, who then commenced to sing 'Ezekiel Saw the Wheel'.

'But it's not moving,' said Alvada, who wasn't as impressed as she might have been. 'I thought it would be moving. How's it supposed to explode the earth if all it does is sit there?'

'If the earth exploded, wouldn't we all be dead? Mama and Daddy and Hattie and everyone?' asked Valada.

'I guess so,' said Alvada grudgingly. 'I guess it's better this way. It does look kind of nice.'

. . . The big wheel run by faith
The little wheel runs by the grace of God . . .

'I think it's the most beautiful thing I've ever seen,' said Valada, who wishes the tail would touch the earth because maybe, if everything wasn't blown to smithereens, she could use the tail like a carpet and walk right up into the sky. A whole lot of folk have taken up Sister Green's song, and now its beat has gotten faster, and the musicians have joined in. Cappy Mitchell's daddy is talking on clarinet to Sister Green, and both of them are holding words with Moses Godfrey on trombone. Usually Seldom Truscott would be joining the party with his horn. Valada just loved to hear Seldom play. His notes scampered and spun around Uncle Moses' like a soft-footed puppy dog, but Seldom's not to be heard when there's a full picnic table laid out. He's not thinking about a star; he's stuffing his face with trotters and Mama Cindy's hoecake. Instead, a big dark-skinned man with a caved-in yellow hat has stepped in, lifting a horn that looks a lot like Seldom's but is longer and sleeker too, and the sound of this horn pierces through the night. It seems to Valada that the dark man is connecting their Chattanooga campground direct to the fan-tailed star. With his sound through her head and fingers, Valada reaches out and feels the starlight.

. . . Better mind, sister, how you walk on the cross,
Way up in the middle of the air . . .

After dinner, Valada didn't want to join in the Buzzard Lope game with the kids too young to go creeping into the shadows. She didn't want to wave her hands in the air pretending to be a bird; she wanted to put her hands on the dark man's horn. She knows she should ask Alvada to go with her, but Alvada's in the middle of the circle pretending to be the cow, and Valada doesn't want to wait. Suppose the man left? So she just walks over by herself, and she's hardly even scared.

56

Most of the musicians are sitting by and under the big cotton-wood tree, passing around a bottle. Some of the older boys are there too, Duquesne Mantee, Lester Morgan. Jeremiah Douglass has brought over that funny banjo he's made himself out of a cigar box and baling wire. Jeremiah is proud of that old banjo, and he can make it do some tricks. Valada had laughed at Jeremiah the first time she'd seen it, but Mama had told her she should be shamed of herself and thankful that the Lord had blessed their family with money for store-bought music. The important thing was to have the joy in your heart, and if Jeremiah had enough joy to make a banjo by himself, then he shouldn't be laughed at but looked to as an Example. You paid attention when Mama talked about the joy. Valada never laughed at Jeremiah again. She still thought his banjo was funny-looking, but she listened to his tricks.

There are a few fancy ladies under the tree, with bright mouths and dresses and shoes the colours of flowers, but no young girls. All the girls not in the bushes are helping their mamas clean up the tables or playing the Buzzard Lope game. The dark man is the first one to notice Valada walking to the tree. He's got the bottle in one hand, and his horn in the other. The horn is sitting low in his lap, between his belly and his legs, shining straight and lavish in the torchlight. 'Now what we got coming up here? You a cute little thing you are. What's your name, honey?'

'Why, this is Miss Valada, one of John Snow's little girls,' said Uncle Moses. 'What you doin' here, pretty? How come you ain't over in the games?'

'Yessir, we some dangerous mens over here. You don't watch out, we'll just swallow you up.' Seldom's eyes are red and watery, and his mouth is hanging on one side as he tries to reach in Valada's direction. 'Come over here, little darlin', and gimme some o' that sweet baby sugar.'

Uncle Moses pokes out his elbow, and Seldom is back on his behind. 'Man, you must be crazy. You mess with one of his girls, John Snow will have you cold and ugly before daybreak.'

'I ain't afraida no fuckin' John Snow. John Snow can kiss my black ass,' says Seldom, but he stays where he's fallen.

'Valada, why don't you run along, darlin'?' says Uncle Moses. 'This here's no place for a little girl.'

But Valada's not going anywhere. Seldom's smelly, but he's not scary; he just gets that way sometimes. All anybody ever has to do is push him out the way. She points at the dark man's lap. 'I wanted to see his horn,' she says, and two of the fancy ladies start to snigger.

'Don't mind them, darlin'. You can look all you want,' says the dark man. 'It's pretty, ain't it?'

Valada nods solemnly. 'Can I hold it?' she asks.

The dark man's smiling broadly now. 'Well, I don't know, sugar. You just a little thing. You think you can handle it?'

Valada nods again. 'I promise not to drop it.'

'I suspect you won't at that,' says the man. 'You bein' John Snow's daughter, you just might have the power, but you gonna have to come over here so I can make sure. This here's my pride and joy.'

The dark man smells like horses and dry leaves. There's a gold-coloured stud on his jacket, but his collar is frayed, and his cuffs are dingy beige. His chin is smooth though, like the horn he is placing in her hands. Her hand can't stretch around the up and down parts all the way, but she likes the way it feels, the press of the push-down parts especially.

'How come this one's bigger than the one Seldom plays?' she asks, and one of the fancy ladies sprays out a mouthful of beer.

'Because I'm a bigger man than Seldom, honey,' grins the dark man. 'So I plays me a trumpet instead of a little peep cornet.'

'You think you the bigger man, muthafucka,' growls Seldom. 'Let's whip out and see who be's the stud 'roun' here! I'll give you big man.'

'Keep your pants on, Seldom,' laughs Moses. 'Ain't no call for all that. This here's a little girl.'

'Ain't so goddam little if she's messin' with that horn,' mutters Seldom, slumping back against the tree. 'Hand over that bottle 'fore I bust me up some heads.'

Valada's wondering why talking about horns is making everyone so crazy, but she's more interested in finding out if she can make the star sound. 'Can I blow it?' she asks.

'Girls can't blow no horn!' says Jeremiah. 'And they got no business trying.'

'I can so blow a horn if I want to!' answers Valada angrily. 'If he lets me.'

'Can not,' says Duquesne. He's looking like Lawrence does when she really wants to hit him.

'Can so!'

'You a stubborn little thing,' laughs the dark man. 'Go ahead and try.'

Valada places her lips into the mouth part, which feels cool and warm at the same time. She blows as hard as she can, but nothing happens. 'See!' laugh the boys. 'Told you. Girls can't play no horn.' The dark man is taking the horn away.

'Please can I try again? Please?'

'OK,' says the man, 'but try doin' your lips like this.' His lips are held tight and a little apart, like a half-open smile. Valada tries her best to copy him, but she's having a harder time getting a sound out of this trumpet than she's had on any other instrument she's ever tried. The ladies are laughing, and the boys are sing-songing, 'Girls can't play no horn! Girls can't play no horn!' but Valada's not giving up, and once she makes her sound she's planning to kick Jeremiah's narrow behind, banjo joy or no banjo joy. She's still trying hard when Alvada comes running up to the tree.

'Come away from there, Valada! We been lookin' all over for you! Mr Harrison's just told Mama that Lawrence's got himself in some trouble somethin' terrible, and we have to leave right now!'

With her sister jabbering away, Valada's kept blowing into the horn and blowing into the horn until, just as Alvada grabs her arm to take her away, Valada finally makes a sound. It hasn't gone to the star, but everyone could hear it, and it was fun. The dark man smiled as he took back his horn. 'Congratulations, Little Snow. You got a whole lot of heart.'

As she runs her sister back to where their mother is waiting, Alvada is a non-stop scold. 'What are you, crazy, hangin' 'round that tree? Daddy would skin you alive if he saw you anywhere near Seldom Truscott! And what you doin' blowin' that man's horn? Don't you know girls don't play trumpets or cornets or trombones neither?'

'Why not?' asks Valada. 'What's so special 'bout horns that they only go to boys?'

'I don't know,' says her sister. 'They just do, is all.' The dark man has started playing again. This time his song is wailing and crying. With Moses' trombone growling underneath, it sounds as though the trees themselves were like to crumple away in grief.

> . . . *Some go to church for to sing and shout,*
> *Way up in the middle of the air . . .*

The fan-tailed star had vanished behind the clouds again by the time Valada and her family made it back home. Miz Harrison said she'd mind the babies so Mama could take clothes and food to Lawrence, but just as Mama was about to leave, John Snow came walking through the door like goblin-magic. Mama had been really quiet till then, speaking softly so Hattie and Lavada wouldn't get upset, even though her lips had lost much of their colour, but when their daddy appeared, she started screaming like Valada had never heard before, screaming and pounding her fists on Daddy, yelling things like, 'You should've been here!' 'My baby! My baby!' and lots of other things Valada couldn't understand. Daddy let her just go ahead and scream until Mama finally kind of folded onto herself just like a doll baby and started to make these little sounds. Daddy took Mama upstairs after that, and then he went out to the courthouse to see about Lawrence, knowing full well that there was nothing he could do.

The girls didn't see Lawrence again for over a year because Mama and Daddy wouldn't take them to the courthouse. The courthouse was not a place for coloured children to be. Every

60

coloured child knew that even if they didn't know why. Lawrence'd been caught thieving Coca-Colas from Nelson's Drug Store with two of his friends, and they all were sent up to the state farm for three and a half years. Lawrence escaped before then, dug a hole under a fence, and ran like the dickens for two nights and a day; but when he got back to Chattanooga, he only stopped home long enough to get some money, not even two days. Daddy wasn't home, so Mama went to Silverstein's and pawned her gold locket necklace. Lawrence knew how much that necklace meant to her, and he didn't want to take the money; but Mama said he had to and stuck it in his pocket. Lawrence hugged Mama hard and cried like Valada hadn't seen him since the time when he'd caught his leg in Uncle Moses' wagon. After that, Lawrence hit the road, and nobody heard neither hide nor hair about him for a long, long time.

> . . . *One of these days, about 12 o'clock,*
> *And this old world goin' to reel and rock,*
> *Way up in the middle of the air . . .*

The Palace Theatre, New York, May 1956

The dressing room feels a good ten degrees cooler with the departure of the Twins, for which Valaida is supremely grateful. The exercise of patience is a discipline to which she has come rather late in life, and, appearances aside, she knows herself to be imperfect in its practice. She is rightly proud of not stepping outside her quiet to put the blondes back into theirs, but the effort has renewed her headache to a point one Coca-Cola is not about to relieve. Like many who have lived their lives on the road, Valaida has never had much time for doctors, so she has not consulted one about her 'spells'. There are things that you know, that late nights, bad air, and worse liquor will eventually take their toll, that the Sweet King is no kind of beautifier, that bug-ridden beds in broken-down hotels are hardly aids to a good night's sleep. A doctor would say, cut out the road, settle down somewhere, and live a longer life; but road people say no, the freedom is the thing. For all the bad air and worse beds, for all the unwashed underwear and lousy food, coming and going when you please makes up for the time you'll never have. Doing what you love in a shorter life, a concentrated life. No regrets for paths not taken. Only Valaida is not on the road the way she once was. She likes her Brooklyn home, enjoys her husband's solicitous kindness, and the day-to-day of watching young Cheryl learn her world.

Now the dancer has begun to stretch. Liz LaFontaine is not so flamboyant as the Twins, not quite so obvious about pissing out her territory, but she is pleased to preen her body before this self-possessed woman, who, rumour has it, was some kind of blazing star, such as coloured people had stars, like Yiddish people had stars, stars in their own little communities, which is to say no kind of star at all; for there is no stardom but the Big Time stardom Liz LaFontaine knows to be her certain destiny, her name in lights on a Broadway marquee, headlining at the Copa, the jewels, the furs. This Valaida Snow, despite her poise, the dress, her fifty dollar shoes, is well beyond the peak of glamour, and how deeply it rankles that she sits so serenely, as if this room were her domain rather than that of someone younger, sleeker, and whiter than she. Better she recognize her obsolescence and politely fade away.

'Did you dance?' asks the dancer, torso draped gracefully over extended leg, fingers tenderly massaging the instep, followed by flex and rotation of foot.

'Didn't we all?' Valaida replies, wondering if she had ever been as ferociously competitive as this self-obsessed young piece. Josephine had been, had to have been, with her too-dark complexion and her desperate needs. Ethel had been and would have knocked this silly chippy down a flight of stairs, wouldn't have bothered to answer, would have just growled and punched. But had she herself ever been so desperate to win, to be the queen of every situation, including every decrepit cubbyhole of a dressing room? She believes not, while knowing that all past years aren't as clear as they might be.

'Was the trumpet part of the act?'

'You mean, did I dance and play at the same time?'

'I had an uncle on the circuit back in the twenties,' says the dancer, studying the curve of her rear end in the dressing room's cloudy mirror, lovingly caressing its prominence, 'a contortionist who played the clarinet. Audiences loved him. I mean, a girl playing the trumpet? Had to have been unique. I know there were the girl bands in the war. The Sweethearts?' Arm up, hand flicked, head peaked around for a come hither look. 'I saw them once with my sixth grade class. That Anna Mae Winburn sure could play, but back in your day. I mean . . .'

Way, way back in your day.

'No,' says Valaida coolly, 'not at the same time. There were those who did, but that was never my style.'

Some things used to work wonders with headaches like this: Mama's helpers, Papa's comforts, direct connections to sweet fogs of bliss, bliss tucked right up onto the borderlines of hell. They say the craving for that border dance never goes away. She could be slow dragging with the Sweet King right this minute, pounding gone, along with her soul. All the Sweet King wanted was every big and little thing, and every big and little thing was what you were ready to give.

'No offence,' says the dancer.

'None taken,' Valaida replies. Her head is pounding. Perhaps it's time to consult a doctor after all. Earle has been after her about it for months, Yolanda has been dropping hints, and watching Cheryl's smile is another kind of joy; but at the moment it is now that must be dealt with. Valaida opaques her eyes, and the dancer has lost what little audience she had.

Hold your gal close to your side
Shivaree, kind of glide . . .

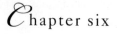

Chapter six

Chattanooga, Tennessee, 1915

Mootch along nice and slow,
Then you to-do-lo . . .

June 2, 1915. She is eleven years old today, a coloured girl with
eight long curls caressing yellow-brown cheeks in Jim Crowed
and crackling Tennessee, and despite now knowing better the
scourges of white folks, white folks' strange unpredictability that
can just up and chomp away your life, your limbs, your family, like
a mad and mangy dog, that's sending trainloads of black folks
streaming up north every week in search of some kind of peaceful
freedom, she sees the world as sunny and sweet and full of possibilities. Valada knows herself to be blessed, and every night in her
prayers, after asking forgiveness for what she's done wrong that
day (and there's always something because she has a too fast

mouth and a manner she's been told is unbecoming to a lady. How many times has she switched her behind before Iola's brother Lester, then pushed him into a horse trough when he's tried to steal a kiss, or promised to keep an eye on Hattie then gone off in some other direction?), she thanks God for smiling on her life. She's got sisters she likes, who are her best friends in fact, and a mama with a soft voice and tender hands. She lives in a house with indoor water, a wicker divan on the porch, and almost always enough food in the pantry. She has three dresses for good, two pairs of shoes, and a beautiful red-brown, grown-up violin. She is very, very lucky for a Tennessee coloured girl.

It's her birthday, and the sky's a brilliant cornflower blue, with a mockingbird singing its always new song that goes on and on, and no one else can copy. Valada figures it must be wonderful to be a mockingbird, making music whenever you want with a song that's never the same. Whenever she practises her instruments, she always tries to make up new ways to play, on the piano, on the violin, on the cello, on the guitar, but she always runs out of music before a mockingbird would. It seems silly that a sassy bird could find more ways to sing than an eleven-year-old girl who's been playing music nearly all her life, but mockingbirds didn't have all the fun. Mockingbirds didn't have birthdays, not birthday parties anyhow. Alvada sticks her head out the door.

'Valada! I know it's your birthday, but could you please come in here and take charge of Hattie? She's running around in circles bumping into things while we're all busy trying to make your party.'

'In a minute, Alva. I'm just looking at my gift book.'

'No, now, Valada, or we can forget the whole idea.'

The book is from Valada's this year teacher Miss Hawthorne. Miss Hawthorne believes firmly in the power of the book and gives every child in her care one of his or her own on their birthday. Her gift to Valada is poems by Paul Laurence Dunbar, a slender volume with raised up letters, and an inscription inside: 'To Valada Snow, one of my lights, on her birthday. You can blaze new roads. Sincerely, Millicent Hawthorne, 1915'. When the day's excitement subsides, Valada may just try to sit still and read; but it's hard to just read when there's music to be played and rhythms to be ridden. She turns a few pages. '*We wear the mask . . .*' a poem starts. What was that supposed to mean?

It's not that Valada doesn't appreciate the gift. It makes her feel particular, like there's a special purpose to her life. Valada admires Miss Hawthorne, who has come to Chattanooga from somewhere up north and says she can think of no better calling than 'to advance the Race through the gift of knowledge'. Miss Hawthorne seems to have no need of family or finery; she has only two sombre dresses, and she lives all by herself. She's only ever seen at school and going back and forth to church, never at a frolic or on Ninth Street or even at a parade. When Miss Hawthorne speaks 'of advancing the Race' and 'representing the Race', her eyes glow fierce behind her steel-rimmed spectacles. Her voice gets clearer, and even Malachi Jackson ceases to act the fool. You don't see that Miss Hawthorne's hair's too short to brush up into a roll, that she's black as pitch, and her nose stretches from here to Athens, Georgia. She is beautiful and strong, and she makes you feel that way too; but Valada wishes that Representing the Race looked to be a bit more fun. How come Representative ladies like Miss Hawthorne and Dr Rogers's nurse, Miss Adams, never wore bright colours, and the only music you ever heard them humming were hymns? When Miss Hawthorne heard kids singing the Mess Around in the playground or saw them dance the Shimmy-Sha-Wobble altogether in a gang, her nose would wrinkle up like she'd smelled something bad, like the nasty old sores on Stumpy Heywood's legs or the calico tomcat that'd been dead for a week. Who wanted to be Representative if you couldn't sing and dance?

A thump, a crash, and a young child's wail. 'Valada! Come and get Hattie now!'

> *. . . Break away then bamboshay*
> *Toddle on as you sway . . .*

Mama is setting out plates for her yellow coconut cake; Hattie is running in with the birthday card she made all by herself (but more carefully after tripping over and breaking Mama's painted flowerpot). Valada and Lavada are four hands on the piano, and Alvada is dishing out the ice cream that had been churned that morning and set to chill in Mr Miller's ice house. Mr Miller wasn't known to do favours for most folk. People said he'd demand the Lord Jesus pay cash on delivery; but he was always there with a smile whenever Mama needed anything. When Daddy was gone, which was most of the time these days, Mr Miller would mend porch doors and a-fix rain gutters, cut back a fallen branch, and ride Lavada and Hattie on his horse Mary Jean. Alvada tended to be kind of hard on Mr Miller, teasing him about the funny way he talked, and laughing behind his back. She said Mr Miller was sweet on Mama, but he was wasting his time because Mama was like the queen in this story Alvada had heard at school, whose husband was a great soldier who went away to fight a war and, though he was gone for years and years, and all kinds of men tried to creep in between her linen, the queen ignored them all because she loved only her husband. The queen knew her husband would return, and when he finally did, he beat up all the men who were pestering his wife, threw them out on their behinds, and took her into his arms. Just like Daddy did with Mama whenever he came home, and no way could funny-talking Mr Miller turn their Mama away from storybook love like that. Valada didn't like to think too much on what it must be for Mama waiting on Daddy so much of the time, but she did figure that it had to be more fun being out in the world having adventures than sitting home cleaning up after a bunch of kids, even if you liked them, and giving music lessons day after day to lots of folk who never practised.

Alvada always had her nose in some book that was making her sigh, always saying she wanted to live like in a book and talking about things like 'grace' and 'destiny'. 'What do you think your Destiny is, Valada?' Sigh, sigh. 'Will it have Excitement and Riches and a Tragic Love?' Well, probably not if you were just sitting around and waiting here in Chattanooga. Alvada would say she was missing the point, which wasn't really to have a wonderful Destiny (because how many people could have that, especially if they were coloured?) but to have beautiful thoughts about it. Then Valada would have to tease Alvada until she either laughed or cried because she just wasn't making any sense at all. Ever since Alvada had started her monthlies, it was as though sense had just left her head a lot of the time. Valada was starting to wonder if this was what being a woman was about, losing your sense like Alvada, waiting like Mama, or being admirable but never having any fun like Miss Hawthorne and Miss Adams.

Valada and Louie have found a lick they like and are giggling together as they try to turn this into a song when the front door hinges creak and a man's steps cross the threshold.

'Did you set a place for me, Etta?' comes the man's voice, and there he stands, with his long fancy jacket, his brilliant-studded stickpin, and his special Daddy smile, just as she prayed he would be. It was good to know that sometimes, when you prayed extra hard, you actually could get what you hoped you would. It didn't work all the time. It hadn't worked with wanting that gold locket bracelet or wishing Mavis Eliot's light hair would turn dark, so's Mavis would stop strutting up and down like she was God's gift to E Street, but wanting Daddy home had been more important than that. Daddy was becoming more like an idea than a real person, some*thing* that made you know the world was larger than Chattanooga because it was out there in it, moving when it wanted when and as it pleased, rather than some*one*, and now you're not sure of just how you're supposed to act.

'I'm wonderin' if my lovelies are at all glad to see me,' he says, with Mama still standing near the table, gripping the cake plates extra tight. 'I'm wonderin' if I shouldn't have stayed my butt over in Mobile.' And then Hattie runs toward him, arms up and squealing, followed by Louie, and he swings Hattie and then he swings Louie just like he used to swing Valada what seems like for ever ago. 'How's my birthday girl?' he calls to Valada over his shoulder.

'Just fine, Daddy,' she replies, and then he pulls a small and floppy package from the inside pocket of his jacket that's the colour of black and red cherries and not as new as it once was. The cuff is frayed, one of the buttons is hanging loose, and Valada wishes to herself that he was wearing the blue and grey one instead.

. . . Start right in a-rocking like a ship without a sail.
That's steppin' on the puppy's tail, ki-yi!
That's steppin' on the puppy's tail . . .

Mama's cake and ice cream had been the best she'd ever tasted, better than Sister Luella Lucinda's, who was always bragging on herself: 'I may not have yo' book learnin', Miz Etta, but, praise God in all his glory, I can surely work my pots. Just taste my coconut cake if you would.' Well, Mama's cake had been much better than Sister Lucinda's pride. Alvada had made her a quilted pocket for treasures into which Lavada had placed her very own prettiest rock, the one she'd found by the battlefield memorial in Chickamauga Park, and Daddy's present had been grown-up stockings the colour of pale buttercups.

'My absolutely favourite colour!' she'd cried, and then wrapped her arms tight around his neck. There'd been stubble on his cheek, and his breath was slightly acrid; but he rubbed his cheek against hers as though he might have really cared.

'But I thought you said your favourite was light purple,' Lavada blurted out, not understanding that sometimes you had to tell a man what he wanted to hear.

'Not any more,' replied Valada. 'This colour yellow's the absolute best! See how pretty they are, Mama! Can I put them on right now?' But she doesn't wait for an answer because Mama's been more quiet than usual this birthday evening with Daddy home. She has served him his plate and filled his glass, but there's no sense that she's actually glad he's come back. She's not wrapping his smiles in her Mama shawls of affection. She's avoiding his

69

eye, and Valada's wondering if there might be some scribbles on the pages of Alva's storybook love. Maybe Mama's finally gotten tired of waiting all the time, but Valada's not going to let this speculation worry away her night. The stockings feel soft and smooth as dandelion down. She is eager to see their effect on her slender not-long-to-be girl's legs, but she is as careful with them as she is with her violin.

Her legs are shining pale gold in the lamp light. Maybe womanhood won't be such a bad deal after all. She starts to twirl and dance. With high flaunting kicks, she is walking for the cake. '*I'm gonna step on the puppy's tail!*' she sings. '*Let's step on the puppy's tail!* Come on, Alva! Come on, Louie! Let's do our dance for Daddy!' She sashays over to her sisters and tries to pull them to the floor.

'But I can't do the dance,' pouts Lavada, ''cause I don't have pretty stockings!'

'Don't worry, muffin,' coos John Snow, happy that the evening's mood might be changing. 'You do your dance for Daddy, and he'll get you pretty stockings, too.'

'Will you play for us, Mama?' asks Valada. 'We always sing much better when you play.'

Mama is holding Hattie close in her lap with one of her sad smiles on her face. Is she not pleased about Valada's golden stockings? 'Go ahead and play for them, Etta,' coaxes John Snow. 'Hattie wants to taste some of Daddy's sugar, don't you, sweetheart?'

'John, it's getting late, and tomorrow is school.' Her voice is soft but tight as well.

'Please, Mama, please! We want to show Daddy how good we've got!'

There's a moment of silence as Mama and Daddy's eyes finally meet, and for the first time Valada can remember, the warm thing doesn't happen between them, the way they used to look that seemed to taste of butterscotch. Then Mama moves over to the piano and starts to play. Too slowly at first.

'No, faster, Mama!' says Valada, needing the music now even more than the moment before. 'Like we did last week.'

Alvada doesn't agree. 'I don't like it so fast. I get all mixed up, and Louie's gonna fall.'

'No, she won't, will you, Louie? It's better faster. We can do it, you'll see.'

And so they start. Though they have spent countless hours working out their steps, their shoulder shakes, and their flirty winks, the sisters are surprisingly shy at first. Performing for John Snow is so much more important than taking their turn with the neighbourhood kids. Mavis Eliot may have her light good hair, and Sylvester Wood flip a mean buck-and-wing, but when it comes to happy oomph the Snow sisters have always been the champs. So many times when they've been out practising in the yard, passers-by would stop to watch and smile, and some would say, 'Sister Etta, you must be so proud of your girls. They all have talent, they surely do.' But dancing for their daddy? Well, their minds are so full of how to do their very best that the first rubberlegs doesn't even fluff their skirts, but then Mama swings the music back into the bridge – she knows her girls can do better than this – and it suddenly moves inside all their bones. Their words and feet are laughing; their little hips are playing games. Lavada puts in a shim-sham-shimmy that wasn't there before. Alvada's bright soprano is soaring over the tune. Valada does a kitty growl under the chorus, kicks high, flops into a split. Then, as her sisters do their bunny truck back and forth across the floor, Valada runs for her violin, has it under her chin in a flash, and she's strutting, and riffing with Mama, strutting, and flicking the bow from side to side, plucking, and joining in with her sisters' song. She pigeon wings back and does a snappy turn and slide. Her body's filled with light. She's away from the birthday tension, inside the joy, and it's better than Mama ever said it could be.

That's steppin' on the puppy's tail, ki-yi!
That's steppin' on the puppy's tail!

71

Her first impression was the smell. Before her brain could find the sense of all the new shapes behind stage of Chattanooga's Paradise Theatre, the strange light, the odd medley of muffled footsteps on rickety floors counter-pointing the gut-bucket thumpings of the house pit band, it had to focus hard on breathing amidst a boggling press of funk. Later she would know what the culprits were, seldom laundered costumes on uncleansed bodies awash in sweats of physical exertion, anticipation, and fear, tobacco of all kinds, the bite of cheap liquor chasing cheaper perfume, old food, melting hair grease, but at eleven years old her brain was scrambling around, frantic, trying to find itself some air. John Snow had told them to stay together near the doorway while he went to find the man in charge, but as the minutes crept by, the sisters had inched further into this dark new place, a real, live goblin world right here in their hometown.

'I can't breathe,' whimpers Alvada, eyes scanning desperately for anything familiar.

'Yes, you can. Otherwise you'd be dead. You're alive, so you must be breathing.' Valada's decided the smells aren't so bad, just different, that's all, as goblin worlds should be.

'It smells like a hundred Willie Seagroves,' giggles Lavada, 'jammed into one big barrel with all their shoes pulled off.'

'Eating year-old bear meat,' adds Valada, 'with swamp water gravy.'

'I'm gonna be sick!' moans Alvada. 'I wanna go home right now!'

'No, you don't,' says Valada firmly. 'Not after all the practising we've done. Not after Daddy went out and bought us all new stockings and bows. You don't want to give them back, do you? And what if we win the contest?'

'We get a whole dollar,' says Lavada, 'and Daddy said we could keep it! Don't you wanna a dollar, Alva?'

'Hush up, you kids! Show a little respect!' Glancing up to the source of the words, the girls give a small collective yelp and grab one another in fear. The face looming above them is split right down the middle, one side corked black as night with sheep wool hair and red, blubber lips, the other pale white folk's pink, with flowing, blond, muttonchop whiskers and a matching mane of hair. 'It's hard enough fightin' wit' them fools up front wit'out havin' to wrestle wit' yo' nonsense backstage!'

'We're sorry,' squeak the girls.

'This yo' firs' time?' The sisters nod in unison. 'Well, let this be lesson number one,' growls Split Face, leaning further into their space, turning his face from side to side. Whiteface, blackface. White face, black face. 'Lesson number two is,' the girls are moving as far away from him as they can, backing into a corner; Valada is lifting up her violin as though it were a shield, 'don't be brushin' up against any o' these here walls in those pretty little dresses, or they'll be black like me befo' their time.' And now he starts to laugh.

'Malcolm!' It's a woman's voice, but almost as gravelly as that of the man with the split face. 'What you doin' to those children? Leave those girls alone.' The woman is surprisingly small and slight. She is wearing a dress with broad faded green and beige stripes that stops three inches above her ankles. Her serviceable boots have seen much better days. She is carrying a trumpet, which she uses to shoo Malcolm into the shadows where the different sides of his face still swivel from side to side.

'You girls here for the amateur talent contest?' asks the woman.

The girls nod. A man has appeared behind the trumpet woman. He is wearing a jacket made from the same faded stripes, as are the small group of dull-complected, snotty-nosed children close by. All of the children carry banged-up instruments, a saxophone, two trombones, a big bass drum, and there's a girl among them, about Valada's size but looking to be a year or two younger, who is also carrying a trumpet, cradling it more tenderly to her body than she would a porcelain doll.

'Us too,' says the woman. 'What all you do?'

'We sing and dance, and I play the violin,' answers Valada.

'That sounds real nice. We after that dollar our own selves, but I wish you sure 'nuff more luck than poor sad Sid out there,' says

73

the woman, nodding towards the stage, where a young man's attempt to sing a rag while playing spoons is being pelted with peanut shells, greasy paper cannonballs, and vociferous abuse until he abandons the fray in tears, his farmhand costume splotched with peanut shells clinging to rotten eggs.

Alvada and Louie are nonplussed by the sight. It hadn't figured in their equations that the Paradise audience might not be as warm as parents and teachers welcoming the Junior Odd Fellows production of *Rebellion of the Daisies*. They're wondering about the appeal of this grown-up theatre thing, but Valada's not worrying about whether the audience will crunch up their feelings and spit them out as chaff; she's tugging the arm of the woman as she's turning to walk away. 'Do you really play the trumpet?' Valada asks. 'You and her, do you really play?'

'Of course we play, honey,' smiles the woman. 'This here brass's too expensive jus' to hold.'

'I want to learn the trumpet, but everyone's always saying that horns aren't for girls.'

'Everyone will talk all kinds of mess, but I say it's a sin to spurn a talent God's gave you. If your heart's dancin' to a horn, then I say you ought to listen and not be wastin' your time worryin' about folk.'

'Could you teach me?' Valada asks. 'I mean, would you?'

The woman smiles again. 'We don't live roun' here, sugar, and we move roun' a lot, but whenever you see me, I'd be pleased to share my time.' And then she too has vanished into the shadows.

'Did you hear that, Alva? That lady said she would teach me the trumpet!'

'She didn't say that exactly,' sniffs Alvada. 'And I still don't know why you want to waste your time with a horn. Did you see how shabby her dress was? I bet she almost never gets paid. Folks ain't gonna pay good money to see a lady with a horn.'

'But I bet she really can play, or else she wouldn't have the guts to stand on up in front of folks. And I wouldn't be talkin' about her dress if I was you. Did you see Daddy's jacket?'

Alvada's eyes cloud up in a way that makes her sister regret her words. 'Don't say that, Valada! We're not supposed to see that, and we're not supposed to say that! You mustn't say that!'

'If you all kids don' shut up, we gonna strap you in a harness an' throw you into the pit!'

. . . We're gonna step on the puppy's tail!

They were up next. They were standing huddled together in the wings while the man doing the introductions was throwing back wisecracks to the audience and somewhere in the banter mentioning their names.

'I'm gonna die!' whimpers Alvada. 'My heart's gonna stop! I know it is! It hurts! My heart hurts!'

Lavada's sweaty hand is bunched up on Valada's dress. 'There's so many of them, Vee! Look at them, and they're all out their seats!'

'I'm scared,' Alvada screeches. 'I'm gonna die! Right here! I'm never gonna have a boyfriend and fall in love and get married 'cause I'm gonna be dead!'

'Quiet, you guys, or we won't hear to come on.' The pit conductor has shuffled his music. Three musicians have laid down their cards; a fourth is setting aside his cigar. 'Here we go,' whispers Valada. 'Get set. Here we go.' On the opposite side of the stage she glimpses a woman in a short, shiny dress throwing back her head in delight as a man in a black and red cherry jacket cups her breasts from behind, then curves his hands down her body toward her crotch. There can only be one black and red cherry jacket in the house. It can only be John Snow with his lips working the neck of a woman not their mama with nary a care to what his daughters might or might not see; but before Valada can take this information to heart, the Introducer throws his arm in their direction. The Piano Man antes up, and Valada and her sisters cakewalk out to centre stage, yellow, pink, and blue stockinged legs prancing high and true.

Even now, with a distance of some forty-odd years, Valaida can remember how her heart felt, how it had not beat out of her chest.

It had slowed. She had felt at the self-same moment to be in and out of the time she lived in, on the stage with her sisters, feeling the thump of its rough-worn wood as they placed their steps, the light warm weight of Lavada's hand on her shoulder when they laced their daisy chain, the damp beneath Alvada's dress as her hand did its kind, but also in a space all her own, where all her senses seemed to work better, where, between the singing and the dancing, the grinning and the clowning, she was knowing that next time there needed to be someplace for her to put her violin like there was at home so her arms could have a few more possibilities.

Come time for her violin feature, Valada had enough notes for a band all her own. She was riding the tune like a trick girl on bareback, her bow flicking sounds into the air like a whip. The house band growled with dismay that such a little slip of a be-ribbonned girl should have such a steady grip on their get-down. The Trombone Man tried to shake her loose, but she righted herself like a cat flying through air. The Bass Man laid down some logs in her path, but Valada tripped over their rolls as light as a feather. But then the Piano Man threw all his bones in the circle, fifty years and countless midnights of spelling out the word. And Valada had to stop. She shrugged to each her sisters, flashed a 'he's got me' grin to the crowd, and saluted the Professor with a respect that said, 'You're the teacher, Mr Piano, but I'll be back real soon to play.' The Piano Man nodded, 'I'll be here for you, darlin',' and escorted the Snow girls back across the bridge to the signifying appreciation of the crowd.

The applause sounded different from that of the church socials and the fraternal halls, daytime clapping that was generous enough but always polite; it smelled different too, fuelled as it was by roast peanuts, corn liquor, and the ferocious desire to grab hold of joy without restraints. This was night-time clapping, night-time hooping and hollering, with nary a nod to God and order. It had a belly to it and an unembarrassed sweat whose spirit mingled with the rivulets of moisture coursing beneath Valada's cammie in the direction of her girlhood. Valada had yet to make her commitment to the Lord. She'd chosen to let Alvada make the trip to the river that Sunday on her own, stating that she'd be along by and by. Now she knew that she would never take that plunge; for this night had been Valada's baptism, this Paradise Theatre stage her river. It might take a while before she could be a full-fledged member of the congregation, but Valada knew from these moments that her Church would be the Night.

They didn't win the contest. They came in third behind a mule that could count and sing and the Jones Family Brass Band, but third wasn't so bad the first time out. Their Daddy had been so pleased that he'd bought them all ice creams on the walk home, saying that the theatre manager had been so impressed with his babies that he'd offered them an intro spot before the contest the very next week.

'Does that mean you'll still be around next week, Daddy?' asked Lavada.

'Would you like that, sweetheart?' said John Snow.

'Oh yes, Daddy, because if you were here next week, maybe you'd get to like it around here again, and you might stay all the way into next month and then maybe you'd be here for my birthday too!'

'You have a birthday? I coulda sworn that your mama and me found you down by the river under a cottonwood tree!'

'No, Daddy! I came out of Mama's legs just like Hattie.'

'You sure about that?'

'Yes, I'm sure! Mama told me so.'

John Snow has scooped his young daughter up into his arms. 'I guess you're right then since your mama never tells a lie.'

Unlike you, Daddy, says the look from Valada that catches John Snow's eye. The look is without rancour, but with a recognition and maturity beyond its years, and John Snow knows he's been seen. He tries a subtle smile of complicity. *You of all the others have always known me best.* Valada says nothing, but does not look away. Alvada's humming has now broken into their song. Lavada joins in and then John Snow as well. His tenor has lost much of its pearly lustre, but he figures that by the simple singing along with their song, his girls will fall in easily with the plans percolating in his brain, of producing whole shows around the talents of his children. His own resources have shown signs of fraying of late. His fingers have been less nimble; his mind less clear. Valada doesn't join in the song, though. She simply keeps licking on her ice cream, her heart still beating slow.

They were better the next week. No longer bewildered by the backstage shadows, Valada had found a man who promised to supply her violin with a box. She was able to make the windmill moves with the ragging waves she'd been working on all week under their daddy's critical eye. Alvada was no longer thinking that the stage was going to bite her, so her smiles were just as angelic as her soul. Lavada didn't lose her place. The Piano Man still taught his lesson, but he did it with a wink. The audience had stomped and hollered, and Salem Tutt Whitney had seen it all. Salem Tutt Whitney! Renowned throughout coloured America for his shows *Silas Green from New Orleans* and *The Wrong Mr President*! Salem Tutt Whitney had just happened to be in Chattanooga that night visiting an elderly aunt, but he was always on the lookout for talent – it was how he stayed on the top of his game – so he'd been in the audience. Talk about your luck!

Mr Whitney'd come to call the very next afternoon. He wanted to design a special slot for the Snow girls in his up-and-coming show, he said, with new costumes and a song all their own. The revue was about to start its way up to Chicago, playing at least ten cities on the way, maybe more. Mr Whitney was a distinguished-looking man with intelligent eyes, graceful hands, and a voice to match. But Mama said no. Her babies were far too young for life on the road, and didn't they have laws up north against children working at night? Mr Whitney admitted that was true; once they crossed the Mason-Dixon Line, the girls would have to miss shows part of the time.

78

Daddy had said, 'Think of the money, Etta. The man's willing to pay them $30 a week!'

'That's all well and good,' said Mama, 'but who's going to look after them between times? I can't just up and go. Hattie's far too small to be moved from town to town, and I can't leave my students. That money we still need.'

'Why, I'll be looking after them, of course,' said Daddy.

And Mama had just laughed.

'When?' she'd asked, her voice deeper and more steadfast than Valada and her sisters had ever heard before. 'In between poker games and throwing dice and keeping time with fancy women? I've already lost one child to the road. Have you forgotten about Lawrence? Your son, John. Gone for good. Maybe dead. You never speak of him, never think of him, and I should trust you with our girls? They're too young to go unprotected into the world. They will stay right here with me.'

Mr Whitney had excused himself then, thanked Mama for her kind hospitality, but there was another appointment for which he was already late. After closing the door behind Mr Whitney, Daddy had turned toward Mama with a look as dark as a tornado sky. 'Woman,' he'd said. His voice was a hiss, a copperhead snake ready to strike. 'You dare defy me before the likes of Salem Tutt Whitney? Get out of here, you kids. Your mother and I have words to say.' But his eyes were too dark to see if his children obeyed. So Valada and her sisters had stayed in the room, too terrified to move at all, too terrified to whimper, as their father moved slowly across the room.

'You dare . . .' His right hand was flexing in and out of a fist, but Mama didn't move. She looked at the fist, then up into his eyes with that not-at-all-happy Mama smile, but with a change this time, like a decision had been made.

'I dare what, John?' Her voice had only the slightest degree of tremble. 'I dare what? You know the life. You live it. For children this young, what does it hold? Ignorance, consumption—'

'Freedom. Cash money.'

'At too dear a price,' said Mama. 'They'll not be leaving this house.'

John Snow turned purple, then pale, and then his hand was no longer a fist. The emotions holding him to this woman, this place, once home, were spent. The tornado clouds in his eyes disappeared; their knives flicked shut. They went flat khaki brown and as distant as the moon, his lips parting into an eerie thing that might have been a smile.

'I'll not be forgiving this, Etta. This is the last you'll see of me.'

Mama's gaze never wavered. 'I saw the last of the man I loved a good long time ago.'

And he'd just turned and walked out the door, without one look around, without a kiss for his children. He just left, and nobody said a word until Mama sent everyone off to bed.

. . . They say this new dance is a scream.
It will make a possum tango
And a tiger scream . . .

The Palace Theatre, New York, May 1956

Hannah Eisenberg slips gratefully into the relative cool of the theatre's vestibule. Walking from the office had seemed a good idea at the time, an opportunity to invite appreciative regard of the legs she knew to be her best feature scissoring amidst the crisp cotton of the peasant skirt, bought from the sweet little shop tucked away in a corner of the Village that only she knew about, her trim ankles wrapped with the ties of hitherto-unworn, red espadrilles; but by the time she'd hit Rockefeller Center, Hannah had been seriously regretting her choice. It was simply too hot. The kind of New York heat that banished all thought from the brain save, 'Where's the next shade?' and, 'If I cross over the street, could there maybe be a breeze?' or perhaps, 'If I buy myself a popsicle, will I manage to get some into my mouth before it melts all over my hand and drips down the front of my blouse?'

It was not supposed to be this hot in May. May was about balmy winds, delicate, yellow-green leaves on the trees in Central Park, and the purchase of lilacs, not bus exhaust fumes melding with perspiration and nestling dark in the pores of your nose, or tar bubbling black and viscous through winter's fissures in the streets, sullying the fire engine red of brand-new espadrilles. The espadrilles had in fact been the worst of her ideas. Slightly small to begin with, they now imprisoned her heat-swollen feet in vices laced with grit, their unworn hemp grinding her sweating soles raw. Her hair's short dark curls are dangling limply against her temples, her Audrey Hepburn coif long since melted away. This was not the way she had intended Paul to see her. She'd had something far more alluring in mind.

After keeping company for the better part of two years, Hannah Eisenberg has not seen Paul Goldman for the last three months. He had taken her home after an evening of love-making in the apartment of an out-of-town friend. After a year of clandestine evenings, Hannah had thought the time had arrived for Paul and her to 'talk'. She was twenty-five years old and ready to move on with her life. A graduate student of Social Work, a sophisticated young woman with liberal attitudes, she was not about to nag her lover about sex. That their passion was mutual was abundantly clear. Why else had she allowed their intimacy to deepen? But he was so elusive, Paul. He simply refused to be drawn on any subject of substance. How could he be so passionate on the one side and so without affect on the other?

In considering their 'talk', Hannah believed that the trick would be to engage Paul in a discussion he couldn't avoid on a topic upon which they'd agree without a doubt. What Jew of their generation would not be drawn on the subject of Germany? Ten paltry years after its crimes of the recent war, should West Germany have been granted status as a sovereign state? Was this not an outrage? She and Paul would discuss then agree how wonderful it was that they

81

had so much in common. One topic would lead to another, and she would be asked the question she craved.

But Paul preferred not to hazard an opinion, not even on the status of Germany. Paul had been his characteristic, passive self, his Adonis brow registering only the faintest traces of emotion as Hannah's opinions had escalated in both volume and tone, until Hannah could stand it no longer and literally shown him the door.

'Enough! No more! Why do I waste my time with someone who refuses to engage with the world?' Because I worship the ground you walk on. 'I refuse to waste my time, Paul Goldman. I want you to leave now, and don't call me unless you have something to say.'

Paul had done as he'd been told. He had left, and he hadn't called. Hannah Eisenberg desires Paul Goldman now more than ever. She does not believe vacancy to be the truth of him. She refuses to believe it, in fact, because Paul Goldman is her future, her ideal match in every way, and she intends, this day, to get him back where he belongs.

The Eisenbergs of New York are a powerful clan, but Hannah is a member of its least affluent branch. Hannah's father, David, like his father before him, is not a banker but an academic. Hannah's home has always been a spacious apartment in Morningside Heights filled with books and light, a grand piano, never lacking a maid. But Morningside Heights rather than Fifth Avenue, on one level rather than two or three, with wood floors rather than marble, framed prints on the wall rather than museum-quality Old Masters. Hannah has appreciated the considerable comforts of her upbringing, but she's always known that there could be more.

The Eisenbergs of Fifth Avenue would never consider the Goldmans of Central Park West and New Rochelle wealthy, but compared to the Eisenbergs of Morningside Heights, the Goldmans were doing more than well. Paul's father, Manny, hadn't come from money. Goldman's Variety Store on 133rd Street and Seventh Avenue in Harlem was the establishment of a pair of Russian immigrants who'd managed to leave the Ukraine before the worst of the pogroms and thus with enough of a nest egg to lease a small store and eke out a reasonable living. Like his older brother before him, Manny was helping out in the store as soon as he was old enough to straighten shelves and see over a counter, but a future in hand-to-mouth commerce was not what Manny saw for himself. Though he managed to stumble out of high school more by charm and guile than application, and had neither the finance nor temperament for higher education, on the odd pleasant afternoon, after a bank delivery, before a pick-up of product, Manny took to strolling through the uptown campus of the City College of New York. Prowling for prey might have been a more apt description, and he came up trumps when he snared Gladys Feltheimer. Unfashionably plump, but pretty and game, Gladys was the daughter of Johanen Feltheimer, a highly successful participant in Manhattan's garment trade. With the studied application that had been missing throughout his education, Manny lured Gladys into pregnancy and acquired her hand in marriage. Paul was born a few months later, in the spring of 1932.

Johanen Feltheimer didn't like Manny much, and thought his daughter a fool for falling into his trap, but he suspended the personal in the face of superior business sense, and this Manny possessed. Guile was well-suited to the business vicissitudes of the Depression, and with Manny as co-pilot, Feltheimer and Sons sailed from strength to strength while much of their competition idled in the doldrums or sank without a trace. In 1934, Paul's sister Dolores was born, and the Goldmans moved into a massive apartment with a view of the Park on Central Park West. It was a far cry from Harlem, but Manny Goldman was not someone who was easily satisfied. Save for her manoeuvring him into affluence, Gladys had never brought satisfaction, and Paul seemed too much like his mother to do much else than disappoint. Manny thought his son soft. As a child, Paul had cried easily. He'd become a good runner, but tended to lose big competitions because he seemed to lack the drive to win. He appeared reasonably intelligent and had done respectably at NYU, graduating with a degree in history. If someone had probed Paul as to his reasons, he might have said because his parents acted as though history didn't exist; but there had been no probing. The history degree had been as disappointing as the unwon races. It was 'useless', and so Paul was working for his father, with no enthusiasm whatsoever on either side.

Hannah is convinced she can change all of that. Whatever criticisms a person might have of Manny Goldman, there was a vitality about him that could not be denied, and there is much of his father's energy in Paul. It was Paul's physical, animal grace that had attracted Hannah in the first place, and his power has been affirmed to her again and again in their intimate nights. Hannah understands that Paul fears confronting his father with the strength he possesses, for in such a clash Manny would surely be destroyed. There was no way that Manny's spent if exuberant vulgarity could stand before the splendid potency of her Adonis. Paul himself might not share this certainty, but Hannah has studied psychology and knows her opinion to be true. It was all so classic really (even if the notion of why Paul should fear replacing Manny in Gladys Goldman's embrace when Manny had long since fled its pillowy abundance presented an enigma Hannah had yet to decipher). Chastened by his failure to contact her after their break, Hannah realizes that the re-claiming of Paul will take a well-reasoned campaign. If he is wary, she must be subtle. And cunning. And gracious. But with the love, support, and prodding of a woman such as herself, Hannah knows that there is nothing of which her Paul would not be capable.

The first order of business was to get her love back into position. For this purpose the Palace benefit has been ideal. Knowing that support of the Appeal was good for business, Manny Goldman could always be counted on for some form of contribution. As expected, he had been more than happy to help with transport expenses via the loan of his car and a driver in exchange for acknowledgment in the programme. Rather than raise suspicion, Hannah had a co-worker call and request the two-day use of the Goldman Oldsmobile with Paul as chauffeur.

'I hope this won't be too much of an inconvenience for you, Mr Goldman,' Karen had said. (Hannah had been standing at Karen's elbow.)

'Him? You gotta be joking! It'll give him something to do besides take up space,' Manny had replied, with a laugh.

Hannah vowed to herself that some day soon Emanuel Goldman would regret laughing at his son, but first to assure her intended that there were no hard feelings. Hannah is grateful not to see Paul in the theatre. It will give her a few moments to collect and tidy herself. There are two thin blondes with pony-tails on stage, throwing rings and bowling pins back and forth to one another as they bend themselves into improbable shapes. Hannah never sees such performances other than at charity events or on TV variety shows at other people's houses. The cultural curiosity of David Eisenberg and Serah, his politically active wife, has never ventured into the realm of vaudeville, and they think televisions a waste of money better spent on books or donations to New York's Neediest Cases. As she asks a janitor for directions to the nearest ladies' room, Hannah swears to herself that when Paul is successful, they will have at least two television sets, one in the living room for the adults and one for the children in the den. Herself an only child often left to her own devices, Hannah would never impose such solitude on a child of her own. Three is the number that Hannah has in mind. Two boys and one girl would be just perfect.

Tempers are flaring in the Palace's backstage area. Two dancers are arguing over whose hand went first for the last cream soda, their well-defined bottoms twitching with indignation. The violin prodigy's mother is screaming for a fan. Her precious princess is on the brink of fainting away. Some joker has taped a thermometer above a radiator that is jammed in the 'on' position. It reads 106, and Henny Youngman had taken one step inside the stage door before disappearing back into his car. He played Turkish baths only on Tuesdays, he said. For this they should call Zero Mostel.

85

He could use its slimming effects. Every air conditioning engineer in the city is on emergency call-out. Eager to spread his misery, Mel Blumberg is shouting death threats into a phone as Paul Goldman enters, followed by a middle-aged man in a suit and a workman, all of them carrying large blocks of ice.

'Where can I break this up, Mr Blumberg?' the younger man asks, relishing the producer's speechless surprise. Blumberg's cigar has nearly lost its clamp on his jaw.

'Aren't you the clever boy, Mr Goldman?' says Lucy, who has appeared from nowhere to clear out a space. 'How the hell did you manage this? I must have called every ice house from Times Square to Lake Erie. "I'd try the North Pole, lady." Nobody had ice.'

'Mr Markowitz here is the father of five daughters,' Paul replies, heaving his block onto the tarp Lucy's provided. 'He helps us out from time to time.'

'You got any idea what it is to keep those girls in dresses?' the iceman remarks, dropping his load with a sigh. 'A Rockefeller couldn't keep up. Next Saturday, Mr Goldman?'

'Any time after eleven, anything they like,' says Paul, offering his hand. 'Their mother, too. I'll be there.'

'It's prom season, Mr Goldman. You're saving my life. You got any more problems, you give Solly here a call. You want we should help you break it up?'

'No, Mr Markowitz, we'll be fine. Don't want you to get too backed up. Thanks a million.'

The iceman grasps Paul's shoulder in leaving and stares lugubriously into his eyes. 'You are saving my life.'

'Ours, too,' grins Lucy, while passing Paul a mallet and chisel. 'Why don't you hand me that jacket? What with those tights and that cape you're wearing under your shirt, in this heat it's got to be too much.'

Mel Blumberg has approached. The dismay in his eyes has been replaced by something bordering on approval, but this he'd never let on. 'You guys planning on yacking until this all is back to water? Things aren't bad enough around here? We should have a flood as well? The trash cans should work for buckets, Sweet Cakes, and remind me to give Clever Boy here a gold star.'

'I'll get the trash cans,' says Lucy, 'but I think he should get a star for each block of ice. So that'll be three gold stars, Mel. Count 'em . . .'

'Don't push me, Lucy,' growls Mel. 'I'm like this close—'

'Too ugly to contemplate. I'm on my way.'

Paul's groin tugs with the unfamiliar sensation of pleasing an older man as Lucy goes off to collect the trash cans. Or is it because the high-buttocked dancers have stopped their bickering to look admiringly in his direction? There was something to be said for general appreciation. It gave a man a rush that could be felt throughout his body, something that's been missing from Paul Goldman's life for years, and all of it due to his concern for Valaida Snow. Mel had been promising ice, but no one could find any, too late, tough luck, no ice available in the whole damn city, and the thought of Valaida Snow cramped in that airless dressing room, with the heat steadily rising and those aggravating females, had somehow brought the thought of Mr Markowitz to Paul's brain.

He'd made the call from the drug store across the street. Markowitz was cagey, naturally, sitting as he was in the catbird seat. He had a million orders, yadda-yadda. There was just no way, until Paul heard himself coaxing out a deal like he'd heard his father do at least a thousand times on the phone. The Lord only knew how loud Manny would yell when he heard about the dresses. Paul would probably end up having to pay for them all himself, making the blocks before him some pretty pricey H_2O, but he would worry about that later. In the meantime he's feeling good and cool, cool as a howling Beat poet in a smoke-filled Greenwich Village dive, even if it's probably only from the ice. As he rolls up his shirt's sleeves, unbuttons its top button and loosens his tie, Paul's wondering how gratitude might be expressed by Valaida Snow. Not with a kiss certainly, but probably a smile, and perhaps a touch from a yellow-brown-coloured hand with its fingers tipped with coral. In the meantime, the pleasure of the dancers isn't bad. God help him if he's not starting to like show business.

Paul is engrossed in his ice by the time Hannah Eisenberg has found her way backstage. She barely recognizes him at first, her always immaculate, reticent Intended in a saturated shirt delineating his arms and back, wet hair hanging about his eyebrows, dark eyes snapping with life, chipping ice into trash cans, and laughing. Near-naked dancers are squirming about him like so many ravenous puppies, squealing with pleasure while slipping ice chips into their cleavages, and Paul in the thick of it, laughing. Hannah wants to scream, '*How dare you?*' even if she's not sure who should not be daring what; but she knows that stridency is not what is called for. Hannah inhales deeply, gathering psychology about herself like a protective cloak. She's been able to revive her presentation. Her cheeks are blotted, her curls and blouse repositioned. Her skirt may no longer be so fresh and crisp, but it is interesting; and her feet are no longer throbbing like they were. She's taken enough little girls' ballet to affect a dancer's walk when she needs to, and this would seem to be a time of need. Throwing back her shoulders, Hannah strolls toward the affray. Paul looks up, and he sees her, but there is no click in his recognition. She advances to greet him with her smile carefully intact, while her brain careens with what is meant by her lover's lack of click.

For the past half hour, Valaida has had the dressing room to herself. Unnerved by Valaida's placid exterior, Liz LaFontaine has vacated in search of fresh air and more admiring attentions. For Valaida, yet another person gone has meant that much less energy spent resisting both the discordant anima of silly, competitive children and the accursed heat; and this is a good thing. It's been a killer, this heat. Valaida hasn't yet begun to perform, and already melting pomade is seeping beyond her hair line, threatening to rivulet down her neck. Her headache has not abated. Her eyes are pounding behind their lids. Her face feels clammy beneath its make-up; her legs in their stockings are sausages aching to burst; and the girdle, the goddam girdle . . . Valaida has been to the big art museum with Cheryl, up on Fifth Avenue, with the big white columns and the marble floors. She's spent time in the Egyptian halls and seen the ancient mummies encased in their painted coffins, looking good and wrapped-up dead as they could be. Valaida's feeling an affinity with those mummies, while knowing that a modicum of relief is right at her well-manicured fingertips. She could remove the stockings, the girdle, wipe off the make-up, confront the world with air circulating more freely and without her masque; but if she gives in to that urge, the game's all done; and Valaida is not done with the game. She'll always be in there doing what she can do, singing, not deferring to the big bad world or young silly children, playing Eugene, and maybe with the attentions of a cute young boy or two. As she's always done. Valaida relaxes into herself. There was something to be said for Egyptian coffins. They were beautiful and sturdy and stood the tests of time. There is a knock at the door.

'Relief at last, Miss Snow. Are you receiving?'

'By all means.'

Lucy's the one who's done the talking, but she just opens the door to admit Paul and his trash cans. 'Three for this room, I think. Those chippies generate a lot of goddam heat. I wasn't referring to you of course, Miss Snow.'

'I didn't think you were.' Young Paul is looking different, and not just because his shirt is damp and clinging to his torso, displaying very nicely its appealing rises and dips. He's straighter about the shoulders, his chin is up instead of down, his eyes still veiled, but less so. 'I've been hearing a rumour through the walls that we owe this miracle to you, Mr Goldman.'

'That's right, Miss Snow,' replies Lucy. 'Paul here's our hero, our very clever boy.'

'Not such a boy,' says Valaida, looking direct into the young man's eyes. Was that the hint of a tremble on the left side of his upper lip?

'Where would you like your ice, Miss Snow?' A little leap of the Adam's apple. Yes, this could pass away some time if you cared to, Miss Valaida. Indicating a space on her table, Valaida is considering what it would take to free a smile on the young Paul's face, promote full tremble of his lips, dance to his breathing. On the pretence of taking a chip of ice, Valaida is about to allow her hand to brush lightly against his when a dark but white young woman appears in the dressing-room door. She looks at Paul looking at Valaida as she steps, hand-outstretched, into the space that is about to be charged.

'You must be Valaida Snow. I've been so looking forward to meeting you! My name is Hannah Eisenberg. I was the one who arranged for my Paul to transport you today. I work for the Appeal.'

Paul looks up startled when he hears the possessive, and Valaida listens politely as Hannah prattles on. 'In your file in our office, I've noticed that you've supported the Appeal a number of times,' she's saying, forcing her cheeks into a rictus of sincerity. 'I wanted you to know how much we appreciate your contributions. It's kind of unusual, I mean, as I'm sure you know, your people aren't usually involved. I mean, why would you? You've got many problems of your own, and I am just so impressed! What you're doing is incredibly positive; Negroes and Jews *should* be joining together. There's so much we have in common, battles for acceptance and understanding, but I was wondering why—'

'Why Miss Snow does something isn't really our business, Hannah.' Paul's interrupting her to offer an opinion, shut her down in fact, causes Hannah's eyes to fly open, her jaw to drop slightly, her posture to flinch out of its dancer affectations. Lucy clears her throat and commences to study a spot on the floor. Hannah is standing between Paul and Lucy and the exit. There's nowhere anyone can go, and the air has just gotten closer. Paul glances at Valaida's hand in a silent goodbye to the coral-tipped fingers.

'I just thought her reasons could inspire others to do the same and that people should know about them. It could help the

Appeal.' Hannah has noticed Paul's glance and realized that what she intends may not be so easy. Her eyes bounce back and forth between this man she desires and this older Negro woman, whom he possibly desires.

'I like to keep some things personal,' Valaida says, knowing that her life's too short to be caught up in the games of Caucasian children. All of them needed to leave the room and her in peace. 'I think most people do.'

'Well, of course they do, but don't you think—'

'No, I don't,' Valaida replies, watching the young woman's brain race through fantasies of fledgling plantation masters and wanton mulatto slaves, pure and innocent white boys learning of lust in a jungle of deep, dark bosoms, and then turns her attentions to Lucy. 'Any idea when I'm going to be up?'

'No,' replies Lucy, 'but I'll go out and ask and be back in a jif. There're other folks waiting for ice, Paul, if you don't mind me saying, as in chop-chop, Clever Boy. Why don't you help him, Hannah? Got to keep our artists happy. That would really be great.'

Hannah is unmindful of Lucy's mischief. Happy to have a purpose, her pique would have been leavened by hope if Paul would only soften his eyes a bit in her direction, but this he has not done. 'We'll be going now, Miss Snow,' he's saying, all eyes on the Negro woman, 'but if there's anything else I can do . . .'

'I'll let you know,' this Valaida replies, calmly, knowing what havoc she's wreaking. Hannah's family is not observant. Her family attended their synagogue on the High Holidays only, and not always then; but Hannah knows the legend of Lilith, Lilith who lived in darkness, enemy and destroyer of the young. Never did Hannah think she would ever meet a Lilith; for what was she other than primitive superstition? Yet here is one before her now, a Lilith virtually glowing with malevolent intent.

'. . . And you won't forget about the pictures,' Paul is asking. What pictures? Hannah is wondering. Of this aging Negro woman? Paul has never collected such pictures! He had teased her about

91

snaps she had collected in her teenage years, of Robert Mitchum and Frank Sinatra, but at least she'd not been twenty-four, and if they weren't Jewish, at least they were white. Why was Paul wanting a picture of this Negro woman who was no one in particular? Dorothy Dandridge she could understand, maybe. Eartha Kitt, she could understand. Maybe. At least they were young and sexy, in a coarse kind of way.

'I won't forget. Nice to have met you, Miss Eisenberg. How nice to gaze on the life you're destroying.'

'Likewise, Miss Snow. I hope you didn't think me too forward,' Hannah replies, vowing to fight this planned destruction of her life, to win.

'Absolutely not. I hope you enjoy the show.'

Once the white children have left her space, Valaida allows herself a deep exhalation of relief. In another time, despite the augers against its sense, Valaida might have decided to play with Paul after the ice has done some work; but other times have been replaced by wisdom. She'll marshall her energies for the business that brought her to this place. Folding her hands loosely across her lap, Valaida wills the pounding of her eyes to slacken.

$\mathscr{C}$hapter seven

Chattanooga, Tennessee, 1917

Steal up-a, young lady, oh happy land,
Won't you steal up-a, young lady . . .

The Snow girls love running down to the river on a warm
summer night when the party boats come through, spreading
news of the rhythms conjured down New Orleans way. The
musicians aren't just ragging any more, they are jassing it too.
Jassing has a thump that centres deep down in your gut, and
notes tumbling all in, out, and around the outlines of a song.
Valada and her sisters love to feel the music jump into their
back-bones, toss it back and forth between them, flipping off
steps and story attitude, and how Valada hungers after making
those horn sounds, holding brass to her lips and sending sparks
up into the sky.

The Snow girls are on their own an awful lot these days. With the never frequent contributions of her husband finally gone for good, Etta Snow had had to think even more about cash. She moved into the parlour to accommodate a second boarder and, when the chance lifted its head, threw reins around the luck of playing piano beneath the screen of the new picture palace downtown. Etta has raised her girls with much love and care and trusts that good sense will guide them in the times she isn't there. For the most part she is right; but sometimes jassing gets the best of Valada, and an hour on the riverbank can't still the hunger in her bones for more of the music than so small a body should stand. She slips away from her sisters on their easy walk back home, hides around a corner when Alvada sees she's gone. Alvada calling, 'Where're you gone to, Valada? Mama trusts us not to prowl the streets like Godless girls lookin' for fancy,' as Valada runs through the alleys to the District, needing to chase more of the night.

Youngsters aren't welcome in the sporting houses and juke joints of Chattanooga, but there's plenty of music to be heard in the streets and alleys outside. Valada isn't the only child listening and dancing in the alley, or the only girl either, but she's usually wearing the nicest, cleanest clothes, and she's had to fight for the right to lap the music up in peace. The children trade steps and rhythm games and sometimes cigarettes, but for the most part Valada just concentrates on the horns, and if time allows, she pays a visit to Antoine.

She decided to name him Antoine because he looks as sleek as a Creole river gambler, like the men she sometimes saw with her Daddy when she was small, with their frock coats, graceful hands, and voices shot through with a diamond brilliance different from the rhythms of Chattanooga's coloured folk. Mr Sackerby wants $11 for this trumpet, which has been in his pawn shop window the better part of a year. Valada hopes she might get him down to $7.50, but with only $2 under her mattress, when and how was only a notion.

Sackerby's Pawn Shop is down the street and around the corner from Morgan's Saloon, the joint Valada and her friends favour for the quality of its music and its wide, almost even sidewalk that makes it easier to hear your taps; but the crowd at Morgan's is rough and ready. More nights than not, some mister rubs up too close to another man's woman, fists and chairs start to fly, straight edges flash, and blood begins to flow. Valada tends not to linger about the fuss. It's the perfect time to visit Antoine in peace, peer into that window, imagining her fingers pushing on his valves, deciphering his chordal mysteries.

'What in the world you doin' in these parts, Miss Valada? Your mama know you're about at this time of night?'

Mr Miller was by himself, as he always seemed to be, except for when he was dealing with customers. He was wearing a black homburg sitting square upon his head, a black jacket buttoned almost to the knot of his tie, and a high, lily-white collar reflecting against the ebony of his chin.

'Is that a Bible you're carrying, Mr Miller? Mama said you always tell her you have no time for the church.'

'I praise the Lord in my own fashion, Miss Valada, and now I think I'd better walk you home. Don't you know what can come to innocence down around these parts?'

Mr Miller wasn't free with conversation, but when Valada asked him for an ice cream from Albioni's cart, he obliged without a fuss.

'Is it as good as your mother's homemade peach, Miss Valada?'

'No, but Mama doesn't have much time for ice cream these days.'

Mr Miller blinked his eyes at that, for more than anything else in the world he has hoped to gift Etta Snow with time. Mr Miller tried his best to coax Etta to his heart when it was clear that John Snow was never coming back, tending her garden as though a fence didn't separate it from his own, saving her the best of everything in his general store; but Etta's heart still belonged to the man who had wooed her. Though she held Mr Miller in high and friendly regard, Etta beseeched him to desist with the hand-picked nosegays and store-bought sweets, which he did, with reluctance; but he never could put a stop to his eyes. Every time Etta Snow strayed across his field of vision, Mr Miller's eyes threw out vast nets of yearning.

'There's a lot of your mother in you, Miss Valada.'

Valada thinks this a silly thing to say since everyone agrees her to be her father's spitting image; but she spends no time pondering the strange ways men's heads turn. She's thinking about Antoine, how he'd feel against her teeth (folks said that teeth were important), what it would take to make him sing.

The next time Mr Miller found Valada in the District, he wasn't walking by himself. He was driving a brand-new Chevrolet automobile and said he ought to drive her home. Valada had never been in an automobile before, so even though she hadn't spent as much time with Antoine as usual, she was happy to take the ride.

'What do you find so interesting in that window, Miss Valada?' Mr Miller's words were so quiet you could hardly hear them with the engine's noise. His Bible was nudged up against Valada's skirts.

'I want to buy that silver trumpet, Mr Miller. I've got two dollars saved, but I'm going to need at least six more.'

The automobile's ride was rougher than a wagon's, but Valada enjoyed the press of plush seats against her thighs and the way everyone just looked to see who was travelling in such style, especially when Mr Miller stopped to get her an ice cream from Albioni's cart. As folk pointed and nudged, Valada knew that she'd be owning an automobile of her very own some day.

'How are you intending to earn your money, Miss Valada?' Mr Miller was looking at Valada hard as he handed her the ice cream, but when she started to lick her cone, his eyes moved down and away.

'Well, there's a talent contest next week, and we win most of the time, but that's fifty cents three ways, so it's not all that much; and I've started teaching Melindy Burrows the piano once a week. Fifteen cents, but it'll add up.'

The automobile shuddered as Mr Miller moved it into gear and then barely avoided a rut. His hands were tensing and releasing on the wheel.

'If your mama permits, why don't you come and work for me?'

If you gonna steal up at all,
Steal that man, don't steal no boy . . .

'There's a lot of your mother in you, Miss Valada,' said Mr Miller after Valada had handed Mrs Dawkins her string-wrapped parcel of maws.

Valada has been working after school and Saturdays at Mr Miller's grocery for three and a half weeks. Mr Miller isn't free with conversation, but he says this so often Valada almost hears it as hello. Only this time his voice has a different catch to it than usual. Valada is twelve years old, but she's been running in the District since her mama's been working nights, and she understands the catch. She looks at Mr Miller, who is looking right at her.

'Do you think I ought to put more peaches in the basket, Mr Miller?'

'Can you manage by yourself?'

'Oh, sure. I'll be fine.'

Valada overfills the carry basket, and one of the wire handles gives way. Kneeling down to reclaim the peaches not damaged by their fall, she hears the soft crunch of a footstep on the chaff-strewn storeroom floor. Sunlight through the slatted walls is slicing topaz through the dust, honey across the pink, tan, and white gingham of Valada's summer dress.

'I'm sorry about the peaches, Mr Miller. I'll be cleaning up soon as I fill the basket back up outside.'

'That'll be fine, Miss Valada.'

The catch has near overwhelmed Mr Miller's voice, and Valada understands. She stands aside from the damaged peaches with sunlight golden across her hair and looks right back at Mr Miller. She fluffs the floor chaff off of her pink, tan, and white gingham skirts, then lifts one side to flick away a small smudge of crushed peach. She knows he will see the white cotton-stockinged curve of her young girl's legs above the modest black leather of her lace-up shoes. She enjoys that his hands are clenching by his sides.

Mr Miller is closer, but he is still across the room. Valada

97

straightens her sleeves, the white eyelet of her cammie showing briefly beneath her shoulder blades, before lifting the full, damaged basket to her chest. The gingham bulges slightly where in future there'll be breasts. The air is sweet with the scent of peach pulp, corn meal, and gently turning yams. She moistens her lips against the room's dry heat. His breath is a fevered rasp. His thing is straining against black wool. His shudder is chased by a quiet moan as she walks by him into the store.

Valada has waited on four customers by the time Mr Miller comes back in the store with a chambray apron over his trousers and his Bible in his hand. She is pleased to be doing a good job for him because she wants her trumpet.

Mr Sackerby didn't agree to $7.50, but Valada was able to buy Antoine for $8.00 and still have $1.50 left over for lessons from Mr Schultz, after Mr Miller put the $5.00 bill in her pay envelope that week.

'How come Mr Miller paid you all that money, Valada? Nobody makes money like that working part-time in a grocery store.'

The sisters were sitting out on the steps of the back porch marvelling at Antoine's length and shine. Across the fence, Mr Miller could be seen hoeing out his garden.

'Mr Miller said he really respected me working so hard to get the trumpet, and that if I wanted it so much, I should get on with it, and I could pay him back as I could.'

Alvada looked suspicious. 'That doesn't sound like the Mr Miller I know. He's always so sour.'

'Yeah,' said Lavada, 'all dressed in black and never smiling, like he was buddy to the Devil or something.'

'Well, he used to smile at Mama, and I'm her kin. Maybe he's still trying to make some points.'

'Oh, no,' laughed Alvada, 'can you imagine Mr Miller as our step-daddy? We'd probably have to tiptoe round the house and whisper all the time!'

'Or a Mr Miller little brother,' giggled Lavada, 'all dark and bald and slack-lipped, just like his daddy!'

Lavada screwed up her face in imitation of Mr Miller's fantasy son, and the sisters fell to laughing as Valada laid aside the soft cloth she was using to rub down her horn, put the trumpet to her lips, then blew out a loud C-D-E-G progression like Mr Schultz had taught her. On the other side of the fence, Mr Miller stood up and looked, his eyeglasses reflecting in the sun.

Antoine grabbed Valada's heart with a completeness that kept her awake at nights. She loved him moving from cool to warm in her hands, her blood rushing up and down her arms and legs, into her girlhood, bulging behind her eyes into the middle of her brain. Mr Schultz said she was going to have learn to control that rush, that if she wasn't careful, over time, it would carry her right away; but she loved the intensity as much as she loved the taste of blood that came to her mouth when she pressed the mouthpiece too hard to her teeth for too long a time. Playing with Antoine was all she wanted to do. It was only at her mama's insistence that she kept up with the piano, violin, and guitar, and soon she was wanting to work it into a routine with her sisters; but Alvada wasn't impressed.

'I don't know why you stay so fired about this horn,' she grumbled. 'It makes you seem like you want to be mannish. It doesn't go with the rest of what we do.'

Lavada liked the trumpet, but Alvada wouldn't be budged; so Valada played her trumpet at the Star of Jordan Picnic on her own. Some people hooted (mostly boys in short pants) and some applauded, and way down the side under a cottonwood tree, a dark man in an old yellow hat nodded his head and smiled. Mr Miller left the picnic right after Valada started to play, which was the last time anyone saw him alive. That night his Chevrolet drove off the Market Street Bridge, which was a strange thing to happen to someone who wasn't a drinking man.

> . . . *I popped my whip, I run my best, oh happy land,*
> *I run my head in a hornet's nest, oh happy land.*

His ice duties complete, Paul has stepped into the alley behind the Palace for a smoke. It's not much cooler in the alley than it is backstage, but at least the air is circulating more freely, and with Hannah gone, Paul can breathe more freely as well. The thought of Hannah causes Paul to squint over his match. What the hell was going on with her? It had made sense for her to show up today; she did work for the Appeal after all, so Paul had expected to see her, not looking forward to it particularly, but thinking it would be painless enough. But after their last evening together two, three months ago, he couldn't have expected her to act the way she did. If he was remembering correctly, she was the one who had shown him the door, never wanted to see him again 'unless he had something to say'. Having always found Hannah nice enough, if a bit tiring sometimes with all of her causes and opinions, and pretty enough, though more in a striking than a beautiful way, Paul hadn't had anything to 'say'. To tell the truth, Hannah's ultimatum had been something of a blessing because she had been part of the rut that has been his life, and Paul knows enough about himself to admit that he probably wouldn't have moved or tried to change much of anything if he hadn't been pushed. He didn't think this habit was something to be proud of, rather, it was something less than useful he'd inherited from his mother.

Gladys Goldman experienced life as though laid back on an ocean of cushions, most oftentimes in an inebriated fog. Paul can't imagine his mother initiating much of anything more than reaching for whatever had been placed directly in front of her. He loves her, but she had a way of sapping a person's energy. Gladys Goldman's indolence had driven her husband Manny out of the big Central Park apartment with the expensive but mismatched appointments into the arms of an endless number of women, before a sales assistant named Bernadette had reeled him into her net. Bernadette (formerly) Nussbaum could be grating to the point of downright vulgarity, but Paul recognized in Bernadette the same kind of crazy energy his father Manny possessed. The same kind of energy Paul had avoided because it was too much and too destructive. The kind of energy he'd been afraid of because he couldn't compete with it. The energy Paul abhorred and craved in equal measure. Hannah's ultimatum had been like the big alarm clocks that used to wake up actors in the twenty-year-old movies Paul sometimes saw on the Upper West Side. There'd be a shot of the alarm clock, ringing off the table, then cut to the actor with his eyes flying open. Paul was actually thankful to Hannah, but he hadn't missed her, so he hadn't called her. He'd had nothing to 'say', so where did she come with this idea of 'my Paul'?

An up-and-coming young comedian joins Paul near the door. His suit is cheap and flash, not cool, but he was said to be a talent. 'Hey there, Paul guy! Major kudos for the ice thing! Talkin' about saving a fella's life! How's about continuing the tradition and letting me bum a smoke?'

'Sure thing. Take a couple if you like.'

The comedian's eyes are darting and his fingernails bitten down to the quick, but he knows how to take a light with a nifty flick-twist of the match and a rock-steady hand.

'Thanks, buddy. You're a champ.'

Paul would like to use that match trick, but he knows better than to try it here and now.

Many of the benefit's acts are out here in the alley as well, some sitting on trash cans, talking little above a murmur, as though loud conversation and raucous laughter would only serve to increase the heat, some counting their way through dance routines, rationing their energies but intent despite it all. The blonde twins from Valaida's dressing room are contorting over one another's backs, oblivious to the alley's dirt and debris. Show people. You couldn't help but admire their stoicism, their self-possession, but Hannah was right. There weren't many Negroes here. Paul couldn't help but wonder how Valaida felt about being one of the – what? Two, maybe three? Paul didn't know too much, but he realized that Valaida wouldn't give him an answer if he were rude enough to ask, not yet anyway. Maybe, if they got to know one another better. How much better, Paul wasn't sure how to imagine. He was feeling this was important. Maybe this was where he could find his path, something to do with bringing Negroes and whites together in show business, maybe doing this thing called producing. Out from under Manny's heel. Maybe Mel would help. The stage door bangs open.

'Clever Boy! You didn't hear me calling? What, you think you do one thing right, and the rest of the day is clover? Get in here!' Mel's voice is a bark, but there's no longer a scowl behind the unlit cigar. Paul grinds his cigarette into the dust with a smile.

Hannah runs into the building housing the United Jewish Appeal, not bothering to pause at the elevator, heading for the stairs. The building's lifts are notoriously slow, and Hannah has figured she has at most twenty-five minutes to spend searching through Appeal Office files before heading uptown to change. The office is empty except for Myrna Fox. Everyone else is either down at the theatre or running benefit errands, but there is normal business to attend to, so here Myrna remains, shuffling papers in the stifling heat, her blouse unbuttoned to her navel, revealing a cheap, greying slip and roaring rivers of perspiration. Myrna is the office rock, fat, solid, and imperturbable as Gibraltar.

'I'm so glad you're here!' Hannah exclaims. 'You can help me!'

'Help you with what? I don't have enough of my own to do?' Myrna is surprised to see Hannah, but doesn't bother to button up.

'You've got to help me, Myrna! You've got to!' Hannah is running from desk to desk, rifling frantically through piles of paper, many of which are sliding onto the floor. 'I need to find out everything we have on Valaida Snow!'

'The lady trumpet player. What about her?'

'Everything!' Hannah has abandoned the desks for a filing cabinet, pulling a drawer out so savagely that it crashes onto the floor, barely missing her espadrilled foot, releasing an avalanche of papers into the room. She then bursts into tears. Myrna waits impassively until the sobs diminish to whimpers.

'What everything?' she finally asks.

'Everything about her,' Hannah replies. 'I think that Marty had a file of all the artists with biographies and clippings, but I can't find it. I want to know why she keeps doing benefits like this one when she's a Negro, and everybody knows that Negroes barely know where Europe is, let alone what happened to us there. I don't trust her! I have to know why she's here!'

'Why does anyone do anything?' The last thing Myrna was wanting this afternoon was the company of one of the Appeal's flightier young volunteers, let alone one in hysterics. Who needed this nonsense? It was too damn hot for nonsense. 'I can't figure out my own daughter, and I gotta hunch you can't figure out that handsome guy you're always going on about, so what makes you think we can know what makes a *schwartze* lady trumpeter tick?' Myrna raises her bulk slowly out of her chair and goes to stand in the midst of the office's new paper carpet. 'You've done enough damage. Go stand over there.' After peering downward for a moment, Myrna picks up a file, much of its contents still scattered about the debris. 'There might be something in here,' she says, handing the file over to Hannah. 'Marty likes her, for some reason. She's probably a good way to fill up space. I think she's done work at the Williamsburg Settlement House, too. More than that I don't know.'

Back at the Palace Theatre, Lucy taps on Valaida's door. 'Fifteen minutes, Miss Snow. I know you don't have any reason to believe me, but I think this is pretty firm. Would you like me to come by and lead you down?'

'That's all right. I'll find my way,' replies Valaida from where she sits in the semi-darkness. 'I don't mind if there's a bit of extra time. I can get acclimated to the band.'

The door eases open slightly, and Lucy pops her head around. 'Anything else I can do for you in the meantime? I've stopped apologizing for the delays. There's nothing I can do about them.'

'Don't worry yourself,' says Valaida. 'I've seen a lot worse.' A whole hell of a lot worse.

*C*hapter eight

Winter, 1919

I'm a jazz baby!
Full of jazbo harmony
That 'walk the dog' and 'ball the jack'
That caused all that talk
Is just a copy of the way I naturally walk . . .

The alley next to the Athens, Georgia Liberty Theatre, is full up with folk gathered around pail fires sheltering against the cold. Squirrel-skin collars are turned up against the wind. Two-toned shoes whirl and stomp in the dust. A pasmala, that's what the step was called, but he was flying it in the middle, jumping one leg over the other as though he was about to trip himself. Valada's studying so precisely she bumps right into a man in a box-back melton coat eating a plate of barbecue.

'Damn, girl! Shit! Watch the way you movin'! This grey wasn't made for red sauce. Goddammit to hell!'

Despite the bluster, Valada's gaze is calm above a dazzling smile. 'I'm sorry about your coat. I was looking for the stage manager of Mr Franklin Dudley's *3000 Miles From Jimtown* revue.'

'Well, you found him,' growls the man, flicking the red sauce off his coat with an elongated pinky nail.

'I know that, sir. I served you at Mamie's Lunchroom back in Chattanooga a couple weeks ago, and back there at Mamie's you were saying as how there might be some chorus openings in the show before too long.'

'Didn't nobody train you better than to eavesdrop on private conversation?'

'Excuse me, but you weren't whispering like it was a secret. I had hoped to get to you before now, but I'd like to show you what I can do, if I might.'

'You don't know if there's a job.' Some curious are clustering, mostly men. The women are further back for the most part.

'No, I don't, but it'd be silly to come all this way and then just stand still.' A tall marrony-skinned woman with a turkey-feathered green hat and stone cold eyes seems the centre of the further back group. Her expression is not friendly.

'Does your mama know you're here?'

'Does it matter if I'm good?'

'There's no music out here.'

Valada lifts her violin case. 'I can provide my own.'

'OK, Short Stuff, you got three minutes.'

One of the men offers to hold Valada's carpet bag before she sets it down. The same when she starts to slip off her coat.

'You sure about this, honey? It's a witch's behind out here.' Further back the Turkey-Feathered Hat has deepened her scowl.

'Thanks, but I'll be fine.' Because she's not sure she can move in the grown-up coat she acquired just before her trip. Underneath she's still wearing young girl's skirts. Valada's been maintaining a smile all this while, but as she takes her violin out of its case, she

105

closes her eyes in prayer to the God she only knows sometimes. *Fire me, Lord, please, now as ever was.*

'Come on, gal! We ain't got all day!'

Bri-i-i-i-n-n-g! Valada spins around on a hard-drawn chord, offers two minutes and forty seconds of her 'Jazz Baby' violin speciality, ending with the leg-over-almost-trip-yourself step she just saw in the alley. She's not had time to catch her breath before Mr Two-Tone Shoes comes running.

'Hey, girl! That's my Over The Top! What you doin' with my Over The Top!'

'And she just about nailed it, didn't she? Just like that.'

'Sure did, and had that cute little hippy thing, too.'

'Time for you to start gettin' nervous, Medill.'

The other men seem to find Medill's upset funny, while a few of the women have drifted closer in to look. Not Turkey-Feathers, though. She's still leaning against the wall, her mouth just set.

'Girl, that is *my* Over the Top! You can't just up and steal someone's stuff! It ain't professional, or neighbourly neither! How'd you like it if I just took that little bow wiggle of yours, called it mine, and you weren't even a nod?'

Valada is genuinely contrite, or appears to be. 'I'm sorry, Mr Medill. I just wanted the job so bad, and what you were doing was so neat . . .'

The Stage Manager's looking amused. Valada goes up to the offended dancer and touches him on his hand. 'I promise not to do it again.'

The dancer looks at Valada's small, paler hand on his and the sweet, earnest look in her young girl's eyes. 'You better put back on your coat, or I'm gonna be feeling sorry for you when you dyin' with the pneumonia.' He smiles. 'You a natural, girl, but you need to work on that left foot. Come around when you got a minute, and I'll help you break it down.'

Valada looks to the Stage Manager, who throws a glance over his shoulder. 'Bessie, take Stuff here and get her Loretta's costumes. That cracker Montgomery must have opened up by now.' He gives Valada an up-and-down as she fastens up her coat and is pleased that she doesn't flinch. 'Ten dollars a week, four shows a day, but you can keep that fiddle in its box. Mr Dudley ain't partial to lady instrumentalists. We're up in an hour. Bessie here will run you through the steps.'

The Liberty is dark and dank and as porous to the wind as a white lawn summer frock, but Valada's feeling like she's entered the first stage to heaven as Bessie hands over the sweat-stained satins and spangles of Loretta's abandoned bits. Bessie looks to be no older than Valada is herself, but she acts as though she's been in the life for ever.

'You'll be in three numbers, at least to start. You'll be a Dancing Dinah, an Oriental Maiden, and in the Bridesmaid Chorus. Dang! I can't find the sash! I bet Loretta took it with her. She was mighty partial to that sash, and it was so cold-blooded how it all went down, even if she was steady stumbling more days than not, but Loretta wouldn't hurt a fly, and just to turn her out that way? Can't blame her for wanting to take a token. She was bigger than you, too. You're like me, still filling out . . .' Bessie's smile is open and friendly despite the fact that two of her side teeth are gone. 'Well, you got your hat pin and that pretty thing on your coat. Maybe that'll work. Us girls'll think of something. Let's get out into some space.'

The Liberty stage is wider than the Paradise in Chattanooga, but there are holes here and there where some of the boards have broken through.

'Yeah, you gotta watch yourself in this house. Medill near crippled himself on Tuesday. Now the routines are all pretty simple, and I could see in the alley that you're pretty fast on the draw. Not as fast as myself 'cause I was born with the gift, but you could put me on my game. The Dinahs start out with a pass, pass, pass with a Wing, double turn for count of eight, then a Lady Time and a point. You know the Time?'

'Uh-huh.' Despite the weight of her heavy winter skirts, Bessie moves with an easy, sprightly grace. Joy has transfigured her muddy complexion, straightened the downward cast of one eye.

'Then after the Point, we kind of shimmy for a while. Shake it, shake it, shake it, and watch the mens just smile . . .' Holding her carpetbag and her violin and her pile of sweat-stained costumes, Valada falls into step beside Bessie, who turns with a grin. 'That's right. That's right. You a natural for sure. Sometimes I think that the menfolks'd be happy if we just stood here and shaked the whole night from our ears to our toes while their tongues hit the floor, but we don't.' She grabs hold of Valada's arm. 'We double-shuffle, double-shuffle, Buck back, and kick right . . .'

The girls are laughing and the dinge is chased with golden light. They part with a little whoop, toss toe-heel business back and forth, and Valada's moved on up to heaven stage number two and fast away from the fate some folk would have her live of teaching school or busting suds and always waiting for nothing much.

'Bessie!' Turkey-Feathers's voice is a rough-hewn whip. 'Where's that salve you promised to replace? My dogs is barkin' loud, and I can't be workin' without it.'

'But I asked you this morning, Mary, and you said you could last to the weekend. There're only fifteen minutes till showtime, and I need to show Valada the basic . . .'

Turkey Mary has walked between the two girls. She was a beauty once, with a tall willowy shape, green-gold cat's eyes in a copper brown complexion, but her once smooth cheek is rivven by a jagged, knotted scar that pancake and powder have only served to emphasize. Turkey Mary's gaze has stilled Valada's joy, moved her senses into wary. Mary's musk is flushed with anger as she fingers the costumes wanting to slip free of Valada's arms.

'These are Loretta's.' Mary is caressing and pulling at the same time. Valada knows better than to move sharply, but is giving nothing away.

'Oh, come on, Mary,' says Bessie quietly. 'We just doin' what Floyd instructed. I loved Loretta like everyone else. She was sweetness itself—'

108

'Don't you talk to me about love! You've barely left your mama's titty! What you know about love! She's gone. I can't find her nowhere. She didn't have no money. She coulda waited . . . and this new little piece of nothin'!'

'Valada don't know a thing about Loretta, Mary. This ain't her load.'

'You just go on and get that salve like I told you!' Mary's eyes are sulfurous coals. Valada exchanges a young girl's nod with Bessie, who withdraws into the gloom. Mary's breath is coming short over rotten stumps of teeth, but she says nothing more. Releasing her hold on the costumes, she turns with a force, looking to send Valada to the floor, but Valada has found balance in the new grown-up shoes she's wearing. A small group of performers had stood witness to Valada and Mary's little scene, but all have now gone about their business save the regal, big-boned woman wearing the black sealskin coat with the leopard skin collar and a great black velvet hat heavily roped with pearls.

'You know what you steppin' into, gal?'

'I'm not sure that I catch your meaning, ma'am.'

'Miss Mary there is parts Injun, Irish, and Geechie, and the meanest parts of all of three. You best better watch your back.'

'Thank you kindly for your interest, Miss Jones, but all I want to do is sing and dance. What can be the harm in that?'

Ruby Jones flashes a knowing smile. Her teeth are there and white. 'You better get a move on, gal. You'll be up before time.'

Valada shivers slightly as Ruby Jones walks away. Yesterday it had been cold in the Chattanooga train station as well.

'Won't you miss us, Valada?' little Hattie had asked with brimming eyes. 'Won't you be lonely all out in the world by yourself?'

'How the world she gonna be lonely when she surrounded by that great big group of folk?' snorted Lavada. 'I just don't see why I can't go! The man was talkin' 'bout chorus girls, more than one, and besides, I can dance better than Valada. Valada, you know it's true! Mama, you should let me go!' But Lavada knew that at twelve she didn't have a chance.

Alvada had said nothing at all, not with words anyway. But even as she pinned her goodbye gift of the homemade brooch on Valada's new secondhand coat, her eyes had been loud with, 'How can you leave us when things are so hard, with Mama hardly working, and the white folks mean as mud?' Alvada's eyes had been shouting. 'You don't care about us. You just want what you want. You're just like Daddy.' And Mama had said goodbye with one of those smiles that used to follow John Snow's back.

Just like Daddy . . .

The Dancing Dinahs went pretty much without a hitch, with Alva's brooch and two borrowed hat pins keeping Valada from catching cold to the men's delight. The Oriental Maidens was more of a challenge.

It started off all right, with a sweet little buzz, buzz, sha-wobble, and Bessie coaching her through the steps. Not knowing what was coming next and managing to jump in just before too late was charging the blood in Valada's arms and legs, washing her through with thrills heading toward rapture. Arms up and out for a Queen of Sheba spin. Round two-three-four, two-two-three-four. With some sharecropper hollerin', 'Plump and pretty pigmeat! Sweetness, fresh and juicy!' Out of the corner of her eye, Valada could see the sharecropper in his clay-caked overalls and 'bama boots trying to walk across tops of seats to the stage, talking about he was gonna get him some. The man didn't get far. He messed a fancy girl's hat, and her daddy slammed him to the floor; but the distraction was enough to put Valada off-step, away from Bessie, and between two of what seemed to be Mary's girls, who were giving up no clues.

Bessie couldn't help her friend from across the stage; there were lyrics to be sung; and before Valada knew she had mis-stepped smack dab into the *Jimtown* camel. No one knew for sure how Mr Dudley had gotten hold of Dora Lee; most figured he had 'borrowed' her from a circus that was about to put her down. Franklin Dudley liked having Dora, thought she was a plus for his show; but he didn't have to work with her. Dora was a mangy, flea-bitten beast that despised everything and everyone except for Floyd the stage manager sometimes. Smacking into Dora gave Valada a whiff of camel breath so foul that her eyes blinded for a second, and she almost lost her food. The camel hissed and mewled, and then snapped Valada's headdress right off her coil, drew blood when she did it, too; but Valada was already having too much trouble with her costumes to let one become a camel's snack. She was in a tug of war with Dora, when Bessie came running up.

'Valada! You lost your mind? You already bleeding and that hellion will take your hand!'

'How'm I going to find another headdress out here in Athens, Georgia? You give it back, you old witch!'

So with the band still going through their number and most of the Maidens still switching through their routine, Valada and Bessie stayed in battle with Dora. The audience, thinking it was part of the show, took to braying and applauding and throwing peanuts on the stage until Dora Lee finally broke loose and ran amok among the girls, scattering them across the boards like so many variegated amber beads.

Floyd was cursing fit to bust, was ready to fire Valada right then and there, except that the audience came up yelling for an encore. No encore took place; Dora Lee had been knocked stupid behind the flats, but folks stayed in a friendly mood, so Floyd was satisfied. After all that, the Bridesmaid Chorus was a cakewalk, plain and simple.

By the end of four shows Valada was exhausted, sure, but exalted as well. There'd been no time to worry about Mary the whole day and night. In between times she'd spent working with Bessie on her steps, hadn't even bothered about food. But come closing-up time, when she was finally sorting out her things in the small corner of the dressing room allowed by Loretta's friends, Valada was greeted by a shock. Her gift brooch from Alvada was nowhere to be seen.

'You must've dropped it,' suggested Bessie. 'With all the running back and forth, things go flying all the time.'

111

Valada searched every musty corner of the dressing room with a lantern. She and Bessie sifted through the piles of dust and knots of hair with their fingers, but Valada knew it was for naught. The rest of the performers would be stirring it up at a local flat after the shows, but Valada said she was tired after Bessie guided her to the rooming-house where the company put up. She settled herself into the unwashed sheets that had once covered Loretta and bided her time till morning.

Breakfast was served at eleven, with the entire *Jimtown* company gathered around one table save Ruby Jones, Franklin Dudley, and Mr Dudley's partner of the moment, who had a table all their own. The mood was jovial when Valada arrived, with everyone tucking happily into heaps of steaming grits and trotters, corn fritters, eggs, and country sausage. Seats at the table looked pretty much taken, but Bessie grabbed Valada a plate and made room on the bench next to her.

'You should have come on out to the flats with us, Valada,' said Bessie. 'This lady from down the way claimed she could shout her some blues as good as Ruby, and she was tearin' the place up too, 'til Miz Jones unpinned her hat and sent sister back to the farm! You ain't never heard the like of those ladies toe to toe! Don't miss Wardell's fritters, better than your mama ever imagined.'

'I'm sorry I missed the show,' said Valada quietly. 'It must have been something,' but her eyes are on Turkey Mary, who's just taken her place on the bench across. Mary seems to favour green, as it complements her eyes. Her skirt is olive, her earbobs are thinking about emeralds, and the jacket over her shirtwaist is a deep, dark green moss with purple lapels, on one of which nestles Alvada's gift brooch. A few of the chorus girls have shifted their eyes and seats uneasily; others smirk at Valada with defiance; but Mary is paying this no mind. She piles her plate with eggs and trotters while nodding her head to coffee, as Valada bides her time.

The Liberty alley is no warmer than it was the day before, so folks are dancing and dicing and gathered round pail fires to keep warm, waiting for Cracker Montgomery to open up the door, just like they were doing when Valada arrived; but it's a different day for Valada. She's a member of the company now, and she wants her gift brooch back.

'You gotta understand Mary, Valada,' Bessie is saying. 'She and Loretta was close. Loretta was her heart, truth to tell, and Loretta never would've started on the hop if Mary hadn't shown the way. Only Loretta had a very fragile constitution. She went fiendish right off the bat, like her very first time. No one's known of it happenin' so fast. I mean, look at me. I ain't nothin' but a slip, and it just went through me like water. Mary tried to get her straight, but Loretta was too far down the track. It's her grief that's making her mean, and, dog, girl, she's got six inches and twenty years of spite on you.'

'I feel for her suffering,' says Valada, 'but I intend to reclaim what's mine.'

Valada leaves Bessie shaking her head, walks direct up to Mary, who has entered into the alley with three of the chorus girls at her back.

'Excuse me,' says Valada, her voice soft and young, 'but I was wondering if you could help me. I seem to have lost something that matters to me, a pin in the shape of a flower made of buttons and stones.'

'You talkin' to me, Stuff?'

'Well, yes I am, because I do think you can help me. In fact, I know you can.'

'You do?' Mary's pose is mystification. She turns to one of her girls. 'Emma, do you believe this little thing?'

'No, Mary, I can't say that I do.'

'So young and bold, and foolish.' Mary's eyes are glassy and adder bright.

'Come on, Valada,' says Bessie, stepping between the two, 'why don't you and me go 'round the corner and practise those moves we were talkin' about.' Bessie tries to take hold of her new friend's arm, but Valada will not be moved.

'I'd like my pin back, Mary, the one on your inside jacket. It's mine. My sister made it for me, and I want it back.'

'Well, I like it right where it is,' replies Mary with a hiss. 'You gonna take it from me, Short Stuff?'

'If I have to.' Valada's voice is steady but very soft. In the alley, dancing and dicing have stopped.

Mary just snorts at Valada's daring, is making to shove the girl out of her way, but her drugged movements are slower than those of a fourteen-year-old dancer. With a dodge and a flick of her foot, Valada sends Mary to the ground, straddles her in a way that keeps the woman's arms by her sides, then, with almost steady hands, removes Alvada's gift brooch from the inside jacket lapel.

There are no sounds in the alley as Valada gets up off Mary, straightens her skirts, and turns to walk toward the theatre, then a collective drawing of breath, followed by a groan of pain. Turning back, Valada sees that the large yellow and black satin-booted foot of Ruby Jones is pinning Mary's right hand securely to the ground. There is a spring knife in that hand.

'Ruby! Please! You're breaking my bones!'

'You gonna leave that child be?' Ruby's voice is reasonable and matter-of-fact.

'Yes.'

'I can barely hear you, Mary. I know nobody else can.'

'Yes!' Mary's voice is a hiss, but it carries.

Satisfied, Ruby nods to the company. The stage door now open, the *Jimtown* entertainers file inside the theatre as Mary's girls help her to her feet.

There was a bit more space made for Valada in the dressing room that day, and one of the girls who was quick with a needle put a tuck in Valada's Dinah costume that kept its skirt more firmly above her hips; but, with the general commotion, there was no chance to thank Ruby Jones until between shows two and three. Ruby's room was a cubby-hole usually used by Cracker Montgomery for bits of sets and peace and quiet for his drinking. Montgomery had not been partial to giving up his corner to that singing nigger bitch, but Ruby Jones didn't perform without a room all her own, and she put behinds into the seats. The white owner of the Liberty could care less about his overseer's racial sensibilities. For the *Jimtown* engagement, Montgomery had to do his drinking in the scaffolding above the stage, from where he amused himself sometimes by spitting tobacco onto the acts. Not onto Ruby, though. Nobody messed with Ruby who put a value on his life. Valada raps lightly on the door.

'That you, Floyd? You sure have taken your time.'

'No, Miss Jones. It's me, Valada. Valada Snow.'

'Valada?'

'The girl from the alley.'

'So that's your name. Come on in, gal.'

Valada opens the door to find a space quite unlike any other in the ramshackle Liberty Theatre. Ruby's sparkling dresses, hats, and wraps are protected from the sooty walls by sheets nailed onto their wood. A braided rag rug covers the splintery floorboards. A mirror and a small table covered with various bottles and jars are folded out of her trunk. Much of the floor not covered by the rug is spotted here and there with sheets of heavy cardboard nailed securely into place. Ruby follows Valada's eyes to the cardboard.

'Keeps the rats out, honey. Those rascals are as partial to silks and spangles as they are to naked toes. I've spent a good part of my years in dumps like this, and I've learned to provide for my comfort.'

Ruby herself is wearing a robe the likes of which Valada has never seen: glistening black, with huge hanging sleeves and images of great, long-necked birds and reeds bending seductively to and fro.

'You like my kimono?' Valada can only nod. 'It comes from Japan. You can touch it if you like.'

The fabric has a surprising weight to it and a tantalizing texture between rough and smooth that causes Valada's heart to beat almost as quickly as the call of a well-played cornet. The scent lifting from the garment and Ruby's great mahogany bosom has a pungent heaviness that is neither familiar nor accessible. It's certainly not the toilet water sold through the South by various travelling medicine shows.

'You've been to Japan?' Valada asks.

The kimono's birds look like they could step from their inky black with a flap of white, pink, and green wings and carry these two dark women away to another place. The great cut-glass stones on Ruby's singing gowns glint and snap in the lantern light.

'Nope, never did get that far, but I've been to Europe and St Petersburg, Russia. Never seen so much snow in all my days, but them folks know what to do with it. They wrap themselves in all kinds of furs, got these big fur hats you've never seen the like of, travel around in horse-drawn sleds with little tinkly bells.'

'I didn't know coloured ever went places as far as that, except for with the war.'

'Foreign white folks the same as the ones we have around here. They love to see niggers sing and dance. I started sailing 'cross the water when I was smaller than you.'

'Were you scared?'

'No more so than you seem to be. This your first time out?'

'Yes, it is.'

'Tell me something, girl, you speak like quality. Where'd you learn to fight like that?

'Where does anyone? But I would like to thank you for your help.'

Ruby is studying this young girl whose pose is polite, but whose eyes are devouring all her stuff. 'You turned your back too soon.'

'I know,' Valada says seriously. 'I won't do it again.'

Ruby smiles. 'I bet you won't at that.' Another rap at the door. 'I imagine that's Floyd come round with my delivery. You need to run along now, but you can come back and visit whenever you like.'

Bessie and her friends invite Valada to join them for food between shows three and four, but Valada says no. She is back at Ruby's door.

I care about you, Alva, I really do, but I can't stay around here and just take what comes. If we wanna fly free in this white folks' world, we're gonna have to find our own way to the sky.'

'But Vee, you ain't nothing but a small young girl.'

'If I'm lucky that will help me more than hurt me.'

Ruby hands Valada a black and purple gown dripping cut-glass beading and a peacock's fan of spangles that folded and sparkled across her breasts.

'Oh, I remember this from Chattanooga!' Valada cries softly. 'When the lights hit, you looked like you could tell the sun to take a rest. It made me happy just to see you standing there.'

'That's part of our job, sugar. Most of our folks live lives without a whole lot of brightness. They loves to see us singin' and dancin', but they want us sportin' finery too. See the shimmer as well as the shake. And I tell you, one of this life's big pleasures is givin' them what they want. Hang the dress over on the wall and come and sit before the glass.'

The room turns closer as Valada moves in next to Ruby. The blueswoman's scent has intensified, and the outside of her nostrils have moistened just a bit as she holds up a compact of light yellow-brown coloured paint.

'Even a fledgling as young and blessed as you needs to learn how to help her gifts. You ever used this before?'

'Well, no, I'm only . . . and Mama . . .'

'A Christian lady, is she?'

Valada nods. 'She isn't like some, though. She loved our singing and dancing, but paint . . .'

'In our profession, it's just another thing you use, like the beat of the Professor's good left hand. Just move it across your cheeks with your fingers, not too much, even like.'

The colour is a good three steps lighter than Valada's natural complexion.

'You're lucky,' breathes Ruby, studying the bloom in Valada's cheek and the small bones at the base of her neck, 'you were born halfway there. Our folks love a pretty pale face smiling at them from across the lights. Some of us have to try harder than others; some of us are out that game before we start. Strengthen the rose of your lips and the snap of those pretty eyes, and you'll be breaking hearts for sure.'

Valada isn't feeling the heat of Ruby's gaze as she tries this pot and then another. The paint has its own heat and its own weight as well. The face in the glass is hers and not hers, the Valada of her own invention, a mask as surely as the paperbag cat face she made for Hattie last Hallowe'en. She raises enhanced eyebrows and purses rouged lips, moves her head from side to side to see what happens to her face planes in the light.

'Where do you get a hold of these kinds of creams?' she asks. 'Not in Athens, Georgia.' She looks forward to getting better at this. There are stages bigger than those in Athens and Chattanooga, with stronger lights and better chances.

'I gotta lady in New York who sends me stuff when I need it. You can have some, pay me back as we go along.'

'Oh, thank you,' says Valada. If she draws a line beneath her eye then looks up with her chin held down, she looks more like Theda Bara than the child her mother knows.

'What you looking for, girl?' The husk in Ruby's voice brings Valada's attention out of the mirror. The big woman's hands flash with stones where rainbows dance about the edges. They are not cut glass.

'I don't know. I just want to do . . . more,' Valada answers. 'I guess what some folks would call freedom.'

'It ain't just for the askin' for the likes of us. You gotta work hard, be ready to step out and stand out.'

'I play the trumpet,' says Valada, looking right back at the woman who's looking right at her.

The Palace Theatre, New York, May 1956

Valaida turns into the mirror to study the state of the union. Her headache has eased, thank goodness, and her make-up has stood up reasonably well despite the heat. Some powder should do it for now. The right eye is red, but she'll wait till the last minute to use the drops. She might as well use the time to sign the young man's pictures. The photos she's carrying in her case were taken, what, three years ago? But that's all right; on a good night, in the right light, they're as close to reality as more than a very select few are allowed to see. Valaida's always been pretty clever about managing publicity stills, the best photographers that would do for coloured, and there are more of them around these days, the best clothes, wigs and make-up just so, and on the touch-ups like a hawk. Photos were just another weapon in the arsenal. If you wanted to slay them, all your armoury had to be sharp. She signs the first photo with no problem – 'To Manny with best wishes, yours in rhythm, Valaida Snow' – but her hand slips right after she's written Paul's name on the other, causing a line of ink to go down the middle of her face. Not because she's bumped her elbow or anything. On its own. With her fingers only barely aware of her pen. This is something new. She's had the odd prickles in her arm, and that weird numbness below her elbow once in a while, but she's never actually lost control of her hand before. This can't be something to be pleased about, but no time to deal with it now. Sure, she could call the Lucy girl and say that she'd taken sick. It probably is time for a doctor, but tomorrow, not today. Today she is here to present. Valaida knows full well that the vast majority of folk in the theatre this evening wouldn't care one way or another whether or not Valaida Snow was on its playbill, but she is here to play, to make them care, to give them a good time and know that she's the one doing the giving. She's already willed her headache to ease. She can will her hand back into feeling; and she does. She quiets herself, relaxes, and in no time, less than no time, the palm of her hand is tingling and fingers responding to her command. Stretch out. Flutter. First and third, second and third, second, second, second, first and second, third. Fine. She pulls out and signs another picture, 'To Paul with thanks. Good luck in all you do. Yours with rhythm, Valaida'. Let the boy puzzle over the difference between 'in rhythm' and 'with rhythm'. Valaida will enjoy watching the wrinkling of his brow. Ice or no ice, it is too damn hot in here. Valaida folds the ruined picture into a triangular fan.

$\mathscr{C}$hapter nine

South Carolina, Summer 1919

They hadn't meant to stop in Redemption, South Carolina. The date had been in Florence; but when they arrived at the Florence Gaiety Theatre, they'd found nothing but a smoldering wreck. Might have been a group of local citizens angered at the notion of their local coloured gathered together for loud good times not dedicated to the Lord. Might have been the theatre owner himself preferring insurance money to the miscellaneous aggravations of popular entertainments. The reason didn't matter. The fact was the date was gone, and it was bad timing too. After five weeks of bad weather, worse houses, and theatre proprietors for whom 'scoundrel' was polite description, pay packets had dwindled from spare to nothing but promises. The *Jimtown* company was restive, hungry as well, so when Franklin Dudley clapped eyes on Ephraim Bailey, an old partner in crime from his Memphis

120

Minstrel days, and Ephraim said that he was setting up a sweet little operation two stops down the way in a nice little enclave of coloured who had their own, would the *Jimtown* company like the privilege of inaugurating its entertainment? Franklin Dudley looked to the heavens and whispered, 'Thank you, Jesus.' Ephraim proposed a seventy/thirty split, but that was nothing but profile. The buddies sparred down to fifty-five/forty-five, the winner to be determined by a throw of dice after the fact, and shook hands with a mutual flash of dental diamonds.

Mr Dudley had just enough cash and guile to transport his company down the track, so when Valada and her colleagues arrived in Redemption to find that the theatre was no more than a shed with a dirt floor, some benches scattered round, and a stage not even near complete, there was nothing left to do but stare.

'Bailey, I'm gonna have your hide.' Dudley's snarl was a decent try, but it didn't carry much bite.

'My hide's awful pretty, but it ain't gonna feed your troupes,' smiled Bailey. 'There's folks around here that'll put them up in exchange for labour, and if some of your lads will lend me a shoulder, the house'll be ready in a matter of days. There're plenty nickels around here, Franklin, quarters, too. It'd be worth your while, and since your sleeves ain't nothing but empty, what else you gonna try to do?'

There was absolutely nothing that Franklin Dudley could say.

Valada had been spending a good deal of her time with Ruby before Redemption.

'Who's that cute little bit, third from the right, with the green sash and the hot little ass?'

'Don't be wastin' your time lookin' in that direction. That there's Ruby Jones's latest young girl.'

Miss Ruby Jones's latest young girl.

How much is she Miss Ruby's girl? Maybe more than she'd tell her mama, maybe less than folks assumed. Maybe not.

As a *Jimtown* star, Ruby found lodging in the small boarding accommodation of Ephraim Bailey's lady love, along with Buck

121

Dancing Sensation Slim Santee, Franklin Dudley and his current miss, while Valada joined three other girls in Samuel Gibson's barn. Nestled into a mound of hay, close up to Bessie for comfort and warmth, Valada couldn't sleep for the noise of country quiet, squeaking crickets, scurrying mice, hoot owls declaring the boundaries of their worlds. Barrell-housing in the distance was more to her rhythm, or the metal clatter of train cars switching rails in their yards; so Samuel Gibson's pre-dawn banging came as an unpleasant surprise.

'There's sacks by the door for the runner bean harvest.' Samuel Gibson was a surly so-and-so, with broad shoulders and features you couldn't cipher in the dark. 'Any of you gals milked a cow in your time?' Lula Brown was too bewildered not to raise a hand. 'You come with me. There's clobber in the kitchen for them that's inclined, but after this morning, them that's interested in eating had best have worked up an appetite.'

'Goddam, he reminds me of my Uncle Cyrus,' groaned Bessie, brushing the straw bits off of her cheek, 'and the reason I took to runnin' in the first place.'

Sarah Gibson's was a gentler soul than her husband's. Taking pity on girls so ill-prepared for field labour, she did her best to fit them out with bonnets against the sun. All the four save Valada had had experience working the land and preferred putting their seasoned feet in the fields to the prospect of ruining precious town shoes and stockings. Following their lead, Valada's soft city pads were stubbed and bleeding in an hour. Bessie kept declaring that harvesting beans was bundling joy compared to the pains and tears of chopping King Cotton, but Valada was not sharing her relief. By the end of five rows, her fingers throbbed so badly from assorted scrapes and scratches that she chose to shred her neck rag into bandage mitts and leave her nape to brave the sun.

'If I were a betting man, I'd wager you've never done this work before.' The voice was a young man's, soft and high, but decisive as well. 'Why don't you join me on this here wagon for a ride to the county store?'

122

The young man's complexion was hazelnut brown under a broad-brimmed straw hat, and smooth and clear as his voice. Mule reins hung obediently between long, tapering fingers. His hands were as slender as his frame.

'That's an attractive offer,' said Valada, 'but I'm hoping for a meal at the end of this day.'

'You'll get your meal,' smiled the young man. 'Daddy always wants someone in the wagon steadying Elaine while I fetch our supplies. Usually it's my cousin Zekiel, but his conversation's nothing to speak of.'

'What makes you think that mine is any better?'

'Your choice of words for starters. You know how to read?'

Valada was wary, but she thought it best to nod.

'So do I.' The smile was too dazzling to refuse the hand reaching out to help her climb up onto the wagon's seat. His grip was young but strong.

'I've never reined a mule either,' she said. His burnt-leaf musk cut through the rankness of the beast.

'But I bet you're a fast learner when you need to be.' And again the smile, more open and honest than a smile had ever been.

His name was James. He was seventeen years old, the Gibsons' middle child, and he loved a serious up-North writer named W.E.B. Du Bois, had a head full of dreams, and hips as slender as his shoulders were broad. Valada had never spent time with a boy like him. Her last school days had been passed running from her teachers' Representative expectations, avoiding worthy activities and schoolmates like the plague. No uplift for Valada Snow! Maizie's Jook was more like it, and hip-swaying to Sonny Jim. With his newspaper reading and plans to reclaim the coloured vote, James would have been far and away too worthy to give the time of day; and Valada would have missed the warmth of his seal-brown eyes gazing her way in utter worship; for James had never even been around a girl like Valada, soft and pretty, swift and sassy, as ready to find the world in a bob-tail's nest or the streak of a falling star as she was to growl a

123

godless blues giving praise to a wayward life. Though Valada's attentions sometimes wandered when he read to her from Dr Du Bois, she understood everything that he said, that James could tell. And she couldn't believe those blues she sang. She was far too perfect for that.

For her part, Valada found there was something to be said for worship, and even more for the sweet taste of hungry, pliant, rose-brown lips as they pulled the breath right out of her body. From eyebrows to toes, breath just gone, electricity in its place, tiny flutters to glancing thunderbolts, and finally she was knowing what the songs were all about, what had kept her mama with her daddy for all those years, what had kept her daddy in the streets. She and James had both been virgins that third night, when sharing songs and dreams of freedom moved them down the inevitable road. James had wept from what he took for love, then stood up and crowed his delight to the moon, taut thighs bulging, his good thing snapped to attention, balls tight and ready for more, while Valada savoured the surge and tingle, with quiet blessings to Ruby for the wisdoms she had shared.

Valada got better at farming, and they both got better at love. Their place was a birthing shed in the far west pasture. Valada taught James to pace his pleasure. James taught Valada to find the world in his eyes. Or at least he tried.

'Come inside me, girl, while I come inside of you.'

'And what you think I'm going to find there?'

'A heart that's only meant for you.'

'So now you can read my mind?'

'Can't I?' Maybe he could. There was a power about him and something as pure as her little sister Hattie's laugh, so Valada would find herself searching until gasping, in spite of herself. There were places you could lean against in James and know that they'd be there. There was brilliance, coursing up and down your veins, curling your feet, filling your head, blinding your eyes until you saw all that you ever knew and all you ever could know, all at the self-same time. What she'd wanted all along but hadn't realized, wouldn't have given the time of day for. Together with playing the trumpet and stepping sassy on a stage. Loving was working on her mind's predisposition.

She took to moving slower and staring out into space with a new woman's half smile.

'Don't tell me you fallin' for that country boy, Valada!' crowed Bessie, having caught her friend finding all in the world that's good in an okra leaf. 'I mean he cute and all, with that smooth nut skin of his—'

'And them pretty hands!' mewed Lula. 'Pretty hands like that shouldn't have no country calluses. Tell me them pretty hands are soft as that thing that take his eyes when I see him look your way. Give me chills all up and down ma body! Can't stand to think what be up and downin' yours. Ooh, wee!'

'He's got nice hands,' demurred Valada. Smooth and rough as this leaf was smooth and rough.

'That'll wrap you right up in corn stalks,' said Bessie, her cast eye all up into Valada's space, 'and drape you down with babies if you give him half a chance. You need to heed yourself, girl.'

Sarah Gibson had borne ten children, buried four, and knew a thing or two about how a body loved. She loved her husband for his constancy and strength, her twins for their childish wiles, and her James for being the best of all their hearts and minds. Her son wasn't speaking on the movements in his life, so she first went to see the girl.

'You know that he intends you for his wife.'

Valada's cheeks went warm. 'He told you this?'

'He didn't have to tell me. I'm his mother.'

Was Valada warm from pleasure or warm from fear? 'You're thinking I'm not good enough?'

'I'm not talkin' about good, child. I'm talkin' about right. James has a light that needs a hearth to keep it strong. You're gonna be a traveller, girl, a firefly flittin' from tree to tree. You can't feed one another, you and James. Your flames'll be gone before you know.'

'I don't believe you,' said Valada, working to keep her fancy free from concern. 'All James talks about is freedom; it's what he reads in all his books . . .'

There was a quiet in Sarah Gibson that stilled Valada's tongue, pulled the young woman's eyes relentlessly into her own.

'You're in the rapture at the moment, child,' the mother said, 'but you're not a fool. You know that freedom ain't the same for everyone.'

That evening under the stars, James's embrace was tighter, fiercer than it had ever been. After his second groans had faded and his pulse slowed to a lighter hammer, Valada was counting on some stillness, a song, a story, a freedom dream or two, until her hand brushed her lover's face and felt a dampness on his cheeks. She raised herself onto an elbow.

'What, James? You're crying?' There was a smile in her concern, and triumph as well, until the intensity of his emotion swept it out of its path, made it scurry away in fear.

'What, James? What?'

His voice came softer and deeper than ever before. 'My mother says you are not for me.'

'Do you believe her?' asked Valada, whispering for worry of shaking loose the question she was ill prepared to answer.

'I believe my heart,' said James, pulling Valada back into his arms, loving her again and so sweetly that she almost believed herself.

It had taken ten days for the *Jimtown* men to bring Ephraim Bailey's shed close to the theatre of his imagination. In those ten days, Valada and her cohorts couldn't have been further from their entertainment life: up before cock crow, work till a meal at noon, then back through chores that never ended, working muscles long forgotten or, for Valada, never known; yet with it all, a surprising peace and ease, the sun's arc dominating their days, rising, setting, nourishing, scorching, clean air, wide horizons. Nature, combining with James's sweetness, had begun to play on Valada's intentions when the *Jimtown* stage manager rode up to

126

the Gibsons', announcing that the company would be back to work the next day to do a few local performances before heading back on the road.

'Work?' crowed Bessie. 'Just what the hell all you think we been doin' here, Floyd? Clippin' our toenails?'

'Can't tell you how glad I am to see you, Floyd,' said Lula. 'A few more days in these here fields and these dogs of mine be lost to all hopes of refinement, forget about dancin' a routine. What you say, Valada? You 'bout ready for town?'

A blast of wind blew up before Valada could answer, sending all the girls skeltering after Sarah Gibson's new washed sheets. The wind was surprising, strong, and exultant in its power. That night, on their way to the pasture, Valada could feel that James was about to ask his question. Stopping, she turned and put a finger to his lips.

'You coming to the show tomorrow?' she asked. His lips were as soft as the silk of Ruby's dresses, and the thought of them caressing her secret places was racing her blood.

'Well, you know Daddy don't hold with heathen entertainments,' said James, kissing her fingers and setting them over his heart. 'I'll have to slip away.'

'If you come and watch, you can ask your question then,' said Valada, feeling the beat of his heart beneath her hand and wondering herself what her answer would be.

Ephraim Bailey's theatre didn't have much to brag about, musicians and dancers not being God's gift to carpentry after all; but there was a tin roof now, a reasonable sized stage, orderly benches able to seat one hundred souls, and an almost new piano borrowed from Ephraim's lady's parlour. The Professor was already at his command post when Valada and her friends arrived, pounding out the rag commotions that had been missing from their days.

'That's right, Professor! Play that thing!' cried Bessie with a grateful shoulder shake. 'Heaven straight on down to Bessie! Yes,

Lord! Save me from country fields, if you would! Ain't it great, Valada? Hasn't your soul jus' been hungerin'?'

'Don't waste your time tryin' to get an answer from Valada,' smirked Lula. 'She so wrapped up in that love thing she ain't knowing this from that. Look at her! Just look at her eyes, like she been showerin' in goofer dust!'

Valada wants to look mad, but she can't, or stop her lips from smiling. 'You need to leave me be, Lula. You're nothing but jealous.'

'Of those long seal brown thighs? Jealous? Me? The hell I am. I'd savour me some country, then cut the 'Bama loose. Just like you need to do. No, don't tell me you gonna stay here!'

'I don't know what I'm going to do,' said Valada with a pensive shrug, because even in her reverie she was astonishing herself. She needed to be thinking about routines after two weeks' break, and all she was seeing in her mind was James' face shining with love-light.

'Don't forget what I said, Valada,' said Bessie, grabbing her friend's arms. 'You better take heed of yourself, or sure as a baby goes to titty that man will drape you down. Farm boys ain't for the likes of us, no matter how pretty they is.'

'Bessie! Lula! Valada! Quit your yappin' and get on about yo' business!' Floyd called from the stage where he was standing with Ruby and Mr Dudley. 'The costumes are around back in the stable. The first show goes up at three. Valada, come on up here for a moment. Mr Dudley wants to talk to you.'

An unfamiliar shyness overcomes Valada as she mounts the stage to speak to Mr Dudley. She can feel that Ruby knows the fabric of her last days, yet still there she stands, considering Valada with a proprietary smile, as Franklin Dudley nods a greeting to whom he figures to be Ruby's latest young girl.

'You wanted to see me, Mr Dudley?' Valada can hardly recognize her own voice for its softness.

'I'm not sure that "want" is the word I'd choose to use,' said Dudley, looking her square in the face, 'but Ruby here has been gnawing my ear for the past ten days telling me I should get over myself about lady instrumentalists and give the show some extra pizzazz. Floyd says that you showed yourself with a violin back in Athens, but Ruby says that you can play a trumpet, too. Is that a fact?'

Blood is rushing so fast into Valada's brain that sight is about to leave her as well as powers of speech. 'Yes,' she manages, 'I can play the trumpet.'

Dudley divides his look between Valada and her champion. 'I guess if you're going to make a fool of me it might as well be in a town named Redemption. We'll give you a chorus at the end of 'Alcina's Wedding'. Work it out with Fess and the boys, and roll your Bridesmaid costume up higher, if you please. If the trumpet don't play, you can at least give these farmers a sight of pretty young leg. We even now, Ruby?'

'It's a beginning, Franklin,' smiled his star. 'I'll let you know your standing in the fullness of time.' Ruby's smile never changed from broad and knowing as she watched Franklin Dudley deal with his musicians. 'You play that horn at all in these past ten days?' she asked Valada without looking in her direction.

'Well, no. The Gibsons, Mr Gibson, he wouldn't have allowed it, and all that work we were doing—'

'It's your choice now, honey,' said Ruby to Valada, while nodding and smiling to Fess and his boys. 'You put that new little love out your mind and take care o' business, or stay wrapped in your little pink cloud and kiss the music goodbye . . . You look after my girl now, Fess,' she called, gathering her skirts up to leave the stage.

'That we will, Ruby,' laughed the Fess. 'We do put a value on our health!'

Ruby pulled a gun from her bag and waggled it in the air. 'And don't you forget it! Ol' Clem has barked many a time in his day, but it would pain me to let him loose on your rump.'

'Pain me a hell of a lot more, Ruby! Don't you worry. We'll set your baby up right.'

*　*　*

Lula was right, after ten days of flapping free in South Carolina loam, dancers' feet were hard put not to bust the seams of their fine city shoes. After ten days of country air, sun, sweat, and dirt, women's hair was bushing back to natural states, laughing at headgear that might have fit a week before. Unwashed costumes felt rank and heavy after ten days of loose garments scorched papery in Redemption's fields. But when Fess and the boys got to cooking, calloused feet tapped, bushy heads bopped the rhythm, and field-worked backs slipped and slid back into jokes and joy. The *Jimtown* company was ready to jubilee. Only Valada was wrestling with torment.

Working up a bit with the Professor was easier than she had expected, after she had managed to get back a decent amount of lip. Fess was from Oklahoma where folks seemed to make their own set of rules about most things. He had worked with a number of lady horn players in his day; so he just got down to business with no palaver about what a girl should or shouldn't do.

'Hold your horn behind your back, nice and coy like,' he'd suggested, 'and when we bridge back to the second chorus, strut on out there and present. Give 'em what have you, darlin'. We'll be steady 'neath you with some growl and catch you if you stumble. If your lip give out, sing a bar, smile pretty, then get on back to business. These ol' farmers won't know what hit them. A cute little thing like you playin' the horn will tickle them right where they get happiest.'

It took a few tries to start presenting on the one, but the odds were that she'd get by fine if she kept her nerve. Antoine wasn't cooperating at first; he was probably peevish from the neglect; but she had washed his valves and rubbed him warm, reassuring him that he was the prettiest man she knew. If James showed up, would he be thinking that as well? If James didn't show, there was nothing to worry about really, except the loss of love and what could or ought to be; but if he did come, what then? Would there be a choice to make?

The Palace Theatre, New York, May 1956

Valaida has arrived in the wings just as one of the chorus boys misjudges his lift of Liz LaFontaine, causing both of them to collapse in a heap onto the floor. LaFontaine responds with a fountain of invective, slapping away the hand of another dancer wanting to help her back to her feet. 'Fucking amateurs!' she's screaming. 'Barney, you promised me! No more of this fucking shit! Fucking farmboys! Throwing me around like some goddam sack of fucking corn! I open at the Sands next week! With my leg in a cast? My back broken? Fucking goddam faggot farmboys!' Barney, the choreographer, has ground out his cigarette and jumped onto the stage, his open vest swinging around an unbuttoned shirt. With hands on both the dancer's shoulders, he speaks quietly, soothingly to the rattled and angry Liz LaFontaine, while the guilty chorus boy limps around the stage, endeavouring to shake the pain out of his arms and legs. The Stage Manager approaches Valaida, wearily shaking his head.

'We're still running behind, I'm afraid, Miss Snow, and it'll be another fifteen minutes or so with Miss LaFontaine. Would you prefer to go back to your room or take a seat front of house?'

'Out front will do just fine,' says Valaida.

It's cooler here in the theatre with so much space stretching back and straight upwards to seat sixteen, seventeen hundred people, still glowing from the refit done some five years before in hope of restarting the glory days of vaudeville. Didn't happen, of course. Times had changed, tastes had changed. Folks who'd paid the dimes week after week for two and a half hours of wholesome family entertainment were staying home to watch the odd juggler or dog act on *The Ed Sullivan Show*. Didn't matter that what folks saw was on a tiny screen with bad reception and then only in black and white. Your living room was comfortable. You could stay in your slippers if you wanted to, and you weren't jammed up against someone else's body odour. One thing hadn't changed, though. The Palace was still the white time, had been when it was

131

the crown of the all-powerful Orpheum Circuit and still was now in 1956; and on the white time there was never more than one coloured act per show. Becoming one of those acts had been a very big deal among Negro entertainers when vaudeville was in its glory. Not only were you revered as one of the chosen few, but conditions were far better than those available on the T.ough O.n B.lack A.sses Toby Time, steadier work, better pay. Not that things were ideal, of course. This was America after all, and se-gregation was a far mightier monarch than vaudeville celebrity; but the money in your pocket had been a decent salve to the assaults on your person. Or so folks chose to present. Valaida really didn't know. This is not her first time at the Palace, but she's only been here since after the war, so well after the crown had lost its lustre. It hadn't been her fate to work the white time as a feature here at home in the States, but she'd done all right, was still doing all right. She hadn't had to step out of show business for more than a couple of seconds, even in the decline. So many people she knew were running elevators, tending bar, mopping up floors, including some who had been shining bright in the white time, and here she was in Palace waiting to do what she could do.

Liz LaFontaine finally nods her head and is sent by Barney back into formation with a proprietary pat and rub on her shapely behind. The number has started again by the time Valaida has settled into a seat, 'From This Moment On', with a not particu-larly interesting arrangement and the band just connecting the dots; but LaFontaine has something. The voracious territorial energy of the dressing room was transformed in the theatre's greater space into that thing some folks called star power, the hunger for everything and everyone within her reach, into a seductive invitation. With legs that did seem to go on for ever and a distinctive voice, not much range, but smoke and velvet all at once, Liz LaFontaine was on the road to conquest, tonight's bene-fit first, then the Sands in Vegas, Broadway stardom, Hollywood, and more than likely it would never be enough. Valaida's off the star road now, but her road had never been the same. Negro show business went a different way for one, had its own rules and byways, some imposed from without, others from within, but then Valaida had never had much use for beaten paths. The way folks knew to go never had the room she'd needed. The only thing she could do was make things up as she went along, which hadn't been as difficult as some folks might want a body to believe, even if at times her heart had been hurting as much as her head was now. Leaving home had not been hard. Travelling and living life with no kind of guarantees had not been hard. Standing still would have been harder. Accepting the way things were, trying to be safe in a world without safety, that would have been hard, and what to show for it all besides a big sackful of regrets? No regrets for Valaida, one hell of a headache, that was for sure, but no regrets.

Chapter ten

Montgomery, Alabama, 1919

September 29, 1919

Dear Alva,

It's been so long since I've written I bet you all were about to give me up for dead, especially with all the white folks craziness that's been going on of late, but I'm not. I'm alive and well and still with Franklin Dudley's Jimtown. We've been travelling all over these states, Georgia, Eastern Tennessee, South Carolina. Now we're in Alabama, and we'll probably go into Arkansas, too. Mr Dudley says you get some of the best audiences in those states where white folks give coloured the worse kind of time. Folks are just that much more interested in coming out to hear some good music and have some big laughs, and that we do!

You'd be very proud of your sister, Alva. Since I started last winter I've gotten a couple of special bits in the show. I'm in that

olio with Mr Blanch Bowen, 'How I Miss My Mississippi Miss'.
Remember that from Chattanooga, with Miss Angeline McGrath
in that dark blue hobble skirt we liked so much? Well, I'm not the
Miss (and I won't be as long as Angeline is Mr Dudley's special
friend). I'm one of the Flighty Friends, but as you remember, they
do a whole lot of singing while all Angeline does is stand there
batting her eyes. But even better, I play the trumpet for two
choruses in 'Alcina's Wedding'! Isn't that just great? It started as
one chorus, but it made such a hit that now it's two. I step out of
the Bridesmaid Chorus and start to play! Mr Dudley gave me a
chance when we were in this tiny town called Redemption, SC. He
figured Redemption was so small that if I wasn't good, it
wouldn't matter. But everyone loved it from the very beginning! I
can't describe the feeling I get when I'm playing Antoine on a
stage, feeling the company all around me and the folks out front
surprised and wondering and then clapping so loud and hooping
and hollering just for me. There's nothing like it, nothing. You
know, for a minute there I was thinking that maybe the stage
wasn't as important to me as I thought it was, but I was wrong.
For me, it's the best thing in the world. I feel like if I did this all
night and day, it still wouldn't be enough.

I hope everything's going all right at home and that Mama isn't
working too hard. Please kiss her for me and Lavada and Hattie,
too. I keep hoping that I'll run into Lawrence some place. I
haven't yet, but please tell Mama I ask about him everywhere I
go, and I dearly believe that her prayers have kept him safe. Me
too.

Remember to have some fun sometimes, Alva.
Your sister,
Valada
P.S. You can keep the violet ribbons I loaned you. They were
better on you anyhow.

After a quick knock on the door of the room Valada shares with
Ruby in the Montgomery boarding house owned by a shady-past

woman by the name of Flo Cochran, it is opened by Bessie, who is all dressed up for some time on the town.

'You comin', Valada? Ruby's automobile is fixin' to leave.'

'I'll be right there,' Valada replies, sticking the letter into an envelope. 'I just want to get this letter off to my sister.'

'Pretty long letter,' said Bessie, glancing Valada's way, but far more interested in the lace and satin frillies spilling out the drawers of Ruby's leather and wood-bound travel trunk.

'It's been a long time,' said Valada. 'I'm not so good at keeping in touch.'

'Better than me. At least you can write!' said Bessie. It's the vanity set she's admiring now, with its tortoiseshell and ivory backs. She holds up the mirror to study her reflection and pat at her hair in exaggerated grand-lady manner.

Having finished with her letter, Valada crosses the room, gently relieves Bessie of Ruby's mirror, and returns it to its place. 'I'll teach you if you like,' she says, with an attempt at a reproving look.

'Waste of time,' said Bessie, gliding airily away. 'I couldn't keep still long enough to learn, let alone come up with something to say. Besides, if I told folks at home what all happened out here on the road, it'd send them to an early grave!' Then she's back onto her friend with a well-placed hip bump. Valada tries to act outraged, but it's impossible when confronted with Bessie pulling a funny face; Valada makes a face of her own, and the friends are overcome with laughter.

'You tell them about James?' said Bessie, catching her breath.

'No, no reason to,' said Valada, who's making a studied attempt to appear nonchalant. 'James is way in the past. To think that I might have been raising crops year in and year out. Okra, runner beans, it's hard to imagine.'

'Not to mention babies.' Bessie's eyes are steady on Valada's face.

'Don't want to hear about no babies!' said Valada forcefully, her nonchalance coming a bit easier at this.

'Sneakin' up to the far pasture,' encouraged Bessie, 'tryin' to play your horn—'

136

'And not knowing what was going to get me first,' said Valada, keeping on track, 'Daddy Gibson and his sermons or the Ku Klux Klan! It was a close call.'

'Yeah, close,' said Bessie, slipping a bracing arm around Valada's shoulder. 'Farms ain't for the likes of us, Valada. You were lucky.'

'Very,' agreed Valada, her eyes looking almost sure as she pulls away from Bessie and pins a new flowered boater on her head. 'We better get out of here, or Ruby'll pitch a fit!'

'That's right,' Bessie exclaimed. 'Time to hoe down! You bringin' that jazzy little man of yours?'

'Yes, I am,' said Valada, picking up Antoine's bag. 'Time to get on out in the world and see what we can do.'

It's taking effort to keep that last image of James out of her mind, James with clouds across his brow on the discovery that his angel frolicked in a show fraught with images that maligned the Race, with crude blackface comedy and bawdy sexual innuendo; and she blew a horn. James's face without its smile.

'But you never told me about the horn,' he'd said.

'You never asked me,' she'd replied.

'But all that talk about dreams . . .'

'Mostly we talked about yours.'

His eyes had filled with tears. Valada felt pain in her chest and suddenly understood that a heart, something she'd always thought just kept going and going until it was done, could truly just break, could shatter like a window or puddle ice under a shoe. Her eyes had followed the movement of every muscle in his face. She'd tried to wipe a tear away, but when she reached up, he'd held her wrist in a grip so firm and hot that she feared her bones might snap.

'Will you stop?' he'd asked.

'Come with me,' she'd replied.

The hand that had delivered her own carefully down to her side was cooling at a speed that she could never have imagined, nor could she have imagined the clog that was rising from her gut threatening to cut off all her air.

137

'*I won't forget you,*' *he'd said before he'd turned and walked away.*

How long had it been before Ruby found her standing there? Twenty minutes? Two hours?

'*Listen to me, girl,*' *Ruby had said, her brace of diamond rings glittering in the moonlight. 'I've loved women, girls, men, and boys, and what I've come to know is that it lasts as long as it does. It's only innocents and fools that think it's supposed to last for ever. It's done here? Well, hell, there's plenty more down the road. You ain't picked this life for innocence, honey. So come on out this damp like you have some kind of sense.*'

Wilbur's was middling as honky-tonks went, not as fancy as some with electric lights adding that extra touch of class, not as lowdown as others. It had a wood floor and windows with shades instead of feed bags and usually glass. Wilbur was particularly proud of his glass, and drunks whose brawling turned the glass to splinters had best have some ready cash on their persons or face a wrath they'd be too dead to remember. Which was why Wilbur was none too partial to farmers since they barely had pennies for the home-made liquor they drank and half the time trying to go on credit for that. The crowd up to Wilbur's tended to be more in the world: iron workers from the mills around Montgomery, loggers in from the turpentine woods, rail men, the gamblers who took their money, and the women who found their joy around that sort of thing. Not school-teachers. Some of the women worked in the mills, some on their backs, but all of them came ready for whatever a night might bring.

Fashion tended to be pretty fundamental at Wilbur's, so the entrance of two automobile loads of *Jimtown* performers in their variegated garb had to draw attention. Wilbur's piano man juiced up his rag, eagle-rocking couples set to dipping extra low, a broad-beamed woman pulled her skirts even higher up her legs and proceeded to whip it and grind it like a man-filled alligator moving onto shore. Her partner whooped and growled as he coaxed her home to Daddy, lamplight glinting on the ebony sinews of his arms, his neck in its open-collared shirt, bulging thighs practically busting through his pants.

'Ooh, baby!' mewled Lula, as the group settled around a couple of makeshift tables. 'I want me some of that prime country ham!'

'Not if you put a value on your life,' said Bessie. 'These sisters 'round here do not play. They'll knife you soon as look at you if you even stare too long.'

'And wouldn't none of us linger long enough to cry at your funeral neither,' said Floyd, shooting his cuffs for the appreciation of a hovering good-time gal. Lantern light obscured the cuffs' frays and smudges. The cut-glass stones at his wrists were sparkling jewels. 'Wilbur!' he called. 'Send on over a bottle of your finest!'

'Hell, I'm just 'preciating the sights is all,' said Lula. 'Ain't nothin' like the body of a hard-workin' man! Ooh, whee! Take a gander at that honey over there! Can't you feel them big arms just a-crushin' you to his chest?'

'Snappin' my neck is more like it,' said Floyd, flipping off a coin for the bottle.

Big Arms seemed to sense the show folks' attention as he sent his partner off in a bravura Texas Tommy spin, then caught and pulled her to his heart before she crashed into Wilbur's guitar player. When she voiced her protest, he gave her a slap and spun her again in complete complement to the rhythm.

'You see what I'm sayin', Lula? You need to pay attention to Papa.' Floyd poured out a round of corn.

'I will when Papa got somethin' interesting to say,' countered Lula, gesturing to Floyd to top off her glass.

'You keep throwin' out that eye, and Papa'll teach you some truth,' replied Floyd. 'You with us this evenin', Ruby?'

'No, thank you, Floyd,' said Ruby, instead pouring the contents of a leather-bound flask into its own silver cap. 'I've still got a portion of last week's purchase. It's a might easier on my vitals than that slop you purveyin'.'

139

'Rupture of your vitals is part and parcel of the charm,' returned Floyd. 'Keeps your mind fine-tuned to the rhythm of the proceedings. Valada, you indulging?'

'I will, thank you, Floyd.'

The air in Wilbur's was a close mix of the sweat of bodies slapping up together, last night's sex announcing from unwashed drawers, the bite of rotgut corn shot through with the exultation of coloured folk grabbing hold of every revel allowed them and one hell of a lot more. Valada smiled quietly to herself. This was the truth of it: she was of the night; its world was where she belonged and thrived; and sweet James was of the day. No amount of love could have overcome that fact. Their happiness would have evaporated with the fall. She was lucky to have learned this truth so soon. *Sweet James . . .*

The *Jimtown* clarinet player had joined forces with Wilbur's piano and guitar, his blackwood's wail piercing through the halflight like the corn walloping Valada's stomach and streaming into her veins. For a moment she was seeing nothing but stardust stretching from her navel, out Wilbur's glass window and on into the sky. *Goodbye, Sweet James . . .*

'You OK, Valada?' asked Bessie. 'That was a powerful swallow you took.'

Valada can scarcely hear Bessie for the burn in her ears, but she's thinking that this music, this heat, this funk, is the best happiness there can be if she can only jump inside. Play her horn.

'Valada?'

'I'm fine, Bessie. I'm fine.' She and Antoine have done turns at *Jimtown* parties, but not just out in front of folk, jumping in like people do. *Time to go.* Big Arms's woman has pulled herself out of his embrace right onto the feet of the broad-beamed Funky Butt gal. While the women start into words, Big Arms has ambled over to the *Jimtown* tables and offered his hand to Lula. Lula is up and gone before anyone can say, 'Watch it!' *Time to try.* Medill is on his feet.

'Well, we'd better have our good time before things turn wild and woolly. Dance, Valada?'

140

'No, thank you, Medill, but I'd appreciate it if you'd walk me over to the band.'

These folks are her friends, but eyebrows are raising. 'You sure about that, Valada? These folks are awful rough and ready.'

Now. Time to try. 'No more so than the folk I been playing for night and day.' On the floor, the Funky Butt gal and Big Arms's ex-partner have moved off from words into shoves. A roar of triumph comes thundering from the gambling room out back.

'Yeah, but up here they out their cages,' said Floyd. 'Go on out there and just dance with Medill like you had the brains you was born with.'

'You saying I'm not good enough, Floyd?' Valada's question is at once flirtatious and pointed. She knows that Floyd would try to talk to her if he weren't afraid of Ruby, which is fine because Floyd is in no kind of way Valada's style, but she knows she can fluster him and so he's good for practice. Out on the floor, the backroom winner has sauntered up to the rough-hewn logs that serve as a bar, jingling coins and calling for action. With a bottle of corn in one hand, he pulls Funky Butt out of her argument with her woof partner and into a lowdown drag. He is almost her match, and his boys are cheering him on down the river. One of them grabs onto Big Arms's ex-partner and commences to drag down even lower, with the piano player following them steady into the gutter.

'I'm not sayin' you not good enough,' replies a flustered Floyd. 'I'm sayin' . . . Damn, Ruby! She's your girl! Talk some sense to her.'

Ruby's attentions would seem to have been on the dance floor drama, but she sends Valada the slightest of nods. Valada had been thinking that she'd be carrying Antoine across the floor in his bag, but Floyd's challenge, the mood in the room, and the corn in her gut has her throwing discretion to the wind. She's pulled Antoine out the bag, is warming his mouthpiece, working his valves.

'You with me, Medill?' she asks. Medill's a mild-mannered man, a dancer who thinks only with his feet. While his feet are playing off the counter-rhythms of the piano player's chords, his eyes are blandly waiting for instruction from whoever will's the strongest.

'Now, Valada . . .' Floyd starts again. Out on the floor, Lula wants a piece of the Funky Butt and Big Arms's partner slow drag competition. Lula's smaller than the others and able to shimmy up and occupy more parts of a grinding anatomy.

'Ah, Floyd, stop yo' belly-achin'! You wanna act the big daddy, get me onto that dance floor,' declares Ruby. 'Let the little girl go on 'bout her business, and see what you can do with this fine brown chunk of North Carolina female.'

'Me and you, Ruby?' Floyd shrugs the good-time gal off his shoulder. 'Shit! Come on!'

Now Bessie is on her feet. 'Y'all ain't gonna leave me over here sittin' by my lonesome? Medill, we walkin' Valada 'cross the floor, then you and me gonna cut some dust and give that Lula hussy some proper competition.'

Nobody's paying any attention to Valada and her friends as they weave their way over to the musicians. It ain't all that often that a bone fide celebrity shares the space of the Wilbur's crowd, so they've moved out the way as Ruby glides onto the floor. The slow drag competition is a blast from the distant past as Wilbur's people crowd all up about Ruby handing out, 'Yeah, uh-huh's' and 'Prove it on him, sister's' as their tonight's Blues Queen works Floyd regally around the floor. Wilbur's piano man and guitar player are as spellbound as the rest of the crowd. They've taken no note of the young girl with a horn newly arrived at their side; they're vamping and vamping for Ruby. Only Roy, *Jimtown*'s clarinet player, has paid Valada any mind, and his eyes are saying, 'Not out here you ain't' as he peels off into another solo.

Now. Valada knows it's time to try. The surroundings blur and slow as she moistens her lips and concentrates on the chords, looking for the notes that are going to swing her up into the tune. Antoine's valves are moving smooth and ready. She's listening so hard that she can practically see the notes. The chord's more concrete than Medill and Bessie's faces. It's the chord, and Roy's

142

fingering on his wood and silver wand; it's the chord, and the piano player's fingering on the keys. Perspiration is trickling down her neck. It's the chord. Valada closes her eyes and goes. She hits her note, and she's on the music. She's riding its shape; she's thrown a bit between its teeth; she's on it; she's dancing on its back.

When Valada opens her eyes, she finds the room has changed its shape. The young girl on the horn has pulled the room for a moment away from Ruby, who's beating time amongst the shadows, nursing a sphinx-like smile.

'Who's the snip?' That's a woman. Probably big, black, and taking no shit.

'Go on, Valada!' That'd be Bessie.

'Go on, girl!' And Lula.

'She can ride!' The big black mama.

'Yes, she can!' A whole assorted bunch of folk.

The piano player and Roy throw each other a nod. Figuring to toss the young girl off their backs, Roy starts scampering up notes and scales like a sure-footed cat. Valada hasn't the chops to follow; so she slips off their riff into temporary silence, licking her lips and clearing the mouthpiece while studying where she'll catch on next.

'Yes, Lord, little mama! Lick my stick, baby, please!' Some strapping strong bass of a man.

Valada doesn't know where the comment came from – she's concentrating on chords – but she smiles a seductive smile before winking at whomever and mounting the wind again. Her blood, warmed by blowing and rotgut, is slamming against her skull, filming across her eyes. The room is red and hot, and if this is hell, then she'll be the Devil's happiest disciple. She's stepping from mid-notes to low with little shake-butt flourishes. She tries to go high; her lip won't hold but it doesn't matter; folks are cheering her on. *James is gone. James was wrong.* She's playing Hattie's laugh and Lavada's sass and little girls' legs kicking up yellow, blue, and pink. Roy and the boys aren't trying to throw her any more. Now they're dancing to the break together, nodding heads, talking eyes, stomping down. And it's done.

She's wet. Her shirtwaist is near transparent, revealing outlines of eyelet below. There's more sweat on her head than after three cakewalk repeats, and the roots of her kinking hair are screaming for a healthy scratch. Her lungs are heaving. Have they ever strained so hard? The room has not stood still. Is that Lula over there between two men that aren't her own?

'That was one hell of a nerve, Short Stuff, just jumpin' in that way.' Roy. His voice is rough, but his mouth might be turning up at the corners.

'But she held tight,' the guitar player is saying as her surroundings begin to take on shape. Bessie's gone over to Lula to try and keep her out of trouble. Ruby and Floyd are heading towards the gambling room in back.

'She needed to, steppin' up in here with that big ol' horn. Little girl needs to be taught another lesson,' growls the piano player, hitting another chord. Roy jumps in and the guitar player, too, but Valada is standing still, trying to get her bearings. 'What you waitin' for, Miss Man?' asks the Piano Man. 'Cute ain't everything. If you come to play, then blow, or sit on down.' Valada flutters the front of her shirtwaist for cool, positions her trumpet, finds her note, and blows.

She'd stopped blowing by the time the fight broke out. Wilbur's was moving toward closing, and nobody was sober, with the possible exception of Ruby, who had continued to nurse her own better quality stash throughout the night. Lula's flirtations had come home to roost when both Big Arms and the Happy Gambler wanted to take her home. Blades came out, and Wilbur had to smack the both of them upside the head with the axe handle he kept behind the bar precisely for that purpose. The Gambler went down easy, but it took some doing to put Big Arms to sleep, and by that time both the Funky Butt gal and Big Arms's ex-partner had contrived to teach the showgirl how to mind her manners. Funky Butt grabbed hold of Lula, and the Partner pulled out a razor, figuring to take a showgirl's scalp. It happened so quick. Lula was twisting and hollering to beat the band; Bessie rushed over and kicked Funky Butt behind the knees; and Floyd reached over and pulled Lula out the way. Only not before the Partner's razor sliced his arm. Blood was spurting every which way until Lula used the sleeve that was already hanging from her blouse to staunch the flow. Now they were all of them piled into Ruby's automobile, hoping to find a doctor who did for coloured before Floyd could bleed to death.

The road out to Wilbur's was more an idea than a fact, and Ruby was driving its ruts as quickly as she dared. Medill was riding shotgun up front, ready to pull aside low-hanging branches and jump out to push if necessary, while Bessie, Lula, and Valada crowded together in back trying to keep Floyd from bouncing with the road and hold his bandages tight. All of their hands were awash with his blood.

'How's he doin'?' yelled Ruby as she pulled the wheel left then right to avoid a big boulder in the road.

'He's still bleedin'!' wailed Lula. 'It don't stop! It's just comin' and comin'!'

'He's still breathing,' said Valada, 'but his hands are like ice.'

'Tear off more of y'all's petticoats,' Ruby ordered, 'and keep on pressin' hard as you can. Two at a time if you have to! And talk to him! Keep on talkin'!'

'Oh, Floyd, don't die! Please don't die!' whimpered Lula. 'I shoulda listened to you. I don't know what comes over me. Music and the liquor just hit me, and I just lose what is—'

'That's all of us, Lula,' said Bessie. 'You don't need to take that burden on yourself. Folks get together for a party, and somehow or another the blood'll just flow. It's nature, is all.'

And part of the thrill, thought Valada, though that was some-thing she wasn't about to say. Somehow the night wasn't complete without its edges, the sharper the better. Sharp heightened all the senses. She didn't have to bring her hand to her lips to taste the salt in Floyd's blood. The scents of Ruby's resolution and Lula's regret were as strong as those of the mule dung squashed with mud under the wheels of the fast-moving automobile and the honeysuckle laced around some distant tree. Only sharp edges did have a tendency to cut; and what Valada has found is that she is not intimidated by the consequences. She is exhilarated. She does not want Floyd to die, but dealing with this real possibility, his blood, bouncing in the night, going towards God knows where, she is feeling more alive, and she is not ashamed. She feels free and glad.

The night is nearly at its end, with clouds low in the sky, and the light to come was going to be grey and not yellow-orange; so what is the eerie glow in the west? Valada leans over Floyd's legs to talk to Ruby.

'What you think that light is?' she asks, not wanting to voice what she already knows in her heart. There has been trouble all over this area of late. Cracker trouble. White folks determined to retrain black men back from the war who'd got in the habit of standing up straight, thinking and acting for themselves, black men trained to kill an enemy who was white. Black families choosing to go North and do for themselves and let white folks work their own tired land, wash their own drawers, take care of their own young. Black folks who owned land or businesses that white folks decided were too successful or they ought to own themselves. Black folks who wandered into the paths of white folks at the wrong time or the wrong place. No matter what the trouble, it was usually black folks that got killed. And white folks' peevishness often involved fires, to barbecue bodies or light up crosses while bodies dangled from trees or were torn apart by chains or gored by red hot iron or mutilated and flayed.

Ruby takes her eyes off the road to follow the direction Valada is pointing and only just manages to avoid two figures stumbling across the road. She has almost brought the car to a stop to make sure nobody's been hurt when she realizes that that would be a mistake.

'It's niggers!' yells one of the men. 'Niggers in a goddam automobile!' Both of the farm-clad men are stumbling drunk, and by

146

the time they have managed to shoulder the shotguns they carry, Ruby has thrown the car in gear and taken off, swerving from side to side, so the first volleys hit on nothing. The second volley is luckier, smashing through the windshield and just missing Medill's head.

'Am I the only one here with a gun?' asks Ruby, eyes steady on the road, and when no one answers, cursing grimly to herself. 'It's in my purse, Medill. You better get it on out. I only got five bullets, so only use them for business.' From behind, the crackers are calling to one another, shooting in the air to attract more attention, trampling through the brush.

'What y'all shootin' at?' they're saying. 'Niggers! Niggers in a goddam automobile!'

How many of them are there? Seven? A dozen?

'How far they git?'

Is there barking? Are there dogs?

'Not but so far on this road.'

No, thank God. No dogs.

'We should catch 'em! We should catch 'em easy!'

No one in the car is wasting energy on hand-wringing, and tears are silent. All the words that need saying are exchanged by hands clenching hands. As first light begins edging the horizon, the sounds of hunters have become fainter, but the automobile engine is sounding louder, more metallic.

'No,' mutters Ruby. 'Not now. Not now.' After one last clang, the car rolls to a stop, and Medill jumps out immediately to see what he can do. 'Don't waste yo' time,' says Ruby. 'Floyd still breathin'?' she asks the wide-eyed women in the back.

'He is,' says Valada, 'but only just.'

Without the automobile engine to muffle them, the hunter sounds can be heard once more, a lot of it laughter.

'We gotta get him offa there,' says Ruby, climbing out of her seat.

Medill's looking toward the not-too-distant laughter. 'But Ruby, he's almost gone.'

'Medill, ain't nobody gonna blame you if you feel you have to go,' says Bessie, 'but we ain't leavin' him for those mongrels to desecrate his body.'

Medill doesn't go. He and Ruby are the strongest, so they take Floyd between them, but neither of them can handle Floyd and the gun as well.

'Any of you gals know how to handle one of these?' growls Ruby, indicating her gun.

When nobody speaks, Valada says she'll give it a try. Ruby's Clem is not a toy; it's a full-size Colt .38 and heavy to Valada's hand.

'The trick is to squeeze not jerk the trigger if you need to shoot,' says Ruby, 'and use both hands.' Which means that Valada's precious Antoine will have to be left behind. 'Bessie,' Ruby continues as the group starts their flight into the bush, 'you and Lula be up front and clear the way. Valada, take the rear.'

Birds deep in pre-dawn conversations, orioles, whippoorwills talking about, 'Where's the food?' and 'This here belongs to me' are near drowned out by the pounding of blood in ears, laboured breathing, the scrape of Floyd's lifeless feet being dragged through underbrush. The group is one hunted animal whose only thought is flight. It doesn't feel the stones tearing at the fancy shoes splitting from its feet or the thorns ripping through the party fineries and gauging at its hide. Its senses are acute. Its muscles burn and its throats are dry as it runs and crouches and claws towards a creek and just maybe survival.

They are lucky. Drunk and sated from whatever butchery they've performed this night, the hunters are not keen to the chase. Some peel off to return to their morning chores. Others group around Ruby's automobile, arguing about who should own it once someone can be found to do repairs. The few that do hunt have no dogs and don't discover the small, branched hollow by the creek where Valada and her friends have found a place to hide.

Floyd dies in the hours they spend motionless in the hollow, waiting to trust the silence long after the last hunter noises have faded away. They do not speak or gaze too long on one another.

They try to sleep or watch the variations of grey blanketing the sky. Their legs cramp. Their stomachs churn. They hear footsteps in the brush, and Ruby cocks her gun. They do not breathe until they see that the feet are small and brown.

The children's father arrives with his wagon under cover of darkness. Three men had been lynched by the mob the night before, two men still wearing the uniform of their country and a man who dared ask to cut their bodies down. It was not safe to venture anywhere near Montgomery. Local coloured were staying well away from the maw of a beast whose bloodlust was seldom slaked by one feed. The father will transport the strangers into the neighbouring county.

After burying and saying a prayer over Floyd, Valada, Bessie, Lula, Ruby, and Medill climb into the rear of the father's wagon to be covered by a manure-stained canvas and sacks of yams. They stink of fear and blood and hunger and shit. They will catch up with *Jimtown*. They will bathe, borrow, and buy new clothes. They will refit their masques, sing and strut and spread their joy, and behave as though nothing has happened. Breathing is difficult under the yams, and Valada struggles to find an open-to-the-outside pocket of air.

The Palace Theatre, New York, May 1956

The stage manager checks over his notes then squints past the lights, left hand visoring a prematurely high forehead. 'Miss Snow? You're up, Miss Snow. And then we'll be sketching out the finale. Lucy?'

'On it, Dennis.'

Standing in the shadows, Valaida smoothes out the curves of her dress. It was a good choice, the cotton sateen. It's done well in all the heat, and her fingers, though still a bit tingly, will be all right, too. Time to step up, and Valaida is pleased. She's going to get on the stage and tell her tale, offer up a piece of her heart. This is what she's come for. She hasn't minded the wait. She's almost fifty-two years old, and she's no longer in a hurry. Her community's tastes have moved in other directions, to sultry song stylists like Dinah Washington, Eartha Kitt, and Sarah Vaughan, to the angular shapes of bop and the hip-rolling riot of rhythm and blues; but tastes moving on don't mean that you have nothing left to say. Valaida's no longer dancing or purveying insinuating cuteness, those days are long gone, but she and her trumpet still have things to say. Valaida knows that she's a filler at this concert, that she'll end up between the performing dachshunds and a panicking violin prodigy, but she doesn't care. As she makes her way toward the stage, she can feel the familiar whispers of, 'What is she doing here?' 'Why is she doing this?' The what and why are nobody's business but her own. There are folks in her community who think she does these benefits only for the work. Negro tastes have passed her by, so she's taking it to the Jews, because what do they know?

People that she's known thinking that her participations in the benefits weren't nothing but a hustle.

'*You can push that nonsense down the way, Val, but don't be looking to sell it over here. You want the work. Ain't no crime, but sayin' you for real? Like Hattie McDaniel was somebody's maid for real.*'

People could think what they want to, including her family, who might know better if she let them. Valaida knows her reasons, some of them selfish and some of them not; just like she knows that she's still looking good at almost fifty-two, and that she still has tales to tell. A gaggle of dancers stands near the orchestra pit, one of them the Negro girl, posture extra-correct, eyes studiously avoiding any contact with Valaida's. Wanting to be the only one, and Valaida letting her stay as separate as she likes, knowing she'll learn that it's not all it's cracked up to be. Being the only one.

The stage manager has been ageing rapidly today. He'd started the morning at something south of thirty-five years old, but it's almost five o'clock, and now it looks like he's moving close to forty. 'Sorry about the wait, Miss Snow. We'd like to hold it to fifteen minutes if that's at all possible. What it says here is "Sentimental Journey". That still correct?'

'It is,' Valaida replies. 'Sentimental Journey'. The song her Earle had selected when she'd started working again during the war as a way back into hearts after all the time in Europe. *'You've been away so long, Vee. This'll let folks know that you're glad to be home.'* The song she'd resisted. *'I don't have a sentiment left, Earle. I only wish I did.'* A simple song, that served at times like this when a band couldn't be depended on to keep up with too much jazz. *'You can do it, Vee. You can do it, and it'll be great.'* A stupid, sappy song, with almost too much truth to bear, that did what it needed to do. Valaida holds up her charts for the stage manager to see. 'I'd like a moment with Freddy, if that's OK.'

'Be my guest,' he answers, already onto something else, calling out into the darkness, 'Anyone seen Mel? Mel? What's the word on Henny Youngman? Somebody tell me, please, that he's on his way back.'

'He's on his way back!' someone replies with a sardonic laugh.

The pit band's musicians are as harried, hot, and tired as everyone else, and they're bored; they're playing cards and smoking, horns resting on peacetime stomachs, unbuttoned sports shirts in a lot of unfortunate colours revealing ribbed undershirts and mostly pasty white skin. Valaida's first task in her allotted fifteen minutes of rehearsal will be to re-ignite their interest. Fortunately she's known Freddy, the music director, for years. She walks in his direction wearing the most radiant smile she owns. 'Hey, baby, what's shaking?' she asks him, with a nice little dip of hip.

'My head in disbelief, Val,' Freddy scowls in reply, but he's liked the little hip shake. 'This is the last time I agree to do one of these things, which I need like another heart attack.'

'You say that every time,' Valaida grins.

'And every time I mean it more. So, Toots, what's it gonna be? The usual? "Sentimental Journey", key of B-flat major?'

'I was thinking something else, but Marty tells me he likes the way it works before a *spiel*.'

'So what's with this *spiel*?' Freddy grins back. 'You been around us Yids so much, you beginning to speak the lingo? I'll give you *spiel*.'

'*Spiel* away, baby, and how about a little thing, here and here,' Valaida indicates in the score. 'What do you think?'

'What? You want us to work?' says Freddy with mock affront. 'Look at these guys! You think they'll pay attention?'

'Please, pretty, pretty please,' replies Valaida, her little girl counter-play dripping with sugar.

Freddy offers a sweaty jowl for Valaida to kiss, which she does. 'We'll be there for you, darling. Simons and Mason, and that hot-shot from Columbia, what's-his-name, Pierson. They're all gonna be here, so we ain't gonna fuck up but so much. You're looking awfully luscious there, Val. When you gonna give me the time of day?'

Valaida looks at her watch as she heads for the stage. 'It's seventeen past four.'

Freddy laughs and starts handing out the charts. '"Sentimental Journey", gentlemen, B-flat major. Ernie, Smokes, take a look at letter B. Pete, Randy, Neal, eyes on the bridge . . .'

As she walks toward the stage, Valaida moves on to another plane. She doesn't hear Freddy instructing his musicians, doesn't notice the whispers of, 'What's she doing here?', the mounting concern over Henny Youngman, or the arrival of Paul Goldman into a seat not far from the stage. She has become aware of her heartbeat. She is blowing Eugene warm, fluttering fingers over his valves. The stiffness is almost gone, so Valaida can concentrate on entering into the song. Some days Valaida has less to say than other days. Sometimes her breath will be short or her head will be hurting, and she finds herself picking up the energy of the blank ones in an audience; but she can feel that today won't be one of those days. Today she'll have a lot of tales to tell. The band will give an intro then she'll announce with Eugene, blues expectations away from that little blonde child, Doris Day, blues the doubters flat out, without ornamentation, then into the verse:

> *Ev'ry rolling stone gets to feel alone*
> *When home, sweet home is far away.*
> *I'm a rolling stone who's been so alone . . .*

Tell a story.

Hannah Eisenberg is calmer now. She is in a cab on her way back to the Palace from her family's apartment in Washington Heights. Rather than on the subway. Hannah is not being frugal today. This day is too important to worry about whether the dollars she is pouring into transportation might be better spent on the witty wicker handbag she'd spied last week in Bonwit Teller's window. It is important that she continue this day more evenly than she's been heretofore. She has showered and changed into the midnight blue shantung silk that will take her through the evening. It is sleeveless under a bolero top, but won't take well to perspiration, so it is important that she maintain her equilibrium, which is why she's taking a cab. For the breeze that can be felt through its partly opened windows. Partly opened, so the breeze won't muss her hair. The cab will stop at Paul's building on Central Park West, where a fresh shirt will have been left with the doorman. It had been Hannah's idea to bring Paul a shirt, but fortunately Mrs Goldman will be responsible for the tip, for today Hannah needs to be smiled at with an admiring gaze that would turn cold if she hadn't a tip. As Hannah's cab speeds toward the Palace, where she will fight off an ageing Negro woman in order to secure her Paul, Hannah needs to feel desirable. She clenches the evening bag that lies in her lap, then relaxes her grip lest her hands begin to sweat. Along with a lipstick and a comb, the bag contains notes from the Appeal office on what Hannah has learned about Valaida Snow.

Hannah too is aware of her heartbeat. It is thumping, beating against her breast like a prisoner who knows he's been wronged.

153

Hannah is torn, for the notes in her bag say that this ageing Negro woman was interned by the Germans during the war, that this ageing Negro woman, with designs on Hannah's happiness, had been a concentration camp prisoner in Denmark, that the German invasion of Denmark in April of 1940 had cut short a brilliant career, that as a coloured American performer of a degenerate music the Nazis despised, this Valaida Snow had been incarcerated, stripped of her possessions, brutalized, that only the intercession of a jazz-loving officer had preserved her life. Thanks to this officer, Valaida Snow had returned home on a prisoner exchange in the summer of 1942, but of course the experience had stayed with her; and this was the reason she worked for Jewish causes. This is how Valaida Snow came to know Marty Engel at the Williamburg Settlement House, where she sometimes worked with refugee children. Like so many of the children, she too was a survivor.

Hannah thinks of all survivors as heroes. So far as Hannah knows, none of her family had been lost in the camps. The Eisenberg diaspora had taken place long before Hitler's ascension, and the Eisenberg money had been put to good use in aid of all in-laws that could be found. It was foolish to imagine that there had been no distant tragedies, but of these Hannah knows nothing. Her family was one of the very luckiest, a fact about which Hannah sometimes feels guilty and always grateful. With her involvement in the Appeal and her mother's various causes, Hannah has, of course, encountered the odd refugee, but by and large Hannah's life has proceeded with little intimate contact with the Horror. So, to be in danger of losing Paul, this most important person to her life, due to the influence of a Survivor and a Negro one at that, did seem to be the cruellest of ironies; especially since Hannah is sure that this woman is not who she purports to be. If Valaida Snow had been in a concentration camp, why won't she talk about it? Hannah knows that a lot of survivors refuse to discuss their experiences, but this Negro woman had talked about hers before. Hannah had seen a clipping entitled 'I Came Back

From the Dead'. So, why was Valaida Snow being so quiet about it now? And Denmark. Hannah had never heard of this Vestre Faengsel camp, hadn't heard of Jews dying in Denmark and neither had Myrna. Myrna had said that it would be years before the full story of the Horror would be known. Things could have happened in Denmark that had yet to come to light.

'The lady's doing her bit, Hannah. Who cares about her reasons?'

Well, Hannah feels it is smarter to care. Why should some Negro woman use the Jews for her own selfish purposes? Especially when her purposes involved the corruption of Hannah's Paul.

Hannah is not an ugly person, and this is why she feels torn. Valaida Snow might be a heroine deserving of Hannah's respect, or she might just be a harlot. She might just be a dark-complected Lilith with designs on younger, happier lives. As a student of Social Work, Hannah has learned how to observe human behaviour and draw reasoned conclusions therefrom. She will use this training this evening at the Palace. She will be dispassionate, scientific. She will only act when she is sure.

On the Palace stage, Valaida is singing, concentrating on the work, studying the band as well as the lyric, with each bar coaxing them closer to her style. Eugene is resting on her hip, glistening at her side. She'll ask for a different gel on her light and hope that it will ease the glare that's assaulting the triangle of brain located just behind her eyes.

Gonna make a sentimental journey,
Gonna set my mind at ease.
Gonna make a sentimental journey
To renew old memories . . .

Chapter eleven

Atlantic City, New Jersey, 1921

> *July 8, 1921*
>
> Dearest Mama,
>
> *I hope you haven't been worried about me. I know I promised to write as soon as we got to Atlantic City, but we've only just yesterday arrived, one week behind time. I admit to being disappointed not to have spent July 4th by the ocean like I said I would (OK, Lavada, you don't have to gloat!), but it just couldn't be helped. That Hudson of Samuel's is just like an old mule. When it decides to stop going, it's a heck of a thing to get it moving again. It got ornery outside of Scranton and just wouldn't have a thing to do with those Pocono Mountains, no matter what Samuel tried, and that was just that! If there'd been a railroad station I could have walked to, I might have just left the two of them to one another. I'm sorry, I know you taught me*

better than that, Mama, but I just don't have your saintly
patience, even when I try.

Anyway, we're here now, staying with the aunt of one of
Samuel's friends who seems to be a very Christian lady. Coloured
can't stay by the ocean naturally, but I mean to see the Atlantic
today no matter what! I hope you all had a fine Fourth of July
picnic. Alva wrote me that Mr Bush had promised to slaughter
and cook up a whole hog! He seems like some kind of catch,
Mama, making steady money and ready to cook up a feast as
well. I hope you're paying attention!

Goodbye for now. I'll send you a postcard of the sea.
Your daughter who loves you,
Valada

The parlour is airless and dark. Mrs Anderson is back for the
fourth time in an hour, dusting and considering Valada's hand as
the younger woman addresses her letter, dusting and studying the
sheen of Valada's ivory silk stockings and the snap of her white
strappy shoes. The clock ticks just off of a 2/2 beat. Valada wants
to smash it with a hammer. She crosses her legs, arching her
instep. Not absently. Giving the landlady something to sniff at. It
is 5:47 p.m. Samuel is two hours late.

Valada craves fresh air and her first sight of the sea, and she has
tired of waiting for her husband, Samuel Lanier, competent lover,
middling tinkler, failing gambler. Mrs Anderson is insufferably
close. Though she wears an effigy of Christ around her neck, her
breath reeks of gin and the copper brashness of her hair hasn't
come to her by nature. Etta Snow might find Mrs Anderson's religion insincere, but her daughter's simmering peevishness would
concern her more. Rather than hammer at the clock, Valada has
decided to leave. Rising to order the canary muslin of her frock,
she nearly sends the landlady sprawling, then offers a hand, as
though it could have been a mistake.

'I'm so sorry, Mrs Anderson,' she says. 'Lost in my own
thoughts, I guess.'

'Not to worry, missy,' replies the woman, disbelieving, eyes narrow with malice. 'I'm a mite sprightlier than you young ones might expect. You on your way out?'

'I'm wanting to get my letter into the mail,' says Valada, using the parlour mirror to straighten her pretty cloche. Mrs Anderson is standing behind her, lips pursed with the desire to put hands around the girl's neck, or onto her hat, or maybe more gin. Probably all three. 'I've promised my mama to be better about writing. May I have a key, please?'

'Only one to a room,' grunts the landlady, 'and your husband's got yours. You want to tell me where you're headin' so's he'll know where he can find you? I lock up at eleven. Unlike y'all show folk, I rise early to praise the Lord.'

'No, thank you,' replies Valada, giving her brim an extra tug. 'You just tell him I said hey.' Samuel or Jehovah, you can kindly take your pick.

Outside the air is humid and heavy, but after the parlour it is bliss. The street is a filigree of blistering black tar. There is no sign of the Hudson. Valada slips her letter into a mailbox and sets her compass for the sea.

Hey, Samuel, where'd you go with your rickety car?
Hey, Samuel, it couldn't 'a' been that far.
Hey, Samuel, you took that much too long.
Hey, Samuel, your baby's upped and gone . . .

That Samuel's days are taking numbers comes as no surprise. His time was always finite. He was always going to be just like his car: flash and promises on the outside with a short-term pleasing ride, but nothing a girl could count on in his guts. His entrance was his strong point. It had been right on time.

Right on time was playing piano in a Tuscaloosa honky-tonk when the *Jimtown* show passed through town on its way to a two-week date in Birmingham. It was little more than a month after the

158

nightmare at Wilbur's, and Valada had been looking for a way out, out of *Jimtown*, out of the South, away from everything that reminded her of the stink of the blood, shit, and fear of those horrific nights and days, Lula, Bessie, and Ruby included. Either that or Valada thought she might go mad.

It never did for 'outside niggas' to encounter crackers on the warpath, so the *Jimtown* company had quit Montgomery in a hurry, leaving most of the fugitives' belongings behind along with props, scenery, and half-consummated fly-by-night affairs. When the women and Medill met up with their companions three days later, folks showed their concern by dressing bruises and sharing clothes, lingering to look for any signs of crumpling, some uncontrollable shivering, say, or yanking at hair, and finding none, said it was good to see they'd made it, while making no mention of what actually had occurred. Mr Dudley took over Floyd's stage-managing duties with a minimum of bluster, and the show just went on. Sometimes Valada would hear a sniffle in the wings or notice eyes glistening too brightly in the gloom, but she knew that if she shared a thought with someone or even a look, her own tears would seep then flood out from behind her masque, and there would be no stopping. She'd end up dry and brittle as last season's chaff; she'd crumble and be gone. So she did just like everyone else: strutted and wriggled and sashayed and sang, smiling broadly to the audience as it stomped its pleasure and guffawed its joy. Only she found too many of the laughs shot through with Floyd's moans, and too many grins in dimly-lit theatres piercing reminders of Floyd's face in death's grip. When she'd finally dared to describe these things to Ruby, the blues woman just humphed and took another swig of rye from a new silver flask.

'Ol' Death sittin' out there in the shadows every minute we're alive. Folks that come to see us know that fact better than we do. Part of our job's to keep everyone laughin' louder than he does and change our shape from time to time to keep him on his toes, him and those pale-assed fiends that do his work.' When Valada said nothing, Ruby looked her way with softened eyes. 'The first time the Demon bites he's like to rip your heart out, but I saw you out there, sugar. You got the steel to be just fine.'

Steel or no, Valada took to avoiding her close friends between and after shows, choosing to hang and jam with the *Jimtown* musicians instead. Even before Montgomery, Fess and the boys had started handing her some propers – 'Hey, the little girl may know a thing or two' – and Roy's account of her blow at Wilbur's had eased her over the line. Her trumpet Antoine having been left in the terror wood, Valada was playing violin for the jamming, or piano sometimes for a laugh when she needed back at the Professor for jerking her chain too hard, but she'd found in the music her best escape from the memories, better than dancing up to frenzy or a pair of warm arms in the dark. The guys all played at wanting entry into her panties, but they were nothing but some talk. She was more like their baby sister.

Samuel Lanier hadn't shared that point of view. Samuel'd joined their table at the Tuscaloosa tonk when Fess got the spirit to strut some stuff and slid him off the bench. Valada had been sitting between Roy, her clarinet buddy, and the *Jimtown* banjo man, when Samuel came over and asked to be introduced. Lantern light playing off his pink silk shirt had chased his nut-brown cheeks with port wine glow. He looked to be a bit older than she was, maybe twenty-six or twenty-eight.

'How'm I supposed to introduce you to the lady when I don't know you from Adam my own damn self?' Roy'd shot back.

'Samuel Lanier,' said Samuel with his hand extended. His nails were neatly clipped and buffed, his eyes making mention to things a girl might care for.

'Roy Lewis,' said Roy, shaking his hand. 'You play a decent box.'

'Thank you,' Samuel said with a quick, little play of tongue over his lip. 'Now if you'd kindly do the honours . . .'

'You don't mean to say the wimmens fall for this okey-doke?' The banjo man was falling over laughing.

'Some do, some don't,' Samuel'd replied. Without a wink. Just his eyes into her eyes.

160

'Samuel Lanier, Valada Snow,' Roy'd said, with a head shake and a wry grin.

Samuel had kissed rather than shaken Valada's offered hand. His moistened lips were smooth. He'd been happy to make her acquaintance, swung over a chair, and bought a round, but he'd got no further than that. Further came in Birmingham.

Valada'd been buying another trumpet after selling the earrings Ruby had given her for her birthday. It was going to take too long otherwise, way too long, and Valada was feeling empty without the horn, like there was a hole in her insides that was just its shape. The trumpet was golden this time, with a mouthpiece too broad for her comfort, but still a fine piece of brass. *James. I'll call him James this time.* The pawnbroker was just telling her about a music store on the white side of town run by another Jew like himself who had no problems with coloured when she found her free hand suddenly being lifted to a pair of lips and kissed.

'Valada Snow, Samuel Lanier.' His eyes still had the charm.

'If my other hand had been free, you might have found your feelings hurt,' she'd said, not about to admit that his kiss had a softness that was pleasing.

'I'd considered the odds,' he'd said.

'So you're a gambler,' she'd replied. This time the shirt was powder blue, his jacket cream, and his breath smelling faintly of liquorice candy.

'It's a living,' he'd said. 'Now what's a sweet young thing like you gonna do with that whole big bunch of horn?'

'You can't be much of a gambler if you figure winning with that card,' she'd replied.

'You interested in playing a hand?' he'd asked. His tone was kin to his sporting man's slouch, cool and relaxed but with a coil of tension underneath. His cuffs and collar were white and unfrayed. The sapphire tack in his lapel flashed in the light like it might be real. Valada turned her attention back to the pawnbroker.

161

'Would you wrap up my trumpet, please?' she'd asked.

'With utmost pleasure,' the pawnbroker'd replied. 'This here's a bargain you won't regret.'

Samuel sat through all of Valada's four shows that day, and she accompanied him to his game that night. Samuel won big with Valada at his side, $400 and the Hudson automobile, and in the come-again match the following night he won a whole lot more. Declaring Valada his luck, he bought her a solid gold necklace and a green velvet coat. He was a fast and furious lover, liking to play at bedroom games, and taught Valada some things about pleasure that James and Ruby had never suggested. After three nights of winning, Samuel thought he should marry his luck. Valada said she'd consider it, if he'd take his luck up North. He'd laughed, bought a ring off a gambling woman, and two days later the deed was done.

Ruby'd been neither perplexed nor perturbed. Her affections had moved from Valada's brooding on to a new wire-dancing beauty with long wavy hair, yellow-brown tiger eyes, and no night toss-and-turning, by the name of Eleanora. With Eleanora pouting at her side, Ruby'd gifted Valada with a diamond stickpin, telling her to remember that the road was long and to use the diamond whenever she needed.

'Ain't nothing wrong with takin' a ride that's offered, long as it suits your seat,' she'd said while Samuel was occupied loading up the Hudson, 'but you know this man ain't drawn for no long haul. Mind the signs, and do what they tell you.'

Bessie had blubbered like a baby. 'I'm happy for you, Valada, I really am, but I'm gonna miss you so,' she'd said. 'You been the sister I always wanted and never had.'

'Don't worry, Bessie,' Valada'd replied as she joined Samuel in the Hudson. 'I just know our paths will cross again one day. You'll be doing some step like nobody else, and I'll be trying to keep up.' But she'd spoken more out of a will to comfort than belief.

162

'Oh, I hope so!' cried Bessie as the Hudson pointed north, waving and waving until her friend got too small to see.

Chattanooga was the newlyweds' first stop. It was November, coming up to Thanksgiving, some ten months after Valada had left home to go on the stage. The drive through the mountains from Alabama had been slow and cold, but the thought of showing off her new grown-up style and handsome husband to family and friends had added another layer of warmth to the throw that Samuel had wrapped around Valada's knees. Only the Hudson broke down on the Wauhatchie Road some ten miles out of town, and their getting hauled into E Street by a farmer transporting hogs to slaughter put more than a little damper on the triumph Valada had in mind. Which is not to say that one and all weren't charmed by Samuel. He was devilish with Alvada, respectful and helpful with Mrs Snow, and thrilled little Hattie with barley sugar candy and piggy-back rides back and forth across the yard. Only Lavada had had a feeling that there might be chinks beneath the surface.

'So you really love him?' she'd asked Valada while they set the table for Thanksgiving dinner.

'What do you mean, "love" him?' Valada was concentrating on how to fit ten people around a table that had always been snug with six. In addition to Samuel, there were Alvada's fiancé, Thomas, the family's two boarders, and Mr Bush, the insurance man who was trying to pay court to Etta Snow. It had taken Valada's sisters two full weeks to convince their mama to ask Mr Bush to join their table, and Valada was hoping he was a good man; their mama deserved an easier life.

'I mean love, like love,' demanded Lavada, stepping into her sister's space, 'like I-love-you, you-love-me, now-and-for-ever love.'

'We have a good time,' Valada replied, moving around Lavada with her attention on the table. 'He's handsome, and he's taking me up North.'

163

'You ain't talkin' to Alva and Hattie, you know, missy.' Lavada could be as stubborn as a puppy with a strap between her teeth. 'You up here so big and bold in your suede-topped shoes and siddity attitude. You even know what love is?'

'Yes, I do,' Valada replied simply, turning briefly to meet her sister's eye.

Lavada's hair was still in long curls, but she could hear the depth in her sister's words. After the smallest of nods, she continued to lay out plates for a decent interval before pinning her sister with a sly sideways glance. 'I guess you know he seems a lot like Daddy.'

Valada did her best to suppress a smile. 'Well, didn't you ever wonder what it would be like to be married to him?'

'Not enough to want to do it!' Lavada had replied, and the girls laughed and laughed till they were gasping.

The first months with Samuel gave few grounds for discontent. True to his promise, he and Valada travelled North, to Louisville, Coventry, and Cincinnati, gamblers' towns all, where Samuel did well. Valada's time took on a different kind of texture, filled with leisure and love-making several times a day, wrapped in silks, whetted with Scotch whisky and French champagne. Her only duty was to sit by Samuel's side whenever he played and watch him win, which she did in high-class bordellos and low-class jooks, aboard gambling boats, behind office doors, among players of every colour, sex, and description, to the tune of rollicking rutgut, elegant ensemble, plaintive blues, or sometimes just the sound of muttered plaints and laboured breaths. Samuel preferred his wife not to play any music, which was fine with Valada for the time being, so long as Samuel continued to win. With Samuel winning, Valada played at being the lady, collecting toilet waters and hats, dressing her hair in new, modern styles, choosing her first diamond rings, warming her hands in a fox-fur muff. With Samuel winning, the Laniers travelled west through the small times and snowy towns of Indiana, and north again, through Gary, and up the

Michigan shore to Chicago. The Big Shoulders. The Bigger Time. Where Valada glimpsed her future, and Samuel's fortunes took a turn.

The first thing you noticed were the lights. They were bright. Like midday pushing hard into spaces that darkness might have felt were his to have. Like all the Stroll was a lime-lit stage, and all its seething humanity players in some fantasy skit where coloured folks walked straight and tall in fine and tended costumes, smiled wide and laughed loud, with clear eyes, money in their pockets, and countless places to spend it. Only it was true. Valada wants to be quiet and just soak up this North, what she'd call True North, the North of her imagination, but her Samuel's dribbling on like a leaky pipe.

'Ed Jones, darlin'!' he's saying. 'Have you an idea what kind of player you got to be to sit down with that man? Why, he and his brothers are the South Side kings! They're strong, baby. Take no kinda shit from no white man, or niggas neither. Don't waste their time with no nickel-and-dimin' bullshit, which is to say I'm one of the select! Sittin' down with Ed Jones! And when I win, when I get my hands around that big ol' pot, you and me, baby! Gonna get ourselves a place of our own, do it up real nice, call it Lanier's Luck, Samuel Lanier and Valada, his Luck. And you'll be showered with diamonds, darlin'! They'll be drippin' all around you like a veil!'

'Hmm,' murmurs Valada. 'That sounds real nice.' There's music coming from everywhere, out of one café after another, from around corners, from vaudeville theatres, from chop suey parlours. That's what they had to be with those strange symbols on their signs, chop suey parlours. Valada wants to know why the Chinese don't use the same letters as everyone else. She was looking forward to tasting some chop suey, but before his game Samuel wanted something he could trust. The Dreamland Café was up ahead, and, yes, the King was playing. His name was on the outside placard. Here in Chicago, there were coloured-owned cafes with outside placards. Some folks were calling them cabarets, an elegant, up-North sounding word. You didn't have cabarets for coloured below the Mason-Dixon Line, you had grin and bear it.

'I want to go there,' Valada says, indicating the Dreamland. She's been hearing about King Joe Oliver. Some folks said that no one compared with him; others said that Freddie Keppard was the man. Everyone was telling her that here in Chicago music was being played like nowhere else. Valada wants to hear for herself. Walking down this Stroll, hearing the hints of this music, is sending blood surging up and down her body, as though it had been pooled in some kind of catchment and the dams had just been lifted. After months of idle tapping, her heart is starting to surge.

'We haven't got but so much time before the game, baby,' Samuel says. 'We could just mosey on up to the club and have a taste there at our leisure.'

Valada forms her eyes into innocent saucers. Sometimes Samuel likes his wife seven years old instead of sixteen, with a tiny voice and an innocent, trusting smile. 'But it's so cold out here, Sammy,' she mews. 'My toes are just curling, and your fingers'll get numb and stiff and then how they gonna pull in all that pretty money? Just for a little, 'ittle while?'

The Dreamland was bigger than any club Valada had ever seen. It was designed to fit eight hundred, and there had to be at least that many people here this night, a few of them white and no one paying them any mind. Worrying about white folk is not the business of this place. Music is the business of this place.

The King is leading his men into what must be their fortieth chorus. They've been playing this one number for at least half an hour and every bar of it tight and hot to smoking. Dancers are standing now and watching the band; dancing has mutated into stomping testimony; all and sundry are yelling their approval, nod-and-grunting their ah-hah's.' Nothing Valada has ever heard before can reach up to the toenails of what she's hearing here and now. King Joe is talking through his tin can mute, trading words with his clarinet man, Jimmie Noone. Jimmie's tone is smooth and romantic, almost dreamy, and the King is pummelling him from the gut. Valada can feel King Oliver's pummel in her lower intestines, can feel it fluttering her ribs, pushing this past winter's idleness up her spinal column through her skull and out the way. Her breath is coming shallow. Her fingers are itching to press some brass. She is indeed three thousand miles from *Jimtown*. The King and his bone man have met and squalled at the break. Jimmie's clarinet is peeling laughter. The crowd is laughing with him. Valada is laughing. This is joy like people say comes from religion or a righteous ball. Valada's cheeks are tingling; her ears are hot. Fess and his boys did all right, but it was always catch as catch can, who was there and feeling however, maybe like playing and maybe not, and then always having to change with whatever and whoever Franklin Dudley threw up there on the stage. Not here. Here in Chicago, in this big beautiful club, filled with folk who knew their music and came out to hear it, these men were deadly serious. Valada had been starting to think of herself a player because she had found her seat at Wilbur's jook, but down outside Montgomery she'd been riding a wily nag. Chicago was the quicksilver, thoroughbred time. You had to know your horn and be ready for what have you. You had to have chops you could depend on. You had to work. Valada's heart is beating through the satins covering her breast. Her attentions will be turning away from hats.

'Baby, it's time to go.' Samuel has his hand on Valada's arm and is standing up to leave.

'Not yet, Samuel.' She's thinking the band may be two or four choruses from the finish, and no way she's going to miss it.

'I told you we didn't have but so much time. You said you understood.'

'Samuel, please!' The King is now wailing through a derby. Hat to horn, the other hand on the pistons. Valada's hands are small, she's wondering if she can learn to juggle.

'I said, it's time to go,' repeats Samuel, his grip tightening on her arm. There is an edge in his voice. Jimmie Noone and the

Bone Man are circling round Joe Oliver's derby. 'Now. We're leaving now.' Valada looks from Samuel's face, with its hint of confusion that she has not yet followed his lead, to her arm, where his hand has begun to damp. Barbarin's drums are summoning High John the Conqueror, the spirit of hope and glory. Some women are howling, 'Yes!'

'I think you need to do this night without me.' The King is blowing clear now, calling the children home. Valada will be following his lead.

'This is Ed Jones, girl.' Samuel's voice is a hiss. 'What I been building up to for months!' Valada can feel his rising anxiety through her sleeve, but she is not leaving this place. She pulls her arm away.

'You do this night without me,' she says. 'I'll see you back at the room.'

If Samuel blustered or muttered or stalked out of Dreamland, Valada is not aware. The King has surprised her. Just when she thought that he was moving towards closing, he turns back into the number with a peal of triumph followed by a virtuoso riffing that takes Valada's breath away. Her gold kid shoes are Vitus-dancing under the table. She grips the table hard to keep from jumping out of her skin.

Samuel had not returned the next morning when Valada rose, unpacked her James, and considered the dulled brass and hesitant valves that her months of neglect had wrought. Whispering apologies, she polished its brass back to brilliance, rinsed and waxed its valves, buzzed the mouthpiece, found that her lips were weak. Cursing her idleness, she vowed never to let such happen again. Whatever the distractions, man or woman, good times or bad, she would remember her lip. She fluttered the valves. Her rings felt restricting and strange. She removed them, then started her scales first, lots of scales. Then chords on to infinity.

She'd been at it for hours by the time Samuel returned, taking only the shortest of breaks to massage and oil her lips before pushing onward. She was still in her nightgown and musty from exertion. Samuel's plum silk shirt was dull with sweat. His eyes were bloodshot. His hand trembled at the effort of uncorking the bottle of cheap corn liquor he carried and lifting it to his lips. Valada didn't have to ask how the game had gone.

'The landlady says that you've been at that thing for hours,' said Samuel, swaying slightly as he considered the horn and her unbound breasts.

'I've got some work ahead of me if I'm gonna get anywhere near what they're playing in Chica—' Valada began, managing not to flinch when he pulled the horn out of her hands.

'If you'd been where you s'posed to, you wouldn' be needin' this horn. I got all the dick you ever gonna need.' The penis Samuel was exposing was only partially erect. Grabbing his wife by her hair, he shoved it towards her mouth.

'Play my horn, baby. Play. My. Horn.' Keeping Valada's head jammed at his groin, he dragged her over to the bed, the violent charge of the moment coaxing his manhood back to life. He thrust hard into Valada's throat. She gagged. 'None of that, baby. Show me what you can do! I've heard what you can do, and I want you to give me some of your best!' Using his legs as a lever, he lifted her onto the bed, scraping her nightgown upwards with the horn. 'You want this piece of brass, baby? I'll give you this piece of brass.'

The horn was still warm from Valada's hours of practice, the mouthpiece moist with her spittle as it slammed at her vagina. Frustrated by the limited penetration of the shank, Samuel twisted and turned it, yanking at her anus, abrading her vulva, while rutting himself against the swell of her swollen lips. Valada resisted the impulse to cry out or clamp down, deciding instead to rush the drama to its climax. Samuel slept immediately, his strangled breathing more in the manner of whimpers than snores. Valada used a plum silk shirttail to rid her mouth of his fluids, then made her way over to the dresser, pulled out Ruby's long diamond stickpin, and poured water into the bowl. Squatting on the floor into the bowl like a child, the stickpin flashing in the light on the carpet beside her, Valada was without thought until it occurred to her that in a manner of speaking, she'd just been fucked again by her James. She found this irony so absurd that she allowed the sleeping man to live.

Samuel wept for forgiveness when he came to and waited on his wife hand and foot for the two days she lay in bed recovering from her discomforts and contemplating her future. Unsure as she was at what had disgusted her more, her husband's violence or his lack of conviction about it, and figuring Samuel was still good for a free room and transportation, Valada decided not to leave for the time being, but it was understood that she now was free to follow her music without dispute. For four months, Valada followed her bands by night and practised her horn by day, graduating quickly from exercises to imitations of what she had heard in the clubs and then her own searching variations on what she thought it was that these men were up to; and for four months Samuel mostly lost at cards. Valada did what she was willing to support his efforts, pawned her rings, then her muff, then most of her hats and some of her shoes, all in an effort to supplement his stakes; but she would not spend her evenings at his side and confine her Chicago to stifling rooms with the tables all the time strewn with broken dreams; until finally there wasn't but $14 aside from Ruby's diamond, and Valada agreed that, as much as she loved this city and its sounds, it was time that they took their leave.

Samuel did better in Detroit, but not by much. The same held true of Cleveland and Akron, Youngstown and Allegheny. He went back to playing some piano, but his note playing had gone as indifferent as what he was bringing to the tables. Nobody who knew music would put up with him for long. By the time that they got to Pittsburgh, Valada had had enough. Gonzala White was in town with her ladies band. Valada slipped James's bag over her shoulder and went and got herself a job. Gonzala and her Big Act didn't conjure, and the vaudeville houses of Western Pennsylvania were nothing after the splendours of Chicago; but Valada was happy to be working and doing for herself again.

170

If Gonzala was disquieted by the way the pert young thing with the trumpet drew audience attentions to herself, Valada chose to pay it no mind, or the he-shes in the Act, seeking to nestle up to her stuff. They weren't none of them a Ruby, so for once, being with Samuel served for a bit of good. But she wasn't making any friends. For the first time in her life she found herself around women without sisterhood, so in Philadelphia's Gibson Standard Theatre, when Valada was going through the riff she'd learned off the B-side of Mamie Smith's 'Crazy Blues', 'If You Don't Want Me, Why Don't You Tell Me So?', and a man in the audience jumped up talking about he was Perry Bradford, the songwriter, and the riff on that record was copyrighted, which was a bunch of junk because how did you copyright a riff? no one had her back when the audience began to crow and laugh. Gonzala had been looking for an opportunity to rid herself of the pert young thing, and Perry Bradford served the purpose just fine.

'There are rules in this life, little lady,' she'd said, 'but obviously you think they ain't yours to follow. Let this be some notice to you that you're wrong.'

Gonzala wouldn't even pay Valada all she owed her, saying she was subtracting two nights worth for aggravation; and Samuel hadn't said a thing.

'What you want to hear from me?' he'd said. 'I told you that horn ain't nothing but a nuisance, but you like you know it all. What is it you knowin' now?'

Valada wondered how she had ever confused what lay beneath Samuel's skin with what might have driven John Snow. Whatever his many faults, John Snow had always possessed a spine. She took to stroking the diamond stickpin, knowing that it wouldn't be hers for long.

That's the Atlantic Ocean rolling onto that beach, with the white folks in their silly bathing costumes bobbing in and out of its waves. Valada's never seen an ocean before, water stretching from here clear to the other side of the world. Way out there,

171

beyond where the ocean meets the sky, there was another side of the world, where things were probably a whole lot different than they are where she stands. She likes the ocean's bigness and the thought of all that difference. She hopes to see it for herself one day, like Ruby did. She likes the smells of sun on sea and salt water taffy, the clack of her heels on the boardwalk, the white of her shoes against the wood, the ocean wind in her hair, the way the yellow muslin flutters under her arm when it is raised to hold her hat. The waves sound just like that big pink and white shell she'd held up once to her ear. *Whose was it, that schoolteacher from up North's, or that first railroad man who boarded, or was it Mr Miller's? Poor Mr Miller. Don't want to think about him . . .*

There are very few coloured on the walk, save for the mostly older men peddling the elaborate wicker taxis and a mammy or two, but Valada isn't letting the occasional hostile look from crackers interfere with her reverie. She is finally but 125 miles from New York City, where she is determined to go, and without Samuel Lanier. Will the diamond bring a better price here in Atlantic City or north in New York? Should Valada try to find work here, or hope that Samuel has some luck and take off with his winnings, but of course Samuel's winnings are nothing to be counted on; so it probably ought to be work . . . There are two coloured women up ahead not dressed as domestics. Why is one of them waving so wildly? Is there trouble? White folks aren't supposed to be so crazy around here, but you can never be sure. Valada looks behind her. Nothing. When she turns back, the waving woman is running in her direction, her taller companion following self-consciously behind.

'Valada! Valada! It's me! It's Bessie!'

Bessie smacks into her friend with a force that almost knocks the two women off their feet. Valada's hat goes flying, and the women are girls again as they pursue and catch the white straw before its capture by the sea. Bessie's friend stands by and watches, reserved and proprietary.

'Oh, Valada, I can't believe that it's you, here!' Bessie's cast eye is drooping lower than Valada remembers, but her dress is smart, and her smile as bright as ever. 'And where's my manners? Valada, this is Frances Porter. We work together in an act, and Frances, this here is Valada who I been tellin' you about and tellin' you about. Valada . . . Dang, I forget your married name!'

'Snow is all you need to remember,' says Valada.

'I'm sorry,' returns Bessie, realizing that white folks were staring and lowering her voice. 'He gone already?'

'No, but blink too long, and he's gonna be!' Valada laughs. 'I was looking for that sign Ruby told me about, and it's just upped and near knocked me off my feet!'

Jealous as she was of Bessie's affections, Frances was none too keen to re-work their act to include Valada, even when she saw that Valada's love for Bessie was not in that kind of way; but there was no going against Bessie's enthusiasm, so Frances had to give in. They decided to call themselves the Jacksonville Trio, even though Valada and Bessie had never set foot in the town. Jacksonville was dear to Frances's heart, and Valada voted with her in an effort to bridge the gap, that and advancing the cash for their new costumes with her diamond stickpin money. They each had three changes in the latest, spiffiest styles, silk stockings with garters, and two different pairs of shoes, which was sensible really with all the dancing they planned to do. As usual, Bessie was the dancing queen, her feet moving so fast sometimes they could hardly be seen. Frances had a beautiful voice and was an able comedienne, ready to mug and pratfall like the broadest blackface clown, though no way would the Trio be smearing cork onto their skin. To keep things moving smoothly, Valada was happy to let it look like Frances was running the act, but in point of fact she designed an ample platform for herself. In addition to the singing and dancing, there was a feature where she played violin, got run off the stage by Frances and Bessie, then came back blasting away on James. In the end that would be the biggest impression, she and her James, which Bessie didn't mind, and Frances, being the oldest and the tallest, just had to figure a way to cope. Frances might have grumbled, but when the Trio hit the clubs after two weeks of practice, they were an instant success, quickly moving from the intimacy of Kelly's Café to lucrative airiness of Egg Harbor, with tips tumbling fast and furious onto the floor.

Valada and Samuel decided to go their separate ways after a month. Atlantic City hadn't been any better for Samuel than the other Northern towns, and he wanted to re-find his luck back home. He swore that Valada had stripped his mojo clean, but he would feel that way. Valada was happy to see the back of him.

> *. . . Got my bag, I got my reservation,*
> *Spent each dime I could afford*
> *Like a child in wild anticipation,*
> *Long to hear that 'All aboard . . .'*

New York, 1922

January 21

Dearest Alva,
Yes, I know that I said Chicago was like a Negro heaven, but that was before I got to New York! I know you say that Chattanooga's just fine for you, but you really have to come see Harlem some day before you die. You couldn't even imagine a place like Barron Wilkins' where we work. Everything is so expensive and refined! You're not even allowed through the door if you're not wearing evening clothes. Every night's like the balls we read about in that fairy tale book Miss Simpson gave us except you know darn well that there were no coloured girls dancing in silks and spangles in those stories like we do here in New York!

We're working hard like always, but here it feels more like play. You feel happy and want everyone to feel like you do. The only little thing wrong is that Mr Wilkins won't let me play my trumpet in the act, too much like vaudeville, he says. What is it with these

men who won't even listen to a girl with a horn? Sometimes I
want to smash everyone of them over the head, but not Mr
Wilkins. I wouldn't have missed working at his Exclusive Club for
the world. You and Thomas need to just get on a train, and bring
Hattie and Lavada, too! I'll meet you at the station wearing your
good luck brooch (of course I still have it). You won't recognize me
otherwise because I'm an up-North sheba now!

   Your loving sister,
   Valada
   P.S. I'm glad you liked the napkins and that Thomas didn't
mind that they were pink.

In Harlem time moves fast and slick. New Yorkers talk fast, think
fast, focus in on the rapid buck. Colours are bright. People dress to
be seen. Birds of paradise, flash, spats, rings on fingers, rhine-
stones on shoes, attitude draping high style around shoulders, and
possibilities seemingly everywhere.

In Harlem, Valada's days are short. She awakes in the afternoon
to light sneaking around the edge of her rooming-house shade to
bathe last night's pretty hanging on the wardrobe door in its New
York dazzle. There is always dazzle about the New York light, even
when it's grey and clotted with weather. Valada will lie listening to
the day sounds of her Harlem street, the fruit man and the rag man
calling out for business, their horses' hooves clomping time for
traffic horn huzzas and sassy little girl voices with their jump rope
rhymes. *Shake it to the east, Sally, shake it to the west.* Maybe there's a
Smith woman's blues wailing from an upstairs victrola as Valada
rises from her bed and always conversation bouncing from one
side of the street to the other and then up into the sky. *Aw, shake it
to the one that you love the best.* Who is no one in particular these days,
which suits Valada just fine. She's smiling as she looks to see if her
pretty has survived its night. She doesn't worry if it hasn't because
there's always another where it came from. If there's a man skirting
about her attentions, maybe she'll let him take her out for a meal.
Maybe she'll go shopping, with intent to buy or just her eyes. In

New York, the possibilities are endless. All it takes is cash, and for cash what it takes is luck and talent, which Valada knows she has. Generally she'll practise her horn. She's bought James a fine case for a home, alligator-looking leather lined with deep scarlet plush. It pleases her, the thought of James nestling in fire. She trusts he'll forgive her for this time he's spending in the shadows. She promises him that it won't last too long.

In Harlem, Valada's nights are the Barron's, where the Trio and the other acts work their shows from just before midnight to 6 a.m. the following day. Barron's Exclusive is a Harlem club like no other, 'a class establishment for the best kind of people'. In other words, rich, and most of the time white, theatrical stars and high-rolling night people, local aristocrats and foreign ones as well. Only light-skinned coloured ever make the scene at Barron's. Unless they were stars like a numbers king, dark-skinned folk didn't tread near the Barron's door. Customers started arriving around midnight, in their chauffeur-driven Cadillacs and Duesenbergs, Packards and Hispano-Suizas. Their downtown appetites sated, they came north to Harlem's darkness for thrills served up as only the Barron could and always, always 'in the best possible taste'. A hundred dollars didn't stretch too far at the Barron's, which for the downtown players seemed to be part of their fun. Sometimes a sport would change a bill into its worth in fifty-cent pieces, and the Jacksonville Trio might find themselves flashing legs in silver showers. The coins could sting and bruise if they actually hit you, but this was the stuff from which dreams were made. Valada hasn't determined the measure of all her dreams, but she knows that they contain dazzle and weight. Just like the silver showers.

March 17, 1922

Dearest Mama,
Sometimes it really is hard being so far away from home. First I
miss Alva's wedding to Thomas, and now I'm missing yours!
This silver candy dish is a small thing, but I hope that when you

use it, you will think of me with love and pride as I do you.
Tomorrow is an important day for your little girl, Mama.
Tomorrow I'll be performing at the Barron's all alone. Frances
finally just got too sick to go on, and Bessie didn't want to keep
going without her, so Mr Wilkins said I could give it a try on my
own! I could use your prayers, Mama. Wish me luck!

All my love to you, Mama, and my best to Mr Bush. (I guess
we don't keep calling him that, do we.)

Your daughter who misses you,
Valada

She has awoken early, shortly after one, and her rooming house,
which caters to night people like herself, is silent save for the
swish of Mrs Levy's broom outside the door. She stretches
beneath the coverlet right down to her feet, revolving her ankles,
spreading out her toes, twisting appreciatively in the pale peach
chemise she left on for sleeping. Its silk is caressing eider feathers
against her skin. There have been damn few hands lately that
could compete with pleasure that it offers. Sitting up, Valada's
glad she stopped early with the Tops 'n' Bottoms; she doesn't
have a head. She's grown partial to the Tops' pleasing combo of
port and gin these last months, and she's often woken with its
effects. The remedy for the Tops has generally been easy enough,
a large serving of Roscoe's chicken and waffles with a hefty wallop
of grits on the side, but that wouldn't have worked today. Today
her stomach has turned acrobatic. She rises to throw water on her
face and inspects the dress hanging from the closet door. It is
almost free of its odours of tobacco and marijuana. Her perfume
remains, but the other funks are fading. Its net didn't tear when it
caught in the taxi door. A bit of its beading is loose, and Valada
should tend to it before the small drip of shimmer turns into a cascading mountain torrent, but her hands haven't the calm for
smallwork. What she needs is a bit of James.

She removes her trumpet from its case and begins to warm its
brass, starts running through fingerings, playing with the pistons'

pressure, trying to transpose a particular riff she thinks she heard the night before. The unwritten rule of the house permits no practice before 3 p.m., but Valada needs to hear some of what she can do, so she sends just enough breath down the mouthpiece to produce a little bit of hum. The routine of these drills is soothing, which is good, for Valada is nervous about doing the Barron's tonight. It is an unfamiliar feeling.

Valada had never seen the Jacksonville Trio as her ticket into the sky. Especially after the Barron refused to allow her trumpet, Valada thought their act lacked that knock-you-over-and-grab-you pizzazz, but she'd valued the Trio's umbrella while she trained herself to the New York time. Stakes were bigger in New York, consequences too, and Valada preferred being part of a group as she felt her way. Only the female complaints that had been plaguing Frances for months had escalated into something far more serious these last few weeks. Finally she could no longer disguise her pain and perform. Frances and Bessie were sharing a room, and they didn't spend money like Valada on so many new dresses and silks and laces that couldn't be seen; so for now there was enough money for Bessie to stay at Frances' side, which was where she felt she ought to be. Which left Valada; and then Brickie stepped in.

Bricktop, Ada Smith, was a singer at Barron's a few years older than the Trio, far more experienced in nightclub ways, and generous with what she knew. She was small like Valada, but light-skinned with the brilliant red hair that had given her her name. She was not particularly pretty, but she had a way about her that just drew folks in and had them thinking that they'd been knowing her for ever. Brickie had said, 'Why don't you try a solo, Valada? I know Mr Wilkins would give you a shot,' and before Valada could decide if this was a good idea, Brickie had hauled her up to the Barron and explained the situation. Valada had felt extra small under the Barron's gaze without Bessie and Frances at her side.

'You ready for this, little lady?' the Barron had asked, his dark expansive face without expression.

'Sure she is!' Brickie'd replied, when Valada'd hesitated a beat too long. 'She's got a beautiful voice and can really work those cute little hips of hers. She'll be great! You won't be disappointed.'

The Barron's eyes had traces of a smile as they gazed downwards into Valada's. 'OK, Miss Snow, we'll see what you can do.' Was it because he'd known how scared she would be?

It was the Barron's white folks that spooked her. Valada told herself that they weren't all of them the hell-hounds that tried to hunt her down in Alabama, that slaughtered black folk for trying to breathe free, and sent young boys to prison for thieving a Coca-Cola, and she was beginning to half-believe it. That was one of the things about being up North. You found yourself around a lot more of them than you ever did in the South, particularly if you went downtown, so you started getting used to them more; and in New York everyone was moving so fast after that dollar there was no time for all the danger-fraught rituals that plagued the South, like who moved out of whose way on the sidewalk or who looked direct into whose eyes. But that didn't change the fact that they didn't behave like folk. Their eyes still bigged or tightened or tensed if you asked them a question most times, like you weren't supposed to have powers of speech that they should understand; and they were an entirely different kind of audience. Valada had never performed primarily for white folks before coming to the Barron's, and she found it an entirely different game. With coloured folk, no matter what the venue, you knew where you stood. If they loved you, the love was demonstrated and warm; if they hated you, you could only hope it was just your sentiments that got hurt. All manner of things could come flying at you with the verbal abuse, peanut shells, pork chop bones, ripe tomatoes, somebody's shoe; but they looked you in the eye while they were doing it. You were part of the family, and they were letting you know how they felt. Not so with white folks.

When you worked, half the time they weren't even paying attention. You'd be out there killing yourself, and they'd be talking to one another, hooting about some joke that was only funny to them, their hands halfway up their women's drawers or down their dresses, as though being in a coloured club somehow excused them from civil behaviour, that and all the money they spent. And when they watched you, you didn't know what it was they were really thinking, or else you didn't want to know. They'd be looking at you dead-eyed, both the women and the men, like you were an animal in some zoo performing inhuman acts, or else they were making like they wanted to get up there with you and do something nasty. It wasn't just that they wanted into your panties – coloured men wanted that too, or they better, it was part of what you played with – but with coloured it was, 'Let's me and you get on with it, sweet baby!' It was folks having fun with each other, person to person; with whites, you got the feeling they thought you were some kind of thing, an animal with no human sense.

But you wanted that money. It was white folks that had the real money, and not only their sporting element, white men with jobs or money from their daddies, who could throw fifty, one hundred, two hundred dollars away without feeling any pain; so you found your ways to deal. You kept changing up, changing up, so they could never get a handle on how you did the things you did. The masks you donned when you hit those lights were thicker than what you used with your own and smoother, so any attempt to penetrate just glanced off into the void; and behind those masks, you took more pleasure for yourself. You revelled in your body in the music, its glisten under the lights, the vibrations in your chest as you sang, the reverberations of your feet hitting the floor. You played off your partners, like birds in a flock or bees in a swarm. You felt communion with the breaths you took, your sweat hitting her, her sweat hitting you, the piano man giving a special lift-off to your steps. And the funny thing was, from behind the mask, you could see that often you frenzied them more when you were into yourself than when you were selling to them direct. It was hard not to think of them as some other kind of being, and tonight Valada would be facing them on her own, going solo for the cash.

180

The soloists were what the Barron's really was about. Moving from table to table, they sang their songs, lingering where the requests and the tips were prime. Interaction was the key to table success, and being what the patrons wanted you to be. Valada had been happy with that stretch of floor between the Trio and the Others. Now she would have to cross it.

The first part of the set had gone well enough. Knowing herself to be neither big enough nor old enough to convince with heavy blues, Valada had kept to lighter fare, innocent songs filled with sunshine and hope, 'Toot, Toot, Tootsie', 'Ain't We Got Fun', combined with a little bit of novelty and Tin Pan Alley love. She has worked out a medley from the coloured Broadway hit 'Shuffle Along' with Harley the piano player, and as she goes into the second chorus of 'Love Can Find a Way', she knows it's time to make her move. Behind the part of her brain that's running the lyrics, she can hear Bricktop's words of encouragement.

'They're not gonna bite you, girl. They're folks, just like you and me; they just have a different style. They think all their money gives them different problems than the rest of us, but it ain't true, so don't you let that confuse you. They're falling in and out of love. They get scared and tired, and they come to us to relax and have some fun. Trouble is, some of them get disconnected from their nature, which mixes them up a bit. Don't concentrate on that. Concentrate on what's the same. They got eyes and ears just like us. They're gonna respond to a pretty voice and a sexy little smile. So go on in there, and get that money!'

Valada moves out of her safety towards the table furthest away on the left, her heart beating so hard she's lucky to find the beat. There looks to be two couples at the table, which should be easy enough, the men with well-trimmed grey hair, florid cheeks, expensive suits, the women much younger, a platinum blonde, a spit-curled brunette, with lavish furs over their chairs even though the night is warm. Chorus girls, probably. Not her business. The man in front is talking to his partner over his shoulder, the brunette's toe working his pant leg towards his knee.

181

'Look, Alfie!' squawks the brunette. 'She's coming to us first!'

The men continue to speak. Valada was wrong about the foursome. There is a single man at the table as well, much younger, a sandy forelock hanging down towards his eyes. He's listening to the men, but he is unfocused. Valada figures he's been drunk for a good long time. It's not all that easy singing over the conversation, but Valada concentrates and keeps on, the smoke of cigars nearly making her retch.

'Have some manners, you guys,' says the brunette. 'How's a body gonna do her work with all this boring business yap! She's got a nice voice. You oughta listen. I like your voice, honey,' she continues, looking towards Valada. 'It's nice.'

Valada hasn't finished her song.

'I like her dress,' says the blonde. 'Where'd you get your dress, honey? But I think it would look better on me in blue. Blue's my colour, don't you agree, Philip? Brings out my eyes. Honey, where did you get your dress?'

Her song completed, Valada sets her smile. 'I've got a special source.' Time to make eye contact. The brunette is smiling stupidly, sweetly. The greys are still on about a deal on Wall Street. The single is looking at her breasts. 'Any requests?'

'But who's your source? Philip, Philip! Look at her dress. I want a dress like that. Can you find me a dress like that?' whines the blonde.

'Sure thing, baby,' Philip answers. 'Anything you want.'

'I want a blues,' cries the blonde. 'You haven't done any blues. Sing us some blues, honey!'

'I tend to leave the blues to the Smith sisters,' says Valada. 'It's more their style. How about "Alexander's Ragtime Band"?'

'But you know some blues,' encourages the brunette. 'All you gals know some blues.'

You gotta be what they want you to be. 'Sure, all of us know something,' returns Valada, sneaking a breath she hopes is not too obvious.

182

She starts in with 'Baby, Won't You Please Come Home?', knowing that Harley will follow her thread. She's not doing so badly because Lord knows she's feeling it.

I've got the blues, I feel so lonely
I'd give the world if I could only
Make you understand
It surely would be grand . . .

The greys have stopped their conversation to stare through their cigar smoke, the one in front taking to a slow and lascivious up-and-down. He's peeling her clothes off with his eyes, tracing on the table what he might be doing with his hands. The brunette slaps his thigh with a guttural chuckle. 'No, you don't, Alfie!' she says. 'You save all that stuff for me!' Alfie adjusts his seat so the brunette's hand can go to his groin.

. . . Baby, won't you please come home
Baby won't you please come home . . .

Valada manages something close to a smile and starts moving around the table, struggling to sway to the music against the beat of her heart. Perspiration is surging under her dress. She imagines it splashing onto her shoes.

. . . Baby, won't you please come home, I need money
Baby, won't you please come home.

Valada's smile is genuine at the song's end. She's relieved that she somehow made it through without a glitch. The front grey gives her a twenty, the one in back's about to hand her a five until his blonde slaps him with an 'Oh, no you don't! You ain't embarrassing me with that cheapskate shit! You give that girl a twenty, and maybe she'll tell me where she got her dress!' A second twenty is reluctantly produced.

'My guy comes here a couple times a week, but I don't know where he stays,' says Valada. 'I wish I could be more helpful. You guys have a good evening.'

She's about to leave when the single grabs her by the hand and pulls her over to his seat. He's holding a hundred dollar bill, but knowing there's something more to it than that, Valada's smile goes slightly wary. She wants to pull away, but his hold is firm. He's mouthing and gesturing silently, 'Come here, come here,' easing her closer. When she is right by his side, he folds the bill with one hand then moves it in the direction of her bosom. Valada wills herself to stillness. He doesn't grope as he places the money in her dress; he does it gently, reverently. Then he lays his head quietly against her breasts. It is the gesture of a child. Valada resists the electricity running up and down her arms, screaming that she slap him across the face and shove him backwards onto the floor. She gives him the slightest beat, clears her throat as prettily as she can muster, then moves on to the next table singing, 'Love Can Find a Way'.

Brickie knew the single. 'Oh yeah, young Van Buren. Boy just loves himself some coloured tits. Had a toffee-coloured mammy, the only mother he ever knew. I've gotten that hundred two or three times. He's harmless. Weird, but harmless. You did OK tonight, honey. So what do you think?'

Valada and Bricktop are at the Smile Awhile Café, unwinding in the wee hours after the Exclusive Club has closed. Most of their fellow clientele are working night folk, mostly legit but not all, closing out their work time in this place that's only for them. The menu is home-cooked food, chased with home-cooked liquor and space where a person could kick back and breathe. A group of musicians is in the band corner, tearing up the joint with a low-down grind. Another musician, sitting at a nearby table, gets so grooved that he pulls out his own horn and joins right in. He's not a bad player, but he misses the chord, stumbles around a bit, then curses out to generous laughter. The musicians give him another

184

try, and he makes good his entry this time. He's not up to their standard, but he jams well enough. The men hadn't been so welcoming the time Valada tried joining in. Early on in her New York time, before she knew more the lay of the land. The Trio had had a good night, and Valada was feeling rightly jazzed; so she had run back to her room and grabbed her James. When she had tried to make her move, she had been on the chord, but the group had gone cold on her. First left her hanging in space, then smashing in with a volume that simply drowned her out. Afterwards the trombone player told her, 'Look here, darlin', you're really cute and all, but this here is serious business. You want to do with us, you can sing, or maybe hit some ivories if you got some real style; but that horn thing ain't gonna make it, not here in New York.'

Valada swore in her heart that someday she was going to blow that clown away. She would find him, wherever he was slinking, and blow his ass away. Not tonight though, tonight she didn't have that kind of strength.

'I said, what do you think, Valada,' repeated Brickie, 'about working solo? Not bad coming up with a blues that ended up asking for money. I figure you're a natural. What do you think?'

'I think that I'm never going to do that again,' Valada replied slowly. 'I hated it.'

'You didn't hate the money,' smiled Bricktop.

'No, the money is good,' agreed Valada. 'I'd be happy to keep it coming, and I thank you for helping me out; but I hated them being so close, like they were pushing up against me, and I didn't have room to move. I've never had our own so close, let alone those 'fays.'

'You'll get used to it,' said Bricktop. 'It's a skill like anything else.'

'No, I won't,' Valada said pensively. 'I'm not like you, Brickie. You invite everyone in, like the club's your own private parlour. That's your style, and you work it really well.'

'You think I'm letting those folks into my real privacy, letting them know everything I am?' Bricktop was looking straight into

Valada's eyes. 'It's an act, honey. It's always an act. Hospitable and friendly just happens to be mine. I saw you tonight. You got past that first table and kept the room interested. You'll find your stride, and you'll do just fine.'

'It's not for me, Brickie,' Valada said firmly. 'I don't want people thinking they can know me that well. I need the line. I learned that tonight.'

'You one headstrong little bitch, I'll give you that,' Bricktop laughed. 'Now, buy us another pitcher with some of that money from your titties, so I can figure what I'm going to say to Mr Wilkins later tonight.'

May 27, 1922

Dearest Lavada,

I miss you very, very much too, and I wish I could have been there to see you win the talent contest at the Royal! Who knows? Maybe someday soon you may be out here on the road with me.

I know Mama was worried when I left Barron Wilkins, but everybody knows that moving from job to job is what show business is about. When we first started working at the Barron's, it all seemed like a little piece of heaven, but now I'm with a show that's even better for me, I think. It's called 'Holiday in Dixieland', we're on the white Orpheum time, and I'm back playing my trumpet, and guess what? Do you remember the trumpet-playing woman we met that first time backstage in Chattanooga and her daughter who looked just like a little brown bunny with a horn? Well, they're both in the show! They're named Dyer and Dolly Jones, we play together all the time, and I'm picking up all kinds of good tips, but you know, just because we both play the trumpet doesn't make us the same kind of person.

I think Dolly would rather play the trumpet than eat enough to stay alive. Nothing else really matters to her. It's like she doesn't seem to care if anyone else is even listening. That's where we're different because I do like the way stage lights feel when they're focusing mostly on you, and I really like it when the audience

really likes you and whoops and hollers and claps (with white
folks it's mainly clapping, but I'm getting used to them I guess). It
comes up and over you like a soft, warm wave. It really is a
wonderful feeling. Another good thing about it is, it usually comes
with some money, and you can buy lots of pretty dresses!

Love and kisses to everybody, and keep practising your steps!
Your sister,
Valada

The Palace Theatre, New York, May 1956

The second trombone has once again lost his place, the music director has hung his head, and Valaida has stopped her run-through because she wants better and knows she can get it. With her minutes ticking away, the stage manager hovering, and volunteers scrambling to organize artists into rehearsal for the finale, Valaida generates the illusion that she has an entire evening at her disposal. Possessing neither the youth, skin colour, length of limb, nor powerful friends of Liz LaFontaine, Valaida understands too much of this world to be peevish. Instead she walks toward the pit and leans over towards the culprit, who has been nudged by his partner, with only the slightest edge of forbearance in her smile. 'What's your name, honey?' she asks.

'Who? Me?' returns the player, his glazing eyes suddenly acquiring a bit of spark.

'Yes, you,' Valaida replies, her smile warm. But expecting results.

'Daniel. Whiticomb. Daniel, Danny Whiticomb.'

'Well, Daniel Whiticomb. Can I call you Danny?' The player nods. 'Well, Danny, if you look at letter F, I think you'll see that your buddy there on the tenor is *ya-da-daa*, but you're *ya-da-Di-da-da-daa*. Is that OK with you?' The player nods again. 'Good, because I need all of your pretty tones givin' me a pillow that I can lean on. If you snatch it away, I'm gonna get bruised, and that's not what you want for me, is it?' A shake of head, with the start of a smile trying to fight with a rising blush. 'Good. I was hoping you felt that way. So why don't we try it again?' says Valaida before the player's blush can turn to embarrassment, the embarrassment into resentment, and the resentment into aggressive sabotage. 'Freddy?' Freddy gives an upbeat, and again they begin. 'Sentimental Journey' in B-flat major.

In his third row seat just left of centre, Paul Goldman watches Valaida in rehearsal, unaware of the hubbub around him, the confirmation that master-of-ceremonies Henny Youngman is finally on his way, the giggles of Haddasah girls in response to the come-ons of every-ready comics, the barking of dachshunds, Mel's mighty expletives, a box filled with programmes ripping from the bottom, its contents scattering up and down the centre aisle. Paul is with Valaida on her journey. *Never knew my heart could be so yearn-y. Why did I decide to roam?* How far did she go and why? he's asking. Why couldn't she have found her satisfactions right here? *Gotta take this sentimental journey.* That lush contralto is rumbling his way, what he'd heard in the car under the laugh, the timbre that had surprised him. She's talking to him, he knows she is, to him out of everyone in the theatre, and the noble intents of just a moment before are swept away before ambivalent but deeply felt yearnings of his own. She's proffered an invitation, she's taking him with her, and here, in this time, she is all that he knows, all that he cares about. Her voice soars towards its home, and she is taking him with her. The break in her *home* is a crease in his heart, and he's wondering why, but he can feel it's for him; this time it's for him, for some reason he's needed. That open vowel in the distance could be Mel calling his name, but the brass is at her lips now, glinting in the light. Yellow-brown cheeks are compressing, and whatever Mel needs is as nothing right now. Notes are sounding from her trumpet, and Paul is mesmerized. His eyes now see only her, the unfeminine stance of her wide-planted feet, the arch of her calves above small, pale-coloured shoes, legs almost straining against the ivory sheen of her dress, the curve of her ass, the arch of her back, the gloss of moisture on her neck above the upstanding collar, a disregarded lock of chestnut hair slipped out above her cheekbone, lips puckered about the mouthpiece.

Paul is not deluded. Valaida is playing to Paul, whom she noticed in a glance when the trombone player first mangled his entry. In the disorder of this rehearsal, it has helped Valaida having Paul there. Time was when the glory of the doing was enough, when Valaida hadn't really cared who'd heard her and how they'd felt, taking as a given that she'd turn heads and throb groins; but those days are in the past. Funny how life was. Time was when most of what Valaida had been was cute and energetic, when most of what she'd had to say was, 'Look what I can do!' Folks hollering and stomping for little more than a wiggle, toot, and smile, but now that she has more to tell, she must work to find her listeners, extend herself further beyond her wall to find the someone who wants to hear. Right now that someone is Paul, and Paul's involvement is her frisson. Valaida is playing Paul. She can feel his thrill, use his energy to her advantage. She knows that a part of this is the desire of a young white man for forbidden brown fruit, all the more tantalizing in its maturity. There is nothing unusual in this, though the desire often creeps up on its yearner unawares. Valaida has been playing to white men for the better part of thirty years, and she is cognizant of their desires, which are often far more predictable than those of her own. At least at this point in her life, when her fruits have been mellowed by time. All men concentrated on what they wanted to see, but looking as they did through their congenital veil of race, white men were more liable to being manipulated by the masque. They weren't as sensitive to the cracks that were observed by Negro men, nor distracted by them either. So long as you didn't scare them. For all their vaunted power, white men could be as skittish as newborn colts whose hooves could kill you dead. But then Valaida never had performed or seduced through terror; she warped her notes through wefts of desires, and so she plays to Paul's. Her playing preens to him, and the pit band is caught up in their momentum, woven into their tableau, and all of this together begets a surge of energy that slashes through the auditorium, catches assembling artists and volunteers off guard, stopping the chaos just for a moment, a sudden wind out of nowhere. There's a moment of what was that? Heads up, looking around, like grazing animals sensing a threat, then the recognition of, 'Oh, just her', nothing, with a shrug and back down to business. But for Hannah Eisenberg there is no 'Oh, just her' about the tableau she sees before her. What Hannah sees as she finds her way into the theatre via the left aisle door is her Paul sitting by himself, in rapt attention, eyes riveted, lips slightly parted, enraptured by the Negro woman on the stage. What Hannah sees is Valaida Snow aiming her performance directly at Hannah's happiness.

Valaida is dizzy after her finish. Her intention had not been to blow in rehearsal as hard as she just has. Her plan had been to set up the design for the evening's performance, feel out the band, put them through their paces – after the heat and stuffiness of the day, reserve her energy for the evening – but the young white man's inquiries had thwarted her design. She'd heard Paul asking just what she was all about, and she'd had to tell him, this evening's version anyway; but now she is paying a price. The stage manager has his arm out as though to beckon her out of the way. She has a sense his mouth is moving, but she's not distinguishing any words. The theatre is a-buzz with activity, but Valaida's hearing is a lot like her sight at present, which is to say pooling back and forth on itself like water in an eddying stream or fingerpaint colours from when young Cheryl used to comb them round and round with her little fingers, threads of red, blue, yellow, green mixing altogether until they ended up like mud, and in the midst of it the notes, splashing around her, bouncing about the bones of her skull, shimmying through her brain. For a moment, Valaida isn't sure of where she's standing, what the weight is in her hand, where her hand is for that matter; so she's not gauging the aggressions of the young white woman dressed in the princess dress of midnight blue shantung silk with a brown paper parcel clutched tightly to her chest.

190

If her antennae had been working, Valaida would have picked up 'white person on the warpath', 'young and delusional white female looking to vent her spleen', and prepared herself for confrontation. After a lifetime of charting her own path, much of it through Caucasian terrain, Valaida knows never to be complacent – when she had, there'd been hell to pay – but now her senses are blurred. That might be Freddy barking instructions at the outermost fringes of her consciousness, Lucy's hand on her shoulder, asking if she feels OK, and the coloured girl dancer might finally be looking in her direction; but Valaida's true awareness is in the music. At the end of her *Journey*. It's where she'll walk to when she feels her feet.

Chapter twelve

New York, 1924

October 17, 1924

Dearest Mama,
I was so excited to hear that I'll be having a new little half-
brother or sister very soon, but are you taking care of yourself?
I'm sure Mr Bush, I mean Arthur, is beside himself with joy, but
Lavada wrote me that you've been very stubborn about letting
her and Hattie help you around the house. You have to stop that!
Mama, I've seen Lawrence. I was coming early to the theatre
after doing some errands downtown, and there he was coming out
of a building across the street. Even after so many years, I knew
him right away. He's well, Mama. He always thinks of you and
promises to get in touch with you soon. A visit might not be so easy
though because, you see, he's crossed over the line, but he was very
happy to see me, Mama, he really was. He's still our Lawrence

despite everything, and he's grown more handsome than Daddy ever was.

Curtain's in half an hour, so I have to go now. I'll write again soon.

Your daughter who loves you,
Valada

It had been almost dusk. She had been coming from a session at the photographer's. Russell had been with her. He'd come along to help carry her costumes. If she'd been by herself the costumes would have been dragging on the ground or getting crushed, and she'd have been worrying about the stage manager yawping about irresponsible chorus girls caring more about their own careers than the good of the show, because if he had his way the costumes would never stray from the rail, like they were any kind of use without the people inside them. With Russell along she'd been able to concentrate on projecting for the photographer. That was one of the sweet things about Russell. He was never always doing something else when a girl needed a man for that male kind of assistance, carrying things that might be clumsy or heavy, or helping her move from one house to another, even if one of his brothers had the car. Russell had stayed with Valada the whole afternoon, kept her laughing so her pictures would be bright and lively, bringing in drinks when the room got close, adjusting the tilt of a hat so her eyes would be shown off just so. It pleased him to know the pictures would show Valada at her absolute best, he said. He wanted only the very best for his girl, he said, and that was some change for Valada, coming from a man. It made up a whole lot for what he lacked in looks.

Russell was a big, dark-chocolate brown, shaved-head bear. Papa Bear, she called him, which he didn't mind in private. A girl could fall back on Russell and know that he'd be there. He kept his wide, chunky feet planted firmly on the ground, not always triple Time-Stepping underneath him like most of the youngblood sheiks travelling through the night life. The youngbloods tended to cause more trouble than they were worth, and Valada had often found more comfort snuggling next to Bessie. That was tender, like grappling with the youngbloods often wasn't, and it was warm, and you weren't all the time worrying about having babies; but it wasn't what Valada wanted to be doing all the time, so it was really nice that Russell was so different from the youngdaddies. Russell was older and settled in himself. He kept up with the times; he played a mean though classically-trained trumpet; but everything he did was at his own pace.

Russell had taken Valada under his wing almost from the start, when *Chocolate Dandies* was still called *In Bamville* and little more than a dream. Mr Sissle and Mr Blake had seen Valada in *Ramblin' Round* with Clarence Muse and Blanche Calloway, and they came to her one night after the show to say that she had just what they wanted for the role of Manda, Bill Slavin's niece, in the new show they were planning to follow *Shuffle Along*. There'd never been a coloured show as successful as *Shuffle Along*, which had run on Broadway for almost two years, and Valada couldn't believe her luck in being asked to become part of its team. Noble Sissle and Eubie Blake were taking coloured shows in another direction. Their shows had plenty of comedy and dancing without playing up to white folks' fondness for never-were plantations full of happy slaves without one brain in all their heads, big fat mammies, and razor-wielding coons. *Shuffle Along*'s 'Love Will Find A Way' was the first love song ever performed by Negroes onstage without a joke. Critics had been afraid that white folks would riot or laugh at such true and simple feeling expressed by a decent coloured boy and girl, but they hadn't. That had been a major break-through. In *Chocolate Dandies*, Valada had several featured songs, each with its own wonderful costume, and lots of dancing. Manda was not a horn-player of course, but Valada was still playing James as much as she could between times. There was so much good music going on in New York these days, and playing for people or not, Valada was wanting to keep up. This was where Russell had been such a big help. When Russell heard Valada was a horn-player,

194

he didn't act like most of these girls-with-a-horn?-never-no-way men. He invited her to come and play with him off hours and was generous with all kinds of tips about fingering and working your lip that he knew from all his years of formal lessons. Maybe with having so many horn-players in the family and all of them good, like his brothers Joe and Luke who were playing with him in *Chocolate Dandies*, he just didn't worry about keeping everything a secret. And it wasn't just about trumpet playing. When Mr Sissle got peeved with Valada's suggestions about people moving around on stage, saying that she was nothing but a young slip of a girl who needed to be grateful for this opportunity and that were plenty of young girls waiting for her costumes who knew not to cause so much aggravation, when Valada's ideas weren't even about making her own part better but for the good of the show because she had learned a lot being out on the white time where there was more money for gimmicks, and who cared where ideas came from so long as they were good ones, Russell had smoothed the whole - situation over until everyone was splitting their sides laughing. And when the show opened and mostly everyone was talking about Josephine, Russell helped Valada not worry too much about Josephine Baker.

'Dady,' he'd said, that's what he called her, Dady, 'God gave you a bushel of gifts of your own, and you need to stop vexing yourself about Josephine. Jo's got one of those flashy kind of talents that are always going to attract a lot of attention, especially if a body's ready to do anything to get it. Most of us are just out there doing our jobs and trying to enjoy ourselves along the way. Josephine's out there trying to fill a hole too big ever to be satisfied. I don't think she had a mother who loved her or anyone else either. You've got no cause to be so hungry.'

'Because I'm loved by a big old bear?' she'd asked.

'And don't you forget it,' he'd grinned.

Russell was sweet. He wasn't like James. No one was like James. But he was loving and lovable, and who knew, maybe she'd marry him. She could certainly do worse, and had.

They had been planning to get the costumes back to the theatre, then head over to the Marshall for some liver and onions before the show. At least, Russell had been planning on liver and onions. Valada couldn't stand liver and anything, but Russell had been trying to convince her that it gave you just the right foundation before a show, kept you steady on your feet no matter what came your way, and she was finally going to have to try some, this evening, just for him.

'But I hate it!' she'd cried, laughing.

'Baby, after all I did for you this afternoon, you owe it to me, you know you do. Damn, baby, a simple request . . . A guy could feel like, like . . . he was just being used.' He was pulling that long, morose face of his, the one he used in the show when he played onstage in the funny hat. Crocodile tears would be next.

'Russell Smith, that's blackmail!' she'd said, her lips poking outward as prettily as she could make them.

'Is it working?' he'd asked, eyes looking slyly upward under his brow.

She'd tossed her head dramatically up and to the side. It was then that she'd seen him. With the sun heading down into New Jersey, the street shadows had been long and hard, which was why she'd doubted her eyes for a moment. Three men were coming out of the building across the street. White men. Nattily dressed. Two light brown suits, one grey. Colourful ties. There were booking offices in that building. Some act, her brain said, and she was going to keep on playing with Russell, until one of the men grabbed his hat off his head to make some kind of point, and the way his chin jutted out, the curve of his lips profiled in the late afternoon sun.

'Lawrence?' she'd whispered. Then louder so it might be heard over the traffic noise. 'Lawrence! Lawrence?'

The man's face had been in shadow when he'd turned her way, then shrugged his shoulders in response to whatever his companions might be asking before continuing with them down the street and away; but still she knew him.

196

'You recognize that guy, baby?' Russell had asked.

'I thought I did,' Valada replied. She wasn't going to get into this with Russell. She didn't know him that well.

'The light plays tricks this time of day, and your eyes have to be tired after all that photographer's flash. I know just what would do you some good.'

'You do, huh?' humphed Valada, back into her role.

'Yeah,' said Russell, maybe thinking of some other things besides the Marshall's liver and onions.

'Well, I may just give you a try,' Valada had said, nestling herself into Russell's fleshy arm for warmth from a sudden chill.

Valada and Russell had been planning to join friends up at Small's after the show. With Russell's car in the shop, they were discussing whether to try for a cab or just go ahead and take the subway when the doorman told Valada that there was a 'gentleman' waiting for her in the alley. 'Gentleman' was doorman code for white man. Coloured men were either 'guys' or 'jokers', or 'bucks', when the doorman, who was Irish, had been drinking more than usual and felt like getting away with what he could. Not expecting anyone, Valada had looked down the alley and saw him leaning against a wall, having a smoke, in the same pale brown suit he had been wearing late that afternoon. He straightened when he saw her and threw away his cigarette, but he said nothing and didn't come her way. His eyes did the talking, and Valada understood.

Russell was disappointed when Valada said that she'd changed her mind about Small's, there was something she needed to take care of, but his disappointment changed to concern when he saw the tears skimming about her eyes.

'Are you all right?' he'd asked.

Valada nodded.

'Are we?' he'd added.

Valada had nodded again. 'I'll see you back home then,' he'd said, and she had managed a smile. There was much to be said for a man with his feet firm underneath him.

Lawrence remained where Valada had left him, smoking impassively, observing the chattering Dandies who passed, not acknowledging their curious looks his way. He straightened when his sister approached but did not embrace her or even smile. He looked older than his twenty-four years, grey-green eyes flecked with gold, long lashes, high cheekbones. Women probably cut their hearts on those cheekbones. Handsome with an edge. Like his father. Valada did her best not to stare.

'You know where we can go?' she said.

'Let's head for the El,' he replied.

He walked quickly and slightly ahead of her until they had moved away from Broadway's bright lights and into the relative shadow of Ninth Avenue where his shoulders and stride relaxed, and Valada was able to walk by his side.

'How long you been over?' she asked.

'Practically since the beginning,' he replied. 'Right after I left home after we escaped the farm. I was hopping a freight out of Knoxville and missed my grip. I was heading under the car. I was shitting myself I was so scared, and that was what almost did me in. That hot then cold feeling on my leg. I figured it was death, and I was telling Mama goodbye when this hand grabbed me and dragged me in. There were three of them, hillbilly crackers not all that much older than I was, headed to wherever they could get to. They shared their food, guided me through train yards. I was going to say, "Excuse me, but I'm coloured. You don't want to be saving my life?" I kept quiet, and life got easier.'

They climbed the El stairs, and he paid both fares. 'Downtown,' he said, and nothing else for a while.

The car was crowded with immigrant workers weary from cleaning midtown office buildings and post-theatre revellers headed south to Greenwich Village for a different kind of amusement than they found in Harlem. Valada never went this direction at this time of night, never saw the dim lights of Hell's Kitchen, the Hudson River's oily black sheen, the Flatiron Building stark against bilious clouds. Her mind was having trouble getting around what must be the terrain of Lawrence's life. He looked aloof hanging onto a strap next to the middle doors, not looking back at her, making eye contact with no one. Inside himself and not very happy. *How many years had he been so unhappy? Why keep passing if it doesn't make you happy? 'If you white, you all right'? It's not looking that way. He's got that set to his mouth and curl of hair not staying put by his ear. Just like daddy.*

Thinking about Lawrence, she didn't notice the white drunk weaving above her until a blast of whiskey near took her breath away. The drunk grinned when she coughed.

'You a pretty thing, you are. How's about you and me? I got ten of Sam's dollars,' he drawled. 'We can make it a night.'

'No, thank you,' said Valada. Drool was splashing onto the lapel of her purple melton jacket. She managed to flinch only slightly as she searched her beaded bag for something to wipe it clean.

'I'll help you with that, baby,' he said, laying a heavy, grimy hand on her breast. His suit was rumpled and reeking of vomit. Valada's neighbours were ignoring her discomfort, showing more impatience as she jostled them in trying to move away from his groping hand.

'We'll call this a promise of things to come,' he crooned. 'You're a cute one, you are. We might make it fifteen. Bet you never seen so much cash in all your days.' The El rounded a curve, and the drunk fell into her lap with a wheezy giggle, hands all over her instead of staggering to his feet. 'Ah, darlin', be a sport,' he was saying as Valada struggled to shove him away. His giggle wheeze continued until Lawrence thumped his neck hard and he screamed out in pain.

'The lady ain't interested,' said Lawrence, his voice quiet, his eyes agate cold.

'What lady?' whined the drunk. The train was nearing a stop. 'Ain't nothin' but a filthy nigger whore, filthy nigger—' Lawrence dragged the man onto his feet. 'What's it to you, nigger-lover? You want one, get one of your own!' Lawrence shoved the man through the passenger scrum onto the concrete platform of the 23rd Street station. 'Nigger-lover!' the drunk was screaming as the car doors slammed shut. 'Fucking nigger-lover!' Lawrence's hand shook only a little as he took a handkerchief from his inside pocket. It was larger than Valada's and better suited for mopping the drunken man's slime. He stood by her until the train reached Christopher Street. There were furtive looks a-plenty from other passengers in the car, but nobody said a word.

Lawrence stayed close as he and his sister left the station, his cheek twitching with emotion, flinching when Valada put a hand on his arm.

'Lawrence, we're both alive,' she said. 'It could have been worse, and it has been worse. I bet we don't have but this evening. How about we leave it go?' The streets in Greenwich Village were narrower than those uptown. There were still old-fashioned gas lamps casting warm yellow light on streets swollen with what could only be described as characters. There were the same kind of uptowners that came to Harlem, stumbling from limousines to speakeasies in the height of moneyed fashion, but also a new group to Valada's experience, varied of race, eccentric of dress, almost as lively as Negroes in the street and mixing with one another, brown with yellow, even black with white, men with men, women in groups, and casually, without fear or defiance.

'I still hate them, you know,' Lawrence was saying. 'I don't let myself carry a gun because I would have killed too many of them by now to maintain good health, and anyway you can't get rid of them. They just keep on coming . . .'

There is a coloured woman standing outside of an Italian coffee house wearing an Indian squaw's skirt and blanket, with tumbling turquoise jewellery, and her hair coiled in braids. She is surrounded by two white men in cloth caps and a Chinaman in pyjamas, all of them laughing. Her eye flick in Valada's direction reveals that the men don't know of the masquerade. 'Don't acknowledge me,' she's asking. 'Let me keep with my game.' A life-long vaudeville act, that's what it was. Back-to-back shows for the rest of your natural days, and this was Lawrence's life?

'. . . they're like rats.'

200

'Well, I'm glad you didn't have a gun on that train,' said Valada, 'because that man's saliva was hard enough on my new jacket. His tired-assed blood would have ruined it completely!'

Lawrence barked a laugh. 'You haven't changed a bit. You the same hard-headed girl you always were, always ready to fight with no thought to how much bigger your enemy was,' he said, grabbing her shoulders for a hug. 'You married?'

'Not any more.'

'Too hard to handle?'

'Look at me. I'm just a little, bitty thing. What could be so hard?'

'That's just what I thought,' he smiled, taking her arm over his. 'We're alike, we two. Settling down just ain't our way.' The stuff of his suit was fine and his arm relaxed, until they were near trampled by two interlaced, drunken uptowners in dishevelled white tie. The drunks looked from Lawrence to Valada with panting tongues and lascivious grins, and Lawrence's body tensed for a fight until Valada whispered, 'One night' in his ear, and they went on in silence. South on Bleecker Street and left into Cornelia. Valada could feel her brother's pressure pulsing under her hand.

'Lawrence, if you hate them so much,' she said quietly, 'how can you live among them?'

'I hated being coloured more,' he answered, his lips rigid with emotion and eyes taking on a sheen. 'I hated the walls all around, and everyone assuming that you were some kind of dumb animal good for nothing more than hard labour and rooting around in the gutter. I wanted something better, and I learned that I could have it.'

'You think this is better?'

'Well, at least I'm still alive. I'm travelling, making money, bedding women who don't know that I'm a nigger. If I lived black I'd'a been dead so long by now my bones'd be dust.' They were approaching a restaurant whose sign contained letters Valada didn't understand. 'We're going in here,' he said, and again his tension started to ease.

Inside the restaurant was smoky and warm and loud with music from an instrument sounding something like a banjo but triangular in shape. The clientele were Characters, men in shapeless coats and soft hats, women following a different kind of style from what Valada had ever seen before, their dresses fashioned from curious fabrics, or no style at all, drab suits and shirts with Buster Brown collars and no make-up at all. Out in public with no efforts to look kicky or hot or even attractive. Like a brood of Holy Roller ministers' wives, but you could bet religion wasn't too high up in their thoughts. Loud discussion rang from most every table, argued by men, some women too, whose eyes were focused, as though, despite the hour, people were not stupefied by booze. Lawrence's face was different, almost relaxed, almost the Lawrence she remembered from Chattanooga before he got brazen, skipping school and thieving from drug stores; almost the Lawrence that would lean up against Mama singing with that angel voice of his. Almost, but not quite.

'You know this place,' said Valada.

'I come here when I can . . .'

'But not nearly as much as you should!' The voice was far more impressive than the frame from which it came. Its owner was a hunchback, but apparently a strong one. Valada thought she heard her brother's bones creak from the force of the owner's hug.

'Max! How many times I have to tell you go easy on my ribs?' growled Lawrence, but the corners of his mouth were up. 'You bust them up, I can't sing. I don't sing, I can't buy your liquor.'

'You don't sing, then you don't travel. Maybe you sit here, and I win back what I have lost at chess.' Chess? Lawrence played chess? Where did he learn it? What, what has been his years? 'That last match, nothing but tricks and flash!'

'Worked though, didn't it?' Now Lawrence was smiling.

'It was beneath you,' sniffed Max from a nose smashed to the side of a face that had to be one of the ugliest Valada had ever seen, but he wasn't offensive like the drunk, and not reacting at all to her standing next to a man he couldn't know to be her brother, though his eyes appeared able to take in all the world. 'You have seen this?' Max continued, producing a newspaper from his pocket with a headline decrying strike thugs in New Jersey.

'I have,' Lawrence said. Valada has seen that paper being sold in Harlem from time to time, mostly by soft-dressed white men, and mostly no one bought it. She never read white papers herself. The theatre critics who bothered to look at coloured shows were all the time talking about what they called 'darky entertainment' and getting upset if you dressed nice or even normal instead of like a plantation pickaninny or some Zulu cannibal. You paid attention to that rubbish and your head could start to hurt.

When Lawrence read such things, what did he feel? Did he read them as a white man, or did he feel himself still coloured?

'You are indignant?' Max was asking.

'I am,' answered Lawrence.

'Then you will join us at last!' Max exclaimed, though his eyes did not see this as sure.

'Man, how many times do I have to tell you that I'm not getting caught up in somebody else's sad song,' said Lawrence, though still with a smile. 'My own is sad enough. Now, are you gonna keep us standing here, or are you gonna let me spend some money?'

Yes, he is still coloured after all, still her brother and her mama's son.

Max was looking at Valada now. 'Always he reduces a situation to its fundamental crassness. He makes me out to be a grasping capitalist, thus questioning my devotions and breaking my heart. But mark my words. He will be ours in the end. Two beers, my friend?'

'From your reserve?'

'Of course. The horse piss we save for the tourists,' said Max with a nod to a table of evening-clad slummers.

Settling into their table, Valada can see that her neighbours aren't the same kind of white folks that filled the nightspots of Harlem, not as much money for one and maybe not so convinced that money could buy anything they took to fancy, which was not to say she was feeling relaxed. She'd much rather be on her feet. She was used to handling white folks on her feet, coaxing them into stupid grins and off-tempo responses to the tap of her feet and the warble of her voice; and if they couldn't be handled, for there was no trusting white folks in a group, then on your feet you were poised to escape. She is glad that at least their table is against a wall. There is another coloured man in the room, a dark-skinned man with thick features and the loose uniform of clothes, looking easy with himself, and there is Lawrence of course, but then he doesn't count. Not everyone in the room is as open-minded as Max, keeping their eyes to themselves and attending their own business. The dark man's skin looks onyx-hard, a shield against white folks' daggers. She can see this in his neck, and here is a place that Lawrence likes. Valada wonders what her brother's life has been. So many questions, no way to start, and no way to continue. There is only tonight.

'Does Max know?' she asks Lawrence, who was again silent inside himself.

'Nobody knows,' Lawrence replied. 'Max knows there's a secret, but I tell nobody my business. I've got too much at stake.'

The beers arrive. They are dark and warm, tasting a little sweet. Not Madden's No. 2, that's for sure. Valada wonders if protection is paid down here in the Village. It might seem like another country, running on different rules, but didn't the Mob reach everywhere? A woman with frizzed-up, bottle-black hair and a long embroidered shawl has taken the place of the triangle banjo. She sings in a foreign language, sometimes speaking as much as singing, arms flinging out, cheeks awash with tears. Funny to remember that foreigners have songs too, and their own sad stories. This song is like a blues. Her foreign lady blues. She could be Clara Smith or maybe Alberta. She believes it that much, more than Valada does when she sings, if she is honest, believes it the way Valada believes when she's playing her James. Valada finds herself believing even though she can't understand a word. There isn't much applause when the song is over, but the woman

204

doesn't seem to mind. White people, Valada's thinking, all the time bottled inside themselves. Bottled up like Lawrence. Lawrence has taken her hand. His is well-manicured, palest caramel cream against her ginger cake. Not so much difference, but all the difference, his grey-green eyes clouded up to storm.

'Mama OK?' he asks, voice quiet, loosening its gruff with beer.

'I don't get home much, well, not at all really, but I think so. She got married again, to a nice man. Mr Bush. I liked him. We have a new little brother. She'd give anything to see you again, but you've always known that.'

Lawrence averts his eyes, not wanting the storm to break. 'Daddy dead?' he asks, his fingers tightening again on hers.

'Not so far as we know. Could be. Might as well be. He left a long time ago.' If John Snow is dead, it wouldn't have been pretty. There would have been blood in it somehow, the blade of some whore's pimp or maybe the splatter of tuberculosis. Yet, the thought doesn't make her shudder, and once she had been her Daddy's girl. 'Something happened to Daddy after we lost you, Lawrence,' she said. 'Even when he was around, he was always on his way out.'

Lawrence just shrugged. 'If it hadn't been me, it would've been something else. He wasn't the holding kind.'

Valada smiled. 'We had to get it from somewhere, I guess.' Valada wants to laugh. With all this talk about home, she needs to laugh; but there's not much laughter in this place, not like she's used to in the after-hours joints uptown, with folks dancing and jamming and howling at somebody's lies. A little bit of music that nobody knows how to react to and a lot of conversation. Maybe this was the problem with white folks. Left to their own, they didn't know how to be loose, so they came to black folks trying to learn how. Only they didn't like learning from black folks, and the resentment kept them peevish. Conversation everywhere, shoulders hunched, hands opening and closing. 'What're they talking about, Lawrence? It all looks so darn serious.'

'Changing the world, the meaning of life . . .'

'Doesn't sound much fun.'

'They tend to think so.'

'Fine for them, but what about you? You having any fun at all, Lawrence?'

'I play them at their own game. They don't know it, and yeah, that's fun. It keeps me howling twenty-four hours a day.'

Poor Lawrence, angry Lawrence. Valada never wants to live this angry. How can you hear the music if you're all the time so angry?

Manhattan Theatre District, May 1956

It feels better here in the diner, more light, but not too bright, afternoon sun glowing through a storefront window lightly frosted with soot. No fluorescents, a shaded lamp overhanging their booth. No air-conditioning, but ceiling fans keeping things moving gently. The waitress' uniform not as damp and wrinkled as it might be. Valaida is grateful to Paul for bringing her here. She'd had to sit out the rehearsal for the finale, which had been just fine with her. The director would have had her hanging around the periphery with her arm around some over-the-hill vaudevillian, with those who caught sight of her wondering, 'Who was she again?' and 'What is she doing here?' Better they stay with the impression made during her one little four-minute spot, short, yes, but under her own control, and therefore as sweet as she had the power to make it. Lucy had asked her if she felt up to performing tonight, and Valaida had just looked at her and smiled because 'not feeling up to performing' was not a phrase in Valaida's lexicon, or anyone else's in this particular line of work, which Lucy knew, so the question was just a formality, like saying 'pleased to meet you' no matter how you felt; but Valaida is glad to leave the finale go. This spell has been stronger than any she's experienced up to now. She's pretty certain that the problem is pressure, as it was for her mother, as it has been for so many in this line of work; so she'll give up the finale in exchange for peace in her spot, hope that the pressure will be satisfied, and then maybe see the doctor tomorrow. Valaida hasn't much use for doctors. Her dealings with them have never been pleasant, but then their business was suffering, so why would they be? *At least this time it is another kind of illness. There'd be no bars, no restraints, no vortex of horror, no screams from the possessed.*

The waitress arrives with their drinks, beers for Valaida and Paul, a ginger ale for Hannah. Paul hadn't been eager for the twosome to become a threesome, but there'd been no putting Hannah off.

'She looks so pale,' Hannah had said. 'Just what would you do if something happened? A woman needs a woman at a time like this!'

If Valaida had had the energy to dance a new fandango with Liz LaFontaine and the bothersome Twins without a dose of fresh air, she wouldn't be sitting across from this agitated young woman with the fixed smile and the too-shiny eyes; but Valaida had needed a bit more space and light as currency for her pressure, so she'd allowed Paul and Hannah to lead her out of the theatre, and here she was, in the midst of some Caucasian melodrama, not looking at this white woman looking at her. The beer felt good though, its cool flowing down the veins of her arms, tempering the heat that had been radiating up from her breasts, to be followed by a chicken salad sandwich. Not such a bad thing, and maybe even worth the aggravation that's about to come, as the white girl parts her lips.

'You're looking better already!' There's righteousness lurking in the hollows of Hannah's voice, beneath the false cheer, cosying up against some menace.

Valaida can sense the menace, knows she should be excusing herself, concentrating on tasks to come; but her thighs are slabs of lead, and she wants the chicken salad sandwich. Drama looming up before her as clear as day, as terrible as the wrath of God, but Valaida's pleasure is her ice-cold beer and a sandwich with chicken, mayonnaise, and celery, with a pickle on the side. It's been Valaida's wont to follow her pleasures. On the road she carved out, they've tended to be worth their price. You just had to be willing to pay. Lady Day on the juke box scratching on about 'Good Morning, Heartache'. Woman possessing five notes, if that, and those wobbling at the knees, and every single one of them a direct hit to your solar plexus, then dropping, splat, into your gut, syncopate-swimming now in the pool of ice cold beer. Valaida will order another beer and another 'Heartache' and assume that the two will float her over the impending drama like a raft, not as effectively as the Sweet King, but buoyant all the same.

'I've never been very partial to beer myself,' Hannah is saying, 'but I can see that it's just what a doctor would have ordered for you. This was a wonderful idea, Paul. How clever of you.'

Paul is sitting across from Valaida in the booth, but not what could be termed 'next to' Hannah. He is as far from Hannah as it is possible to be without appearing rude. Though Hannah and Valaida have noticed this, Paul has not, but Paul has not been without sensitivities this afternoon. He had been the first to notice Valaida's disorientation at the end of her rehearsal, had reached her side before Lucy, and guided her off the stage. Unsure of her footing on the steps, she had taken hold of his arm, her yellow-brown fingers skimming the flesh of his wrist before resting on the rumpled cotton of his sleeve. He'd offered to carry her trumpet, but this she'd folded up against her like a wounded wing. But though there seemed a distinct vulnerability about the lady, her health perhaps not being what it might, Paul would never confuse her with some helpless, damaged thing. She generated too much excitement for one, and there was an unexpected muscularity to her arm when it rested against his own. Paul wondered how old she was. She looked hardly close to forty, but she had to be older. His father's admiration had been for a woman, not a child, and that had been more than twenty years ago, so Valaida Snow could be older than his mother. But there was no slackness about her person. The cheek that had brushed his shoulder briefly had been firm. There were no lines about her eyes. Perhaps from blowing the trumpet? Paul has so many questions he'd like to ask: Who are you? Where have you been? Why did you go there? Were you playing for me? Is there some little place in your consciousness for me? Is there something I can be for you? But he has no idea of how to start. The woman he faces seems content enough. She is the serene she has been through-out most of this day, her serenity at once palpable and impenetrable. Her attentions are not here at this table. Maybe in the song? Paul hasn't understood the appeal of Billie Holiday. She sounded so destroyed. The drugs, they said. Negro musicians and their drugs. They seemed to wear them like a badge, like some medal of maxi-mal cool. Paul had once thought of dabbling, but hadn't known how, had been far too afraid if he was honest with himself. He wonders if Valaida has ever done drugs, but no, she looks far too self-possessed. Another question to ask, but maybe not the first one. Considering that question causes Paul to smile, not in and of the question itself, but because yesterday the question would never have occurred to him, and if it had he might have been stupid enough to ask it; but today has taught him different. A further smile as he sips his beer, which is tasting as good as any beer ever has. He's going to call Mel Blumberg tomorrow, see if he can't start picking his brain over lunch, even finagle out a job. Couldn't hurt. Time to start.

Valaida hasn't noticed Paul's smiles; but Hannah has. Valaida is rapt up in the music, and Hannah is wrapped up in Paul. She knows that his smiles are not for her, but she is managing to main-tain her own, for she is her mother's daughter after all. Serah Eisenberg is strong. It took strength to work herself out of the Lower East Side. It takes strength to contend with an ailing, finicky partner and still have energy to try to change the world. From the time she was a babe in arms, Hannah was witness to all manner of strike committees, town meetings, picket lines, cru-sades offices, her mother always in the midst of the action, never just tolerated as the wife of a man with money. Serah Eisenberg was clear-eyed, forthright. Hannah's underarms have begun to moisten, and she worries for her midnight blue silk, but she knows herself capable of following her mother's example. 'Whatever are you smiling at, Paul?' she asks. 'You've seemed to be having a lot of fun today, and with all this heat! What has been going on?'

Paul looks in Hannah's direction for the first time since their arrival. She's been acting strangely today, but she's looking pretty in blue, and he probably wouldn't have worked this day if it hadn't been for her. There's no reason that she shouldn't be among the first to know. 'I've made a decision today, Hannah. I'm going to stop working for Manny. I want to go into show business.'

Hannah's mind races as she contends with her surprise. Her Paul? In the notoriously unreliable world of show business? This is not what Hannah has in mind, but Paul's eyes are so happy, confident even. Her response must be reasoned and clever. 'And do what?' she asks, widening her eyes slightly like the *shiksa* girls she sees in movies.

'I don't know exactly,' Paul replies. 'Probably producing, once I know what it means. I've noticed what you said today about so few Negroes appearing in regular shows. I mean, you never see them, do you? In this day and age, how can that be right? I don't know. Maybe that's where my road will lead.'

Now Hannah smiles, for it is this Negro woman after all. Her task has just gotten easier. 'And what do you think that your parents will say?' she asks, her voice all modulated concern.

'Gladys won't notice,' Paul replies, 'and Manny will probably say "good riddance".'

Now is the time, Hannah thinks, to make her move. 'It's never easy working for family, especially for someone as opinionated as Manny. But Paul, everything about you is good and true, and everyone knows that "good and true" aren't words that describe producers.'

A three-inch furrow has appeared on the beautiful brow. Hannah wants to kiss it away and be wrapped into arms appreciating her concern, that know they are hers alone. 'I'm flattered you think so highly of me,' Paul is saying, 'but you can't believe that the garment business is moral!'

210

'But there are limits!' Hannah exclaims. 'Ethical businessmen have rules, but in show business . . .' Fighting a rush of anxiety, she wills herself to confront her adversary. 'Miss Snow, you're older and wiser. You've been in this line of work for a while, and Paul obviously thinks very highly of you. Do you think that he has what it takes to make it in show business?'

Valaida has not been listening. She's given the waitress another quarter for the juke box, and the needle has just reconnected onto Billie's 'Heartache'. While the children have been chattering, Valaida's been ruminating on needles and Billie, thanking Christ that she herself has managed to stop puncturing herself with steel. She'd done her legs because of the trumpet, so upraised arms weren't covered with wounds, but the toll on her knees and ankles . . . Even now, beating time could summon up phantoms of pain. And the constant craving. But she'd beat it. With Earle's help, she'd stopped. Despite the constant craving. *Wish I'd forget you*, Billie sings, *but you're here to stay*. The young white faces are looking in her direction, eyes bright and hungering. With the menace sitting between them like some big, bad dog. Time to see if he was going to bark. 'I beg your pardon?' Valaida replies.

Hannah plunges on. And the dog starts shifting its weight to one paw, then another, one paw, then another. 'After one day of hauling ice around the Palace Theatre, Paul here is thinking that he wants to make show business his career. You've been in this line of work for what seems to have been a while, and I was wondering if you thought he has what it takes.'

The dog's pelt is long and matted, and he drools. 'I think that a person ought to follow his or her heart,' Valaida says carefully. In all her years of proximity to American Caucasians, Valaida has subscribed to the wisdom of avoiding involvement in their intimate affairs, yet here she sits, her head stretching forward toward the maw of the dog like she wants to be bitten. 'If show business is the direction the man's heart is heading, then so be it. Who am I to tell someone not to follow his dream?'

'Even if that dream is based on delusion and bound to mean disappointment?' the white girl persists. 'Paul's a person of honesty and integrity. How could he survive?'

Paul and the menace beside him fall out of focus as Valaida looks direct into her eyes. *It's been a lifetime since you've looked into a white girl's eyes. And never, ever, as often as she might have wished.* 'Just what is it you're wanting to say, Miss . . .?'

'Please, call me Hannah.'

'I'd rather not.'

'Eisenberg,' mutters Paul, whose attention has become riveted on rubbing condensation off of his glass.

'Just what have you been wanting to say, Miss Eisenberg? Is there something about me that's agitating you?'

'I don't care about you, Miss Snow,' Hannah declares, somewhat flustered now by the Negro woman's audacity. 'It's Paul who's my concern. Paul is a good person, a good man, who doesn't cheat and lie, and your business is filled with people for whom lying is as natural as brushing their teeth or tying their shoes, who'd do and say absolutely anything so long as it furthered their career.'

Stop haunting me now, Billie sings. *Can't shake you no how;* and the dog has opened his jaws. His fangs are green. His breath is foul. Valaida's head is pounding again. Her stomach is roiling. She should leave this place, but her vision is blurring. She cannot find the door. Earle had warned her about this. '*Go on out there if you must, Vee, but just don't get confused.*' He'd asked her if she wanted him along this time for company, as he always did, but she'd said no, like she always did. Because she'd learned that negotiating American white people was usually easier on her own, so long as she didn't let her guard down. It was the headache and the heat. She'd just wanted some air. The dog's slathering tongue is midnight blue.

Paul's attentions have left his glass. 'Why are you bringing Miss Snow into this, Hannah?' he's asking. 'Why does what you're implying have anything to do with her? You've been acting crazy all day long!'

212

The exasperation in Paul's voice causes Hannah to strike with less finesse than she'd intended. 'Miss Snow knows full well what I'm talking about!' she cries. 'She's been playing with your affections all day long, and you've been falling for it, hook, line, and sinker! She's a prime example of everything I've said! She's a liar and a cheat, who'd do anything to help her career! Ask her about her time in Denmark! Ask her!'

'I'll do nothing of the sort.'

'Then I'll ask her myself!' Hannah declares, turning to hurl her disappointment in Valaida's direction. 'You've told people that you were in a concentration camp in Denmark, haven't you, Miss Snow? I saw the clippings in Marty's file. But there were no concentration camps in Denmark! No Jews died in Denmark because the Danes helped them all escape in October of 1943 and not by pulling them out of concentration camps that didn't exist!'

The dog's snout is buffeting her ribcage. The air is close. Valaida can no longer feel the fan. The white girl's eyes are glowing hotbeds of emotion. The white boy's eyes are shaded. There's a pocket of oxygen near the centre of the table. Valaida wills it towards her lungs. 'Jews were not the Germans' only concern, Miss Eisenberg,' she says quietly. 'The Nazis invaded Denmark in 1940. They hated our music. They called it degenerate. I was there. I couldn't leave the country. I was incarcerated. I was in prison.'

'So, you admit it! Prison! Not a concentration camp!'

Hannah's voice is shrill now, and ricocheting through the void left by the completion of Billie's heartache. Paul grabs Hannah's arm to calm her down. The blue silk of her dress is no longer crisply pristine. Paul's face is a mask of disbelief. 'Stop showing your ignorance, Hannah!' he hisses. 'Do you think every German crime was committed in a camp? Do we know that every camp was like Auschwitz and Buchenwald? We weren't there. We don't know. We were lucky. Our families were lucky. Who are we to stand in judgement of someone who was there?'

Believing that Paul is lost to her now, Hannah abandons herself to her sorrow. 'Yes, we were lucky,' she sobs, 'which is all the more reason to fight for the memory of the Jews who did suffer and die. How dare you use the suffering of Jews to promote your career, Miss Snow? How can you be so unscrupulous? If you had known one person who did actually suffer, had been penned like an animal, stripped of every dignity, died in fear, had the gold in their teeth melted down into ingots, the skin on their backs flayed and tanned into lampshades, you couldn't be so crass! You'd have your eyes fixed on the heavens for fear that God would strike you dead!'

The chicken salad sandwich arrives, its aroma blocking Valaida's access to her little pocket of oxygen, and she realizes that if she remains in this booth she will faint dead away. Her legs know this as well and allow her to rise. 'It's rather close in here,' she says, gathering up her purse and horn. 'Thank you for the beer, Mr Goldman, but I'd like to get some air. You'll excuse me, won't you?'

Hannah's sobs are being masked by the next juke box selection as Valaida's legs conduct her through the diner's door toward any place save where she is. *If you'd known anyone . . .* Despite her head's pounding, Valaida welcomes the blasting vehicle horns of rush hour traffic. Anything to eclipse Hannah's words, which are echoing in her brain. The blasting horns are a Midtown Manhattan version of a New Orleans funeral line. *If you'd known anyone . . .* Escorting Valaida toward a better place.

> *. . . She rambled all around*
> *In and out of town*
> *I said she rambled, Lord,*
> *Until the butcher cut her down . . .*

*C*hapter thirteen

Shanghai, China, 1926

. . . And didn't she ramble, ramble
She rambled all around . . .

It was Shanghai where it started, if she thought about it hard,
China where her world broke out as surely as John Bubbles
moving from a wing step to a slide, and that slide just going and
going on a floor that went for ever; a floor like in one of those
musical motion pictures where hundreds of dancers just kept
coming, up and down stairs, in and out of rooms that couldn't be in
any theatre if you thought about it, but you didn't; and then here
came Bubbles, spinning and tapping, fast and furious, in and out
of arches, on and out for ever because there was always somewhere to go so long as you had the energy and the skill to keep on
tapping.

Her first sighting of China wasn't land but water. She was out on promenade, which was what she had done on board whenever the band wasn't rehearsing, rather than playing cards or shuffle-board or drinking booze outside Prohibition then sleeping it off like most of her friends. It was September, just at summer's end, but the air was still warm enough to wear a dress of light peach lawn along with the long rope of white beads that looked well with the dress even though they weren't real pearls. After three weeks on water, Valada had still loved the sea's salt-sharp winds against her face and the feeling of constant motion, whether it was soft and soothing with water whooshing against the ship with the sound of sand sliding in a box, or violent to the point that most other folks were whimpering in their bunks, not knowing if they'd rather puke or pray. Valada liked looking out over the water for whales and dolphins and the sun's play on waves, and so she'd seen the Pacific's blue suddenly suffusing with brown.

'It's the Yangtze,' said the steward who had followed her puzzled gaze. 'China's big river. It's just a matter of hours now.'

Soon the ship had turned into the river and was gliding by land-scapes that probably appeared in geography books that white children must have had, rice crops growing out of fields of water, small boys on the backs of gigantic bulls people were calling water buffalo, stark, jagged hills in the distance dotted with trees in unfamiliar shapes, with the smells of sewage chasing the sea scents away. The decks were crowded with passengers now, chattering, pointing and laughing with excitement, save for the Chinese men in steerage who were standing, most of them, but still as pensive and morose as they had been the entire journey, with even the young man with the pretty mouth, who had followed Valada with his eyes whenever he could these last three weeks, ignoring her now, even though she had positioned herself for his easy inspection. The young man's attentions were on what had to be his return, and, looking past him, Valada was thinking, This is different, this is definitely different. This isn't America. This is someplace else, as farmland gave way to first mud huts, then factories and docks until there appeared a long stand of buildings that could easily have been in Chicago, or New York, if Fifth Avenue buildings had gone up on the Hudson River, only not with these funny boats, small flat ones, some with little huts, some without, and larger ones with sails like fans, and Chinamen everywhere because this was where they were from. Valada was neither chattering or laughing as the ship was man-oeuvred into its dock, but her heart was all thumping heebie-jeebies and her hands two cushions for pins as she wondered what she would find here, how she would play here, because it wasn't just all about having a good time any more. Valada was wanting to move on.

The *Dandies* had been wonderful, but the *Dandies* had collapsed and died on the road with Mr Sissle and Mr Blake owing wages to everyone for weeks, and it had been just as well because Valada's Russell had started talking about babies. Russell'd been getting all kinds of domestic for a while, taking to cooking on hot plates and preferring moonlit drives at midnight to hitting the flats for drinks and laughs after a show. Russell was sweet, and he was kind, but his way of looking at life tended to be from the side when Valada was wanting to be flat up in life's face; and when Russell started getting all misty-eyed around street urchins then looking in her direction, there just was no help for it.

'*Russell, honey, if I told you once, I've told you a thousand times, my life's got no room for babies.*' To be tied down to one place, dirty diapers and colic like her own mama had been, still was. '*I made that decision when I was still in pinafores, and I haven't changed my mind.*' Or ever would, but Russell couldn't curb himself when she asked him to, so he had to go. With the *Dandies* dead, Russell found a job in Fletcher's band along with his brothers, which meant he'd be travelling all over the country with his ex-wife Leora, who was Mrs Henderson now. Well, anyone could under-stand that was too much to expect from a girl. If Russell's feelings were hurt when Valada broke the news, she was moving too fast in the opposite direction to know.

* * *

Chicago was her first stop, where the clubs were stronger and the lights brighter than they had ever been. Money was just jumping into the pockets of folks who knew a thing or two in Chicago, and Louis Armstrong was teaching things about horn-playing that no one had ever imagined. Russell had been really good on trumpet basics you couldn't do without – tone control, working your lip, finding your pitch and holding to it – but Louis . . . well, there really were no words for what Louis did with a horn. Justice Taylor had heard Louis and thrown his horn up at the ceiling, smashed it to smithereens.

'*Damn, man, that horn's your life! Whatchu do that for?*'

'*What was I supposed to do? Play? Play what? Play how?*'

If you could work your way past the shock, all you could do was listen hard and work towards as much of his magic as you could get your mind around, let alone your lip and fingers, which is what Valada did. She got better on the horn, and she had fun while she was doing it, there in Chicago and in other towns as well, spending time with folk who liked to enjoy themselves. But she wasn't moving on, and folks were moving on.

Lovely Florence Mills, who had starred in *Shuffle Along* and was sweet and kind, with never a bad word for anybody, had conquered England with her bird-like voice, pixie steps, and wistful personality, and Josephine prancing around half-naked was causing Parisians to lose their minds. White women who'd always prided themselves on pearly white complexions were said to be basting themselves with oil and trying to roast themselves like poultry. Now Valada wasn't thinking about performing in no more than a few bananas and a smile because she had a few more things to offer than crossed eyes and bobbling titties. Josephine Baker could not even carry a tune, but Josephine had moved on while Valada had mostly been biding her time; so when word went around that Jack Carter was back in Chicago looking for a band to join him and Teddy Weatherford in Shanghai, China, Valada figured that since she'd been aching to get across some water and had a fondness for chop suey, she might as well give it a shot, and come August 31st she was on her way to where she was now, which was nowhere near where she ever had been before.

They went by rickshaw to where they would be staying, one not large man dressed in rags, a tweed golfer's cap but no shoes, fast-pulling Valada and Jack and two of their trunks past hundreds of other contraptions just like his, automobiles, bicycles, and trams, weaving in and out of a blur of hod-carriers and vendors and pedestrians of every racial description except their own. There were brown men with red cloth wrapped around their heads directing traffic, Chinese girls in tight silk dresses that were cut all the way up to their hips, china-doll toddlers wearing shirts but with their behinds naked to the wind, white children in blazers, pleated skirts, and straw hats, white men in suits talking to Chinese men wearing blue coats down to their black cotton shoes. Food seemed to be cooking everywhere and none of it smelling like chop suey. Markets were selling vegetables in baskets and birds in cages, and Valada swore she saw some monkeys in cages next to the vegetables as well. What she was hearing out of folks' mouths had to be language but none of it was sounding like words. You couldn't figure out beginnings or ends. It was more like stringed instruments being plucked and strummed, and Valada found herself wondering if the Chinese didn't have catgut and wires instead of tongues, though that was probably like thinking that coloured folk had tails and rutted like hogs. Jack took charge when they arrived at the house where the band would be staying, which was a very good thing because only he could decipher the pidgin English of the Number One Boy.

'How can you call him that, Jack? That man's sixty if he's a day. It's not respectful. We'll be acting just like white folks!'

'Chinamen ain't us, sweetness. They don't seem to mind, and they get the last laugh anyway 'cause they'll be robbing us blind. Whatever the crackers think, this ain't nobody's country but these here Boys'.'

Valada's room is short on light, but large and airy. The furniture is fashioned from red-brown wood with black iron fittings in the shape of flowers. She feels off-balance without the sea moving beneath her feet. Outside her door the easy-coloured laughter of the band guys mingles with caged bird squawks and vendors' sing-song floating up from the street. Somewhere in the distance a gong is sounding. There is a scent of burning wood transfused with a perfume that reminds her of Ruby's bosom. *She has lost track of Ruby. Was she singing? Was she dead?* Valada is not in America any more.

The Chinese didn't know what she was. Not Chinese, of course. Female, probably, but beyond these nothing that they could classify, even with effort; and so they stared. When the band ventured beyond its neighbourhood streets, there was pointing and laughter or gasps of fear. Any pretext was used to touch their hair or skin, but even though many in the band were darker than Valada, it was for her that the greatest disbelief was shown, as if it were natural that these strange, dark-skinned animals that walked up straight like humans would display as males, but that a female version stretched credulity just too far. Women would brush against her breasts to see if they were real; little boys would try and peek up under her skirts; but Valada realized pretty quick that it wasn't about her being a nigger. The Chinese didn't know that Negroes were niggers. The Chinese didn't know that Negroes existed, and they couldn't have cared less. This was a new sensation, being around people who weren't coloured and, outside of being curious, didn't give a damn about what she was doing there. She was just one ant in the swarming hill that was Shanghai. So long as she didn't burn the place down, nobody cared what she did. For some people, Alvada for example, this indifference might have been frightening. Alvada had always been a hand-holder, a lean-up-against-er. Alvada withered without connection, be it a vice or an embrace. But that had never been Valada, and in Shanghai, for all its crowds, Valada was feeling herself in whole new reaches of space. Hers for the taking.

The Jack Carter Band had been brought to China to entertain white people. Valada didn't know how white people came to China, but it looked like, as usual, it was to try and run the place. Unlike many of the hotels and clubs in Shanghai that catered to white people, the Plaza Hotel, where the band was appearing, did let Chinese through the doors when they had the cash, but the audiences were always overwhelmingly white. In that way the place was a lot like Harlem, where the Cotton Club and Connie's Inn had followed the Barron's lead in not letting most coloured folks through the doors of the clubs that clogged up their own streets. Shanghai, in fact, seemed more like Harlem than Harlem was itself. Harlem's night-time mask seemed to be Shanghai's day and night reality. It was the Harlem of folks' imaginations, where everything was possible because nothing was familiar, with nobody who knew you looking over your shoulder, at least if you didn't happen to be Chinese. The white people in Shanghai were mostly Europeans, but when it came to the Chinese, a lot of them acted just like home-grown crackers. Valada saw white people cursing and kicking and spitting on Chinese in their own streets, not all of them of course, but enough to make an impression. These same white people knew Valada and her friends were coloured, but they seemed to be too busy treating the Chinese like niggers to worry about a few of the real thing. The guys in the band laughed about this all the time, tickled to death to see some other poor bastards catching white folks' hell for a change. Valada didn't think it was all that funny, but then, back home in America, she stood less chance than the guys of being lynched, raped maybe, but with at least some odds of staying alive. She had to admit she appreciated this Shanghai relief. It was part of why she was getting this sense of so much space, into which she could run and then take off and fly.

As a seven-year show-business veteran of twenty-two, Valada knew she was never going to be simply part of a band. The hot second she'd spent with Gonzala White had been proof of the fact that wherever, with whomever she was, Valada was always going to show out. Showing out wasn't something that she had a whole lot of control over, even if she had wanted some, which she didn't. It was a thing that came from a place well-deep inside and sang right alongside the music, saying, '*Push it. Play it. See what you*

221

can do.' Playing Manda in the *Dandies* had fed that thing some healthy meals, but she'd been confined by what Mr Sissle and Mr Blake wanted. Finally, here in China, she was able to do whatever she could and pleased in a place that was far from a dive, before an audience who really couldn't tell shit from Shinola, so if you tried something, and it wasn't what it ought to be, they loved it anyway because whatever you did was 'authentic coloured American jazz', so long as you kept smiling and they got to Charleston at some point during the proceedings, when, back home, folks would have been all over you with abuse.

Valada had to admit that some of her notions had fallen flatter than Lu Cheng's pancakes for that dish with the dark sauce and duck, but others, like doing the last choruses of 'Blue Heaven' pushing through the audience on her knees, were working an absolute charm. Moving through this audience with the trumpet was not the same as working the Barron's tables. First of all, you weren't begging for tips, so nobody got the notion they could buy you, and if hands or looks got too familiar you could blast the transgressor with the trumpet, which not only stopped him short, but guaranteed laughter, wonder, and applause. Valada was relishing this power on her plate. This was her idea of the manna from heaven, summoned by James as surely as Gideon's trumpets summoned victory from the Lord. Manna's hoodoo placing her dance steps surer, her riff runs truer, all of it coming from a mind-tripping, gambolling head-over-tail free; and then she met Karol, her first trip across the line.

She didn't know his name at first, just that he'd been staying around to see them. He was hard not to notice because he was there most sets, leaning against a door or a column near the back, grey-brown jacket thrown over the satin of his Russian orchestra costume. Baggy wine-red trousers stuffed into high black boots, high-necked shirt buttoned not down the front but across a shoulder, embroidered sash around the waist. Others of the orchestra often stayed as well, but not for every set like Karol. His hair was light, not yellow-blond, but not brown either, combed back, full, with ends resting behind his ears. Not the way American white men wore their hair, so far as she'd ever noticed. He sat one night, and her slides brought her past his satin knees. She turned and trumpeted in his direction. He laughed, eyes glowing, and then waited for her outside.

She was with the guys as he approached. That's what had become their habit, sticking together outside the hotel in one knotted group, like covered wagons huddled together against a frontier bristling with Indians. Not one of them would have described this huddle as fear, more a preference for what they knew rather than venturing out into the stares. They liked their lives the same despite a place; playing, eating, drinking, sleeping, practising, shooting the shit. What they were getting out of Shanghai was closets full of beautiful suits. Tailoring the Chinese could give them fast and cheap and expert. *Those silks, those beautiful silks! Of every colour, of any design, textured or satin, for dresses so plentiful that you could pile them up and roll in them, toss them in the air like autumn leaves . . .* The Chinese could keep their food, that weird noise they called music, even their women. Most of the band had sent for their wives and girl-friends once they found they'd be staying a while. Only Jack was interested in venture, Slick Jack who had brought them, Slick Jack who knew the place; but Slick Jack liked to move solo because Slick Jack liked to play. Jack and Valada had played on the boat for a minute, but Jack was a wanderer, from this man's wife to that man's daughter to that daughter's cousin to that cousin's friend. English, French, Russian, Japanese. It was the more different the merrier for Jack. Valada's only play in Shanghai has been the occa-sional tumble with Jack, which, with no strings and many laughs, was what she is pleased with for now because she's been happily loving her James, but she has been thinking of starting to venture herself, slipping loose from the wagons, trying out the frontier.

'You,' she said, bemused, moving herself a little free of the group.

'Me? Yes, I hope so.' His English was accented but clear, his smile confident but not cocky. 'Karol Dimitrivich Glazonov.' A movement of the heels, a bend from the waist, a 'Get this' from the guys. 'At your service, mademoiselle. As you must know, I find you swell.'

'Swell, huh?' She smiled. He was slender but solid and out of his costume, the stuff of his suit old and yet fine, a white man looking at her but without that 'I wanna fuck you, animal' thing. *Different here. Not America.*

'The playing. The whole show. I never tire of it,' he said.

'That I've noticed,' she replied. A flush of red beneath the pale but not moving into fluster.

'It brings me great joy,' he went on. None of that lay-it-on-me, take-me-to-the-pussy stuff. Stillness.

One of the band guys grunted. 'That's my belly talkin', Val. Y'all shit or get off the pot.'

He didn't know what to expect, which was in his favour. 'We'll be having supper back at the house,' she said. 'You can join us if you like.'

They shared a rickshaw.

'You speak Chinese?' She arranges her skirts so as not to caress his leg, not her usual, but right for now. *He is still a white man.*

'We've lived here seven years, my family and me, since the Revolution. We are White Russian.'

'That I can see.'

He is puzzled at first, then laughs. 'I mean as opposed to Red. You know politics?'

Valada shrugs. 'I sing and dance. I play the trumpet.' Ahead are two rickshaws encircled with loops of brightly coloured electric lights, their precious cargoes, two silked china doll prostitutes, looking to be twelve or thirteen years old. Karol gives them no glance.

'Have you seen Shanghai?' He sits still beside her with no sense of 'gimme', pale, smooth hands still, but not a faggot. This she can sense.

'Besides between our house and the Plaza?' Her look stays in the street, not in his direction. She is not in the habit of looking at white men.

'You must allow me to show you,' he says. 'It is a city like no other.' There is a different melody to his voice, the Russian more than like. She's never had a different accent so close to her before. She found herself playing with its notes as James's case slipped towards the floor and Karol's pale hand almost brushes hers. Hearts do not thump as they re-settle the case. Instead there is stillness.

He played the triangular banjo in the orchestra, the balalaika it was called, but that his heart was the violin, he had learned at the age of three. After hearing Karol play, Valada refused to show him what she knew. In Karol's hands the violin was a live thing that sang and moaned and scurried and screamed, its voice travelling into the pit of her in a way no violin had ever done, not even her own when she was first in its thrall, its tentative vibrations tickling her neck. Karol's play was not in the language Valada used. It moved off and against itself; it slid between times; but its stories were the same, love, loneliness, victory, search. Valada sometimes thought of taking bits of what he played. That might go on a trumpet, and that, and that. But mostly she listened, and sometimes she was in her mama's parlour on the afternoons after music lessons when her mama would get that smile and then sit down at the piano.

'So you know Bach?'

'Not to meet him on the street.'

'But you've heard this, I can tell!'

'There was someone who used to know him, but then she changed herself.'

'Did she know Schubert as well?'

He had studied to be a soloist before the Revolution, intending to travel through Europe, even to America perhaps. It wouldn't happen now. He and his family had no country and thus no papers, like all of the Russians who had found refuge in Shanghai. Once his family had been rich, but all their money had gone to escape.

'Escaping what?'

'Escaping the Bolsheviks. They were killing everyone. You did not know?'

No, Valada didn't know. How could she know, always on the road as she was?

'Was it not in newspapers?'

Newspapers? Lawrence was still the only person Valada had ever known that read the newspapers besides the theatrical columns, but had it brought him any joy?

'Yes, I know what you mean. Sometimes it's better just to live.'

'Why are so many of your people so down on their luck?' When despite it being China, white people seemed to be in charge? You saw Russian men pulling rickshaws, Russian broken-down whores fighting Chinese children in the streets for tricks while other whites enjoyed laughing in their faces.

'My father is a duke. He was a scientist, a thinker, but here he works as a doorman. He wears a great fur hat and a purple coat with braid and brass buttons. He is the Grand Duke Dimitri, Clown of Russia. My mother stares into space, fondling her last piece of lace. My sister wants privilege and so gives herself to men. We have no way out. Shanghai will be our end.'

Valada didn't believe it. 'It doesn't have to be, not if you don't let it,' she'd say. 'My end could've been picking cotton or teaching school, looking over my shoulder for lynch-mad crackers, but I'm not there, am I? I've made my own way. I'm in Shanghai, China, and this is just the beginning.'

He would laugh, shake his head. They were almost the same age, but he seemed so much older, world-weary was what he called it. 'You are so lucky to be free of history,' he'd say. 'All those centuries can give you such a weight around the heart. It's in the way you play the music. It's to be American, I think.'

He didn't know about being coloured, and she couldn't bother to tell him; so finally there was nothing for it but to move to another plane.

He is muscled but soft, and smooth and pale. His nipples and penis are pink. His scent is at once sharp and sweet. The hairs of his groin are wisps instead of springs. He marvels that her hair is strong and lush, that her lips go from deep brown to pale magenta; but aside from these, it is as it is. He is a man. He stiffens, he moves, he thrusts, he comes. There is no big mystery, except possibly the sameness.

For a while Karol became a constant. Valada saw Shanghai, and a lot of other Russians. Evgeny and Vladimir, Nikolai and Gyorgy, Masha and Ludmilla, Sergei and Rivka. Different kinds of names for different kinds of folk. Entertainers mostly, or seamstresses and waiters, who would have been students if the world hadn't turned, and now lived too close to its edge to worry about the colours people came in. They lived only in this moment, and if you're into this moment, come on! The Russians laughed and argued more like coloured than the whites Valada were used to, but their energies seemed to come from somewhere around their chests rather than black folks' closer to the ground. Their music was that way too. Sometimes, when the vodka was flowing, Valada and her new friends would try and interweave their styles, but it generally ended in disaster unless they began by singing and dancing. Buck and wing into fouetté turns, charlestons into kazotskies. 'Vercherneeny Zvony' into 'Go Down, Moses'. After voices, feet, and arms had found some common meter, it was amazing how similar different people could be.

The band's women didn't look too kindly on Valada's ventures when they came to Shanghai. They called it acting mannish, which of course went along with the trumpet, and they didn't hold with her Russians, calling them trash just like the English people and the French. Valada didn't care. She started sprinkling her numbers with the odd Russian curlicue, and friendly, pensive times with Karol, with the odd playful romp with Gyorgy, who was wilder than Karol and always ready for a laugh. Sleep became an activity incidental to Valada's time. Novelty was her refreshment, and it was suiting her music fine. She was buzzing the stars with her music.

I'm coming at you, Louis! I may not be with you, but I've got you in sight! And can you step like this, Louis? You know you can't!

But increasingly Karol was needing something else.

It was late winter when Karol opened the door. He had not played with his orchestra that night, which had been happening more and more. Gyorgy was warning that in 'playing with the smoke, Karol was playing in the fire', for who knew how long the orchestra leader would be indulgent? Musical counts were as grains of sand on the shore of Shanghai, said Gyorgy. 'The prince will find someone who stays out of his shoe.'

Karol was sitting at a good front table. He wore black and white. Formal tails, stiff white front and collar, fake pearl studs, wide black lapels. The fairy prince he might have been had history not turned over on itself. He was shining, beautiful, as was the young woman at his side. Valada had avoided them, but he touched her during her slide.

'This is Nadia, my sister. Join us,' he said. The sister's dress was celadon with ivory figures; her bracelets were real diamonds. Valada blew a triple-tongue break, and Karol led a cheer.

Nadia had been dressed for display by her lover across the floor. She was nineteen, once a pianist, and manoeuvring for a visa. The lover was a Belgian diplomat. If he took her out of Shanghai and she prospered, she would send for her brother. At their table, gay determination shrouded disbelief. After the lover reclaimed his sister, Karol took Valada by the arm. For his escort services that evening, he had earned three hundred Shanghai dollars and the use of a private rickshaw.

'Now we go someplace special,' he said.

The place was in Nantao, the old Chinese part of the city. It was raining. The British soldiers at the Settlement gate looked young and miserable, as though they'd rather be nestled up against sing-song girls in the Fuchow Road than tending the barbed wire that kept the girls' countrymen at bay. The barbed wire was new enough not to be rusted and dull. Its glitter in the torchlight complemented the red turban of the policeman who questioned their intent.

'Trouble tonight, *sahib*,' he told Karol. 'Students are rabbling. The big men will not be standing it for long.'

'We have an appointment,' said Karol, waving the man away

with a gesture Valada had never been close to before, for she had never known a person whose life had once been full of servants. The barbed wire's scrape grated on Valada's spine as it was moved. She pulled her monkey-fur collar tighter about her neck until it prickled against her nose. She'd thought the matching hat would be too much for someone her size when she'd bought the coat. She was regretting that now.

The rickshaw man made detours to avoid street demonstrators with their make-shift banners and photographs on placards and the shadowy dark-clad men who followed their every move.

'Do you know what they show in the pictures?' asked Valada.

'Burnt villages, chopped-up people.' Karol's reply was without emotion. 'You have been right in the way you've lived, Ladishka. It is better not to know about such things. Tonight we will not know in the best possible way.'

It was a street like any other in Shanghai: a few flickering gas lights illuminating stone gates to the row houses; the little store-fronts of merchants who sold only one thing, like pink baby hats or fresh-smoked eel or green umbrellas. The rickshaw man was to wait. A faint, sweet smell was in the air. Karol led the way down a narrow flight of stairs. His hand was not still as it twisted a knob on the wall. The old man who opened the door had long fingernails that were stained with black.

The walls were hung with embroidered silks and appeared to drift in the gloom like rippling water on a Tennessee August night. Golden branches glinted through the haze. Karol and Valada were led to a low-sitting table. The pillows covering the benches on which they sat were also silk and embroidered. Valada is aware of forms reclining about the den. Occasional murmurs and sighs are the only sounds. A young girl kneels next to their table and pre-pares the pipes, scooping the sticky black paste into a small silver dish, cooking the paste over lamplight until it bubbled and popped, transferring the paste into the small ivory bowls. She offers the first one to Karol, lit match at the ready as he holds it to his lips. He turns the pipe towards the flame, draws deep, and then smiles. 'Oh, Ladishka,' he says, 'I am so happy to share this joy with you,' then little else for a good long while.

Valada drew deep. Jack had described the technique: '*Like you some little pickaninny back on your mama's titty.*' But Jack wasn't one for sharing, and Valada hadn't been about to ask him. You couldn't trust Jack, anyway. He was likely to up and leave you in some dive of an opium den if something better caught his eye; so Valada had waited for Karol. She drew again, and her lips throbbed with a phantom memory of James's metal jammed hard up against her; then the memory was gone, taking with it the trumpet pressure behind her eyes. She drew again, and the pain from the bruises on her knees seemed to swell, spread down her shins, up her thighs, and then it too just disappeared. She could hear herself breathe, like she was inside of her own lungs. Her hand brushed against her dress, and its sequins clattered like the little cymbals in tambourines. The back of a hand touched her cheek. Whose hand? A girl's, like Bessie's hand, *but softer than Bessie's hand*. Like little Hattie's hand. *Hattie's little-girl hand after letting loose a firefly*, but cooler than Hattie's hand. She is laid down and unshod, a firm small hand lightly pressing her sole. She is loose and light. She is floating on the haze and then in the haze. Is this swimming? No, water has more press. And it is wet. Her dress would be clamming to her body, but it isn't. It floats around her. It is swirling around her. She turns her head. Her eyes are slits. There is gold. She is moving toward her star, but not quickly. In a sparking shower of golden light. Yes.

Afterwards, it wasn't like booze. There was no head. She felt buoyant, energized.

'You liked my gift, Ladishka?' The light in the stairwell was dull and grey. It was still raining. Karol's collar was no longer so stiff and white. In this light, his faux pearls were dull, the stubble on his cheeks ageing him years, yet Valada was feeling closer to him than she had in a while, protective as well. He was vulnerable, this man, and had given her much.

'It was nice,' she replied. 'More than nice.' She slipped her arm through his. This place she would be wanting to re-visit before time.

230

'I was happy to be able to show you this way, Ladishka. It is not always possible.' Obviously not, for the bulk of Karol's escort payment was gone. 'We can only hope that Nadia's Belgian friend remains sweet.' Popping sounds were coming from the street, which was strange because it was far later than dawn, too late for the firecrackers chasing away devils on the river. Not that these sounds were coming from the river.

Night soil pots were turned over in the streets, their foul contents slushing in the puddles. A mound of what looked like sacks with legs was piled at the end of the street, and their rickshaw man was gone.

'Do you know where we are?' asked Valada.

'If we make our way to the river,' Karol replied.

It wasn't just shit in the puddles. Valada was avoiding what she could see of brown in the water, but it was impossible to miss everything, and much of it was red. A blood wash was seeping into the yellow satin of her shoes. The bodies at the end of the street had no heads. Their necks were severed clean. Valada and Karol were transfixed by the sight. Spinal cords were creamy white inside vertebrae. Some heads had been cut off above the hairline of the nape. Some of the hair remaining was long and luxuriant, if tangled with blood, some was shaved stubble. Karol looked upward, attracted by a creaking above their heads, made an intake of breath, and tried to shield Valada's eyes.

'What? What?' The heads. In birdcages. Hanging from telegraph wires. Others on bamboo stakes, leaning against walls that were slashed with blood. Eyes open. Mouths screaming. Most of them young. Women too. Valada couldn't scream. She had no sound.

'To the river, Ladishka. We should not stay here.'

She should have been afraid, but it did not feel real. They passed through street fights on their way to the river. First they'd see the women, carrying pots and baskets of steaming food to makeshift barricades behind which workers and students with torn jackets and bloodied bandages stood at the ready, armed with old pistols, long knives, axes, and clubs. What the defenders prepared for was found but streets away, men with white armbands, longer knives, and better guns, butchering anyone with a weapon and without an armband and others who stood too close or protested too loud. Noise was all around and thunderous. There was no more yellow in Valada's shoes. It should have felt real. The screams were Chinese, but they were real. The blood was real. The fires were real. The shit was real. She should have been afraid, but it didn't feel real. Maybe because of the opium. Maybe because they seemed to move unnoticed through the noise and fires and blood in their soiled evening clothes and not-black hair. They were shoved against, but not pummelled. The noise was around them but never at them. When they huddled in doors, Valada could feel Karol's heart, which was not racing.

'Was your revolution like this?' she asked.

'No. Then they wanted me,' he replied.

At the river, terrified Chinese struggled for boats, but Karol's last dollars worked more wonders as room was made in a sampan for the Western devils with the not-black hair. Little more reality on the river as their tiny sampan joined scores of others winding their way around the great grey battleships that had been schooling in the Wangpoo for months, bristling flags and cannon like so many whales masquerading as porcupines. Porcupines going to a dress-up ball. Watching fireworks. And applauding. Sailors were applauding. Gesturing anyway. A sailor looked down at the river directly at Valada. Right into her eyes. He wore a funny hat. With a pompom. Maybe he was French. He saluted. And then he laughed. Their overcrowded sampan was taking on water. Children were crying. The water stank of oil and sewage. It sloshed against her toes. It was freezing. This was real.

She ripped her dress climbing out of the sampan. Bugle beads hitting her frozen shins like buckshot. The gate is pandemonium. As though the Settlement can be the only deliverance from hell with desperate Chinese, crowds of them, screaming, pleading, being beaten away.

She has been here six months, and still Chinese is only noise. No sense of where words begin and end. Only noise, with a dominant treble. Violins sawed off the bow. But with its own special rhythm. Chinese rhythm. Up in the air somewhere. Her ears pricking to its beat.

She has never seen or heard of terror like this, not even when folks spoke of East St Louis and that place in Arkansas in the summer of 1919. Black folks tended to go to ground during a riot, raising their heads after it passed, maintaining their place. Here was terror that sent folk rushing out their homes wearing such clothes as they could throw onto their backs, carrying the chicken meant for next week's supper, the bedclothes that had been slept on for generations. Nothing but rags most of it and them clinging to it like life itself, as if these sorry shards would be all that could connect them to what they'd been. And all this trouble coming from their own kind. Chinese butchering Chinese and nothing between them but an armband. Hard to grasp for a coloured girl coming from a place where you could be pretty sure that deadly enemies were those who didn't look like you. If she'd thought about it, she might have recognized this as war; but she didn't because her feet were cold, and all she really knew about was singing and dancing and playing the horn.

The Settlement wants no parts of these people. Last night's contingent of turbaned policemen and feckless recruits has been augmented by a variety of European volunteers and the Settlement's own Chinese henchmen. A man runs forward. He wears the silks of a merchant but has the build of a peasant. He has mass, few teeth, and eyes howling with fear. He is clubbed by police, but he does not fall. He knocks a trunk from a woman's hands, displacing the toddler tied to her back. One foot on the trunk, the next on a man's shoulder. A steadying hand on the man's head. A foot on the stone tower. Both hands on barbed wire. Dragging his body across the wire. Ripping the silk and his abdomen with it. Tumbling onto a platform. But then grabbed by volunteers before he can leap away to safety. Lifted up and thrown

233

back into the crowd. Swallowed, beaten, and trampled by the crowd. To gunfire syncopating on Chinese screams.

Only Westerners are being let through the gate, and every one of them searched. Valada is searched by a young British soldier. Thoroughly, roughly, his hands slashing into her armpits, fumbling across her breasts. But it is not sexual. He is too frightened. His dreams of sing-song girls in the Fuchow Road are long forgotten. He hates the Chinese now.

It is late afternoon by the time Valada and Karol clear the gate. They are hungry and tired and slathered with grime. Still there are no rickshaws. When they reach her door, he squeezes her hand. His eyes have not focused in this time. For him, the day was never real. *It was beautiful, Ladishka. Do not forget.* No, no, she would never forget.

Valada hardly saw Karol after that. They never repeated their visit to Nantao even after the shooting stopped and the warships left and the money was there to do it with grace. She never found out what the fighting was about. People argued about Communists and whispered about gangsters, but it had nothing to do with her. Those things were not her worry. What she did was sing and dance and play the trumpet. Karol never went back to the orchestra. Through Gyorgy she knew that he continued in the thrall of the Divine Lotus.

'*She's his only love, Ladishka. He lives only to find her, embrace her. He has no pride, doesn't care where she takes him, but who's to say what is right in these days and times? Who's to say?*'

Ludmilla reported that Karol's sister Nadia lost her Belgian then found a Swiss, lost her Swiss then found an Argentine. The Argentine may have been lucky, for then there was no news of either brother or sister. Valada sometimes passed the club fronted by the Grand Duke Dimitri, who always looked grim below his high fur hat. Maybe because his children had left him. Maybe because of his life as a clown. By summer Valada had tired of Russians. Their fatalistic desperation was no longer fun, and they couldn't wash enough. Which was not to say that she had tired of

234

Shanghai, with its money and freedom and its cascades of applause.

After a year in the East, some of the band opted to go home, but not Valada, because here she was developing her style and moving on. She brought some home to China by inviting Lavada to join the show. It wasn't always easy having Little Sis around, asking questions and talking sass; but they laughed a lot, had fun with clothes, improved their singing, and Valada stayed out of the dens. Which was good for everything, but she never did forget.

Manhattan Theatre District, May 1956

In Manhattan, Valaida sips vodka in a darkened bar. After the unpleasantness with Hannah, she was needing some relief, and not only of her thirst. She concentrates on alcohol's numbing effects and the piano patterns of Art Tatum emanating from the juke, seeking to purge all vexations from her mind, the physical throbbings, the irksome memories, but she's not succeeding as well as she might like. Hannah's words are pebbles on a shore, tumbling about in the onslaught of spirits, but remaining resolutely there. *If you had known anyone.* Valaida is hungering for relief. There is a man she's known from another time sitting at the bar, in a grey suit with a beige knit shirt, and a silver lighter in a languid hand. He has the relief Valaida desires in the heel of his shoe. After all the time that has passed, Valaida wouldn't need a syringe. A little bit of powder on the back of her hand. A sniff. A rush. Then peace. For a while. *If you had known anyone.* Valaida sips her vodka. She needs to resist her hunger. She has been clean for so long. She has been enjoying her life without the Sweet King. She has promised Earle. Promised herself. But in the midst of this relentless, harrowing pain, she wants to sing and play the trumpet. She wants to tell her tale tonight. How will she manage without relief? The man is but fifteen paces away.

It takes Paul's eyes a moment to adjust to the gloom, as it has in the five establishments he tried before arriving here, but his persistence is rewarded. The lady sits in a middle booth, the trumpet case by her side, still in her shades despite the dark. The coral paint on her nails appears blood-red in the diminished light. Her lips are looser than they have been, as though part of a mask has succumbed to flesh. Her lips tell him it might be safe to approach, and that's what he chooses to do.

'You're alone,' he says after a beat, at the edge of her booth. Her shoulders are not held as straight as they've been throughout the day. She has looked upwards, but there is no way to see her eyes. 'Mind if I sit?' The head is still at first, then shakes ever so slightly.

'I'm really sorry about what happened with Hannah,' he continues. 'I have no idea what came over her. Well, maybe I do, but it has nothing to do with you. Would you like something else to drink?' Another shake of the head. The music changes to Thelonius Monk. Valaida's still working on Monk, but now his style's right on time. Stabbing and lyrical all at once. Her heart beating against the stabs. The young man orders a drink.

'I wanted you to know I understand that there's always more than one version to any story. There's no real reason you should want to speak to me ever again, but if you cared to tell, I'd be interested to listen.' The young man's manner has changed. He seems less frantic, more mature, but Valaida has never been profligate with her counsel.

The grey-suited man has paid his bill and left. Valaida licks her lips, which will need some tending before the performance. This performance will require a reach. 'Everything you need to know about me is in the music,' she says.

Paul wants to intrude, but understands better. 'If you'd prefer to be alone . . .' he begins, with a start to rise.

'No,' Valaida replies, with the smallest intake of breath. 'No,' she repeats. 'If you wouldn't mind sitting here for a bit, what I'd really like to do is close my eyes.'

II Fugue and riffs

Chapter one

Denmark, 1942

Metal scraping against metal. They have already delivered lunch. They are looking at her again. A voice calls out a question. Female as always. Grating as the metal. She cannot understand it. She is shivering too hard. Her cramps are too painful. Her head is buried in the grey wool that covers the cot. It is rough. Her knees are at her chest. She rocks against the cold and pain. The fabric of her garments is unforgiving, the black canvas of the tunic, the trousers that match it. The chemise is rough across her nipples. Never has she worn clothes so harsh and unforgiving. Even the costumes of *Jimtown*, heavy with salts and grime not her own. Even as a child, when money was at its scarcest. The voice again. Valaida raises her head. Everything is grey, the concrete walls, the corner sink and the bucket below it, the tin plate on the ledge, the mounds of food it contains. The food reeks of lard and heavy grains. Her stomach seizes from its odour. 'My medicine,' she whimpers. 'I need my medicine.' There is no answer. The slot grates shut. Valaida rolls onto her other side. The strip of sky is grey. She closes her eyes, and still the grey remains. And the craving. And the pain from the craving. This place. What is this place? All of its sounds are in echo, clangs and scrapes and whistles and guttural shouts in a language she is not understanding.

She had been looking for Alois. She had been in Den Rote Okse waiting for Alois. She'd had the silver in her handbag, a fork, two knives, a spoon. She'd wanted to pay Alois this time. No more favours. No more, 'Keep your silver for food, Valaida,' and then him wanting her to suck his dick. Alois had been away for days. Valaida hadn't had the strength to coy him away from a favour. She'd give him the silver instead. Her medicine was more important than food. Alois understood this, and he always delivered. He was her angel, black-haired and bearded and smelling of fish oil, a strange sort of angel, but her salvation all the same; only Alois had left town, and Valaida was facing the rages of Hell. The barmaid had not been helpful. '*Han er nord paa,*' she'd said. He is in the North. '*Jeg ved ikke hvornaar han kommer tilbage.*' I don't know when he's coming back. '*Ikke dag.*' Not today. '*Eller morgen.*' Or tomorrow.

The waitress had spoken Danish. Den Rote Okse was in Copenhagen. Is Denmark where she is?

She had finished the ersatz coffee that felt like sand on her tongue and tasted like dirt, counted out three pennies, and left the café that had been no warmer than the street. It was March, but there were no signs of spring. Puddles were covered with ice. She'd shivered so violently that she'd feared for the safety of her syringe against the silver. She hated the syringe, but how could she replace it if it broke? So much easier when she'd been able to drink the Eukodal from its half-litre bottles. The taste had been foul, but its effects immediate, smooth, and sweet; but now the Eukodal source was long since gone, the apotheke closed, its proprietor jailed. Vials of morphine were easier to move from place to place, in a coat lining, in a hat. Alois had his sources and not just for medicine; for meat, for sugar, for cigarettes, anything, so long as you could pay. Like many denizens of the Copenhagen district of Istegade, who worked hard and played harder, Alois had no fear of the Danish police and laughed at the German occupiers.

Germans. Germans had come to Denmark. Is she in Germany? Have they taken her away to Germany?

Istegaders like Alois made no judgements about how people lived their lives. They reminded Valaida of the night people in Harlem or Beale Street or on Chicago's South Side, and so she'd felt as safe among them as she could feel trapped in a Copenhagen occupied by the Germans with their death pins, and she a coloured woman with no licence to work, no money, and this ever-constant craving. Time was that Valaida travelled all over Copenhagen, all over Denmark. She'd been a glamorous star in Denmark, but not any more. In the end, she'd seldom strayed from the cramped spaces and working people of Istegade.

Valaida's feet were frozen blocks, which hurt when they hit the concrete. She wished she could find some music to fill part of the void she was inside, but she had heard nothing inside for days. She needed her medicine. Valaida still sang for Alois sometimes, for he couldn't have cared less about work permits or any other kind of law for that matter, but she didn't play the trumpet. Her lips were chapped and flaccid, and her trumpet long since gone, like her gowns were gone, and her jewellery, and her trunks, and her silk-satin negligées, and her lace-trimmed step-ins, all gone to pay for living. In the slaughterhouse at the far end of her street, oxen bellowed on the way to their deaths, their misery as rank in the frozen fog as the stench of their blood and urine and shit. The water from Valaida's eyes was freezing against her face. Her nose was running. She needed her medicine.

They had been waiting at the hotel. They were Danish, not German, and they wore no uniforms. '*Fru Val-eye-da Snowberry?*' they'd asked. The name on her passport. The name from her marriage to Nyas, and always mispronouncing, and as if Snow and

Berry were all one word. '*Fru Val-eye-da Snowberry?*' She'd cried out and crumpled onto the floor. 'I'm sick!' she'd cried. '*Jeg haed kalve!* I'm sick! I'm sick!' Their hands had been upon her. Fru Asmussen had twittered about the background with her broken English and the once-pink knitted shawl that was always around her shoulders and stank of cats. 'They are *Fremmdepoliti*, Val-eye-da, Alien polices. They say you do not come to the *Ministerium*, *som behoeved*, as required. You miss two times! They take you now! I tell them, no, you sick. They do not listen! I will look for you, Val-eye-da! I your friend! I take you care!'

Valaida had had no strength to kick and twist. The men's hands had felt like iron on her arms as they escorted her to their van. One did the driving, and one sat behind with her, as grey as the frozen fog, grey skin, grey eyes, grey coat, grey expression, but Valaida had felt too sick to be afraid. She cried because now she'd never see Alois. If that were true, life would be far too hard to bear, and they might as well go ahead and stand her up against a wall. Their bullets would bring a blessed release from the cold and the grey and the emptiness and the craving. But they hadn't shot her. They had brought her to their Ministry then transferred her to a room with cold grey walls. She'd been too sick to understand anything that they were doing, even when an officer had spoken to her in English. She was a problem for Denmark, he'd said. She needed to go back home to her country. He talked about the war and Sweden and money and papers. With her body trembling with craving, Valaida could not understand. She told the officer if only she could have her medicine, she would understand so much more. The officer had closed his mouth hard, looked down at her file, gave a wave of his hand, and she'd been taken away to be stripped and prodded, then dressed in chafing, ugly clothes that did not fit.

Beyond the scrapes and the clangs, Valaida hears a new sound in the distance. It is a chord. F, A, C#. It's getting closer. F, A, C#. It's a train. F, A, C#. 'Take me,' she whimpers. 'Take me, too.'

242

Chattanooga, Tennessee, 1928

The train chord. F, A, C#. The train chord. In America, going home to Tennessee. After so much time on the road, after two years in the far Far East, can Tennessee still be home? Mama and Hattie. Never Lawrence. Lavada and Herman getting married. The train chord. On the Southern Pacific out of Oakland, California. In Pullman cars. Valada in one cabin with her finery. The lovebirds in another. The big country gliding by. Through the Rockies and across the Northern Plains. Snow on the outside and she cocooning herself in silk. An occasional nip from her cinnabar flask because Prohibition is still the law. The Porters loose-limbed, elegant in their grey uniforms. Happy to be doing for their own. Ivory smiles in copper against charcoal grey, in toasted biscuit against charcoal grey. Broad, proud shoulders, long, rangy legs. Rushing crosstown in Chicago from Union Station to Dearborn and the Dixie Limited. The train chord. F, A, C#. F, A, C#. No more Pullman. No more pretty Porters. It's *Plessy* on the Limited, Jim Crow all the way.

For the first time in two years, Valaida is surrounded by her folk. Butterscotch, sealskin, chocolate, plum. Women swaddled in furs or worn and weathered worsted, with witty cloches hugging marcelled waves or shapeless felts squashed down on naps. Baskets of fried chicken and potato salad shared with those who'd travelled too far to prepare.

'Praise God! Did you hear that? These chil'ren been to China! China, can you imagine? And going home to see they mama . . .'

Clapping games warming the children. One sister's hum being taken up by seven. *Comin' for to carry me home . . .* The rail car rocking on springs that have ridden better ways. Home. But Chattanooga? F, A, C# . . .

'Oh, they're beautiful, Valada! What do you call them? Jade? Mama, did you see? Valada brought me these beautiful bracelets!' Hattie's grown plump, but she's the tallest of them all with innocent eyes prancing with dreams. *'I'm gonna be on stage just like you and Louie! I've got*

a dancing act with my friend. We sing the blues and everything! Last month we came in fourth at the Liberty, but this month we're gonna do better! Can I show you? I want to show you! Mama, will you play?' Hattie's pitch is close to true, but her steps are not.

'*You could help her, Valada. It would mean so much.*' Alvada's eyes are tired and sweet, like their Mama's. Thomas has a steady job sweeping up at Wheland Foundry. Alvada's sure he'll be made a stoker soon. Children tumbling around the apron she has on most all the time. '*I try, but I was never as good as you. If you could stay and give her that extra push . . . You've been missed, you know.*'

Arthur, Jr is dark brown and blunt-featured like his daddy. Not a Snow, but her Mama seems happy. And makes no requests. Chattanooga is a swaggering boom town after China. Rhythms are rough and ready. People laugh out loud and get knifed and shot. Hattie is happy to hip-shake to please the crowd.

'*You been around white folk too long, Valada. Our folks like it straight.*'

Music is coming from everywhere, from portable victrolas and radio sets. Only not at 222 E Street, 'cause Daddy Arthur don't allow it.

> *. . . I don't care what Arthur don't 'low*
> *'Cause I'm gonna shimmy shake anyhow . . .*

She had to leave Chattanooga to chase the music. The music was pumping out of New York. Ethel Waters with James P. Johnson and Clarence Williams. And Louis on 'Melancholy Blues', sliding up and down his notes like it was no kind of effort and every one of them a shoe to your plexus. Air kicked out of your lungs, just gone. Fletcher Henderson thumping from the Roseland Ballroom with Russell singing pretty. *Her big old Russell bear. Sounding so sweet.* And Louis, 'Struttin' with Some Barbecue' to a place that was 'Hotter Than Hot', finding his own time, playing slower, playing faster, but always right on it. Blim-blim-blim on top, right up there where the horn shouldn't go, never had, not like that, and always on it, always. The Duke from the Cotton Club every night. Before she went to China, what had he been, Mr Edward Kennedy Ellington? A piano player with a sometimes band, and now broadcasting national? Every night. The music flying through the sky, and Louis Armstrong streaking beyond it. Valada and the guys had coasted in China, blown unchallenged and bought suits, while back in the homeland sounds were looping through the loop. Louis' opening on 'West End Blues'. Notes a sun shower of golden raindrops bouncing off your eyelids and rippling into your ears, then easing into a blues strong enough to strike a Smith woman dumb. Trixie, Clara, Bessie, Mamie. And their sisters. Because the sound was so perfect, the story so true, and she not able to take James out his case because of Arthur's pressure. Arthur couldn't stand it, even when she stuffed a mute with rags.

'I know she's professional, Etta, but my head just starts to throb. You don't want me to die, do you? On account of some piece of brass? Let her play the violin or piano. I ain't got no cause with them, and besides, that horn's unseemly. It's not gonna bring no good.'

She had to leave Chattanooga, go North after the music.

'How can you go, Valada, with Hattie's do next week? Your nieces and nephews don't even know you. And you won't be back, will you? You gonna break Mama's heart.'

But never a mention of where Lawrence might be. No words on his desertion or worries about his soul.

The dress Valada wore to Lavada's wedding had been designed by Madame Plietskaya of Shanghai, peach silk-satin inter-stitched with pleats of ecru crêpe-de-chine, tumbling into points with lace-covered satin shoes to match. This was to be her last day in Chattanooga. She was on the 6 a.m. Dixie Flyer in the morning, and she meant to leave Chattanooga with a vision in its mind. Her dress was prettier than the bride's, but this was not her fault. In Shanghai, Lavada had been too busy playing with Herman to keep up with the needed fittings. Madame Plietskaya was an artist, and Madame Plietskaya had been displeased. She took Lavada's money and bunched cream satin into awkward bows up to her ribs. Lavada hadn't cared at the time – '*Herman's just gonna tear it off anyway!*' – but she'd cared on her wedding day, and Alvada had cared, and Hattie had cared. '*How could you, Valada? This is her day, not yours!*' Lavada said nothing, but her eyes could have cut peach silk to shreds, then pierced through flesh to slice a vital organ. Hattie and her friend performed sweet songs Daddy Arthur approved of with Alvada at the piano, and only Mama was at the door before dawn to kiss Valada good-bye.

See you, Chattanooga. You're no more home,
No more home of mine . . .

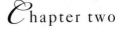

$\mathcal{C}$hapter two

Denmark, 1942

She knows where she is now. She is in a prison called Vestre
Faengsel. It is in Denmark not Germany, in Copenhagen, but miles
from Istegade where she lived. She is in a cell. She is by herself.
There is a cot and a sink and a plate and a cup. There is a window
that only allows you to see a small strip of sky. There is a desk with
a book of hymns and a Bible, both of them in Danish. Valaida has
been in Denmark for almost three years, since before the war, before
the Germans, before everything turned grey; but she reads almost
no Danish, so the Bible will be no comfort. Much to her Mama's
despair, it was never Valaida's habit to seek solace in the Bible, but
she would have been willing to try now if It had been in English; but
It is not. Perhaps God is taunting her for her lack of attention, but if
He is her Mama's God, can He be that cruel? If He is cruel then He
must be angry. But why is He angry? What has she done?

247

Her body is shaking, her stomach is cramping, her teeth are chattering. She needs her medicine. Her fingernails are broken stubs. If she had her nail file she could make them presentable, or maybe stab her throat. If she stabbed her throat, they'd bring her medicine. They'd have to bring her medicine, but she cannot stab her throat because they've taken everything away. Valaida rocks on the cot and looks at the floor. Her shoes are ugly. They are black, with heavy soles and straps like a child's. They don't fit her well, and they have been worn many times, probably by many people. Metal scrapes against metal. They will not have her medicine. When she asks, they never answer, even if she asks in their language. Valaida continues rocking and doesn't bother to look up. She stares at her ugly shoes. She grips her ankles tight and tries hard to find some music. She grips her ankles until the pain feels like starlight.

Zulu man is feeling blue
Hear his heart beat a little tattoo
Diga diga doo diga doo doo
Diga diga doo diga doo . . .

New York, 1929

New York is faster, sparkling brighter, flashing more money than ever was. Harlem is jumping harder, black folks walking prouder, eyes level, steady, being about the city that is the centre of their world. Staccato clean taps riffing 'round gut-bucket moans ending on a laughing vamp. New York. Four years Valada's been away. Valada needs to catch up, and so Valada works. She takes a room off of Lenox Avenue in a house catering to the life with no Daddy Arthurs and music going all the time. She runs into friends, Bessie, Maude, her trumpet buddy Dolly Jones, who crows with delight and falls into embraces.

'*Valada! Girl! Is that really you? I thought you might be dead! Lord God, I missed your face!*'

Everyone looking plush because good jobs are all around, silk stockings undarned, cute little animal heads dripping off shoulders.

'*You want a job, Valada? You could find a job in a minute, over to Small's or to Tillie's or downtown at the Alabam. Everybody's buyin', and we got rhythm for sale!*'

But Valada doesn't snatch a job, and she doesn't run and party, at least not like she could. The road this music's travelling is not for the faint of skill. Valada wants to be a master, so she pulls off into the shed.

She buys a brand new Victrola and an armful of records, Louis of course, but the Duke as well to get close to Bubber Miley's wailing, and Fletcher for Russell and his brother Joe and Rex Stewart and Coleman Hawkins on tenor and the way the Redman had of bringing it all together; but it always came back to Louis. Louis' Fives and Sevens, Louis with Clarence Williams, Louis with Bessie Smith. Louis, Louis, Louis. She'd listen hard while buzzing her lips and warming up her James, taking notes in her mind, forming the pictures in her mind, plotting the fingerings in her mind, and then she'd start to blow. She is twenty-four years old. Her muscles have developed. Her diaphragm is strong, her cheeks are firm, her mind is ready, but she'd coasted in China. There'd been no challenges in China. She can't keep up. She's finding herself behind the beat. She has to work her keys. The 'Heebie Jeebies' in every key God imagined and the ones that are Devil's own. And then faster, faster. A fast that goes past your thinking direct into your fingers, fingers hitting the valves like good clean taps, dancing. Rhythm coming from the dancing, telling the stories with the dance, and she can dance. She always could dance, but these tempos are tripping her up. Tell the story, but faster, stronger.

Another trumpet. She needs a new trumpet. She wants a warmer, clearer tone, faster action from her springs. This James has been her heart, but it's time to leave him go. He's not growing like she's growing, can't travel this road she's on. He held his own in China, pulled her back in China when she'd fickled with a Lark, but now he's done. Past his day. She could change his springs and fiddle with his valves, but his tone's his tone. He was sweet and tender, young like his namesake, like his owner. Valada caresses his contours one last time, then packs him up and trades him in without a sigh to help her buy a Martin. Louis' trumpet. She calls him Ernest because that is what she is. Ernie's warm, responsive, and along with the dance, she's hearing the story in her mind, singing in mind, and she gets closer. Not there, but closer. Only it hardly even mattered because the scene hasn't changed in New York.

There's still no place at the Nest Club for a chick with brass at her lips. '*A honey? With a horn? No time, no way. No time, no way!*' Now if she were as bad as Louis, she would have gone ahead, shoulders squared while she took Ernie out his case, breathed him warm, the sweetest fuck-you smile to the fellas before she took her lead and blew. But she wasn't as bad as Louis. Nobody was. But the guys could play in if they had something to offer. They could do what they could do. She had something to offer, but she wasn't as bad as Louis, so she had to sit still on the side. New York.

Sometimes she practised with Dolly Jones. They'd sit up in her room, listening to the records, playing out, trading fours.

'*Why don't we form our own band, Valada? Just forget these men! I got a friend Clotel who plays a demon clarinet. She handles saxophones as well, and plenty sisters play piano. We could do it. What do you say?*'

No. She said no. No more girl bands, never again, not after Gonzala White. That was no way into the stars, no way up the comet's tale, in some sideshow girl band, no matter how hot the playing. A girl band at the Savoy or Small's or Connie's Inn? A girl band making records? Valada had to laugh.

'*But at least we'd get to play, Vee. Isn't that all that really matters? If you love the music, just to play?*'

No, Dolly, Valada wants to be on the comet's tale. China had been fun, but China was nowhere near the stars. This is what Valada's learned in returning to New York, and every other week she's reading newspaper scoops on Josephine. Josephine in feathers at the *Folies Bergère*. Josephine Baker and her pet cheetah, Josephine with her gold nails and designer gowns, Josephine dressed in tweeds talking about how much she loves the country, fishing and riding. Like she ever held a rod in her hand, at least, not the kind you fish with. Josephine, the star. Valada wants to find her move. She's going to have to leave New York. But where to go? Back to Chicago? Or what about Paris?

The world is going to Paris that summer, the coloured world, too. It's in the air. Go to Paris. Challenge Josephine. And Bricktop's in Paris. With her own club. Doing well. Valada has always admired Brickie. Could she hip her to a path? *Blackbirds* is going to Paris, *Blackbirds of 1929*. Bessie will be there.

'*Oh, come, Valada! Do come! You could get you a job in the chorus with me, no sweat. It'll be fun.*'

Sweet Bessie, but Valada's done with the chorus. How many years has she been out of the chorus? You don't go backwards, not even to go to Paris and work for Lew Leslie. Valada wants to meet Lew Leslie because Lew Leslie is a maker of coloured stars. Lew Leslie made Florence Mills a star, and now that Florence is dead, folks say he's always looking to find her equal. These days his star is Adelaide Hall singing 'Diga Diga Do'; but Adelaide isn't Florence, and he won't back her for ever. Valada wants to meet Lew Leslie, but not dancing in his chorus. On her own terms, doing what she can do.

'*Valada Snow? You are Valada Snow.*'

She and Dolly were at the Lenox Club catching Bessie on her last night in the line. In between numbers Dolly was still going on about forming themselves a band, and as much as she loved Dolly, Valada was thinking of wringing her stubborn little neck.

'*I'm not changing my mind, Dolly. I'm not even listening to you any more.*'

The man was black, dark, dark-complected and not all that comely, but there was a refinement to his baritone and his bugging eyes were pleasant and smart.

'*Yes, I'm Valada Snow. Who's asking?*'

His cuffs were made of some soft fine stuff under an easy draping jacket of toffee cream. Handkerchief linen maybe. Not what you picked up in Harlem. His table companions were pretty-boy members of the fast crowd's faggot elite, no females need apply; so why was he over here talking to her?

'*My name's Cas McHenry. I saw you performing two, three years ago at the Sunset in Chicago, that bit you did with the shoes.*'

She'd used seven different pair of shoes with dancing styles to match, soft shoes, taps, Dutch clogs, Russian boots. She'd done it on a dare, and it had turned out to be a wow, cascades of coin coming her way every night. Louis had caught that act a number of times, which was how she got to meet him, him and his buddy piano player, Earl Hines, who was also dark-skinned but very cute, tall, slender, with pretty dimples in both cheeks.

'*Your act was something, really something. I thought you had more talent than I had seen in a long time.*'

Her head was feeling fuzzy. She needed to watch the cut-rate booze. '*That is very nice of you to say.*'

His eyes tell her he's not finished; so what's the punchline, Mr Bug-Eye Boy?

'*I know this might sound strange since you don't know me from Adam's uncle, but I'm here from Paris to find a vocalist for the summer. Would that kind of job be of interest to you?*'

Ka-da bang. Just like that. Castor McHenry. Conservatory-trained pianist from Oklahoma. Father a high school principal, mama a French teacher. Educated folk with money, acres of farm land, and horses to ride. Twenty-five years old and living in Paris, taking Valada to Paris. Cas and Valada to Paris. Just like that.

Chapter three

It is too terrible. It is worse than anything has ever been, worse than the fear in the Alabama woods, than the emptiness when Lawrence went away, than the pleurisy she had as a child. The preachers had said that Hell was never-ending. Just as she hadn't read her Bible, Valaida had never spent much energy on listening to preachers. During the sermons of her Chattanooga Sundays she had concentrated on the rhythm of their words rather than what they were actually saying, tapping her heels, bopping her head, but she is remembering those words now. This torment is never-ending. This torment must be Hell. They don't help her; they barely talk to her, and she sees almost nothing of them; but they won't leave her alone. Opening the grate, sometimes she sees a flick of eye, sometimes she hears breathing, sometimes she catches their odour, sometimes they call her name – 'Fru Snowberry?' – but they never respond to her pleas for help. They don't care about her tears. Smoking would make her calmer, but they will not let her smoke. The gate closes, then hardly a moment to recover from the last invasion before the iron grates open again. Everlasting torment, that's what the preachers promised if you didn't follow the godly path, and Valaida hasn't followed the godly path. God is angry. *Mama, help me!* Everlasting torment.

Despite the cold, she had been happy to go outside the first time they'd opened her cell. At last she'd see another human, for she'd heard of prisons and jails; she'd seen them in Big House movies. You saw other people in the yard. After the endless, pain-wracked hours in the solitude of her hell, she'd see some other people. They'd be sharing cigarettes, playing cards. Some of them would look at her in blank amazement. She knew a few would mutter, '*Neger*', but others she might even recognize from Istegade, and they might welcome her as they had there, haven as it was for those outside law and polite society. Valaida'd taken no notice of how her shoes rubbed against her heels as she'd stumbled down the concrete steps toward the yard, nor how the stairwell's chill gave hint of the outside's bitter cold; she'd thought only of possible haven. But there were no others when she stepped out into the air. Her yard was a high-walled, pie-shaped wedge with nowhere to sit and commune with cards, cigarettes, and idle chatter. There was nobody else, there was only her. 'Why?' she screamed. '*Hvorden?* Why? I'm not a bad person! I haven't done anything!'

'*Gaa!*' came the answer. '*Gaa.* You walk.' But Valaida couldn't walk, she could only cry. She leaned against the pie walls, crying. She turned herself down the wall, crying and crying, until she vomited. She was still against the wall when her half-hour was up, with no strength to move when they summoned her to the door. A twitch of the shoulders was all she could manage. Her mind was vacant. There was only pain. Even with the guard's hand under her armpit, she could not manage the concrete steps. She stumbled, bruised her knees, cried again and vomited again. When she was returned to her cell, she could only curl on her cot, face to the wall, eyes open, but seeing nothing, because there was nothing in this Hell to see. She didn't scream a few hours later when it was time for her second half-hour out of doors. It was misting and dark enough that the sun seemed already to have set although it was probably no later than three in the afternoon. Valaida could feel the mist settling into her hair, kinking it further. She could feel droplets of water on hair shafts. She didn't have to cry, her hair was crying for her. She drooped against the pie wall until her time was up. In the stairwell she felt as though she was drowning. Her chest was heaving, she was fighting for air. Now she screamed. She didn't want to drown here, she didn't want to die here. She gulped for air and gulped for air, then choked on saliva and found herself shaking. One guard was not enough to return her to her hell. Valaida shook, and she shook, and she shook.

The man before her is probably a doctor. Neither his hands nor his eyes are kind, but they are thorough as they probe and peruse her. All of her senses are fuzzed, her eyes from crying, her ears from the unceasing noise of this place, the bells, the tappings, the gratings, the off-key singing, the groans, but she can decipher the word '*medicin*'. This is a very important word, in fact the most important word, in all the world. With *medicin*, Valaida just might survive this Hell. '*Medicin*,' Valaida manages. '*Jeg behover min medicin.*' I need my medicine. '*Vaersagod.*' Please. '*Vaersagod, vaersagod.*'

Neither the doctor nor the guard reply. Perhaps they haven't heard her; she has barely heard herself. Her mouth is dry, her lips are chapped. She has less strength than sound, and they refuse to understand her. '*Medicinmisbrug*,' says the doctor. Medicine misuse. Iron hands on each arm walk Valaida back into the torment that will last for ever.

She is on her hands and knees when they release her, and remains there as the door clangs shut. The floor of this hell is cold and hard, its finish granular beneath dull paint. Valaida can feel the

255

grains imprinting themselves on the flesh of her hands. Pressing harder on the grains brings a different kind of pain, diamond sharpness that is a distraction from her twitchings and the dull aching of her joints. There is a strip of brightness on the floor two feet before her. Distractions are a good thing. Valaida rocks into the grains and their diamond pain; and the pain brings her music.

Il existe un cité
Au séjour enchanté
Et sous les grands arbres noir
Chaque soir
Vers elle s'en va tout mes espoirs . . .

Paris, Summer 1929

Valada emerges from Chez Victorine and turns left instead of right. Midsummer night doesn't last long in Paris. At 6:15 a.m. full sun has long since washed away the dawn. It'll be a hot one today, but right now a pleasant westerly breeze sneaks round the curves of the rue de Bruxelles, fluttering Valada's dress about her knees as she pauses at the Boulevard Clichy before crossing with the measured gait of someone who's been on her feet for hours selling genuine coloured rhythm to the jazz-crazed patrons of Gay Paree. If she'd turned right instead of left, Valada could be joining the *Blackbirds* gang at Brickie's after hours or maybe Mitchell's American Restaurant further down on the rue Pigalle for 'sausages and hot cakes just like the ones you get back home'.

With so many of the clubs employing Negro American musicians and the *Blackbirds* troupe performing over at the Moulin Rouge, you could mistake Montmartre for Harlem. And it wasn't just entertainers you kept bumping into on the streets. Coloured folks calling themselves writers and artists, and others, who said they were travelling just to travel, flocked into the district day and night, finding their comforts, as ever, in being among their

256

own. To the point that sometimes Valada found herself wondering just where in the hell she was, in Paris or on Seventh Avenue uptown, until she adjusted her point of view to see the domes of the Sacred Heart, perched up there on the Butte just like a crown of giant meringues. There was no Sacré-Coeur in Harlem, or twisting streets that turned in on themselves so mysteriously you lost track of where you were going, but in the end maybe you didn't care so much because you'd find yourself looking at some pretty little fountain or maybe a church, old like you'd never before known old. People said that China was old, but Shanghai hadn't looked old like Montmartre, with its cobble-stoned sidewalks and streets, its wood-below, crumbling-stucco-above shops. The Shanghai streets had been straighter, its buildings looking less like they'd been there since the beginning of time. More like home in a strange kind of way, even though in China there was no way of deciphering the signs, and in Paris at least there were letters you recognized and words you could try to say.

In the solitude she finds in turning left instead of right, Valada has more attention for the particulars of Paris, the shops on her way up the rue Lepic, with their cow tongues in jelly and their cheeses rolled in ash, the intricate ironwork of window balconies, and actual windmills like you saw on plates. It's not often that she encounters coloured wandering the steep climbs of the Butte. Her friends and folk tended to find their accommodation in the small residential hotels of the Flats. Among the free-wheeling citizenry of Montmartre's night life, a body could just as well be on the South Side of Chicago, the difference being the language, and then only just. Valada would be down there herself if it wasn't for Cas. She could be giggling and gossiping, unable to distinguish good from bad champagne or *filet mignon* from *c'est la vie*. Castor McHenry has been her difference.

'You can find a room in the Flats if you want to, but I only ever use this place to practise or when one of Alistair's family is in town. There wouldn't be a question of me cramping your style,' he'd said.

257

Cas' rooms in the Impasse Girardon have a baby grand Steinway, Oriental carpets on the floor, and walls covered with paintings that don't look to be about anything that Valada can recognize. Books are everywhere, in shelves, on tables, on the floor, next to the toilet, a lot of them in French. There's liquor standing around in cut-glass bottles, next to glasses refracting the day's light into rainbows, pillows on the day bed embroidered with mythical beasts; but more than all of the parts, a grounding peace. Valada never knew that a Negro could live this way, but then she'd never been around a Negro like Cas. Their trip across the Atlantic had shown her that he trod a different path, one that led her into surprises, many of which she found pleasing. She wasn't going to turn his offer down for a dark, dank hotel just to be back around the familiar, and besides, they had begun to love one another. Cas McHenry, the best friend she'd ever have.

Their love began on board the *Île de France*. It was Cas' habit to travel the Atlantic on ships of the French Line. The food was better, he said, and the Nordics more liable to leave you in peace. For this in particular, he'd always enjoyed the *Paris*. It was smaller and less grand than its glamorous younger sister, but after a number of crossings, Cas appreciated the older ship's cosy familiarity and knew many of its crew members well. A fire on board the *Paris*, however, had forced a transfer of Cas' reservation from the *Paris* over to the French Line's queen. The *Île de France* staterooms were renowned for their spacious luxury; and if Cas and Valada were going to be working with one another, and only one stateroom was in the budget, it seemed only right that they should share the luxury rather than split into smaller cabins for the sake of a propriety neither one of them possessed. And so they did, travelling like the brother and sister they each wished that they were closer to.

'*You're a twin? I can't imagine there being two of you around.*'

'*Not identical.* Her name is Polly, Pollina.' Who alone in their family knew where Cas found love, but not why he couldn't suppress it since she had managed to do so herself.

With its frosted glass and patterned carpets, its marbled columns and gilded rails, its splendiferous dining room and longest bar, the *Île de France* was a palace dedicated to rich folks' pleasure. Valada and Cas were not the only Negroes on the trip. They shared First Class with a diplomatic delegation from Dahomey, upright-looking gentlemen in stiff collars and sombre suits, and there was a brace of bourgie boys in Third. But Valada and Cas were the most visible Negroes by far. Having paid their tariff, the last thing Cas had in mind was sitting discreetly to the side of white folks' attentions. Like Valada, his equilibrium was unaffected by the sea, and he intended to exploit all that the liner had on offer. After their morning rehearsal and again after lunch, the two would embark on another chapter of what Cas called their *Île-iad*, up to the bridge to chart the horizons, to the stern exploring the mail plane to the point of clambering into the cockpit, down to the engines and the churn of the ship's colossal machinery. Cas had an enthusiasm for the mechanical and a way of thinking that Valada had never seen in a Negro man before. He stood her right up next to a turbine.

'What does this say to you, Valada?'

'What I'm saying is, I don't want to dirty this dress. Cleaning on this tub costs a fortune.'

'It says, "Progress!" Can't you hear it? It says, "Keep me in mind, and you'll know freedom is possible."'

'Cas, what it's saying is, "Chug-a, chug-a, chug-a."'

'You're limiting yourself to the known, Valada. You keep saying that you want to be up there in the sky. Fly, Valada! Fly!'

'Cas, it's saying, "Chug-a, chug-a, chug-a."!' But despite her laughter, beginning to feel what he meant and appreciating that he saw the sky was the place she belonged.

They plugged chimera in the shooting gallery, rode till dizzy on the merry-go-round, danced the tango in the afternoon with a drama that would have dared any sheik into a run for the money. It was Valada's first flirtation with dance apache-style, and she liked to pull it her own way with the odd Black Bottom break.

Valada's breaks tended to confuse both the band and other dancers, but they always sent Cas into cackles of delight. A good deal of their time on the voyage Cas and Valada spent in laughter and, all of their time, the white people around them stared, sometimes in wonder or confusion, sometimes in anger and disgust. Valada was unaccustomed to being just two against the world all day long without a break. On the Shanghai travels she had been part of a larger group, which made the eyes beyond their own easier to ignore. On the *Île de France* at times she felt the scrutiny starting to press; but Cas never let the staring inhibit his living in any way.

'Of course I know they're there,' he said one afternoon. They were promenading the boat deck wearing their masques of carefree smiles, watching the white people watching them. 'But I like to think of them as trees in a forest. You know the trees are there, especially when the wind is stirring about their leaves, but you don't waste your life worrying about whether this one's going to grab you from behind or that one's going to fall on you or if the other one's fruit is rotten. You go about your business, continue along your way. You may even find one you like enough to lean on for a spell, with a trunk shaped to your back, fragrant blossoms, and sheltering leaves, or again, trees may not be to your taste; but if you spend your time worrying about when they might transform themselves into dragons, you'll never get anywhere. They're nature, that's all, just another part of God's creation.'

'Like hurricanes and boll weevils,' countered Valada.

'Or the Grand Canyon and the Mississippi River, challenging things to deal with, but possible, possible.'

'You find the forest friendlier in France?' asked Valada, waving to a young steward who has been smiling shyly in her direction.

'For the day to day, yes indeed,' said Cas, 'because the truth is your average French person has other things on his mind than how he feels about Negroes. Their history isn't tied up with how they feel about Negroes. They went through a war that killed over a million of their men, left another million cripples. You see its evidence everywhere, men with crutches, women in black. If they're thinking about history, they're thinking about that, and maybe, when they see one of us, that a lot of Negro troops helped them win when they finally did. And as for the rich, like the people in our part of this floating pleasure dome, well, they're pretty much the same everywhere. They believe that they own everything and everybody, that nobody's human that isn't like them; but for the most part they're harmless on this side of the water. They're too busy trying to stay what they call "amused" to do most people any harm.'

'Does your Alistair know you're human?' asked Valada, looking beyond two women considering her without discretion from her shoulders to her shoes. She craved their pale, light jersey pleated frocks with the geometric initials, but not the pinched expressions on their red, bee-stung lips.

'Alistair's life hasn't been all blessings, so he knows a few things about want and living without respect,' Cas replied, his eyes taking on shadow. 'At least, that's what I'm choosing to believe.'

'Does he know he's a tree?' asked Valada. A blast of wind vibrating rigging sounded a middle octave B flat.

'That he'd take as a compliment,' Cas returned with a laugh. Then he'd offered his arm, and they'd gone for a cocktail; for Cas dearly enjoyed his drink.

For all his French-speaking, roundabout-thinking elegance, Cas McHenry could play some blues, he understood performance, and he pushed Valada in rehearsal like she'd never been pushed before. They were testing what they could do together, building up their store of numbers, combining Tin Pan Alley with coloured Broadway and uptown blues, Paris sophistication with bring-it-home-to-Mama heat. They used the piano in a remote party room, and sometimes staff on their break would watch. The entertainment level was usually high.

'Sometimes I think you have more talent than you know what to do with!' That's how Cas was liable to start. 'Just what in the hell do you think you were doing with that song?'

261

'What do you think I'm doing?' She, straight into attitude, hands on hips, elbows pokey. 'I'm singing it!'

'I'm getting nothing!' A piano chord for emphasis, usually a thirteenth. 'You're not telling me a thing!'

'I'm giving you stuff! I'm giving you tune and eyes! I'm giving you good-God-Almighty!' A lowdown grind for provocation, generally followed by a sideline snicker.

'I don't want your hips, Valada.' Maybe a Fauré arpeggio for patience. Valada learned about him sometime later. Castor loved himself some Fauré.

'Of course you don't, you goddam faggot, but not everyone I'll be singing to will be looking to find some dick.' Often a steward interrupting with towels and beverage. Cas had taught her to say, '*Merci.*'

'You sure? You never asked me what kind of club this was.'

Valada wanting to strangle him, but somehow managing a kind of laugh. 'What do you want me to do, Cas? I'm killing myself up here.'

'I don't want your death on my hands. I want you to tell me a story.'

'I'm telling you a story!'

'You're giving me noise!'

'This is me, Cas! I'm energy! This is my style! This is what you saw in Chicago, that you said you liked.'

'Give me the energy, but I want some heart.' And if he suspected any real upset, up from the piano, for an arm around her shoulder.

So she worked on heart. She worked hard on heart.

'Tell me please, just what note was that?'

'I don't know . . . A flat. ' A G flat bang on the piano.

'G flat, Valada! Not A! G! You know the difference! You can hear it! You can sing it! Use your head!'

'You wanted heart. I'm giving you heart!'

'I want it all, Valada! Everything you have. All of it!'

'I'm going to wring your scrawny neck! One less nigger in the world, who would care?'

'No me, no Paris job.'

'Forget you, Cas McHenry! I was working when you were still in knickerbocker pants. I will always find a job! I don't need you for a job, you bulge-eye viper!' But she hit the next G flat.

More and more *Île de France* staff were finding the practice room during their breaks until, on the fifth day out, they were joined by the Second Purser. The Purser applauded the music, laughed at the back and forth, then invited Cas and Valada to provide cocktail entertainment that evening in the bar. After some questions in a French which both surprised and pleased the Purser, Cas looked to Valada, who nodded, and then said, *'Nous serons là.'*

'You were looking very pleased with yourself, talking all that *parlez-vous*. It doesn't make you a genius, you know. People I know say they manage without a word.'

'That's just what they expect of us, Valada. You get that much more of an upper hand if you manage to keep them guessing.'

'And if you can't keep that stuff in your head?'

'That doesn't apply to you, Valada. All you'd have to do is decide you wanted to try.'

'And if I didn't?'

'Then you'll regret it. Being lazy has a way of coming back at you. You want to add a trumpet feature this evening?' That was Cas, a regular old Mr Whip and Bait.

'I thought you said the trumpet couldn't be part of the act. You won't be knowing where it will go.'

'I never know where you're going to go, Miss Valada. That's one of the things I like.'

He pushed her past where she thought she could go, and that was one of the things she liked.

Cas decided to spend some money on the night that he and Valada began to love. The cocktail set had gone well. Many of the assembled would be seeing them again in Paris at Chez Victorine, and Cas thought it time for Valada to make her entrance to dining not in one of her Shanghai Russian creations or hot-off-the-truck

Harlem specials but a bought-from-the-shipboard-salon Paris gown. Valada was drawn to an iridescent-spangled, here-I-come confection, but Cas steered her to a simple Lanvin, a cool column of almost gold. There was no budget for jewels, so a silk flower at her neck.

'You go for less, Valada, and they'll know you know.'

'Know what, Mr Expert?'

'That you don't need to try hard. Who you are is quite enough.'

They created a minor stir as they descended the staircase into the salon. There were the usual eyes, holding longer this time, some whispered asides, the odd fluttering of applause. Valada was glad for her trumpeter's diaphragm keeping her upright and still, for her dancer's feet stepping sure in defiance of her nerves and the ship's subtle sway. There was some champagne from the Purser waiting at their table to which Cas gave an approving nod.

'You'll like this,' he said, holding his glass towards Valada for a toast.

'Cas, you know how I feel about all this fancy food,' Valada replied through a dazzling smile displayed for the curious. 'Just please give me a pigfoot and a bottle a beer.'

'I've already ordered you *pieds du porc grillé*,' Cas said as their glasses clicked for a toast.

'Yes, but what are they going to do with them? They never seem to be able to just leave their food alone.'

'Valada, tonight, a favour. Dinner in peace? No complaints? And wine, I'm thinking of an effluence of wines.'

'How much is that?'

'A lot.'

'Well, after enough of it, I'm not gonna care.'

They were finishing their pre-dessert sorbet when the drunk dropped his handkerchief. Cas was starting in on a story of his first misadventure with too much corn liquor, involving a piano recital and a dowager's lace bosom. They were hilarious with the effects of the Purser's champagne and four half-bottles of fancy-labelled

264

wines, two red, two white, Cas' continuing futile attempt to bring Valada to share his love of the fruits of the vine.

'Cas, you're wasting your time, and money.'

'I didn't drink all this by myself.'

There'd been no thought as Cas had offered the handkerchief to the white man, home-trained manners was all. Someone drops something in front of you, you're closer to the object, you pick it up. You don't think about it, you pick it up.

'*I was thinking that you could use it to shine my shoes.*'

They had noticed this drunk man from time to time. He was American, with the elegant profile and luxuriant hair of a motion picture star. He and his wife, who was not so beautiful as he, were travelling with a party intent on the ship's most expensive pleasures, high-stakes gambling, extravagant liquors. Most of their companions were American, but not all. The man's face was flushed, but his smile agreeable. The smile was accustomed to getting what it wished, and now what it was asking was the most natural thing in the world.

'*I figured that that has to be what you're doing in here,*' the smile said. '*This frog ship is so damn classy they dress their shoeshine boy in dinner clothes so he'll be available and close but won't spoil the décor. Has to be the reason I've been seeing you every place I go. I know they haven't been expecting me to share my first-class crossing with a pop-eyed coon.*'

Cas' hand was not shaking as he folded the handkerchief, the ebony of his fingers sharp contrast to the snowy linen with its milky stains. Only a twitch at the corner of his left eye belied the strength of any emotion as Cas handed the handkerchief to a junior waiter who was standing close by, with a casual comment in French. The drunk demanded a translation which the waiter delivered fearfully.

'Monsieur has suggested that I give Monsieur's cloth to the chambermaids to be used in the cleaning of toilets.'

Cas was not a strong man; all of his limbs were spindly, and sometimes Valada thought that a strong wind could carry him off over the ocean like some pickaninny kite; but he showed no fear when the drunk lunged for his throat. As two larger waiters restrained the man, and the Second Purser convinced his party to retire to the lounge, Cas adjusted his lapels and poured himself the last serving of wine. The Purser was stony-faced when he suggested that Cas and Valada might prefer to take dessert and coffee back in their cabin and became even more so when Cas refused. Cas' expression, save for the twitching left eye, was a portrait of calm all the while, despite the drunk's spittle and the Purser's disdain; and Valada had never felt such admiration for a man in all her life.

They went to bed that night without a mention of what had happened, nor anything else if the truth be told, each taking a solace in the ritual of caring for their possessions. The new Lanvin gown was carefully pinned to a satin hanger, the silk shoes stuffed with tissue paper. Cas' sapphire and platinum cufflinks were rubbed with a cloth and returned to their case. They whispered good night and slipped between their sheets as though nothing out of the ordinary had happened, for indeed nothing had. Cas seemed to drop off immediately, but Valada was finding peace more elusive. The wind that had been building throughout the evening had changed the ship's gentle drag into a powerful Eagle Rock, and the cabin was noisy with the clatter of toiletry bottles rattling against one another in the frames that kept them from sliding and shoes flying off their racks to time step against closet doors. Valada was just convincing herself to leave all the ship's business to God and slip into sleep while the going was good when she heard new sounds, a brush-brush-brush and a click-click-click. She sat up in bed to find Cas fiddling with the cabin door. She called his name, but there was no answer as he strode into the corridor clad only in a white cotton nightshirt and the silk stocking cap he pulled tight over his hair every night to ensure it kept its wave in the manner he preferred. By the time Valada had pulled on a robe and shoved her feet into slippers, there was no one in the corridor but a nurse come to minister to a seasick passenger moaning loudly from within the stateroom across the way.

> *I see the lightnin' flashin', I see the waves a-dashin',*
> *I feel this boat a-crashin', I am trying to spread the news . . .*

When Valada finally caught sight of Cas, she would have giggled if she hadn't been so concerned. He looked comical, her friend, with the white shirt flapping about his spidery black calves, thin, ashy feet flopping against the ship's custom carpet, progress as steady as could be despite the increasing pitch of the waves. Like he was in a haunted house olio of an old-time minstrel show, only this act wouldn't be for the amusement of their own. When he got to the end of the present corridor, Cas paused as though listening, and Valada was able to run up and take his arm.

'Cas? Let's go back, Cas. You don't want to go out there.'

But he cried out, 'No!', pushed her away, so violently that she stumbled, and then he turned left. He was heading for the long bar.

'*No, Cas! No! You don't want to go in there!*' There was nothing for her but to follow.

There were very few passengers in the bar that night, the less hardy and more sensate having long since retreated to the womb-like assurances of their staterooms. But dinner's beautiful drunk was there, sprawled out in a corner, vomit splotched yellow-orange across the starched bib of his dinner shirt, a woman not his wife caressing his brow. Some eight of his fellows were finishing the last of a large bottle of cognac, when one caught sight of Cas.

'*Warren, it's the coon! Wake up, man, it's the coon!*'

Cas noticed nothing as he strode straight through the room, not their hooting monkey noises or the roasted peanuts they threw his way or their falling in behind him like some bacchanalian procession crowing, '*Hey coon!*' inviting others they encountered to '*Follow the coon!*' Valada didn't waste her energy entreating the

267

group to be less bestial, but shadowed her friend as closely as she could. The tormenting numbers had almost doubled when Cas turned out into the heavy weather of the deck. In the cloud-broken moonlight, crewmen were securing everything they could find against the increasingly mountainous dimensions of the sea. Torrents of spray had rendered the pitching deck as slippery as glass, and giggling revellers found themselves careening into railings and collapsing onto chaises longues; but Cas' barefoot progress was sure as he headed relentlessly toward the stern. It was the mail plane that he wanted. He reached its platform and started to climb. Valada could see that he was heading for the cockpit. She screamed at him to stop, but her cry was swallowed by the wind. Her friend's saturated nightshirt now clung to his skinny shanks, fully revealing the contours of his genitals, at which the inebriants pointed, hooted, and laughed until at long last the crest of a wave smashed onto the platform, knocking Cas off his feet and out of his trance.

He was disoriented and terrified as Valada helped him to right himself 'Polly?' he asked.

'No, Cas, it's Valada.'

'Oh, Valada! Oh, God!' Valada removed her robe and wrapped it around her friend before guiding him off the platform and onto the deck, where a ship's officer was urging the throng to retire into the safety of their cabins.

'You must forgive them, mademoiselle. Strange things can take hold of the most civilized men on ships. I'm sure they were just having a bit of innocent fun.'

Valada had her own version of innocent fun in mind as the officer summoned a seaman to wrap her and Cas in blankets and escort them back to their room. She wanted to level the whole forest of them, all these white people. She was feeling like her brother Lawrence. Mow them down, pull them up by their roots, chop off their limbs for kindling, and immolate their souls. Maybe then she might feel like smiling, but forgiving, no, or forgetting either. Once back in the privacy of their stateroom Valada prepared a hot bath, which she shared with Cas, for he was panicking without her near. They shared the same bed that night, huddled together, his back to her front, and Valada realized she had never felt so ferociously connected to a man. The strength of emotion made her dizzy but did not ease her into sleep. That did not come until after daybreak. The storm persisted the following day, so their remaining in the cabin drew no particular regard. Their quiet persisted as well. They dozed and played cards. Cas read, Valada practised her trumpet. They needed few words. Their eyes and subdued smiles said it all. Valada was the one who was broody on the next and last day of the voyage when the day dawned bright. She didn't know if she could assume her role.

'I'd like to take your razor and slit a few throats, but I can't because it'd be messy.' And they'd just keep coming, that's what Lawrence said: '*They just keep coming . . .*'

'They might make you walk the plank.'

'And I can't swim.'

Cas took Valada's face in his hands, his slender fingers resting at her temples. 'When we look at them and smile, they'll never know what we have on our minds. What they don't know, they can never control. We've got the upper hand because they don't know us, and we do know them. And it's not all of them. They'll never make me believe that it's all of them.'

'You can say that after last night?'

'If I couldn't, I'd go mad, and I won't give them that power.' Like they have over Lawrence. Valada doesn't want to be like Lawrence.

'So now, Miss Valada, will you join me for a turn around the deck?'

The clouds were billowing white, sunlight sparkled on the sea, and the atmosphere tingled with anticipation of privileged summers awaiting the boat's beautiful people in France. As they walked by the tennis courts, Cas and Valada were approached by the Second Purser, smiling expansively, hands outstretched. He'd had so many compliments with regards to the cocktail performance, would Cas and Valada consider repeating their set this last evening? Cas and Valada smiled, said, yes, and the evening was a great success. As if nothing out of the ordinary had happened, for indeed nothing had.

Valada's mind was on Lawrence on the train from the *Île de France* to Paris. Looking out the window at fields divided by trees shaped like paintbrush tips, villages made out of brown and beige stones, ponds filled with lilies, wondering how Lawrence lived as something he despised, how he sang and danced for people whom he thought should all be dead, whom he'd like to kill himself. How did Lawrence do it? How did any of them do it? She'd left the Toby Time behind because she wanted to move on, to the star and the money. She sang and danced for white people because she wanted to move on. She entertained people who didn't think she was human, who were ignorant and dangerous because they didn't think she was human. Was the star really worth it? Could the money buy that much? Her eyes were tearing. She turned away from the window to search her bag for a hanky and found that Cas was looking at her. He'd put down his book. He handed her the handkerchief from his pocket.

'We do it because we must, Valada, and we do it because we can. We do it because if we didn't tell that story we'd get sick or die because that's what we're supposed to do. That we can do it gives us a whole hell of a lot more freedom than most people in this world, monied white people included, so that makes us lucky. We're in a first class coach to Paris, and we're God damned lucky.'

'So now you're a hoodoo?' asked Valada.

'Just thinking out loud,' Cas replied.

$\mathcal{C}$hapter four

Copenhagen, March 1942

They opened her door, but this time they didn't take her into the pie-shaped yard. She was handed a parcel that contained her own clothes. She didn't know what this meant. There was neither smile nor smirk in the expression of her guard. She was directed to change. Her own clothes' softness and hint of perfume might have brought a sigh of relief, except she didn't know what this meant. Release was too much to hope for; the guard had neither lent a hand when she'd wrestled with the twine, nor turned a back in deference to her modesty. Was she to be handed over to the Germans? She didn't bother to ask a question, for they never answered her questions. Valaida followed the guard's broad back down the corridor, past other cells, which, in this moment, were as silent as tombs, but which Valaida knew to be occupied. There was usually so much noise, the tapping, the off-key singing, the groans.

Why the silence now? Were other prisoners sensing a terrible fate? Valaida shuddered from fear and the need for her drug, but there was comfort in shoes that had been made for her feet.

She was sat in the back of a van with a different guard, a man this time and relatively young. He too was completely closed-mouthed, but Valaida could feel his eyes shyly on her as she struggled to maintain her seat over the jostling cobblestones. If she'd had the energy to engage his eyes she might well have seduced some answers, but she was completely bereft of the necessary will to bend his curiosity into her power. She was weary of young white men's curious eyes. Relief was her only interest, and this he couldn't supply. When the van finally came to a stop and its engine switched off, the young man finally spoke. '*Vi er her*,' he said. We are here. '*Det universitetshospital.*' The university hospital.

The university doctor was more gentle in his pokings and perusals. His voice was firm but not cold, and so Valaida could hold better onto his Danish. 'I'm afraid I have little English, Mrs Snowberry,' he said. 'Would you prefer I spoke French?' Valaida shook her head no. 'You are suffering from medicine misuse. Can you tell me how long you have been misusing medicines?'

Valaida's eyes flooded with tears because she didn't know how to answer. She had only ever used her medicine because she'd needed it to do a job, because it had taken care of the pains. How could that be misuse?

'How long have you been misusing medicines, Mrs Snowberry?'

In Valaida's confusion her tears became sobs, and with the sobs she began to shake. She could not stop shaking. She shook so hard that she slid off of the examining table, but not onto the floor because the doctor broke her fall. 'Get her into a bed,' he said. Into a bed.

The bed is in a very large room with a very high ceiling. There are beds on both sides of the room, more than ten, more than twelve, and there are women in the beds. She is in a room with other people. Her bed is narrow, but wider than her prison cot. The

272

sheets are almost white and starched. More than two hands replace her clothes with a hospital gown, sponge her down, and lay her into the sheets. The pillow has a bit of softness, and there are windows all along the room. Light from the windows is checker-boarding the walls. A woman in white supports Valaida's neck with an experienced arm. '*Drikke dit, Fru Snowberry.*' Drink this. The liquid is thick and bittersweet. Valaida can feel its track into her stomach, and then relief branching into her limbs. Not complete, but something, something. At last, she is warmer. The light on the wall is bright.

> *. . . J'ai deux amours*
> *Mon pays et Paris*
> *Par eux toujours*
> *Mon coeur est ravi . . .*

Paris, Summer 1929

Valada's world and work expanded on the Butte of Montmartre. Cas made her read music and get back to the piano.
　　'*You're rusty, Valada, and you shouldn't let this go.*'
　　'*You know, Mr McHenry, I already have a mother.*'
　　They passed hours playing a notation game of their own devising. They'd play a record on Cas' grand victrola and then see who came closer to writing the music down. The loser had to cook the before-work meal. Valada burned down-home and Cas cooked French-ified. Both acted as if they wanted to outrage the other, but both, in truth, only wanted to please. The laughter continued. When Valada heard Cas' footsteps on the steps, she would feel her heart begin to open and start to bubble inside. It was passion, but unlike any that she had ever felt before. Riffing out from her mind rather than throbbing up from her parts, complementing as it did the high dimensions of his mind and not the aggressions of a hunt. For the first time in her life Valada had the feeling that

here was someone who really knew her, who had looked at her, could see her and liked all he saw, what he knew to be true as opposed to what maybe ought to be there, what he thought might be there, or not really caring one way or the other because the chase was the thing. She'd never even suspected that you could know someone this way, or even paused to think about it really, at least not after James. If Cas had been drawn the usual way, he might have become the love of her life; but then maybe he was the love of her life because there was no question of getting entangled between some sheets, because Valada isn't interested in entanglements. Valada has no time for entanglements, so Cas is damn near perfect, and she seems to add joy to his life as well.

Cas loves Paris, but he misses his home. Paris allows him to be who he is, has brought him luxury and love, but Cas misses the family who couldn't begin to know him, when family had earlier been the fulcrum of all his strength. Valada hails from home. Valada knows Cas, yet loves him, knows him in a way Alistair never can, and embraces him. Valada even gets along with Alistair, and Alistair, with his supercilious mouth and febrile brilliance, is not an easy man. The second son of an English baronet, shunted off from early childhood to avoid familial embarrassment, Alistair has cultivated an acerbic wit and streaks of perversity that have fazed many comers, but not Valada. In the face of Valada's lack of dismay, Alistair stopped trying so hard to be difficult and instead tried to convert her to the religion of the new art. It didn't work.

'I don't see the point,' she said. 'If someone says he's painting a tree, I want to see a tree. If I have to look at a woman's naked body hanging on some wall, then I should know it's bosoms on her front and not some blocks of wood.'

Exhortations about people trying to represent all sides of a thing at once and artists taking their inspiration from Africa and the pagan rhythms of jazz did not impress.

'I know you're not going to sit here eating my food telling me I get my music swinging from some tree. You need to be afraid that I won't cut you up and throw you in the pot.'

274

The truth was that Valada has little patience for talking up and down about what an artist painted, a dancer danced, or a musician played. If you couldn't do a thing yourself, then you couldn't be an expert no matter how much you thought, and how many 'isms' you could name. Cubism, Expressionism, Surrealism, Futurism, and Cas not just humouring Alistair, but as enthralled by the words as he. On the mornings Valada suspected there might be too many 'isms' on the Butte, she would come out of Chez Victorine and turn right instead of left.

Valada nurtured what she played from by turning right instead of left. Food was the sweet familiarity of Bessie's laughter as much as catching up on the dance moves missed in the Shanghai years and a platter of sausage and grits. The *Blackbirds* flocked together doing for one another, firing hot combs, massaging pulled muscles, loaning a string of beads for a date with the boy who'd been lingering by the stage door of the Moulin Rouge. Sometimes Valada would stay down in the Flats until just before time to change for the night. She'd loll about Bessie's bed, enjoy the firm curves of Bessie's back, and not wonder for a while how she was going to catch up with Josephine. Which is not to say they didn't talk about Josephine. The *Blackbirds* talked about Josephine. Even more so than in New York, everyone in Paris talked about Josephine.

Josephine is not in Paris during the summer of '29. She is touring the world with her Italian, Pepito, whom Bricktop has dubbed the 'no-account count', so Valada is unable to challenge Josephine in person for the coloured crown of Paris, though what would she have done if it had come down to that? A duel in Montmartre at sundown had landed Sidney Bechet in jail, and besides, unlike so many of her colleagues, Valada didn't carry a gun. A cutting contest on who could fling the best Black Bottom? But Valada keeps hers covered, if not insulated, so what kind of playing ground was that? There'd be no contest again in singing. Josephine could barely carry a tune; but then Josephine's appeal didn't flow from her voice. The allure that had been driving white men to suicide and madness seemed to be based on things that

275

had no foundation in the real; yet every coloured woman in Paris had to contend with the phenomenon of Josephine. Was she as abandoned and *sauvage* as *La Bakaire*? Did she spread her legs as wide? Wiggle her posterior so seductively? Did she smile so sweetly, titillate so suggestively? Or if she was not so magnificent a beast, was she as welcoming and understanding as Bricktop, *la patronesse extraordinaire*? Did she soothe the egos of the rich, indulge their high jinks no matter how outrageous? Valada knows that she falls into neither camp. Her body is not the instrument she manipulates for public pleasures, but then Valada couldn't take off her clothes for audiences even if she wanted to. Her body's flirty but not long-limbed and slinky, and she wants more attention for herself than naturally comes a hostess' way. Singing and dancing and playing the trumpet and now sometimes the piano as well, this was the way for Valada, but Chez Victorine is small. All the Montmartre clubs are smaller than the most intimate Harlem clubs, and although the customers claimed to come looking for jazz, what they really wanted was background music for their own personal the-atricales. In so little a space, Valada's energy is loud. She's worked on temperance with Cas, but the truth is that she chafes at having to mute both her horn and herself, and Cas is not sympathetic.

'You are so impatient, Valada!' is what he said. 'You haven't been here but a month. You could stay here, develop your own fol-lowing. More space would come. You'd find it easier to be yourself over here, you know. It wasn't white people keeping you from playing your horn back home in the Nest. The French don't have so many notions about what a Negro woman should or shouldn't do. I know they have these strange ideas of what we're supposed to be, but they don't care about us or those ideas enough to take the time and trouble necessary to keep us in a box.'

Yes, Valada has felt this, but deep down she doesn't trust them. How can you really trust anybody who can't or won't comprehend who you are?

'You seem to like the living, the perfume and dresses and the Perrier-Jouet. You can't tell me it's so bad.'

No, she can't say it's so bad, but Valada is impatient. She wants to shout from the rafters ideas she's been developing on the Butte. She needs to be in a show. Doing the right things in the right show would force the men at the Nest Club to listen. One of the reasons she's come to Paris is to impress Lew Leslie, the maker of coloured stars, who is in Paris with his *Blackbirds*. Now it's time for Valada to catch the impresario's eye, but Cas is not impressed.

'Just what do you want from Lew Leslie, Valada? You don't hold with Josephine running naked in the jungle, but it's OK to dance in front of a giant watermelon with your head wrapped in a rag? I thought you left the South to keep the cotton out of your hair, and now you want to work for a man that makes his money keeping us down on that plantation. You're beyond that, Valada. That doesn't have to be your style. Stay in Paris. You'll do better in Paris.'

'I want to show Lew Leslie what I can do, Cas. There's a party for the *Blackbirds* next week at a place called the Salle Pleyel. It's being given by some big society women. People I bet you know, Cas, you or Alistair. Lew Leslie will be there, Cas. If we performed at that party, he would see what we can do.'

Cas had riffled through three measures of the sonata he was composing. He'd been working on the piece for more than two years, and in these weeks, with Valada around, he had finally progressed because, he said, she'd pushed through the wall he'd put up between Paris and home.

'I couldn't find the way to combine the bits of my life before now, but with you around I've been hearing how to gumbo.'

'Creole's not really my style, Castor. In Chattanooga we were more partial to fricassee.'

Cas' expression was pensive at the piano and just a little bit sad. 'I wear cork for no one, Valada, not even you.'

Valada placed her yellow-brown hand on her friend's coal black cheek. 'I don't think cork will be necessary, but maybe just a touch of white around your lips?'

Copenhagen, March 1942

Valaida opens her eyes. It is dark but not so dark as it was in the prison. Once again, she is unsure of where she is. She turns her head. There is a lamp on a table at the end of this room, and a shadowy figure sitting close to its light. She begins to remember. She is no longer in the prison. She is somewhere where someone gave her relief; but the relief is beginning to fade. She is feeling the hunger. She wonders what would happen if she approached the figure at the table, but in this bed is more comfort than Valaida has felt in months. The figure looks at its wrist, closes a book, and stands. It is slender, skirted, and moves quietly from bed to bed. Not a guard, a nurse, sometimes just looking, sometimes murmuring, sometimes placing a hand on a torso or brow as she makes her rounds. Valaida pulls herself to an upright position, for she is hungering and cannot wait her turn. The nurse looks over, but continues as she'd planned. Tears are streaming down Valaida's face when the nurse reaches her side.

'You are hungry, Mrs Snowberry?' Valaida nods in response. 'I am instructed to give you something, but only a very small amount.'

Valaida's tears move into small sobs of relief. The milk is warm when it comes, with only the faintest trace of bitter; but in the tasting Valaida is already better. Better.

> . . . *Ma savane est belle*
> *Mais à quoi bon le nier*
> *Ce qui m'ensorcelle*
> *C'est Paris, Paris tout entier* . . .

Paris, Summer 1929

The *Blackbirds* party at the Salle Pleyel. Valada had heard of Paris parties from her *Blackbird* friends, parties where Negroes provided amusements for white folks' frolics, with not all of the music being performed from the bandstand, or all of the stepping disporting from the dance floor; parties where high-toned coloureds pretended they were French, with poetry readings and cocktails passed around on trays. Parties all night long and through all the days, as though work was not a factor in a citizen's life. Valada had entertained constant revellers at the Chez Victorine; but these parties were not her life, not as a nightclub entertainer. Valada's parties tended to be in the morning and far more subdued. Laughs before noon over hotcakes and beer, behind the after-hours shutters of Montmartre's small clubs; girls' games played in scanties in the rooms and halls of Montmartre's small hotels. The Salle Pleyel party was a departure for Valada in Paris. More like the glitter of First Class on the *Île de France*, with the same interior expanse of First Class on the *Île de France* but a great big difference in the numbers of coloured flaunting the glamour, striking the poses, sharing the laughs. Elegant white women were passing the trays, aristocrats according to Cas. ('The Vicomtesse de Noailles? I can't believe this, Valada. Shit, the Princesse Murat!') White people were there in their glamour and their numbers, but they were the onlookers for once, seemed on the defensive for once, laughing too brightly with scurrying eyes, skirting the edges, drinking too quickly, choking on food, as if perhaps overwhelmed for once by the exuberant good spirits of dark people resplendent.

The Salle Pleyel foyer is high and wide, with a domed rotunda, geometric tile-work and wrought iron railings similar to those on the *Île de France*, in the style Cas has explained as Art Deco.

'*It's about living in modern times, Miss Valada. It's to do with speed and beauty and the future all at once.*'

Right for tonight. There's space here in the Salle Pleyel, space equal to Valada's energy, space where she can show out. Move on to her future.

Cas had been willing to put on a show. He didn't need to, this she knew. At season's end, Cas and Alistair planned to travel the northern hills of Italy then maybe on to Turkey. '*Alistair has a fascination with the cruelties of Byzantium.*'

Valada didn't understand Cas's references at least a third of the time, but she understood that he needn't attract more custom to Chez Victorine. Cas planned to compose after this season and away from Paris. '*This party won't go on for ever, and things may get messy when it's done. I'd rather be someplace where the music won't be drowned out by the din.*' The show-out at the Salle Pleyel Cas was effecting just for her.

'*I'll never forget this, Cas.*'

'*Don't think that I'll let you.*'

They'd chosen 'My Special Friend is Back in Town' by Andy Razaf, a lyricist that gave a body any number of things to play with. It was good that they had spent so many hours working on their routine because aside from performance order, there is no order to this party and no stage either. The performers just took their places on the floor and grabbed for the attentions of the circulating revellers around them. More challenging than any venue Valada has played as yet, and with more at stake, but she is feeling calm as she takes her place next to Cas. They exchange a smile, and he strong-arms the first chords with all the weight of his classical training. Heads turn, and Valada's smile becomes more flirtatious.

She starts out humming to Cas' tinkling, beating time to the tinkling, her trumpet not in sight. '*Hmm-um, hmmm-um.*' Her smile getting broader now, more in the know. '*Hmmm-um.*' Until . . .

It can rain, it can snow, it can sleet, it can blow,
Hey, baby, I don't give a hang!
You can read it in my face something soon
Will take place,
I'm saying good-bye to the gang . . .

Then Cas coming in with a 'what you say?'

. . . I'm acting like a nut,
No, I'm not crazy, but
My special friend is back in town . . .

280

Valada is back and forth against Cas' baritone, flirting 'round the lyrics until she can contain herself no longer. She is sashaying around the floor, putting down steps as complement to the lyric.

Of course, when we meet on the street
Merely stop to say,　　　　　　[flippity-slap!]
'Howdy do. How are you?　　　　[pasmala-stepping]
After that, be on your way . . .　　[shoulder shake with a
　　　　　　　　　　　　　　　　　pretty-feet scissor]

She's twirling around Cas' bench to pick up the hidden trumpet, Cas following her with eyes that are saying, 'What is this girl up to?' She's blurting out a fanfare so now everybody's taking note. She's alternating song lines with brass measures, with everyone taking note, cosying up against Cas and the guys with everyone taking note. She's sitting down on the piano bench, and now Cas is scared.

. . . Take back this, take back that –
After all, they're yours.　　　　[careful placement of the
　　　　　　　　　　　　　　　　trumpet on the piano]
Take your dog, take your cat,
Or he'll think you're Santa Claus . . .

Taking over at the keyboard, with Cas looking. 'Damn!'

Excuse me while I laugh
But I just hid your photograph.
My special friend is back in town . . .

She is singing the sass, accompanying herself on the piano.

. . . If you don't see no lights
Don't you ring my bell tonight,
My special friend is back in town . . .

She finishes with flourishes that are the fruit of Cas' cajoling, looking triumphant into his eyes with the party wild applauding. Cas is smiling, 'You did it!' and Valada is knowing, 'Yes.'

. . . My special friend is back in town . . .

Returning to the party after her dress change, Valaida's blood is surging with adrenalin and the fizz of good champagne, surging down to her fingertips and all around her scalp, as though she is wearing a skullcap full of starlight. The silver lamé of her knock-off Lucien Lelong is slapping against opalescent silk stockings, her legs still moist with the sweat of her performance as she moves through a gauntlet of accolades with Cas at her side.

She recognizes the bourgie boys from the *Île de France*, and then, up ahead, there he is. Lew Leslie, looking at her. She'd spotted him during the performance. It hadn't been hard. He'd been standing apart from both the white guests and the coloured, keeping his own counsel with his expensive, ill-fitting suit and a whiskey in his hand. No canapés, no champagne. Looking. Dark hair plastered across a low forehead and piercing eyes, looking. *Yes, look at me. That's what I want, Lew Leslie, you looking at me.* Cas escorts her into position then eases away into the crowd.

'Valada Snow. I liked what you did. With the trumpet and the singing. Then the piano. Very classy. You always work as a pair?' There is no music in his voice. His expression is neutral.

'No, my work with Mr McHenry has been just for this summer.' Valada measures her smile so it is pleasant but not too eager, relaxes the muscles around her lips, willing them not to quiver.

'So maybe you're flexible as well as versatile. You work New York?' His fingers are thick. There is hair on his knuckles and his eyes do not waver.

'Don't we all?' Her heartbeat is pronounced but slow, her voice pleasant and even, or so she hopes.

'Then why don't I know you?' Is the look predatory? No. That's not said to be his game, trading in coloured pussy.

'Who's to say? You keep busy. I've been travelling.' She can feel eyes watching, Cas', others', and some making a point not to see.

'On the T.O.B.A. circuit?' Now his eyes consider the package, without heat or innuendo, as he might consider a statue. Valada tenses the muscles in her behind, then her legs to create the subtlest rippling movement beneath the silver lamé.'

'Not for years and years. I've done a lot in Chicago, but also Batavia and Shanghai.' She pulls her shoulders quietly backward, lifting her breasts just that bit upward, willing her eyes to be at once passive, energetic, and direct. His return to neutral having finished their inspection.

'You don't say? Shanghai. China. Lot of Chinks in China.' It is where they come from. 'Well, Valada Snow, I usually have something going. I may keep you in mind.' Nothing else, but then Valada had gotten what she wanted, and that wasn't conversation. Cas returned to her side as Lew Leslie threaded his solitary way through the Salle Pleyel and the *Blackbirds* band started in with 'Papa Dee Da Da'. Valada could glimpse two brown-skinned young men over Cas' shoulder in top hats and tails, one of them carrying a cane.

'So, will he be finding you a place on the plantation?' Cas asked.

'I've been really loving you tonight, Castor. Don't force me to change my mind.'

'My apologies, milady. Did he like you?'

'I think so.' The boys, they were hardly more than boys, were now together across the dance floor. The taller one, with the cane, strutted with a head-high kick, toe pointed, slim, elegant, a freeze and a melt in perfect time. They were good together, freezing and melting, kicking, freezing and melting, but the taller one was the show. Cas has followed Valada's eyes.

'The Berry Brothers. Very sharp, very cute,' said Cas. 'Especially Ananias.' He was the older brother. Nyas, he was called. Valada had been hearing of the Berry Brothers. They'd been causing waves with good reason.

'Not your taste,' said Valada.

'But possibly yours,' Cas replied.

283

'Not this evening,' laughed Valada. 'I'm not planning to cause any confusions this evening. Your arm please, Mr McHenry.'

'At your disposition, Miss Snow,' said Cas, offering an arm, then covering it with his hand. His eyes are too bright, effort bright, but Valada chooses not to notice. 'Might I suggest a triumphal process around the room and then a cleverly turned Black Bottom.'

> . . . *Le voir un jour*
> *C'est mon reve joli* . . .

Cas took Valada up the Eiffel Tower on her last day in Paris in the summer of '29. She hadn't been before. Time was so limited in the world of nightclub entertainment, outside attentions as well. Valada's glimpses of Paris had been restricted to the Butte, broader than most of her *Blackbird* friends, but in truth not so broad at all, for where was there room for Paris in a mind filled with notes, steps, and ambition with only the smallest niche for affections? Here, in Paris, Cas has occupied the fair portion of that niche. Valada was happy to have her arm lightly through his as she viewed the grey, sand, and green symmetries of Paris. It was a beautiful city, but the comfort of Cas' affection was more appealing to Valada than the visual glories of Paris. She would miss this friend, whom she could sense, even through her ambitions, might be the best she would ever have. They lunched on a tourist-crowded *bateau mouche*, ignoring the normal hostilities of their white compatriots to savour the wonders of Notre Dame and the Île-St-Louis. The breezes were gentle, smelling of old water, white wine, and *pommes frites*.

'You could come with us,' Cas said. 'Alistair told me to ask you again. You could work on your music as a woman of decadent leisure. There's no guarantee that Leslie meant what he said.'

'Gotta make him mean it,' Valada replied. 'He's provided an opening. It's my job to work the key.' She placed a hand on one of his. It was warm, but dry. 'It's not easy leaving you, you know.'

'The truth now, Valada. I'll have flown out of your mind as soon as you hit that boat and start playing with that boy.'

284

'He's young,' she grinned.

'You'll make him older,' Cas replied. They had held hands tight across the table, so tight that rings bit into musicians' fingers, and still they didn't stop. They'd interlocked fingers and savoured Paris.

After their boat trip on the Seine, Cas and Valada walked the streets and boulevards in the area of the Champs-Elysées, coveting the luxuries, gossiping about the crowds, cutting an impromptu one-step to a busking accordianist and the amazement of a crowd. At the salon of Jeanne Lanvin, Cas purchased for Valada her first bottle of Arpege, to complement the dress from the *Île de France* and 'to keep me with you from time to time', but he needn't have worried.

Valada started to play with Nyas Berry on her voyage back to the States, found Lew Leslie wasn't ready for her in New York, and so travelled back through Europe as the girl lead in a Louis Douglas review, but she never lost her sense of Cas McHenry, at once as sweet, complex, cutting, lingering, challenging, and reassuring as the most personal of perfumes.

. . . J'ai deux amours
Mon pays et Paris . . .

hapter five

Copenhagen, March 1942

She is feeling safer here, here in the closed psychiatric ward of the National Hospital, the *Rigshospitalet*, safer than she has since she started understanding the meaning of war, ten months after she and her man and manager Earl Sutcliffe Jones had arrived in Scandinavia from Paris.

She'd had a good run in those ten months. Three months in Sweden and Norway, including some of her best recording ever in Stockholm with white boys that knew their way around their instruments, praise be to God, and were capable of stomping it down. Not thinking about the war rolling out further south. That was one of the reasons to get the hell out of Paris, to get away from the constant, tiring talk of the It's-coming! It's-coming! war. Jumping across that little strait of water from Sweden to Copenhagen and six glorious weeks in its National Scala Theatre.

The audiences just loving her, really happy that she was sharing with them what she had to give, with less of the intellectual blases that sometimes set the tone further south; she singing well and blowing up a storm.

Everything going well, right into the following year, so well that she and Earl decided to stay on in Denmark when the American Embassy suggested they leave, go home to the United States because the 'situation in Europe had become too dangerously volatile to ensure the safety of American citizens'; but when had American crackers ever had anything constructive to say about the 'safety' of their darker compatriots? No, Valaida Snow Berry and Earl Sutcliffe Jones were doing just fine and dandy, thank you. They preferred to stay where work was plentiful and the white folks were friendlier. Things were quiet on the work front in the early months of 1940, but nothing wrong with that. It was good to relax every now and again, and her medicine was easily come by. Why ever should they worry? Like Earl had said so many times in so many places, these white folks' arguments had nothing to do with them.

They had awakened late as usual on 9 April 1940. Valaida had heard what she'd imagined to be thunder in the early morning hours, not that April was a month for thunderstorms, not that thunderstorms were a common feature of Danish weather, but it was hardly an hour for analysis. She'd turned over and gone back to sleep. There'd been other noises as well not long thereafter, poundings on the door, a muffled cry, Danish that was hard to distinguish: *Krigs* or *kridt*? *Tysk* or *tis*? *Tis* meant pee, which Valaida went to do, after which she'd climbed back into bed and sleep once more. When she and Earl finally arose, it was the preternatural quiet that had struck her as strange. Danes were not Parisians or Shanghai Chinese or New Yorkers; they weren't given to boisterous noise in the streets; but Copenhagen was a city. There were cars and trucks. There were horses and carts. There were bicycles and their bells, the sounds of footsteps on pavement; but this day there was nothing. As neither Valaida nor Earl was given to parting curtains or opening shutters – 'We don't need no curious crackers intruding their noses into our business' was the way that Earl put it, and Valaida had to agree – so Valaida and Earl didn't learn the source of the silence until they went out for coffee at their usual café, only to find it closed.

The entire street was virtually deserted save for the odd clutch of elderly and children standing near doorways. No, cowering near doorways, not standing, fear as palpable to them as the walls near which they stood. All of the surfaces were littered with small green leaflets, printed in what looked to be Danish, so neither Valaida nor Earl bothered to pick one up. There was a rumbling noise again, sonorous and steady, and, as Valaida and Earl walked in the direction of its sound and the closest large avenue, they found themselves joining an ever-increasing throng of sombre Danes, looking far paler than usual even for them, looking, in fact, like shrouds on the dead, pushing their bicycles, saying absolutely nothing. Valaida and Earl saw the trucks when they reached the avenue. The rumbling came from the trucks, which were filled with German soldiers, *tysksoldaten*. *Tysksoldaten* with guns were lining the streets, some with grenades at the ready. Some Danes, Nazi sympathizers with armbands and broad smiles, were moving among the *tysksoldaten*, serving them pastries and coffee, but they were comparatively few. The majority was silent, wide-eyed, dumbfounded. Earl's hand was wet when he clutched Valaida's arm. The white folks' war had come to Denmark.

It hadn't been so bad to begin with, not what you'd choose for yourself naturally, but not what you'd come to think of as 'war'. The Germans told the Danes that they were 'protecting them' from the aggressions of Britain, 'preserving their neutral stance' in a war that was not their concern. All that the Germans wanted in return was complete cooperation and access to the butter and bacon that the Danes produced in such abundance. No one with any sense thought that that was all there was to it – it sounded like sharecropping when it was explained to Valaida, which never had been or ever would be anything but false grins and broken promises – but 'cooperating' meant that war in Denmark was not what Valaida had seen in newsreels of war in Spain or Abbysinia. There were no bombs, no shootings, no buildings in flames, no screaming babies in ragged clothes, no staggering lines of refugees. In Copenhagen there were just Germans everywhere, with their guns in hand, their tanks all over the streets, their helmets that made them look the evil knights in one of Alvada's long-ago storybooks, their flags, their attitude. They stared whenever they saw Valaida and Earl, stared longer and harder than any other European white people had ever done; but in the beginning Valaida convinced herself that it was just a matter of degree. How different was walking between a bunch of Germans from walking down a Southern sidewalk lined with crackers just hoping that they could find some excuse to lynch you? Not so different, easier in fact.

On April 10th, the day after the occupation, Valaida and Earl, who lived as man and wife, were questioned by Danish police of the Alien Division, the ones who spoke fluent English. Strictly routine, they were assured. The United States was not at war with Germany, and so as American citizens, Valaida Snow Berry and Earl Sutcliffe Jones were not enemy aliens. Given the situation, it would be advisable for them to leave Denmark at the first opportunity, complicated now, of course, by the new situation, but in the meantime, Valaida would be permitted to work when things went back to normal. As though occupation was some visit from relatives you'd rather not be bothered with. White folks did love to wrench around the meanings of words. In the meantime Valaida and Earl would be issued with ration cards like everybody else. Very decent white people, the Danes. You had to give them their due. Valaida had flashed the best of her smiles and before too long, as promised, she was back in work; and, in her work, there was much to enjoy.

If her audiences had been appreciative before the Germans arrived, they seemed absolutely ecstatic to be in her presence now. To the Danes, particularly the younger ones, jazz music seemed to be more than entertainment, it seemed to be providing them a particular kind of release. Folks said that the Nazis had no truck with jazz music, that they called it a product of lower races, Jews as well as Negroes, and this, among the Danes, seemed to become part of the music's appeal. Listening to it, dancing to it was a way to get back at the Germans. Valaida had never seen white kids reacting to the music like they did in Denmark after the Germans arrived. She'd seen newsreels of American white kids lindy-hopping with energy and flare, but she'd never seen that kind of ability in Europe. Moving to jazz and blues rhythms just didn't seem part of what European white people could do, but something had gotten into the blood of these young Danes. They would come to the clubs and concerts dressed in what looked to be uniforms, brown stetson hats and long jackets over bright yellow or red sweaters and baggy slacks for the boys, short skirts and equally bright sweaters for the girls, with funny cork platforms glued to the shoes on the feet of both sexes, and from start to finish they would be up and dancing as though their lives depended upon it. Taking to the music and dancing in a way that reminded Valaida how folks did back home, as though music was the one way that they were allowed to feel free. Food came from this kind of public.

If Valaida had been sometimes falling into wondering what it all meant these last couple of years, moving from country to country, city to village, half the time playing for Caucasians who hardly knew up from down, then performing for these Danish kids washed that kind of ennui away. They'd come up to her after performances wanting her autograph on their school caps. When they saw her in the streets, she could feel a shy reverence in their regard. Oftentimes they smiled, sometimes they dared the occasional wave. It made walking through German soldiers a bit easier to deal with, because they were nerve-racking, these Nazis, with their tailored uniforms, cold stares, and the sense that they could do with you whatever they pleased; but with this Danish public,

Valaida had a sense that if the Germans pounced, she would have a safe place to run to, and in return she wanted to give the Danes all that she had to give. She found herself spending less time with Earl and his substances and more time with her music.

Which made it all that much harder for Earl. Occupation was a tough one for Earl, who had never done well under anyone else's rules. Black men had always had to be wary of white men in America, but at least after slavery-time a body could roam, hit the rails or the streets, breathe the air, be slick or act the fool. A body had a number of choices. Occupation was about the limitation of choice and had brought with it curfews, as in everyone off the streets at 8 p.m. Wherever you were at that time was where you were supposed to stay until six the next morning. Being cooped up in one place indoors every night was just not how Earl lived, but Earl was afraid of the Germans. No shame in that, most folks with any sense were afraid of the Germans; but Earl hated the fact he was afraid. He wasn't about to admit to the fear, so as weeks passed into months, he became more irritable and evil. Even more than before, he spent the bulk of his moving hours in the taking and commerce of substances. While substances as such weren't illegal in Denmark, making a nuisance of yourself was. When transport back to America became possible that August in a ship that was leaving from Petsamo, Finland, Earl was not given a choice by the Alien Division; he was deported.

The authorities had wanted Valaida to leave as well, but she had contracted to perform for three weeks in the northern Denmark city of Århus from which the club-owner refused to release her. With her complete cooperation. The special circumstances of the Occupation had contrived to make Valaida a star in Denmark, and what would be waiting for her back in the States? Better to stay where she was actually loved, and she had been tiring of Earl anyway with his stupors and impotent complaints. She had ways to the medicine she needed for her pains, and there were other, more winsome ways for her to spend her time.

Talk about your handsome misters
That you don't see in the pictures,
Yes, he's that way, lovable and sweet . . .

She'd seen the young man at a number of dates. He was hard to miss if you had an eye for beauty. Tallish, high-browed with an abundance of golden hair, a lush mouth for a Nordic. Quietly but expensively dressed, a bit in Cas' style, but without the faggot flair. He had a concentrated way of listening, without the frenzy of the lindy-hoppers. She'd found herself smiling whenever she saw him. Unlike Karol in Shanghai, he asked to be introduced. Norbert Nilsson was his name. He immediately invited her out for a coffee, and she just as immediately complied. He spoke an elegant English. There was a scar near the cleft of his chin. He knew and respected the music. He saw, in its amalgam of intellect and earth, the key to salvation in the damned century in which they lived. In close proximity, his eyes were serious and green. Valaida found both them and him appealing. They began spending time together, which increased after Earl was sent home.

With Norbert as her guide and curfew amending the rhythm of her days, Valaida was introduced to Copenhagen in sunlight, the beauty of its formal gardens, the fairy-tale details of its palaces, the expansive dimensions of its squares that were managing to maintain their grace despite the intrusions of German troops and tanks. It became fun, thrilling even, to adopt the silent resistance of the 'cold shoulder' with Norbert at her side, to walk through formations of German soldiers as though they didn't exist, ignoring the bicycle-riding bands of Danish Nazi youths with their leather boots and chin straps, their aggressive Nazi songs. Norbert even got Valaida on a bicycle for the first time in her life, leading her out into the countryside to picnic in a meadow. Swans, wildflowers. Like one of Alvada's storybooks. They had returned to town by tram, though. Trumpet-playing and singing had blessed Valaida with sufficient wind for all kinds of exercise, but her behind had not been prepared for two hours on a bicycle seat. Sitting was not her preferred activity for more than a day, and for this she'd demanded contrition. Norbert's contrition was like the young man himself, serious, innocent, and tender; and, innocently too, he brought Valaida as his guest to a family lunch celebrating the visit of a favourite aunt and uncle.

The proportions of the rooms in the Nilsson home were unlike any Valaida had ever seen. The ceilings were high, the windows long and many-paned, the floorboards were laid out in geometric patterns, the walls painted subtle shades of blue and grey. Porcelain and silver vases tumbled with flowers. Portraits glowered from gilded frames. Norbert's family was old and prominent and more than gracious given its utter dismay at Norbert's companion. They were ten around the damask-covered table, Norbert's parents, the surgeon and his wife, the aunt and uncle, three younger siblings, an elderly woman whose relationship was never clearly explained, and then, of course, Norbert and Valaida themselves. Valaida silently blessed Cas McHenry, her time on the *Île de France*, and hence her familiarity with the phalanx of cutlery on either side of her hand-painted plates. Conversation was subdued. There were a few smiles, occasionally, from the children, in her direction, but no laughter. Valaida had never been in a white person's family home before, and as she chewed her food as delicately as she could muster, she had a feeling of contrasting strength that this was not something to be repeated. She fought against shifting about in her seat. She was finding the entire experience decidedly strange. Soporific and strange.

After the dessert of hand-picked berries and cream, the family retired to a salon, where Norbert was cajoled into joining his mother, his uncle, and younger sisters in the playing of some favorite piece of chamber music. Norbert's hand had been on Valaida's arm while his sisters pleaded their cause. His fingers pressed into Valaida's flesh gently before fetching his viola out of its case, a gesture that did not go unnoticed by the aunt who was distributing the parts, who flicked a glance to her brother, Norbert's father, who gazed resolutely in turn at both his son and the guest, who had the temerity not to lower her eyes. The family members were accomplished musicians who played with concentration but, again, no smiles; and Valaida found her mind and eyes wandering as notes wove back and forth through the rarefied air. The pattern in the sheer white curtains looked to be some kind of vine. The pale window frames were reminding her of bones. What in the world was Norbert thinking by bringing her into this place?

The heavy gold of the old woman's earrings had lengthened her lobes until they seemed more like tongues lapping against the slack flesh of her neck. Was he getting confused about the nature of their relationship? No, no, he couldn't be that foolish, but how could Valaida know what might be running through a Danish boy's mind? The younger daughter was playing the cello with flair, holding it between her knees like some high-spirited pony, bowing it with flicks that brought to mind a riding whip in the hand of an actress with piled-up hair, in one of those movies where the women wore voluminous skirts. Or one of the prostitutes Earl would frequent when he had an appetite for welts on his back. Thinking of what Earl would make of the Nilssons produced a percolation of laughter that Valaida stifled with a cough, which came during a quiet passage in the music, resulting in uncensored glares from older Nilssons that caused cramping in Valaida's stomach as she valiantly fought to suppress her desire to roll. Norbert's surprised look from over his viola brought a leak of urine to Valaida's crotch. After normalizing her breathing, Valaida again looked Dr Nilsson straight in the eye. *You needn't worry*, her look said. *I have no desire to be a lady, which I will be making plain to your son the moment we pass out of your door.* Dr Nilsson nodded and relaxed his shoulders, and without further ado, the music continued pleasantly to its closing.

> . . . *No one else can hold a candle,*
> *What a precious thing to handle,*
> *Yes, he's that way, lovable and sweet . . .*

During her sweet summer of 1940, Valaida chose not to study on the meaning of war, or conceive that war could nudge the world of an entertainer on top of her game; but changes came with the fall. As the days shortened and the temperature cooled, Denmark's outdoor venues closed. Work was still to be had, but the feeling of brightness was gone. The normal winter withdrawal of the Danes had been exaggerated by the war. They had to use that much more energy than usual worrying about themselves, how they were going to deal with rationed food and limited fuel, how they were going to hold on to sanity and integrity while being 'protected' by the Germans, and had that much less energy with which to be infatuated with a coloured girl who played a horn. Valaida too found herself withdrawing into the darkness. She was less often in the company of upstanding young Danish men, her musicians, who, after Earl's departure, were insulation between herself and the Germanized cold. She spent more time by herself, comforting the pains that were increasing as the temperatures dropped, and more time with the few who understood the demands of such pain; but she was known, really known, by no one, and for the first time in her life Valaida felt darkness seeping into her core. Her days often began with an unfamiliar tightness around her heart, something known by others through millennia as worry.

Of course Valaida had felt strong concerns over the years, concerns about her music, about proficiency and respect, concerns that the clothes she wore presented her to the world in the manner she desired; but worry, day-to-day, how-am-I-gonna-make it? worry, had never been part of her make-up. She had lived, for the most part, in luck's very good graces. She'd never worried about where the next meal or the next job was coming from, never worried about her appeal or ability, despite the many perils of the vagabond life she led, never been inordinately worried about her physical safety. There was always the possibility of things happening if you were coloured, but an attractive, intelligent woman generally had options available. That the odds were in her favour Valaida had taken for granted. She'd never worried about physical safety until the winter darkness of 1940 when she found herself alone in a country of Caucasians that war had divided into the fearful and the feared. When autumn became winter, in the twilight weeks of 1940, worry displaced luck as Valaida's constant companion. Her heart started to pound whenever she encountered Germans. She walked around rather than through them, took circuitous blocks just to avoid them. They made her feel vulnerable and weak and small, when she and her music had never been about feeling vulnerable, weak and small. Her music, her life, had been about brightness and making it through. Moving from vulnerable to strong for the work that was her life increased the pains Valaida felt in her arm, head, and soul. She found these discomforts unbearable without relief, and so she had to worry about maintaining a supply of what brought her ease.

The window shadows in Valaida's hospital ward are leaning sharply to the left, which means that the time of afternoon relief is near.

'You maybe should've gone while the going was good.'

You heard voices in this place, particularly just before the medicines were distributed, because every woman in these beds is gripped by her own version of hell, and when the balms run their course, the voices often break through, declaring their misery or their anger. Valaida understands.

'It comes to this? You lying up here in the company of a bunch of crazy white women? The Coloured Queen of Rhythm? You should've gone while the going was good. You didn't want to miss the fun? How much fun you having now?'

All of the voices exclaim in Danish but not this one, and Valaida pays none of them much mind because she, too, is wanting her medicine. It is better being here in the *Rigshospitalet* with its thick walls and locked doors between herself and the Germans, with food placed before her on trays three times a day. It is not wonderful food, but there is no wonderful food in this second winter of the war, and she has not had to go out and do difficult things to find it. The only problem is with the medicine. They bring it to her, but it is never enough. She tries to explain that she needs more, but they refuse to understand. Valaida is now eating as much of the not wonderful food as she can manage, thinking that, maybe if she is stronger, she will find a way to make them understand.

'You're kidding yourself, Miss Valaida. I hate seeing you here, I really do, but you're refusing to get a hold of the reason they have you here.'

Valaida's wondering about this American voice, but she's more interested in getting her medicine. In the far corner of the ward the very tall and thin Danish woman has begun to scream and claw at her belly and breasts. Valaida has understood enough Danish to know that the woman's pain has to do with dead children, children that were killed or children she killed herself, and that it happened long ago. There's a lot of bad luck in this room, which is another reason Valaida finds solace here. She can see that she is not the only one.

When a black cat crosses you, bad luck I heard it said . . .

apter six

New York, September 1931

. . . When a black cat crosses you, bad luck I heard it said,
One must've started 'cross me, got halfway and then fell dead . . .

She turns on the light and sags against the door. The room is tiny
and airless, but she dares not open its soot-caked window. The
alley's stench of summer-baked refuse would do her stomach no
good at all. Better to sit down and catch her breath, calm it all
down, her racing pulse, her quivering legs, the persistent feeling of
her insides wanting to fall outside. She is damp between her legs,
but she won't change the pad until just before her opening
number, 'Rhapsody in Black', shoving as much gauze up her
vagina as she can manage and still move. If yesterday was anything
to judge by, it will be a messy night. She'll be needing to gauze up
with every costume change, more so for the dancing, praying that

298

the dam won't break when what she needed to be concentrating on was putting on a show and what she really wanted to do was just lay down and die. No, not die, never die, but sleep, yes. Sleep until the gauze in her vagina stopped sopping up her life's blood, until her legs stopped quivering, her insides decided to stay where they were designed to be, and Ethel Waters was struck dead by lightning or maybe a stage lamp crashing down from overhead. Valaida, for she is Valaida now, would like to lie down, just for a moment, but she doesn't dare that either. Her body might believe that it had a right to rest, but since it does not, she sits down before the mirror and removes her hat instead. She has looked better. Her eyes are glazed, her cheeks flaccid, her lips pale. She hasn't had much appetite. Bright and wholesome will take a lot of paint. She pushes her hair back with the make-up band, all the while staring in the glass at the 27 year-old fool, Valaida not Valada, who got caught by nature even though she knew better.

> . . . *Yeah, my right hand's raised to the good Lord above*
> . . . *Yeah, my right hand's raised to the good Lord above*
> *If they was throwin' away money, I'd have on boxing gloves . . .*

Like many girls on the circuit, Valaida has never been too regular. Folks speculated on the wages of irregular hours on top of bad food, rotgut booze, and a touch of the clap now and again, but nobody really minded. Motherhood wasn't high on most girls' lists, and months without monthlies meant that much less worry about seepage onto costumes and kicking up your heels. But you watched yourself. When you took men as your pleasure, you kept your vinegar or your Coca-Cola handy. At the first notion of trouble, you got hold of some vanilla extract or some pennyroyal from a drugstore, which is what Valaida had done; but this time it hadn't worked. Maybe if she had been dealing with a full man instead of a half boy, she wouldn't be in this state because what-ever or whoever might catch his fancy, Nyas Berry just loved himself some Coca-Cola, would take Coca-Cola any day over the finest Scotch whisky or Beefeaters Gin. So on that morning back in June, when Valaida reached down to the floor to do her douche with Coca-Cola, all she came up with was an empty bottle. Since Nyas was half boy, he hadn't let an inconvenience or the thought of where that bottle may have been damp his feelings down. He'd laughed that he was sorry and proved it on her as he could. Nyas could prove as well as he could dance. With his firm hips, smooth-as-a-girl's chest and tapering thighs, Nyas Berry was a proving fool, and Valaida had enjoyed herself, trusting to the way her luck had always been, until she'd felt that twinge round the beginning of July. The little bugger had attached itself to her womb and simply wouldn't let go no matter what she'd tried, which was everything short of throwing herself down a flight of stairs. There'd be no broken bones keeping Valaida off this Broadway stage and ceding victory to Ethel Waters. She'd die first. She almost did.

An idiot she wasn't. She wasn't about to trust herself to just any old woman with a catheter and an orange stick or a knitting needle dunked in wood alcohol. Valaida wanted the doctor with the paste that got squeezed up your canal with a bulb syringe, which was then packed with gauze until eighteen hours later the deed was done. Some mess, a few cramps, and you were back to your life because Valaida stands firm by her conviction that she will never be like her mama. There'll be no squalling infants tugging on her heartstrings and tripping up her life. Alvada could do it for all the Snows as far as Valaida is concerned. But by the time Valaida had traced the doctor he was on vacation up in Martha's Vineyard where the high-class hincties spent their summers, wouldn't be back till after Labor Day, and Valaida knew that she was running out of time, was past time, really, for things to be easy, so she decided to try iodine, only nobody seemed to know how much you were supposed to take. All anybody said was that you took some, waited a bit to feel if anything started happening, and if it wasn't, take a little bit more. Which is what she did.

The iodine had tasted so nasty it had been hard to know if what she wanted was what was happening since the taste alone had been enough to make her retch. So, how to know if the heaving she was feeling was exaggerated disgust, or the baby taking its leave, or her body telling her it was dying when it turned out to be all three? Thank goodness Bessie had been there, and thank goodness that the apartment they were sharing was up on Sugar Hill, where doctors were scattered up and down the avenue like dandelions on the banks of the Chattahootchee River. So at one o'clock in the morning, when Valaida's delirium moved on into shock and Bessie found that Dr Polk and Dr Williams in their own building were not at home, she was able to run right next door to 411 Edgecombe and summon Dr Metcalfe. Dr Metcalfe strode over with a grumble but no quibble, pumped Valaida's stomach and scraped her womb clean of residue, pronounced her a 'very lucky little lady' and prescribed bed rest for a week, all the while knowing that Valaida, like any other Negro entertainer, would be on her stage again that night.

What had been her confusions? Her mama imploring her to keep the baby. Alvada telling her not to bother. *'You'd be a wretched mother, Valada. There's no love in you, none at all.'* A faceless crawler mutating into Nyas who, acquiring breasts and a pussy, turned again into Bessie, all in the shadow of a towering Ethel, wearing Valaida's Rhumbola costume as a bloodied apron over her own. Ethel howling with laughter with thundering applause at her back. Not the floating pleasures of an opium haze. Wrenching pain. Foul fluids and fetal tissue, ruby-red gelatinous, thicker than blood.

The problem about living on Edgecombe was that you didn't get much privacy. Columnists from the Negro press were often hanging around the lobbies looking to pick up gossipy tidbits for their readers on the secret lives of the Race's social and entertainment elite. So it was that Dr Metcalfe's coming and going caught the eye of Cedric Walker of the *Amsterdam News*, who then nailed Bessie on the second of her forays out for milk.

'Aren't you Valaida Snow's roommate?' he'd asked. 'Is she ill? Will she be able to perform tomorrow? Is there any truth to the rumour that she and Ethel Waters don't get along? What about her and Ananias Berry?'

'I've got nothing to say to you!' Bessie'd cried.

Piqued by the brush-off, Walker waited for Dr Metcalfe until 4 a.m. 'What's doing with Valaida Snow?' he'd asked the weary doctor whose cuffs were spattered with traces of blood.

'Got herself into a little trouble,' Metcalfe answered.

'Love problems?' queried Walker.

'You might say that,' Metcalfe replied.

It was announced on the front page of the *Amsterdam News* as a suicide attempt. As though she would take her life and cede victory to Ethel Waters! John and Etta's child? No time, no way, but suicide was more acceptable to the public than killing your baby, or so folks said; and Valaida Snow was a public person now. *It's what you wanted, was it not? It was part of the path to the star.* Better for folks to think she had tried to kill herself because, though everyone was killing babies, in her world anyway, no one dared admit it, and on top of this, Nyas believing the lie because she hadn't bothered to let him in on the problem, because he might have become as foolish as he was young, getting notions of a spitting-image toddler as part of a dancing act. So be it. She could live with the lie and its adjustments, providing, of course, she made it through this second night, which right now was feeling like an order higher than the sky.

Yesterday's show had been a disaster. She'd walked in rhythm rather than danced. Whole verses of lyric had simply vanished from her brain, in their place this conviction of her insides falling outside. Trying to blow a trumpet with her mouth a metallic-tasting desert, benumbed chops barely managing a treble call or two. Arms too weak to conduct the band, barely moving from her sides. Trying at least to smile. Not knowing if she'd succeeded. The applause after her numbers weak and wondering. Friends picking up the slack as they could, the Choir, Nyas. In 'Dream of the Chocolate Soldier', Eddie Rector had bid her stand while he placed his taps in quadruple time, *tap-pa-ta-ti, tap-pa-ta-ti* like she was inside a wreath of splintering glass. But no sympathies from Ethel. Hell no. Ethel had revelled in her lapses. Valaida knew

302

this without ever seeing her; she was gloating in the wings. Valaida could feel her. There was no way a body couldn't feel Ethel when Ethel was around because everything about her was big, her stature, her talent, her territoriality. The way she just stood there and grinned with the audience secure in her hand. Lew Leslie's *Rhapsody in Black* was a case of Valaida Snow versus Ethel Waters. Ethel Waters was a bitch, and Ethel Waters was winning.

As Valaida lines up the make-up and combs she will be using, a knife stabbing up through her vagina to her heart nearly takes her breath away. Wincing, she withdraws a stick of rolled-up weed from a silver case, lights up, pulls in the smoke, holds it, hopes. Valaida is not a viper as a rule. She finds marijuana's slowing influence a hindrance to her performance style. Sure, Louis smoked all the time, but Louis didn't *dance*. Nobody was worrying Louis Armstrong about not having nimble feet; but the weed's easy numbing had been emolient last night. Without it, the pain would have been impossible to manage. Valaida pulls again, and the vagina knife withdraws.

It was, all of this business, down to Lew Leslie. Leslie hadn't been ready for Valada in the autumn of 1929 because he was in the midst of planning the latest version of his *Blackbirds*, that of 1930, starring Ethel Waters with Nyas and his brother Jimmy among those along for the ride; but *Blackbirds of 1930* had laid a great big egg. Audiences were wanting something new after the Crash. They were sick of the tired old plantation stereotypes, blacked up faces and watermelons and skits based around the inability of Negroes to speak anything resembling proper English. Leslie took the shaft deep in his pocket and decided it was time to change his spots. 'The Negro is fitted for better things,' he announced. He'd produce a 'symphony of blue notes and black rhythm' against a background of respect. (He had no money for sets.) This new show would present a new kind of Negro girl of higher learning and better background, who, when she danced, would 'show rhythm and grace, but not suggestiveness. Her dancing will be artistic'.

Valada was back from Europe; she hadn't finished grade school but she could read and write. This time Leslie came looking for her. *Rhapsody in Black* would be built around newcomer Valada Snow, who not only sang and danced, but played the trumpet and piano and conducted both the band and choir in the perform-ance of her own arrangements, 'all of which gives the audience a chance to see that Miss Snow is really an accomplished young woman'. This was what Lew Leslie declared to all who asked. The big chance. To be the next Florence Mills, but in her own special way. Valada on her pathway to the star. Thank God, thank Cas, thank the Wanderer back in Chattanooga with the yellow hat and beat-up horn, thank Dyer Jones, thank Bessie, thank Ruby, thank everyone she'd ever known. Only Leslie had forgotten his obligations to Ethel Waters.

Ethel appeared during rehearsals saying that Leslie had prom-ised to build the show around her, which was probably true because Lew Leslie was strictly one of your small-time hustlers, desperate and shifty despite his willingness to work hard. Why else had he been forced to earn his money off of black folks? Leslie tried to duck and dive.

'Oh, we've got plenty of room for you, Ethel! You'll come on here and here and here, with some of your off-colour songs.' Valaida can still see him, his eyes scurrying, his thumb working a finger wart on his right hand.

Ethel was having none of it. She put her big-ringed lawyers on the case, and soon songs were commissioned from Mann Holliner and Alberta Nichols. Good songs. Songs you could build a world around. Songs that had Ethel on stage by her lonesome, creating her worlds, relieving the audience of their hearts. Ethel's numbers were quieter and earthier than the rest of the show. She was a washerwoman, a dance hall hostess, a spurned but still loyal lover, all with a common touch. Ethel operated from a still centre and the audiences loved her, thinking that they knew her. But they didn't, not by a long shot. Ethel wasn't warm; she was mean as a wounded she-bear. She couldn't stand any female smaller, lighter, or prettier than she was. She'd throw a chorus girl down a flight of stairs for even looking at her man, when half the time she had her own little girlie on the side. And if the smaller, prettier female had talent, she'd better really look out. You didn't think she would do violence on you for real, but Ethel's aura had a menace that could unnerve a body, throw you off your game, until soon you were being what she wanted and less than you were. It was downright spooky.

Valaida was not a superstitious woman, but sometimes she wondered if she shouldn't get herself some *gris-gris* protection against Ethel's power from one of the conjure women on 134th Street because Valaida spent a lot of energy resisting Ethel's will, energy that might have been useful deflecting Nyas' youngblood sperm. With conjure protection against Ethel, could she have avoided this whole inside-falling-outside mess?

But it is a waste of time to be thinking this way because Valaida is a modern woman. She'd changed the spelling of her name because she wanted it to look more modern, less country. *'I know folks have known me without the "I", Mr Leslie, but I think the new spelling is so much more sophisticated and refined, don't you? Just like you say our show is going to be.'* As her dresses were. As she wanted to be. As she saw herself. 'Looking every bit as ritzy as a Vanderbilt or an Astor,' one reviewer had gushed, which was what she liked to hear. But too ritzy and sophisticated for her audience, perhaps? 'A puzzle to audiences who are wondering what she will do next,' another judgement read, with a bag of 'histrionic tricks'. But these same critics were disappointed to see 'the Negro taken out of the jungle in *Rhapsody in Black*'. They were not to be listened to; besides the fact that if Valaida ran her life and talents according to what other people wanted her to be, she'd still be in a chorus or tending a bunch of babies or curled up in the dust, defeated by Ethel's thrall. And she wasn't. She was here, in this tiny, airless dressing room that nevertheless was hers alone because no matter what Ethel Waters was trying to prove, she, Valaida, was a star, smoothing cold cream over her cheeks, preparing them for the illusion of bright and modern and wholesome, with eight numbers of a show to do, her insides wanting to fall outside,barely slowed by the hits of weed.

A knock at the door. 'Valaida? It's Sherman. You decent?'

She is decent, and he is right on time. Slick in his honey-brown suit and yellow shirt, wide brim stylish on his gassed-out head. Handing her the little packet between two long fingers with sharpened nails. 'How much do I owe you?'

'Five dollars does the trick. You want me back after the show?'

'Tomorrow will be soon enough.'

'As you like it, sweetness.' Valaida works the packet between her fingers. The feel of the powder is fine, but she won't use it until just before time, a frosty pick-me-up for Miss Snow, to keep her better on her game. Not forever, but for as long as the weakness lingers, the legs feel encumbered. Buzzed, she'll worry less about the bleeding, feel its moistness less, feel her stomach seizing less, and, with luck, the shortness of breath. She blends the Madame Walker No. 4 with the No. 3 in the normal ratio, but she'll be using more highlighter on her cheekbones than usual, brighter lips, stronger eyes. To distract from the death heads lingering behind her slackened cheeks.

What was it that Ethel did? She could say her words, but so could Valaida. She had a voice, but so did Valaida. Was it the stillness? Valaida is not still, she is fast. She likes action and lots of possibilities. She gets as much of a thrill being inside the sounds she makes with her voice, horn, and feet, enjoys the manipulation of them as much as the joy she can give and get from an audience. More so, if she's honest. It's more so than any other love or sensation, what Cas called 'heart' up against the heights of pleasure inside the doing, and 'heart' not winning. Ethel was unencumbered by this dilemma. She stood and delivered; the people received, sighed, and cried.

Legs a-tingle with cocaine, buzzed, bleeding, and benumbed, Valaida stands in the wings waiting for Ethel to complete her final

306

number and go on with Valaida's own. Ethel ends her song. There is a moment of quiet, and then howls and applause as the crowd explodes. Ethel smiles and bows her head in what the unknowing mistake for modesty. She raises her arms slowly and wide as though to gather up all the love, lets fly a majestic kiss, and strides regally off to the wings, invading Valaida's space, whose presence she ignores. The cries continue and Ethel returns to centre stage. Again with the wry smile and the slight bow of head, and they can't get enough of her. She is a bitch, and she is magic.

Valaida is thinking she must work harder, that she will have to work much harder if she's going to have a chance of winning this one, when she feels a presence behind her, then soft lips applying a kiss to her ear.

'Don't worry about her, Valaida.' Nyas. 'You don't have to be thinking about her. She just wishes she had everything that you got, your looks, your talent.' The warmth of his hand is a comfort at the small of her back. 'And I'll always love you, Valaida.' His voice more vehement now, more immediate than Ethel's applause. 'You don't never have to worry about that!'

For a moment Valaida's insides rest, forget to fall outside. Her heart slows its cocaine-fuelled beat, her mouth and brow are no longer so tense. She accepts her lover's kiss to her neck with a smile, unaware of Ethel's final invasion-into-her-space exit into the wings. When the band launches into 'Dream of the Chocolate Soldier', out she strides onto the stage with eyes dancing toward the audience and, despite still quivering legs, the energy ready to grab them.

Rigshospitalet, Copenhagen, March 1942

The bitter-tasting milk makes thoughts of luck retreat. The light softens, and muscles release. Valaida runs her tongue across her lips. They are chapped and weak. In the safety of this ward, she could make them whole again. She no longer has a trumpet, but perhaps someone here could find her a mouthpiece. Maybe the young doctor who must be a student, whose eyes have considered her with kindness. If the young doctor came soon, while her medicine was still fresh, Valaida thinks she could manage a smile. She would smooth back her hair when she saw the doctors enter the ward, and while they stopped at her bed, she would smile and she would gesture. She could make him understand and want to help her, if they came through while the medicine was fresh, because she's always had a way with sweet young men. Who'd enjoy themselves. For a while.

You're not the kind of a boy for a girl like me . . .

$\mathscr{C}$hapter seven

New York, 1931

. . . For you're just a song and a dance
And I'm a symphony . . .

Valaida didn't hear Nyas the first time he proposed, pretended not to anyway. Nyas, in his timidity, had bowed his head and bit his lip, so like a boy with a confession for his mama that she'd had to resist the urge to simply laugh and embrace him.

'There something you wanted to say to me, baby?' she'd asked.

'Not now,' he'd replied. 'Maybe later.'

Better never, she'd thought, for why in this world would she want another marriage when the last had been a disaster and her heart was hardly designed for fidelity? But he surprised her when it worked, was waiting in her dressing room with a bouquet of yellow and white chrysanthemums. It was December.

'I wanted these to be roses,' he'd told her, his voice husky and hands shaking ever so slightly, 'but they said I'd have to wait another day.'

'You in some kind of rush, baby? What you have that's all that urgent?' she'd said, reaching a green-gloved hand to caress his cheek. 'You're looking kind of flushed. I hope you're not coming down with that grippe that's going 'round.'

'No, I'm fine. I've just got . . . I been thinking hard on how to do this, Valaida, and I didn't want to wait. I couldn't wait. If I waited . . . You have to sit down.' He places her in a chair and the flowers in the lap of her silver fox-trimmed tweed coat, and she's thinking, don't you do this, Nyas. Don't do this. We've got a nice thing going here, good times, no strings. We shouldn't mess it up, and he's down on one knee, reaching into his inside pocket, bringing out a box.

'I love you, Valaida. Don't say anything yet, please, just listen to me. I love you, and I want to marry you. I know you think I'm just a boy, but I'm not a boy. I'm a man, and I know my heart. I will love you for ever, and I want you to be my wife.' The ring is beautiful, three diamonds, all large enough to see, the gift of a boy, or man, with an urge to spend. His eyes are brimming with hope and tears. She allows him to slip the ring onto her finger.

'Have you talked to your daddy about this, Nyas? I have a feeling he won't be so pleased.'

'This ain't my daddy's business. It's our business, you and me. I'm sick of him trying to run my life like I was still some thirteen-year-old kid. He'd keep me in harness till I was forty if he could. Do you need a church wedding, Valaida?'

'A church?' She'd coughed as a means to suppress rising hilarity. 'No, honey, I've got no need of a church.'

'Because I know about this town in Pennsylvania. Raymond told me about this town, Media, in Pennsylvania. We could go down there after the show and have everything settled in time for the show tomorrow. Eddie's gonna lend me his car, but he doesn't know what for.'

'I didn't know that you could drive, Nyas.'

'Well, I've never actually done it, but I've ridden and watched enough times. How hard can it be?' He'd started grinning that grin, the one that showed out after an on-the-money backflip into a split or after he'd given her to holler particularly loud and long. 'So, what do you say? Valaida Snow, will you marry me?'

So, how long was for ever?

. . . You said that you never would doubt me . . .
But I'm telling you, you'd be better off without me . . .

Rigshospitalet, Copenhagen, March 1942

Sleeping during night hours does not come easily to Valaida, even with medicine. She's spent too much of her life coming alive at this time, tuning her energies to peak after the work-a-day world has been happy to find its rest. She has revelled in the manner that light plays in the ink of night. Valaida has always sought to be in that light. She looks longingly at the pools of yellow that have been formed by the nurse's lamp, imagines herself dancing in its glow. Imagines herself moving. This is the one way in which her prison cell was superior to the supervised safety of this ward. She could move around at will. There was no one to talk to, but she could whisper her songs, stand up and move her feet, beat out regrets with the rhythms of her feet. On this ward, she can move her feet half-time underneath the sheets, but it isn't the same. But then nothing is the same.

. . . I'm just the kind of a girl, who would never be square . . .

'But you robbed that cradle anyway.'
Again the voice. No English-speakers about, and no reason she can think of not to answer.
'What?'

'You robbed that cradle anyway.'

'You?' At last, here, someone who really knows her.

'Who else around here is going to get some truth out of you, Miss Valaida? You robbed that cradle.'

'That's just not fair. Nyas wasn't but eight years younger than me. You'd think he was my own grandchild from some of the things folks came to say. Eight years difference is no big thing. Men have been doing it, keep doing it, all the time, chasing after that sweet young meat. You can't tell me that's not true. "Ooh, sweet baby, come on over here to Papa!" So how come the world decides to rest on my case?'

'The world picks its own times for understanding. You decide to walk your own road, and you want the world to come along? You wouldn't like it, Valaida. You'd find the path entirely too crowded and have to be shoving folks out the way; and whatever you tend to do or don't do, shoving's not your nature, that much I 'll always give you. Did you love him?'

'Why are you all the time so concerned with the little details, Cas McHenry? Why can't you just take in a happy picture and accept it for what it is?'

'Then paint me a picture, Miss Valaida.'

'I can't do you one of your broken-up, crazy pictures with things all split up around themselves.'

'I'm not asking you for that.'

Valaida looks toward the lamp-lit table where the nurse remains deep in her book, and no one else is registering anything. She allows herself a genuine smile, and enjoys its feeling in her cheeks.

'He was beautiful, Cas. Not just in the way he looked, but in the way he did what he did. The precision of it. Somersault into a split, turn, split. Flying tumble into a split, pull up and a flip on the last note of the music. Arms always alive, shooting out energy along with the legs. Perfection. I loved that perfection.'

'You're telling me what he did, not who he was.'

'You never change, do you? Always in a person's face, always pushing.'

'Did you love him?'

'He was sweet, Cas, and innocent in the midst of it all. His smile, even when he was doing grown and raunchy, had a baby's sunshine in it. It was warm and bright and clear, and he adored me. He thought I was some kind of sepia fairy princess, had me remembering who I was before I really moved out into the world . . .'

'He reminded you of that boy James from Alabama.'

'I told you about James?'

'You told me everything.'

'Just about.'

'Just about? Touché. Just about. But tell me you weren't thinking back on that birthing shed in the Far West Pasture, that farm boy's firm brown thighs, those sweet as molasses lips, the calluses on his hands from chopping wood and hoeing cotton . . .'

'That was a difference right there, those calluses.'

'Do tell.'

'You're acting deviant.'

'I'm true to my nature.'

'I've missed you, Cas.'

'And I've missed you.'

'Will you ever forgive me?'

'The calluses, Valaida.'

Valaida's own hands are moving downward, past her belly.

'Nyas' hands were as smooth as a baby's, but there was a ridge of horn on his left cheek from hitting those splits.'

'How'd it feel against your hand?'

'Use your imagination, then rev it up a touch. Do you forgive me?'

'Don't be asking if I forgive you when you need to be asking if Nyas will leave you go. Did you love him?'

'I found myself trying to be his princess.'

'But I bet his daddy wasn't thinking that way.'

'Well, Daddy Berry had his particular confusions. Mr Berry looked at me and saw a girl as young and pliable as his dancing children, took to calling himself my manager, like I needed someone talking for me and taking my money after all those years of doing for myself. I'm afraid this little girl wasn't made that way.'

313

'You came between a father and his son.'

'Nyas brought that pot to me, not the other way around. Nyas was looking to me to help him become a man. You had to know that that was part of why he had wanted me there. I was cute and fast and cuddly, but I'd been grown a real long time. I suggested that he might think of parting from his baby brothers, at least from time to time, especially if he wanted to be working with me. No coercion, not much anyway. His decision. He made it, and was better for it.'

'For all the toying you did with his feelings?'

'I was made for the music, Cas, not to be living inside some fairy tale.'

'Oh, Miss Valaida, there's so much for us to discuss.'

'I'm not sure I'm going to want this, but right now I've got nothing but time.'

$\mathcal{C}$hapter eight

Rigshospitalet, Copenhagen, April 1942

They would have known who she was if they had seen her in the chapel. There was only one of her in the country, and who else could she be? So she's turned down the offer to attend Easter service in the hospital chapel because yesterday she'd caught sight of her reflection in a window. Bright sun, the first spring sun, had been streaming in through the windows. Valaida had stepped up into the warmth and seen herself in the glass. It is only in the last days that she would have known what she was looking at. She'd been too ill before then, too preoccupied with her worries, too grateful to be out of the prison, off the Nazi-occupied streets and in this ward. Knowing that the Germans were on the outside and she was on the inside, that food and medicine were here inside arriving on a dependable schedule had calmed Valaida down to the point that she could look sometimes now beyond her immediate cravings and fears. To see what? Sunken cheeks, hollow eyes, hair on end and matted all over her head. Repeated splashing with ice cold water had brought some life back to her complexion; she had felt the face blood rushing and its muscles tensing and relaxing, tensing and relaxing. She could almost feel herself returning to herself; but there was next to nothing that could be done about her head. She'd spent the majority of Holy Saturday fighting her matted locks with what the nurses had to offer, an inadequate comb and brush designed for Nordic hair, the bristles too short, the tines too short and close together. Her eyes had teared from the effort, and at the end of the taming, with no pins and no oils, there was nothing she could do but braid it down along her scalp like some sharecropper's wife. It felt better, yes, but no way would she allow non-crazy people to see her. A Coloured Queen of Rhythm had her pride, after all. Better to sit on the outer edge of the ward's own special Easter service because there are no expectations here.

The woman who mourns her children sits directly across from Valaida. Her eyes are distracted, but not clouded. There are cords in her neck, and her hands are tightly clenched. Four other patients are slopped about in their seats, eyes half-closed, mouths drooling; a fifth is conducting quiet conversation with the ceiling. Valaida has no idea what the minister is saying. His voice is a droning monotone, but she enjoys the slashing purple of his neck scarf, and she can see that his eyes are a deep sea-green. He is moving toward the jug of dark red liquid on the table decorated with a white tablecloth and pale-green-budded branches. This is the reason that Valaida is sitting here, to be closer to the pretty table. She has missed pretty these last months with all the grey, and the nurse holding the basket is the one who reminds her of Henny. She has the same square shoulders, clumsy wrists, and soothing hands. The basket contains bits of bread. The minister is pushing bread gently into one of the slobbering mouths, murmuring words Valaida would not understand even if she could hear them.

'But you know what he's saying, don't you?'

316

'I never went under that water. Never got baptized, never did communion.'

'But you know what he's saying, don't you?'

'I didn't give my attentions to preachers, Castor. Mama and Alvada did enough of that for all of us.'

'But you know what he's saying, don't you?'

'"This is my body which is given for you. Do this in remembrance of me . . ."'

'Because your mind could always fasten onto a lyric, Miss Valaida. The communion charge is as much a lyric as any other. Has its words, has its rhythm. I knew it had to be down there someplace. And what was the song that Henny always used to sing?'

'Henny?'

'Yes, Henny, Valaida. Henny Thomsen. Your Henny. You know she's on your mind today. What was that song she'd sing?'

'I don't remember.'

'Yes, you do.'

'No, I don't.'

'Yes . . .'

'"I can't dance, I've got ants in my pants. I can't dance, I've got ants in my pants."'

'Ahh, the first Parlophone recording. A masterful piece of work.'

'Think what you like, but they loved it over here. They were always requesting it. All those blinking blue eyes wanting the "crazy Ants in Pants". Used to drive me around the bend.'

'And what about Henny?'

'She drove me there, too.'

Let's go down to the drummers' club
You take the streetcar and I'll take the sub . . .

Denmark, 1940–41

She'd been a chorus dancer. Not a very good one, at least not by Valaida's standards. With her chunky wrists and ankles, she was not a naturally graceful girl, but she'd tried hard, thrown herself into the routines with an almost frightening abandon. She wasn't the prettiest girl in the line, either. Her hair was too mousy, and her face was too broad; but you watched her because you knew that she cared and was trying to understand. In the early summer of 1940, she and Valaida had been working in the same revue in one of the Tivoli Garden's many outdoor restaurants, where the Danes continued their determined 'cold shoulder' toward the German occupiers. Let the German 'grasshoppers' in their grey-green uniforms and the black-uniformed SS wander where and how they pleased under the multi-coloured fairy lights. The Danes were taking no notice. They drank their beer and munched their herring and applauded their performers with even more of a studied disregard than they exhibited towards the invaders in the everyday streets. Tivoli was Denmark's wonderland. Every wonderland had its ogres, but they lost much of their power when you paid them no particular mind.

Valaida had first really noticed Henny against a grasshopper background. Henny's dancing to Valaida's music had been blocking the view of a table full of soldiers. The soldiers kept gesturing at her to move, and Henny had kept on ignoring them to the considerable pleasure of all the Danes in her vicinity. Valaida had mentioned her to Earl at the end of the set.

'Did you see that girl dancing right up by the bandstand? The one that was driving those Germans crazy?'

'You mean that chunky, farm-girl looking broad that's always throwing the chorus off their game?'

'Well, I think she's cute. I like her spirit.'

'And I think all this nasty fish we're eating is turning your brain to grits.'

Valaida saw Henny again in Århus later that summer, after Earl had been sent home. Bands at the Århushallens performed on a platform overhanging the dining-room floor. Henny had been standing throughout the set, moving to and into the music, arms outstretched, having herself a righteous ball, and when Valaida had taken her bow, Henny's hands had been clasped against her heart. She had been at the end of the autograph line after the show, holding two of the flyers with Valaida's picture that had been posted around the town. Her cheeks had been flushed, her complexion dewy and smooth.

'Are these both for you?' Valaida had asked.

'Both for me?' Her English had been hesitant. 'No, no. They are for the sons of the brother of my father.'

'Your cousins.'

She smiled now, broad and crooked and completely without guile. 'My cousins! Yes, my cousins! Hakon and Otto. They like you so much!'

Valaida had allowed the girl to stand very near as she signed the small posters, close enough to smell her scent that had a trace of over-ripe peaches, close enough to sense the rapid beating of Henny's heart. 'And you,' Valaida asked, 'do you like me, too?'

Henny's flush had deepened and spread across her thin-strapped shoulders. 'Me? Oh yes! I like you very, very much! Very, very much! Ants in my pants! Very, very much!'

She was delightful. It had been a successful afternoon. There were egrets by a pond in the distance, and the sun's light was still full gold in the northern sky. Valaida was feeling good, and there was nothing to do but laugh. Henny was taken aback at first, but then she smiled and dared to go on. 'Would you teach me?' Her eyes were grey, with little yellow highlights.

'Teach you what?' Valaida replied.

'The ants in the pants. I try so hard, but I cannot. I cannot—'

'Show me,' said Valaida.

'Just so?'

'Just so.'

Her movements had been all over the place. Valaida put a hand on Henny's side. 'No, still here.' The girl's flesh was quivering. Valaida's other hand went to her hip. 'And more here. Try again.' The girl's breathing had changed to rapid little gasps, but she tried again.

'Better,' said Valaida, 'but you must practise. Remember. Still here. More here.'

'I will practise! Ants in my pants!'

Copenhagen had been the next time, after the summer idyll, after Valaida had shown Norbert the door. As the world was taking on darkness and Valaida was having more needs, Henny somehow always managed to be around. Valaida began to depend on her, to decipher the ration system, to keep performing clothes in shape, to shop for food. Henny was always willing and asked nothing in return save the odd smile from Valaida that Henny knew was just for her. If Valaida's attentions had been wider than her own worries and pains, she might have seen that Henny was in love; but what Valaida recognized was that Henny was good for what ailed her. Henny's hands had a magic touch, delicate and firm at once, always sensitive to where the need was strongest. Then came the night after the newspaper interview.

Valaida had been the person expected by the interviewer, all bouncy and gay, when she'd been feeling anything but. The days were short and cold, jobs were scarce, the Germans everywhere, and Valaida was without protection. After the interview, Valaida's shoulder had begun to throb with an intensity she hadn't experienced for a while. As was increasingly the case, curfew that night had stranded Henny in the lobby of Valaida's hotel. As was increasingly the case, Henny had accompanied Valaida to her room, doing whatever might be needed, mending a hem, setting a wig, polishing a horn, anything, everything, on the off-chance of extracting a smile. Valaida had taken some of her medicine, but it hadn't come to full effect. She'd needed Henny's hands massaging her shoulder. As ever, Henny had obliged, and then she'd reached for the Eukodal.

'Let me try some,' she had said.

'It's medicine,' Valaida replied. 'It's not for everyone.'

'It makes you smile,' Henny said. 'The worry goes from here and here.' Henny's hands had brushed across Valaida's brow and

320

down her cheek. 'I would like to smile as you smile. I would like to smile instead of worry.'

The yellow in Henny's eyes had turned to fire, and Valaida chose not to venture down beckoning roads. 'Help yourself,' she'd said. Henny had brought the bottle to her lips, grimaced slightly, and then gulped. 'Careful!' Valaida admonished. 'You have to be careful. This medicine is strong. It's not for everyone' But Valaida was already floating. She was already in her relief and didn't murmur when Henny swallowed again and again.

Henny's hands resumed their massage, but Valaida's blouse was obstructing their work. Henny put three fingers on the button above Valaida' s breast, and Valaida nodded yes. When Henny's hands moved across Valaida's bosom, Valaida's nipples stood erect. Henny's hands cupped Valaida's breast, trembled against Valaida's nipples, and Valaida whispered, 'Down. Down,' she repeated, 'down,' undoing her buttons down to her crotch, slipping a hand up Henny's thigh, parting her lips, caressing her centre. The pubic hair was fine and sparse, unlike any Valaida had known. Valaida found Henny's mouth, where Henny's lips were also trembling. Valaida kissed them lightly then moved across to her ear and whispered, 'Down.' Henny was sobbing, with what? Joy, perhaps, possibly fear. Valaida had no interest in determining which as she showed Henny the way towards what could become Valaida's heart. What Valaida knew was that her pain was gone.

On the *Rigshospitalet* ward, the minister and his goblet have reached Valaida, who is hesitating, out of superstition or a sense that there may be a few inviolable rules? The minister is accustomed to the rhythms of this ward. He lingers for a beat, but is about to move along.

'Go ahead and take the wine, girl. "This cup is the new testament in my blood. Which is shed for you?" You know you're going to need any help there is to be had. Henny loved you, Valaida, with all her heart and soul. You have to take your hat off for a love that strong. You have to give it its due.'

'*I love you, Valaida.*' There had been crushes before, a special school friend, a particular teacher, but nothing like this. What this was came only once in a life. '*I love you, Valaida.*' This was not the direction Henny's life was supposed to follow. There'd been a young man these last six years, a carpenter's apprentice. Their families had known one another for generations. He was devoted. He even understood the dancing. There were expectations. She was the only daughter. Her mother had been embroidering trousseau linens for as long as she could remember. '*Tell me you love me, Valaida.*' She'd wanted too much. Valaida had told her time and time again that love was not something that she, Valaida, spoke about. Which was not to say that she was never tempted. There was a tenderness and fire to Henny's kisses, a sympathetic sweetness in her embrace that stirred and soothed Valaida more completely than any medicinal concoction. Valaida could feel Henny dancing on the outlines of her heart. She could feel Henny's touch toying at the locks leading to private chambers in her brain. '*Come to me, Valaida. Just as I have come to you.*' Henny was too much.

Henny declared her love for Valaida to her family, and her father threw her out of the house. Called her an *uhyre*, a monstrosity, declared her worse than a whore; but Henny's heart was not broken because her future was with Valaida. '*Tell me you love me, Valaida.*' Valaida could not speak of love. There was no room in Valaida's Denmark darkness for love, but she let Henny move into her room in the Hotel Rio because Valaida relished Henny's sweetness and fire, and where else could Henny go?

'This is not for ever,' she told her. 'Whenever I can, I'll be leaving this place.'

'You'll be taking me with you.'

'I will not take you with me.'

'You'll be changing your mind.'

'I will not change my mind.'

'You will because you need me and you love me, even though you will not say this.' Henny wanted too much.

At the beginning of February, Valaida was working at a small club called the Prater, and Henny at a similar club close by. Henny kept on coming by Valaida's work and coming by Valaida's work until Valaida thought that Henny needed to learn why not to cling and probe. There was a man. No one special. A former grocer growing rich on black market pork and grains. He had as much soap as he needed, and so his hands were usually clean, his Caucasian musk usually acceptable. He enjoyed the jazz. Valaida allowed him to kiss her in front of Henny, then shared his bed for two nights after Henny had thrown a table and smashed a chair.

When Valaida returned to the Hotel Rio, Henny's body was already gone. She had been found by a fellow dancer when she hadn't shown up for rehearsal or the performance that night. She had drunk an entire bottle of Eukodal.

'*This medicine is not for everybody.*'

'*I want to smile as you smile.*'

Valaida didn't attend the funeral; she knew that she would not be welcome. She felt hollow but could not cry. As punishment for her involvement in Henny' s death, her work permit was revoked and her ration cards curtailed and the Danish darkness turned to pitch. Five months later she was allowed to work in Sweden. Her lips were virtually gone. She pawned her trumpet, and there was only pain. No sweetness anywhere.

Rigshospitalet, Copenhagen, April 1942

The minister is delivering his Easter benediction to a small suffering congregation who behave as though nothing has changed in their world.

'*You remember this part, Valaida? "I am the Resurrection and the Life. She that believeth in me, though she were dead, yet shall she live." A lovely sentiment, I always thought, and to the point right in through here, with desperation, war, and self-delusion all around.*'

'*You saying I'm kidding myself?*'

'You say you didn't love her.'

'Like I told you, Cas, I was made for the music. Not for living some fairy tale. Nyas had his version, and Henny had hers. I told Henny that we couldn't be forever, that all I wanted to do was get out of this place. Why couldn't she understand that?'

'Maybe she thought she could offer another way.'

'I didn't want another way!'

'You didn't mind her being your own personal little oasis.'

'So she goes and kills herself? Why did she kill herself, Cas? Why? What kind of people are these that go 'round killing themselves for no reason? You don't kill yourself, Cas. You deal with what you're given, and you keep on going.'

'You're a fine one to talk.'

'I'm moving out of this place, Castor.'

The minister has left the ward, and the nurses have removed the cloth and branches from the table to return it to its daily use, but it is still Easter in the courtyard, where patients and their families sit on wooden benches or perambulate in the sun. Many hold bouquets. There are no flowers or perfumes on the ward. The odours here are of disinfectant, funk, and bodily wastes. The ward is larger than a cell, but Valaida is still a prisoner. She is not allowed outside. She is stronger now, but her legs are soft and her knees aching from inactivity. She cannot be outside, but she can move. In the afternoon, patients are allowed to move around the ward. Their shuffling and shambling has annoyed Valaida no end, for she wants to move in rhythm. On the outside, in the Nordic streets, a body cannot move in rhythm without being taken for insane, but there are no such strictures here. Valaida needs to move in rhythm to chase Henny's pain away. She needs to dance Henny's blues out of her mind. She needs to dance in reminder of what she's been and shall be. Valaida is a prisoner, but she has at her disposal the freedom of the insane. Any freedom is better than none and Valaida takes it. Within herself she finds some music, she marks its time, and then she dances. Folks are watching, as well they should, because Valaida Snow is the Coloured Queen of Rhythm; and she's dancing.

The Grand Terrace, Chicago, 1933

She enters for her last singing chorus with the sweat of the dancing choruses streaming down her torso, the double satin of her costume only just not clinging to her bush, grateful that no fabric shields her privates from the little bit of air shifting up between her legs. Her scalp is throbbing from thirteen stitches snaking down the back of her head toward her neck, and shouldn't she have known better than getting into an automobile with Thomas Fats Waller when, lovable as he was, the man simply stayed drunk? She'd found herself resorting to the happy dust again, and it had done its business, numbed her pain throughout her show, because it is her show. She has produced this show. She had responded, 'Yes, I can,' when Ed Fox asked, 'You think you could handle this, Valaida?' Fox might have been thinking money saved in the ongoing wage dispute with his old producer, but Valaida was knowing her answer as Opportunity. She'd taken those Hollywood musicals as inspiration, the elegant black and white of their costumes, the lines of dancers in shifting patterns. She had selected the music, got some new numbers written in fact, drilled the chorus girls, showed the Earl Hines band to its advantage, and herself as well. The audience has loved it, been stomping down for more, and now, as she's preparing for her last chorus and the blessed relief of a backstage recline, Earl is beckoning her to the bandstand and his white Bechstein piano.

'Come on up here, Valaida,' he's saying, teeth flashing bright in that pretty black walnut face of his. 'We got something for you.' One of the band walks forward holding a gleaming handful of brass, the other musicians vamping as he makes his way through the stands. *No, you don't! Not my trumpet! Not now! Not with my lungs heaving from the effort of five tap choruses against a line of teenage girls!* Earl is smiling. All of the guys are smiling, but not all of the smiles are friendly. *Goddam you, Earl! Goddam you!* Valaida's smiling, too.

'Ladies and gentlemen, I think you'd agree with me that in this little bundle of dynamite resides one of the Race's foremost female stars.' The crowd of brown and white sporting folk looks expectant, and the band is steady vamping. Smiling and vamping. The mirror ball above the show floor dispersing a Milky Way of starlight. *Not now, Earl! Not with my lips still tingling from the chill of that damn cocaine! My heart's thumping so hard, I'd be hard-pressed to find a beat.* But Earl's going on. 'This girl's got more talent than she knows what to do with. She's not only one hell of a little performer, she produced tonight's show all by herself. Who needs Hollywood when here in Chicago we got the Grand Terrace?' *Don't do this to me, Earl. Where's your heart, for goodness' sake?* Valaida's eyes pleading, and Earl's smile speaking mischief. 'Now you already know that this little lady knows her way around a horn, but usually she's strutting her stuff out there on the show floor.' *You bastards! Now you gonna let me in after all these weeks of keeping me off the box?! You chittlin'-eating, mamma-jammin' bastards!* 'Tonight, me and the fellas would like to invite her up on the bandstand for an extra special encore of our great new number, "Bubbling Over With Beer". Come on up here, Valaida! Don't go shy on me, baby!'

Valaida steps up to accept the trumpet to the kind of applause she figures Christians heard on their way to meet the lions. Her head's throbbing strongly as she breathes into the mouthpiece and works the valves. The house before her is swimming, and Earl, steady talking.

'Now, I have to tell you, ladies and gentlemen, that it's not every musician that holds with honeys blowing from a bandstand. A few might even tell you it's damn unlucky, but tonight we're making an exception for this little lady here, because I think you'll all agree she's a veritable Little Louis. You ready, Valaida?' Valaida's nodding smile is a bright bristle of stilettos. 'All right then,' crows Earl, 'Here. We. Go.'

Valaida never knew where her wind came from that night or where the lips that had been numbed by cocaine found their burr. With her lungs raw from choruses she had danced, with her belly heavy from the evening's pot roast dinner, with the stitches on her

326

scalp outlined in heat like a salamander in flame, Valaida listened hard and entered the music. She knew 'Bubbling Over'. She had wrung it out of Louis Dunlap and Charlie Carpenter for this her show. She had scatted its changes to the chorus girls. She knew where it had been, and where it could go. After the melody's intro and Earl's left-hand-to-right-hand cascades of piano sound, her space was opened and Valaida jumped in. She blew. She felt the horn in her hands surrounded by a shaft of golden light, and she blew beyond herself. She entered the music and saw its symmetry all around her. She saw the chords, embellishes, the references to other songs as plain as day behind her eyeballs, and she used them. She jumped from bar to bar like a benzine-fuelled billy goat. She didn't miss. She hit her peaks and whinnied in triumph. Her stitches split with the force of her blowing, and blood came snaking down her neck. She didn't notice. She was aware of nothing but the construction of this architecture of sound. She traded fours with Cecil Irwin and Walter Fuller and eight after eight with Earl. In the nebular light of the Terrace's mirror ball, she flew with men who had backed Louis Armstrong at his best.

At the end it was as though she didn't know where she had been. The crowd was on its feet. Purple Gang mobsters were throwing hundred dollar bills on the floor. She was drenched now, her makeup gone, the roots of her hair on their way back to nature, and her costume beyond redemption, soaked as it was by her Niagara of sweat and blood. She had played. She hadn't just acted cute and entertained; she had played. Earl lifted her arm high and squeezed her hand as they took their bow. Earl Hines is known as a ladies' man with good reason. He and Valaida would have some memories to love around in this night, but they won't recapture the ecstasy they reached on the bandstand in this music. Nothing could.

She had been right to leave *Rhapsody in Black*, but would she have left if it hadn't been for Nyas? With reviews piling on top of each other praising Ethel to the skies and talking about, 'Valaida

Snow is a puzzle. You never know what she's going to do next,' her husband of one year had kept on her about it for weeks. 'Why do you keep putting yourself through this, baby? Why you keep letting them play you for second fiddle when nobody in the world can do what you do? Sure, Ethel can sing, but she never was no kind of dancer. All she did was shake, and she's too old and lazy to do that no more. And can she play a horn or a piano? Can she conduct a band?' No, Valaida would think, which is why I'm finally going to get her, but into that thought, here would come Nyas. 'There's no beating Ethel on this one, baby, and I'm sick of seeing you having to put up with all her guff. You're not happy, baby,' he'd purr, a slender finger playing under her chin. 'I want to see you happy.'

Valaida had been stubborn, but Nyas had been right. All through the months in *Rhapsody*, she had been going through the act of happy, spending the good money they'd been making on gorgeous gowns, apartment furniture, and an $8,000 orchid-coloured, chauffeur-driven, Mercedes automobile. Living high. During a time when the country was wrestling with catastrophic depression, Valaida and Nyas were neck-high in furs and dripping diamonds, being a couple folks wanted to look at, be like, living a life of winning, when night after night, in town after town, Valaida was coming in second best. But she wouldn't have thought of leaving if it hadn't been for Nyas. She would have hung on in there, kept on fighting, striving to get that win, when, for her, victory came from stepping outside the battle.

It had been easy. Lew Leslie was grateful to see her go. The ongoing feud with Ethel had greyed his hair for more than a year. *Rhapsody* would continue just fine without Valaida, and he'd be saving her hefty pay check. Valaida thought she maybe should feel offended but instead found herself breathing a sigh of relief. For a minute Daddy Berry had thought that he was going to run their lives, weaving Valaida into the act that he had devised for Nyas and brother Jimmy, but Valaida quickly disabused him of that mistake.

Rather than slot herself again into someone else's idea of where she should be, she and Nyas formed a snappy duo of their own, trading on the magic they had managed together in *Rhapsody* despite the strife; and bookings were easy to find: the Lafayette in Harlem, the Howard in Washington, DC, the Regal in Chicago. And, after so many years working this night life on her own, Valaida found that there was protection in her married status, more so than even the serious time spent with Russell. Folks might tease her about cradle-robbing, but with a ring on her finger Valaida found the terrain a lot less testy. Folks had affection and respect for Nyas, so behaved with care around his lady. Men played at being wolfish, but she had to deal with their bites a whole lot less, and without wasting so much energy playing cute and helpless or cute and sassy, hot little mama or sweet little lamb, 'I could do this if you help me, Daddy', deciding whether to lift her skirts or keep them tight around her knees, Valaida was freer just to fly. Her talents blossomed with Nyas' ring on her finger. She stopped comparing herself to Ethel Waters or Josephine Baker or Adelaide Hall or Nina Mae McKinney, and became what no one had ever seen before, Valaida Snow, the coloured girl who could do it all.

Rigshospitalet, Copenhagen, April 1942

The effect of Easter celebration has been two-fold on Valaida's ward. First a sun-washed calm that seemed to imply that God had seen fit to ease the suffering of His troubled on this day that honoured His glory, followed by a general agitation among the patients after day had conceded to night. As though all understood that darkness was the truth of it. With the darkness, Valaida was compelled to bed like everyone else, but she had found solace in her dancing and a reacquaintance with night as an intimate friend. There had been moments in this day that had nearly approached contentment.

'So, Nyas helps you find a new life, and you return the favour by fucking Earl Hines?'

'I've had some peace this evening, Castor, and I was beginning to enjoy this night. Do you have to be so crude?'

'Just trying to get your attention because I'm picking up a pattern here. Miss Valaida using people according to her needs, then discarding them like worn-out stockings once their use is past.'

'You're trying to put Henny and Nyas together, but they were two different things, and I've explained to you about Henny.'

'You saying you didn't use Nyas? I'm here for you, my darling. Explain to me about Nyas.'

'Earl Hines and me had nothing to do with Nyas. Nyas could have come into the Terrace if he'd wanted to. Ed Fox had wanted to hire our act, both of us together, but Daddy Berry was raising so much hell about how Nyas had deserted his brothers, and the family was going to starve if he didn't do something to help them out, so Nyas agreed to go out with them for a few weeks. Mr Bush had passed away leaving nothing but a pile of debt, so we had taken in Mama and Arthur, Jr and Hattie, which meant that Lavada was all the time coming to call after her East Coast jobs, even though she still wasn't speaking to me for 'ruining' her wedding. Ruining her wedding? Four years after the fact, she didn't have anything else to worry about? Treating me like some kind of crimial in my own apartment. It was too crowded in New York. Fox said that he would be happy to take on just me, so I went to Chicago.'

'And stayed for months.'

'Yes, I stayed. Why did you stay in Paris? Because it worked for you. Chicago was working for me. A body could move easier in Chicago than in New York. It wasn't so stuck on itself, didn't have so many rules about who could do what and where. It let me play my music, Cas, and that's what it was about with Earl and me, the music. Do you know how it felt finally to play with guys at the top of the game, guys who'd played with Louis? To be right down in the trenches with them instead of all the time "toot, toot, smile, smile, take me serious, please"? They pushed me like you pushed me. I got better with them, really starting to say things of my own. Yeah, sure some of them were still up there talkin' about, "She ain't all" *that much", but with Earl on my side they had to put up with me. I will always be grateful to Earl for that. He'll always have a piece of my heart.'*

'Even though he left you out there standing on your own?'

'They're not brave, Cas, none of them. Women are brave. Ruby was brave. Bessie Smith talked trash to a whole swineherd of Klanners, turned her back on them and lived. My mama was brave, standing up against my daddy even though she loved him. I'd just as soon as slit Ethel Waters's throat as look at her, but she is no kind of coward. Men? Outside of you and maybe my brother Lawrence, not a one I know about. I try to get Earl to stand up to that slave contract he was under . . . Fox throws me out on my ear, and Earl does absolutely nothing.'

'Ed Fox was run by Al Capone. Standing up could have gotten Earl killed.'

'And I wasn't risking anything?'

'You don't want to know this, Valaida, but most gangsters don't see young, pretty women as threats.'

'Daddy Berry didn't agree with you. I'm just out of Chicago when he pulls my first husband out from under a rock to file a bogus charge of bigamy, chasing me with bailiffs, getting me arrested, all because he thought I was the only reason Nyas wanted to go his own way.'

'Nyas took you back despite what his daddy wanted, despite the fact that you playing with Earl was no kind of secret. He wasn't a coward.'

'If not then I was his backbone.'

'Just when was it, Valaida Snow, when your heart took on this chill? You've got the right name, sister. Your ribs are a regular Arctic Circle. Nyas loved you, Valaida, and you were careless with his love, like you were careless of Henny's love. You've had a habit of carelessness, my dear. You gave that interview to the Amsterdam News talking about how sad your life had been and how bad your family had treated you, how they were taking advantage of you, when it hadn't been anything like that. You were more than careless, you were selfish and cruel.'

'I was desperate! That man wanted me in jail! I missed the music, Cas. It was a horrible pain that kept tearing at my gut, like a vulture pulling flesh off of a carcass, but I was still alive; and nothing I found to do

331

seemed to help it go away. I'm feeling it now, the ripping. It makes me crazy!'

'Is it the music you're missing or your "medicine"? It seems to me that you've betrayed the music just like everything else.'

In the night-time shadows of her ward, Valaida is hearing a new kind of sound, a mewling like some terrified kitten. It is close to her, as though on her chest, but she knows there are no cats in the ward. No animals are ever allowed in the ward.

'You're crying? You?'

'Why are you tormenting me, Cas? Why? I'm all alone in this German-overrun God-forsaken country. I'm in prison, for goodness' sake!'

'You're in a hospital.'

'Nobody knows where I am or cares!'

'I care. Why else would I be here? But you're feeling sorry for yourself.'

'Yes! I'm feeling sorry for myself!'

'Don't yell at me. I'm trying to help.'

'I need my medicine!'

'Your drugs, you mean.'

In reaction to Valaida's cries, the ward nurse has left her book and padded quietly to Valaida's side. *'Fru Snowberry? Goer det ondt?'* Are you in pain? *'Fru Snowberry, du skal vaere stille.'* You must be quiet. Other patients are waking in response to Valaida's disturbance. Some are sitting upright, others have begun to weep. *'Fru Snowberry, du skal vaere stille!'* When Valaida does not respond to her entreaties, the nurse rushes to the front of the ward and rings a bell.

'They're going to restrain you.'

'I fight against them, they'll sedate me.'

'No, they won't, darling You've had today's quota. You're on your own.'

'You're the one who's cold, Cas, like death. You're trying to strangle me, when you said you loved me, for who I was, and you were the only one ever, the only one.'

'That's your carelessness again, Valaida. What about your mama? But you never gave her a thought when she was alive. Couldn't spare any

332

tears for her, just as you had no tears for Henny. Etta Snow Bush wasted her love, but I guess mothers do.'

'You don't know what I feel! I loved my mother. I loved her.'

'You did?'

'I betrayed her, Cas. I acted as though she was nothing.'

'She found peace in the end.'

'But not from me.'

'There you go again, bringing it around to you. If you loved her, then you wouldn't care how she found her peace, only that she did. Can you love, Valaida? Aside from the music, can you love anyone? Why are you crying?'

'I hate you. I miss my mother.'

In the ward, Valaida hears rapid footsteps, then feels strong hands on her legs and arms as the orderlies begin with restraints. Rough canvas corsets her wrists and ankles, grinding against bruises that are already there. Valaida bucks and kicks because she must, although she knows it all to be futile. She screams because just maybe someone will really hear her, find her, take her away. She screams again and hears more words in Danish. *'Tilstaekkelig!* Enough, Mrs Snowberry, enough. *Nok!* You upset the others.' She hears groans in the darkness, other weeping moving towards tantrum. Something metal crashes to the floor. Valaida feels hot. Her face is damp and oily. Her scalp is itching. She is sobbing. Her tears are hot. *'Fred, fred.* Peace, Mrs Snowberry. Peace. *Fred.'* A cloth is cool. A hand is calming. Her cries turn into whimpers.

. . . I didn't know what year it was
Life was no prize . . .

hapter nine

New York, 1934

. . . I wanted love and here it was
Shining out of your eyes . . .

Etta Mae Bush found her peace at a Marian Anderson concert. She was nearing sixty, suffering from both pressure and diabetes, but she was still a music teacher. Teaching was Etta's pleasure but a necessity as well, for the money sent her by her daughters never lasted an entire month, when it was sent and not late or completely forgotten. Arthur, Jr was twelve and strapping like his father. Despite the Depression that had shaken Harlem to its core, Etta prided herself in keeping Arthur, Jr fed. She had found pupils among the children of her neighbours on Harlem's Sugar Hill, so many of whom had pianos. Most of the pianos were larger than those Etta had known in Chattanooga but, despite their grandeur, just as frequently out of tune. Etta had yet to find a musician among her students, but among the mothers she had acquired one friend. Lou Anne Riley was a doctor's wife, twenty years Etta's junior, a club woman who would have loved sponsoring Etta into any one of her organizations, but Etta Mae Snow Bush had never been a joiner. She had never learned bridge, had never had the time, but still Lou Anne wanted to cultivate her company. Knowing that her Ruth had a tin ear, no aptitude for the piano and less interest, if it was possible, Mrs Riley continued with the travesty of Ruthie's lessons in order to offer up a cup of tea to Mrs Bush after the hour and enjoy the serenity of the teacher's company. Marian Anderson's concert had been a planned activity for one of Lou Anne's clubs, but her little boy was home sick with bronchitis, and Lou Anne wouldn't be able to attend. Etta had volunteered to baby-sit, but Lou Anne had refused.

'Come now, Etta,' she'd said. 'How often do you get a chance to go downtown, and the Lord knows that you'll appreciate the music better than I would! My ear for music's only a little better than Ruthie's. Now I know you know that's true.'

Etta agreed not to argue any further and so found herself on a winter afternoon at the Town Hall in downtown Manhattan for the concert of a woman she admired at least as much as she did her daughters. Sitting in a fine seat in the orchestra section, Etta was a cloth coat among the furs, a brown skin among far fairer complexions, and she was wondering if perhaps her acceptance had been a mistake when the recital began. In the very first notes, as the singer's burnished contralto caressed the first aria's first words, Etta recognized a place she could only sense as home, as though after years in a wilderness she had finally stumbled back onto the path that might have taken her beyond her life as deserted lover, mother, spouse. Her sigh preceded a cascade of tears, born not out of regret but of joy.

It was during the concert's twenty-five minute interval that Etta heard the laugh that struck her as familiar. Never having been a drinker of spirits or wine, Etta was hugging the wall of the

Town Hall bar, occasionally sipping the orange crush her daughter Alvada had insisted she allow herself to buy. In exchange Alvada would make sure Arthur, Jr did all his homework before heading into the street to find grocery bags to carry and thus a few pennies to contribute to the family's shallow coffers. Arthur was a fine boy, steady like his father, and yet he lacked . . . Etta hesitated to contemplate, let alone put to words her knowledge that Arthur lacked the fire of his long-since-gone half-brother Lawrence, for she felt it the greatest of sins to compare one child to another; but Etta has missed Lawrence, the first of her babies to survive and then the first of them to leave. With Lawrence living across the line, Etta knew that she would never see him again, never embrace him, never smell his scent. Arthur, Jr was steady and kind, but he would never refill the hole Lawrence had left in his mother's heart. Etta's eyes were tearing from the thoughts of Lawrence, struggling to hold on to the solace she had found in the recital's Mozart and Bach, when she heard the laugh from across the room, rippling, like a tumble of bells. No longer of silver alone, clad in bronze perhaps; but familiar. Etta followed her hunch to a copse of clever hats, edged through silver foxes and cigarettes brandished between carmine-painted fingernails to certify that this laugh could only be one she hadn't heard for the better part of forty years.

The woman whose laugh this was Etta found to be swathed in mink pelts, bestuck with brooches, and immensely fat, her still keen features embedded in the now yellowing alabaster pudding of her face. But her eyes were the same. Tourmaline. Flashing with delight, if tempered now by the irony that also played about her crimsoned lips. The woman felt Etta's presence, looked in her direction, and the air between them stilled.

'Allegretta?' Etta whispered.

'No, it can't be . . . you?' the woman replied. When Etta nodded, Allegretta Simpson gave a cry of such pleasure and relief that all conversation in the bar came to abrupt and absolute surcease. With all eyes trained on her considerable person,

Allegretta plunged through her club fellows, with all the force her bulk allowed, to clutch to her breast Etta Mae Washington Snow Bush, her long-lost friend, her childhood heart, with a laughing, crying urgency that near suffocated them both.

Seating was re-arranged for the recital's second half in order that Allegretta and Etta might enjoy Miss Anderson's last soaring renditions with their arms tightly entwined. Rather than travel uptown to the Hotel Theresa for her club's Chicken Newburg dinner at which the revered Miss Anderson was expected to join them in dessert, Allegretta spirited Etta to a small Italian restaurant on the city's Lower East Side, where she, Allegretta, was well known to the owner and could trust that he would do nothing to embarrass her darker friend. Drinking red wine from wickered bottles, the two women talked long into the night. They sang Miss Anderson's praises, proud that she had realized the goals of musical greatness to which they had long ago aspired. Etta admired Allegretta's wide-ranging travels and good works. Allegretta was humbled by Etta's fortitude and envied her her children.

'You're so lucky, Etta,' she said, 'with so many people who love you, you don't have to worry about being old and alone.'

Etta could only smile. How to say that for all her children, there were no such guarantees? Lawrence, her light, was gone for ever. Valada was always somewhere away. Now she was in London, from where she wired money and the occasional note that was warm but brief, doing well it seemed, and never wanting to be reminded of all the grief she'd caused. Lavada too was on the road, often in shows very much like her sister's. The clippings she sent home were favourable, but that she was always considered as just less than Valada had caused clouds to form across the heart that had once been so much like a warm summer's day. Hattie had long since returned home to Chattanooga, for she was a southern girl to her bones who'd never found sense in the big city's crowds, concrete, and bitter cold. Only Alvada remained attendant to her mother, but with her Thomas gone and four mouths of her own to feed, Alvada had more than enough cares of her own.

'Allegretta, why didn't you ever marry,' Etta asked, 'with all those handsome beaux forever hanging around your door? Sometimes you needed a scythe and a pitchfork just to make your way to the street.'

Allegretta laughed. 'All those boys were really just after my daddy and what he might do for their pockets, like I was some medieval princess coming with a big fat dowry and a job guarantee. They couldn't stand my chatter about singing in St Petersburg on the one hand and "What you going to do about this Jim Crow?" on the other. They were all the time trying to smother my talk with kisses. Well, I wouldn't stop talking, so they finally stopped coming! I figured, "Good riddance," and went on about my life.'

'You've never regretted it?' asked Etta.

'Oh sure,' said Allegretta, 'sometimes at night, when I have trouble moving this fat around, and don't know if I'd rather keep on breathing or have another slice of pecan pie; but I really can't complain. Turns out that I did have a dowry after all. I've been able to hold onto the house, help finance some Negro trouble-making, and have a great big heap of fun along the way.'

It was late, past midnight, the other diners long since gone, the candles scalloped flaps of melted wax. Etta and Allegretta were holding hands across the table. Etta knew that she must tear herself away, be fresh for Arthur, Jr in the morning, to decide which way to prepare beef knuckles and beans for their meals, to cut down Dr Riley's old jacket for her son's coming baptism, but a force as strong as her duties kept her firmly in her seat. After forty years of distance the friends couldn't stand the need to part.

'Come with me, Etta,' Allegretta finally said. 'Come with me to Washington. Bring Arthur. Bring Alvada and her kids, too, if that will make you feel better. They can stay with us or have a place of their own. I've got so much room and more than enough money. We're both of us lonely, and I just couldn't stand losing you again. Why don't you come with me? Please?'

And Etta said yes.

Etta felt her pressure ease when she and Arthur, Jr walked through Allegretta's door. Some things had changed. The lighting was no longer gas but electric, the furniture a jumble of fripperies and bows and eccentric gestures to the modern rather than the elegant unity of Viola Simpson's style, and there was no sullen European maid; but Viola's treasured Meissen tea set remained. Missing one cup, chipped and repaired, it still stood testament to long-past, grace-filled hours, lace-trimmed handkerchiefs, bustled skirts. And there was the piano. Amidst the clutter of magazines, newspapers, scattering pillows, exotic knickknacks, the piano's wood glistened, its ivory glowed. When Etta touched a key, the sound was true.

'I've kept it ready,' said Allegretta, coming up from behind and placing a hand on Etta's shoulder.

'For all these years?' Etta replied.

'The memories were precious,' said Allegretta, 'and I always had hope.'

Etta slipped out of her travelling coat, took her seat on the bench and commenced to play. 'Do you remember?' she asked.

Allegretta nodded. 'Meyerbeer,' she replied, then listened for her entry and commenced to sing. Her voice was a throaty warble, not at all what it had been, but there was a peaceful pleasure in the doing. When the song was done, Allegretta took Arthur, Jr into the kitchen for a sandwich, then returned to help Etta move into her room. The sun was bright, and the curtains were brocade. Etta Washington Snow Bush would be living and dying in peace.

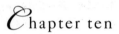

$\mathcal{C}$hapter ten

Vestre Faengsel Prison, Copenhagen, April 1942

Fange Nr. Valaida Snowberry
14 April 1942

Inspector
Please excuse me. I wrote you a letter one time before, and you did not even answer it. Won't you be a gentleman and kind enough to answer this letter? I have not committed a crime. I am here in prison because the police are sending me home to America. I beg you please to let me have my needlework that is now in the garderobe as it is very good for the nerves, and it makes one very nervous just to sit alone all day and do nothing. Please be kind enough to answer me this time, as I feel sure you would not like your wife, mother, or sister to be thrown into a prison when they have done nothing besides being American and not able to get home.

Please say yes, or at least be kind enough and gentleman enough to answer me.
I am, dear sir,
Yours sincerely,
Valaida

The ride from the hospital had been uncomfortable and long. With the ration of gasoline, many vehicles were now hauled by old-fashioned horse-power instead of driven, but rather an eternity being tossed around in the rear of that paddy-wagon than returning to this place.

She'd asked the guard watching her, sitting with her in the rear of the wagon, if the Germans were still in Denmark. '*Er alle tyskerne stadigvaek i Danmark?*' He had not replied, but his eyes had clouded. There had been no change. She caught glimpses of buildings through the high, narrow, barred windows of the wagon, and of branches without buds. She wondered where the flowered branches used in the Easter service had come from because outside in the world there had been no new growth, no changes. She could hear life outside the paddy-wagon's walls, a child crying for its mother, a snatch of someone practising a piano, heavy leather boots marching in formation, life as it had been. She was no longer shaking from illness, but what did it matter if there had been no changes?

She could smell brewing hops from the Carlsberg factory across the road when they'd walked her into reception. She could hear the whistle of a passing train during the intake inventory as her personal possessions were taken away one by one. *1 fur hat, 1 fur coat, 1 pair galoshes, 1 pair shoes, 1 dress, 1 garter belt, 1 pair stockings.* The prison uniform scraped against her flesh as she climbed the stairs toward her cell carrying her face cloth and her dish cloth and the comb that would never get through her hair. *1 chemise, 1 woollen jacket, 1 pair stockings, 1 pair trousers.* Her cell is number 47 this time, closer to the wall that abuts the Jewish cemetery. A cemetery, a train, and booze enough to drown in, all tried and true vehicles of escape. Parked right outside her doorstep, and not a

341

one of them available to take her for a ride. There was space on the ward, but there is little space here. There was light on the ward, but there is little light here. Rather an eternity in that ricketing paddy-wagon. Rather the rugged road to Hell than actually getting there. The prison noises are as they had been, clanging iron, ringing bells, tapping pipes, everywhere and always. The noise is slamming against Valaida's soul as relentlessly as it does her eardrums. She suspects that she could really go crazy. She has to get out of this place. The hospital would be better. She must command the warden's interest, she must make him understand. She must get him on her side.

'Needlework? How very domestic, darling! I never would have guessed.'

'You've followed me here?'

'I am where you are. I care for your heart. So, tell me, do you think these other broads are plaguing the prison governor with their personal tales of woe? This place is a monument to lost luck, after all. Everyone here has to have a story.'

'I'm not worrying about the "other broads", whoever they are. I'm worrying about me. I don't deserve to be here. I'm just waiting for my passport, so why can't I do that in the hospital? The hospital's where I belong. I'm sick, you heard them say that. I don't belong in a prison. I haven't done anything wrong'

'So what about all that silverware they found at the bottom of your suitcase?'

'You'd rather I'd starved?'

'What about swindling all that Eukodel out of that poor apotheke chap? He's on trial for that, you know. What, a girl has to do what a girl has to do?'

'I hate it here, Cas.'

'There's not much to like.'

'I mean, I really hate it here. I hate this noise. I hate the smell. I need to get out. I need more air. I need pretty things. I need living in the night. I need . . .' Valaida's breathing has become laboured, her voice a whisper. She is gripping the side of her cot, her eyes glazing with tears. 'I don't know how long I can last here, Castor.'

342

'I'm not accepting that talk from my girl, Valaida. You will last as long as you have to. You will deal with what you've earned, and you'll last as long as it takes. My girl does not give up. You may want to strangle her, but she does not give up. Come on and give us a tune, why don't you?'

'I don't have any music. It's all gone away.'

'My girl's music never goes away. It's always there for the finding. On your feet, Valaida.'

Her vision blurred with tears, Valaida rises slowly from her cot and begins to pace.

'That's right, baby. There it is, right before you.'

Valaida's chest is tight and her throat narrowed with emotion, but she begins to hum and then to step.

'Blackbirds, London, 1934.'

'Uh-huh. "Walking the Chalkline".'

Goddam, what came next, the circle kick and slide? Valaida's knees aren't enjoying the prison clogs against concrete, her ankles neither.

'I do hope you were better.'

'I was, you smart-ass, but then so were the circumstances.'

'They liked you in London.'

'They loved *me in London. I was a sensation in London. I was the Queen of the Trumpet and the Coloured Queen of Rhythm.'*

The circle kick and slide, a little better this time.

'Blackbirds of '34. You were on that man's plantation.'

'Not me. I was wearing silk.'

London, Summer and Autumn, 1934

. . . Let's go down to the drummers' club
You take the streetcar and I'll take the sub . . .

Lew Leslie came calling again in the spring of 1934 but without Ethel Waters this time. Ethel was ensconced in the white time by then, on Broadway, in the movies, pulling down more zeroes than

343

a producer like Leslie even knew how to write. Two years could have been two hundred. The difficulties of *Rhapsody in Black* weren't even a memory. Leslie needed Valaida for London, her amazing talents, her sophistication. There'd be no competition this time, no shadows on her star shine.

'You'll knock them dead in London, Valaida. You'll be as big a hit as Florence.'

In 1934 Florence Mills was nearly seven years gone, but Lew Leslie was still seen shedding tears for his departed star. A whole lot of folks thought he had genuinely loved her; some said he kept her picture in a pocket against his heart. Next to his wallet was more than like, said others, but no matter.

Valaida was ready. Her music was tighter than it had ever been afer the time at the Terrace with Earl in Chicago, and Nyas had taken her back.

'Don't ever do me that way again, Valaida,' he'd said, with an emotional generosity Valaida couldn't begin to understand. 'There's only so much that a man can take.' This with a fire she couldn't help but find appealing. After the battles with his father and the embarrassments of the bigamy case, Nyas' eyes were less young than they had been, but hungering for her as they had from the beginning, still with a vacancy of understanding, still seeing only what he wanted to see; but again, no matter.

Valaida promised to be true. She told herself that she was ready for his devotion this time, maybe not to remain his princess, but she was ready to be his queen. She enjoyed the laughs they had together, the smiles over the breakfast table as they sat opposite one another in matching robes. She savoured the bend of his young dancer's body, the sweetness of his scent not yet polluted by dissipations. Intertwined in the firm, silken mahogany of Nyas' flesh, Valaida renewed her grip on joy.

'Mr Husband,' she'd call him to make him particularly happy.

'Mrs Wife,' he'd reply with that grin that sometimes reminded her of another.

Husband and Wife flourished again together, renewed their act

344

together to enthusiastic notice. They began by singing and dancing together, then they'd trade their specialities, Valaida on the trumpet, Nyas on his feet, with Nyas' rhythm and acrobatics spurring Valaida on as well or better than any big time band might have done. They improved one another and revelled in their prowess. Husband even convinced Wife to form her own girl band for a while.

'You playin' so well, baby, just as strong as anyone out here. Folks ought to really hear you, and you know these men ain't never gonna really let you stand with them and blow. Won't be no kind of freak act. You've got entirely too much style.'

Valaida tried it for a while, but none of the girls could match Nyas' feet. When Leslie guaranteed good treatment for Nyas as well in *Blackbirds of 1934*, Valaida travelled with her man to London, the name Valaida Snow Berry on her passport, and London greeted her with open arms.

When the Blackbirds arrived in August of '34, Louis Armstrong had just departed England after being there for most of the year. The English were just crazy about Louis and, finding a beautiful young woman who played a trumpet with much of his style, they just wanted to go wild. Not as the French had gone for Josephine, for the English were not the French, and Valaida's clothes after all still clung firmly to her curves. The English did not lose their reason, rather they seemed to want to know her and, ignorant as they were about life across the Atlantic, you could tell them anything that came to mind, no matter how outrageous, and they believed it, swallowed it whole, hook, line, and sinker. You had to bite your lip to keep from laughing as you watched your lie go down. Everyone loved Louis? Well then, Louis became Valaida's teacher, taught her everything he knew, sat her by his knee, and then marvelled at her prowess.

'Where were you born, Miss Snow?' The English could make neither head nor tail of Chattanooga. 'Was that California, Miss Snow?' Then California it was, orange trees and beaches, sunshine and movie stars, when Valaida's only experience of California had been as a staging post for China. *Blackbirds* gave her a similar show-case to that she'd had in *Rhapsody in Black*. She played the piano and trumpet, sang and danced, as herself and in character, once again conducted 'Rhapsody in Blue', but this time, for the English, she wasn't too much. The English didn't object to her versatility, they celebrated it. The English didn't seem to have so many hard and steadfast rules about what Negroes should or shouldn't do. Sure, there were occasional references to 'pickaninny exuberance', and there was a photo of Nyas captioned 'the Coon with the twink-ling feet', but they never used those terms about Valaida. Valaida they only admired with respect, her amazing talent, the elegance of her gowns, her form riding horseback in Rotten Row, her aspira-tions for racial leadership.

'You, a Race Woman? The Negro Joan of Arc?'

'I did say that it might have been too extravagant an ambition.'

'Extravagant an ambition? You weren't talking that way back in Jimtown, Miss Valaida. You'd gotten very grand, my dear, very, very grand.'

'You Cas McHenry, with your nonsense paintings and your mouldy old wines, who are you to call me grand? So I started using a few more words—'

'As though you were a character in some play by Noel Coward.'

'There's something wrong with expanding who I was? That's what you always wanted from me, wasn't it? Not be limited by what people expected of us as Negroes? People used more words in England than they did back home. Why shouldn't I? I knew what they meant.'

'I'd have hoped that you'd be honest.'

'I believed those things when I said them. Why shouldn't I be a leader? People listened to what I was saying, not just the Blackbirds, the English people, too. These white people respected me, Cas. They appreciated me as an artist, and they found me intelligent, too. Why shouldn't I want to use those things to fight for our people?'

'No reason at all if there had been some sincerity to it, just one little grain, Valaida. Some Joan of Arc who ignores everything going on around her that doesn't have to do with her self. Some Joan of Arc, who won't

stand up for her friends. Bessie calls you in tears, desperate for your help, your oldest friend, and what do you do?'

'I'd been up all night playing trumpet in Soho! I couldn't make sense of what she was saying, then she takes off for a ship out of Liverpool before anything could be done. I could have done something if she had waited . . . No. No, the truth of it was that Bessie wasn't up on her game. She wasn't keeping pace with Nyas in "Your Mother's Son-in-Law". Her rhythm was just off. I don't know why. She kept complaining about her ear. It was his first big number. It had to be on it, and she was driving him crazy.'

'Bessie Duncan saved your life, Valaida, and you didn't lift a finger, you with all your clout.'

'I'm not listening to you, Castor! The Blackbirds time was wonderful, and I won't let you take it from me now when I need it most! I won't! I won't!'

London, January 1935

. . . Let's have a party, and let's spread good cheer
You bring the pretzels, and I'll bring the beer . . .

Her taxi pulled into the crescent-shaped drive of a large white house on a quiet wooded street. When she entered the foyer she was greeted, and addressed as 'Miss Snow'. A young man offered to carry her trumpet, but she refused.

'I look out for my baby, thank you very much.'

'As you wish, Miss Snow. Shall I lead the way?'

There was open staring from those she encountered in the corridor on her way to the studio, but their eyes held no hostility. Curiosity, admiration, a fast intake of shallow breaths from the young man who guided her around a corner. She wore the chestnut gabardine coat with the large red fox collar over the chestnut Mainbocher because she knew there might be photographs. The reptile shoes she'd bought two days ago on Bond Street were pinching a bit, but they looked so good over her finest silk stockings that she hardly felt the pain.

'This way, Miss Snow. May I fetch you some tea?'

Nyas had stayed in bed. 'This is your show, baby. You know I need my rest.'

It was not the first time she had been in a recording studio. The first time had been with Earl's band during the Grand Terrace time. Earl had been generous, kept the band in the background so that she could show what she could do, done her a real favour, knowing what he'd be getting in return. Too bad she hadn't been able to do a favour for herself. They weren't letting her play a trumpet, so she'd wanted to show what she had for a song, problem was that she'd thrown everything she could think of into one three-minute slot. She'd been fast, she'd been slow. She'd warbled like a sepia Jeannette MacDonald, jived like herself, and gotten down into the gutter with the lessons she'd learned in her time with Ruby Jones. It was an arrangement that they'd often played in the club, one that was usually greeted with great hoops of appreciation, but when she heard the recording, unwrapped the brown paper, blown open the sleeve, put the shiny black disc on the turntable of her new bought-for-the-occasion travelling record-player, she'd not only wanted to die of shame. She'd had to wonder if audiences had only been applauding her way with the number because they were too far drunk to distinguish good from bad or else wanted to hurry her on her way. That had been nearly two years before exactly. She'd learned from that lesson, and these London sessions were hers.

The Parlophone producer wanted to record her after seeing her on the Coliseum stage in *Blackbirds*, hearing her on radio, seeing her playing her trumpet in after-hours Soho clubs.

'There's never been anyone quite like you, Miss Snow. It would be a privilege to bring what you do to a wider audience.'

Like she was both a talent and a lady. Like there was no irony in speaking with her, doing business with her as you would with any lady. Made her want to act just like a lady, who knew just how to present what she could do. This was still the Depression, and she knew herself to be an experiment. Valaida Snow was an unknown quantity surrounded by a little bit of commotion. The company wasn't about to risk but so much money. There would be one take for every song, and no chance to hear what she had put down. She'd have to concentrate and be precise, run though the numbers as many times as the session allowed, hold onto her pitch when they went to shellac, and her nerve as well.

An orchestra was being recorded in the villa's larger studio. Valaida had heard just the edges of its thundering sound as she'd passed. There was another world in there, a world she sometimes glimpsed on its way to the opera house in Covent Garden. The world Cas wanted for his own. She wondered if he had ever finished his sonata. *'You got me started again, Miss Vee. Now it's up to me.'*

Things would be quieter in Studio Two. Parlophone was providing her band.

'We'll get you the hottest jazzers London has to offer. A couple we have in mind worked with Louis Armstrong on last year's tour. I say, can't get a better recommendation than that, now can you, Miss Snow?'

Six young men, bright-eyed but bashful, stood with their instruments when she entered the room.

'This is Billy Mason, Miss Snow, Duncan Whyte, who'll be your second trumpet, Buddy Featherstonehaugh, tenor saxophone . . .'

'Just call me Valaida, fellas. Thank you for being here. It's a pleasure to meet you.' They'd already been working the arrangements, so why were they looking so scared?

The producer had selected the material. 'In keeping with your effervescent personality, Miss Snow, we looked for something upbeat and happy. We think you'll have some real fun with what we've found.'

'I can't dance, I've got ants in my pants . . .'

'Pretty swell, don't you agree?' By Clarence Williams, but not at his best. 'We hope that you're as excited about this as we are.' Well, a song was what you made of it.

Valaida never lost her smile. 'I can't wait to get to work.' She laid her brick red gloves across her handbag and took her trumpet out of its case.

The first two sessions were touch and go, with two sides working and two just being too bad. The band knew their way around their instruments, most of them anyway, but white English musicians were not American Negroes. Rhythm and the blues were not natural to their blood. They kept trying to drape the music around their shoulders like some bulky, variegated cloak that dragged along the floor and often made them trip, especially when they tried to wrap it extra tight. Valaida realized that this was the tariff on her opportunity to record. No one in America had shown her this kind of interest, no company had been wanting to give her a try, no musicians willing to back her up. The musicians on this chilly, damp island were happy to play with her and for her, delighted in fact, but they would never be able to feed her. She'd have to spend her time feeding them to help them rise to a level that let her deliver what she had. This truth she felt, but she couldn't waste energy wondering what it might mean to her future. She accepted the price, never once losing either her patience or her smile.

'You're really saying something here, Buddy. Now, if you could only smooth it out a touch, get out of that buggy you've hitched a ride on and into that smooth-running Swallow I saw you eyeing the other day! Yeah, I saw you! That cute, little two-tone. Why don't you drive it on down my street, open the door and take me for a sweet little spin?'

'Duncan, you're holding a whole heap of horn right there under your jacket. Don't let a little thing like me embarrass you into dropping what you already have. Step right on up here and show me what you got!'

The horn players gained confidence, got better. The rhythm section, well, it simply didn't make sense mourning the loss of

Earl Hines, or a vaudeville pick-up band in Greenwood, Mississippi on a Tuesday afternoon. The one thing these English fellows could do was keep a steady time, so she took to thinking of them as some double-dutch jump ropes that hit the pavement *slap-slap, slap-slap* right on the beat, that weren't going to change unless one of them got tangled up and fell over. Their time was as even as a metronome, so she showed out between its hits. Despite the rejects of the first two sessions, the company seemed to be pleased with the results on their throw-away songs.

'*You're not only a great talent, young lady. You're a real trouper as well, and we're very happy that you've come to join us at Parlophone.*'

The third session, one month later, featured numbers you could bite into. *It had to be you . . .*

Valaida was having a very good time. She was loving London, loving the appreciation of her public and the beautiful gowns this appreciation was affording her to buy. She was loving the Cockney cabdrivers and the gentlemanly police, the white-trimmed brick buildings, the well-kept public parks, the charming flat she and Nyas had found in Regent's Park, with its tiny little fireplaces and deep, heavy tub, away from the bustle of the theatrical West End. For the first time in her life she wasn't living right in the night life. Bars and hustlers had been replaced by trees and pale, quiet children in the care of uniformed nannies. Valaida awoke to birdsong rather than the rivalling tumults of car horns and street vendors, and she would have thought of staying in London if Nyas had been disposed; but Nyas wasn't sharing his wife's excitement over England. Nyas never wanted to sight-see, said he had no interest in 'dead white men on horses and boring old piles of dirty stones'. He was only slightly enthused by the new canes, suits, and gloves Valaida bought for him in the shops off Piccadilly (though he did find pleasure in the custom-made shoes). His spare hours seemed to be spent with his buddies in the cast, drinking whiskey, shooting craps, and counting the days until they returned home.

'*Baby, I'd give my best silk shirt for a decent steak and a cold Coca-Cola!*'

Valaida suspected that maybe love involved the exercise of patience as well as passion and that she might change his mind into settling one day in a place where their talents were appreciated and where they were treated with respect, but mostly her mind was teeming with the music.

'*A wonderful time in London. Not thinking of anything beyond yourself.*'

'*Oh, Cas, please, I was finally doing what I could do.*'

London, Spring 1935

It was already April. After days of persistent rain, a bit of sun shone on the draperies. The table was strewn with music and press cuttings. Valaida was checking the pads on her trumpet. Nyas was wearing his grey herringbone.

'*Baby, I was thinking about asking Mr Culpepper if I couldn't record that song I've been working on. I figure it's about ready, and it being mine and all, the guys won't be ready to do much more than vamp. I could get a good solid solo in, like the one I lost when "Poor Butterfly" didn't work. I'm going to call it "Imagination". What do you think?*'

Nyas had been studying the racing form, having a last piece of toast, not like the English liked it, browned on both sides. It took longer, but it pleased Valaida to accommodate her husband.

'*Think? About what? Oh, that song you been playin' with. They seem to love you down there. They'll probably give you the shot.*'

'*You wanna come keep me company? You know more about music than all those ofays put together.*'

'*Me? No, sorry, baby, I gotta meet a guy.*'

He didn't kiss her goodbye before he pulled on his gloves and adjusted his hat. The grey homburg with the two-inch black band. There was a rash across his cheekbone. His nostrils flared. The soft wool of his jacket caressed his back with grace when he turned. The moulding around the door glistened in the sconce-light.

'*I'll play it to you, Nyas.*'

The entry door slammed shut. He was already in the street.

The cab ride to the studio had been especially pretty. Trees were beginning to flower. Window boxes were being renewed.

I imagined that I was rich, and that I did receive
A cottage full of bliss in a land of make believe . . .

She'd placed her hand against Culpepper's tie, looked intently into his eyes, deferred to his infinite wisdom, and willed him to answer yes.

. . . My only inspiration is just my imagination,
And I make believe, I make believe . . .

The band was more than willing to let her have some room. Parlophone was pushing her as a singer, but her musicians knew she was more than that.

'*We're all better for playing with you, Valaida. You're as good as anyone we've ever heard. You're right up there with Louis.*'

'*Don't lose your reason now, fellas.*'

'*Just tell us what you need.*'

Culpepper agreed to postpone 'I Must Have That Man'. Valaida agreed only to sing on the date's three other songs.

. . . I dreamed that I'm in love, and that on some sunny day
The man I'm thinking of, he'll come and pass my way . . .

She was thinking of Nyas. Who would have thought that she'd ever have come to that? Ruby Jones would have been howling, her sisters dropping their jaws.

. . . Love and imagination. Imagination and love.
You dream and dream and dream and dream . . .

She'd wanted to use the words she'd started using since she'd come to England, but some of them were long, their consonants in difficult places. Her words weren't scanning easily. Her enunciation was feeling heavy. Was she hearing too much vibrato? Maybe she had sung better. But never with so much of her heart.

. . . There are certain dreams, just like a ship without a stern,
No matter how you steam, you can never make a turn.
My only inspiration is just my imagination, and I make
*   believe . . .*

When she'd finished the lyric, Duncan held out a platform, and Valaida took off. She wasn't flying like she had with Earl. She felt like she was climbing through the branches of an old spreading tree. She was fighting her way to the light. Webs and leaves were blocking her view. She could only sense which way to turn. She dug down, below the perspiration trickling from her armpits, past her technique, into the deepest, knottiest marrow of her core. From deep within her being she could hear someone wailing. The pain of it was near unbearable. It stifled her breath, made her choke and stumble while her fingers worked of their own accord. Her eyes were closed, but she saw colours. The insides of her eyelids were streaked with green and scarlet until suddenly everything blazed into a radiance of white. She was there. She had made it.

And I make believe . . .

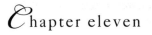

*C*hapter eleven

Vestre Faengsel Prison, Copenhagen, April 1942

Fange Nr. Valaida Snowberry
15 April 1942

Inspector
My dear sir
Did you forget to ask Mr Weine if my passport has come from
Sweden, also if he knows when the ship leaves for America? I
received no message from you so I'd thought you'd forgotten.

Also, please tell me if you can help me, by moving me into the
hospital, as you promised me, if it were possible, you would. I
hope it is possible, as I am getting more sick every day, and I'm
sure that it is only my mind. I'm sorry to worry you so much, as
I was surprised this morning to find you such a nice man, but if
you don't help me, no one will. All of the nurses in the hospital

but one speak English, and here I understand no one and no one understands me. Please help me if you can.

    Sincerely yours,
    Valaida

There's an unevenness of paint on her wall. About eight inches above her cot and maybe five inches from where she lays her head, the brown thins to reveal a grey-green underneath. It's more pleasing than the brown, a pond of soothing cool. About eighteen inches further along there's a small raised line of something imbedded in the paint. Probably hair from a paintbrush. It looks like a scar, or maybe a fossil. Valaida had seen fossils one day in a museum in London. The day had been sunny when she'd cajoled Nyas into walking through the pretty crescents and squares of South Kensington. Valaida had loved the white, joined-up houses with their fluted columns and brilliant flowers. Nyas had been willing to humour her until it started to rain. They'd run into a museum, a huge fort of a place, which had on display huge skeletons of animals that had once roamed the earth – it was hard to imagine that anything live could ever have been so big – and cases of flat rocks that held the imprints of other crushed and long-dead things. Mostly birds. Some fish. Some strange things on legs that were almost like animals she knew but not quite. The birds had been caught in the mud, and the mud had been buried and pressed until after many long years it had turned to stone. You could not only see what was left of the bones. You could see feathers as well. Little raised-up lines.

    'It's not but a few hours since you met that man. You think he has nothing else to do but deal with your little problem? You've lost all track of time, and those nurses were not English-speakers.'

    'Two of them were.'

    'You need to be careful, darling. You know that your record of convincing men of your sincerity and good intentions has not been all that great.'

    'It hasn't all been my fault, you know. It could have something to do with the quality of the man.'

'Which could have something to do with the way you've made your choices.'

'I chose you.'

'And where has that gotten you?'

Los Angeles, March 1936

I've got the world on a string
Sitting on a rainbow . . .

Valaida drives through the California sunshine. It is late afternoon, the sun slanting across the Pacific clear and strong, its white gold blaze just now taking on hints of orange as it slides across the snow capping the San Gabriel Mountains. Her Hollywood meeting has gone quickly and well. She has secured two more appearances in movie shorts for herself and Nyas, with a small company, it's true, but then the big companies only used Negro women as maids or squaws, if they were light enough, and no way was Valaida going to spend a day sitting on the ground with some feathers in her hair. The music shorts were fun and painless and got shown around the country. More folks would get familiar with what they did, and that could only be for the good. Valaida is feeling pleased with herself, so she has decided to take the long way home. She loves to drive this road that joined the canyons, the snout of her pale yellow car before her as her trumpet protrudes when she plays, the Pacific Ocean beyond Beverly Hills on her right, the mountains beyond the valley's orange groves on her left, the silk lining of her skirt slipping against the silk of her hose as her feet shift confidently between the accelerator, brake, and clutch, her fingernails tapping against the luxury of the solid ivory steering wheel. Valaida had never really enjoyed driving before this time in California. She'd always preferred being driven, until the accident with Fats convinced her that knowing the workings of a car might prolong her life – better her behind the wheel than

357

some blind drunk fool – but before California, she never did it out of choice. Rather a smartly uniformed chauffeur squiring her between hotel and club, holding the door and taking her bags if she'd shopped, bystanders craning their necks with wonder at who this coloured woman could be with the casually elegant air and the long fine limousine; and she's always sensed something vaguely sinister about Eastern roads outside a city, as though a skulk of Klansmen might be lurking behind a haystack waiting to rampage across a cornfield. Not so in Southern California. Here, in the space and light of the Los Angeles hills, Valaida feels free. More than free. On top of her world. *What a world, what a life . . .* And there's reason.

For nearly six months Valaida and Nyas have been working at Frank Sebastian's Cotton Club, performing in a show she was brought in to produce. Always on the lookout for new talent for his club, which, like its Eastern namesake, featured 'only the best in sepia entertainment', Frank Sebastian had caught Valaida and Nyas' act at the Lafayette in New York not long after their return from London. He'd liked the interplay between wife and husband that sweetened their versatility, found clever the way Valaida had woven a line of dancers into their spot. Compliments backstage flowed into drinks at the Hotel Theresa. Sebastian knew about Valaida's work at the Terrace in Chicago and asked her what she would want to do if she had a whole show to produce for an audience of movie stars.

'We're right down the road from MGM and Culver,' he'd said. 'They're in there every night, Clark Gable, Joan Crawford, Dick Powell, Claudette Colbert.'

'Anything I wanted?' she'd asked.

'Within reason,' Sebastian had replied.

'How big a reason?' she'd asked.

'Pretty damn big,' Sebastian had replied.

If she'd been watching, she would have noticed the swelling of the problem right there at the Theresa. Nyas had been by her side that night, but neither she nor Sebastian had paid him much mind save to acknowledge the certainty that he'd have much to give the dancers. While Valaida and Sebastian had enthused about picture numbers from *Footlight Parade* and *Dames*, argued the merits of Dorothy Fields's lyrics versus those of Andy Razaf, Nyas had slouched and drunk and smoked. Valaida had occasionally smiled in her husband's direction and caressed his knee, but Nyas didn't smile once after they'd left the stage that night. Valaida might have noticed her husband's eyes that evening to be glowering or opaque and his mouth to be grim; but she hadn't been watching. She'd been concentrating on selling herself to this white man, who seemed pleased to hear what she had to say, whose eyes could keep her in view without spending too long on her breasts. She was using language and confidence she had practised on white men in England, and what's more she was enjoying herself. She'd felt herself glittering inside a circle of starlight. She hadn't had time to keep watch on her husband.

The richest offer of their lives arrived less than one week later. Four figures a week for a minimum of four weeks. Four figures a week for all these months. Crazy money in a depression. Money for champagne and fine whiskey, beautiful clothes and fancy cars. Money for servants and parties and even for the gambling Nyas seemed to enjoy so much, and still some left over to send Mama and Arthur in Washington; but money alone wasn't the source of Valaida's satisfaction. Every night she appeared in a show of her own devising, where even the costumes had been designed to her specifications. She had supervised both the dance and vocal arrangements and imported a chorus from Chicago when she found that some of the locals couldn't play up to her standards. Unlike Lew Leslie or Ed Fox in Chicago, Frank Sebastian was a gentleman who treated his talent with respect. His place might be called the Cotton Club, but Valaida didn't feel like she was on a plantation. Coming to work was a pleasure, even on days that might have started off poorly, with Nyas peevish or pouting, or her knees wishing that she would just stop.

Once she walked through the door of the club, started exchanging hellos, checking that all the performers were present and ready to give their all, Valaida would feel renewed. She could feel the light inside her body coming up from her tail bone across her shoulders, into her head and down her arms. It was bright and strong and better than sex. It didn't pierce her brain like playing the horn could when it was right, which was fine because no one could live for long inside that kind of ecstasy. It braced and lifted her like wings. Valaida was up in the air, and it felt like she could fly for ever. For the first time in her life, she was not itching to be some place else or comparing herself to somebody else. She didn't perform for the dream merchants, hoping they'd make her a star. She knew they had nothing she wanted. Nina Mae McKinney had been given a five-year contract after wowing them in *Hallelujah!*, but in five years the moguls hadn't come up with one thing that they thought she could do. Nina Mae was like Valaida, small, pretty, caramel, and smart, neither a maid nor a squaw, and Nina Mae was sitting around half-crazy with boredom and frustration while Valaida was living her own movie every night. Valaida didn't trust that it would last for ever; but in show business you thought about right now; and she is satisfied, serene.

> . . . *I've got a song that I sing*
> *I can make the rain go*
> *Anytime I move my finger . . .*

The San Gabriel snow is becoming tinged with violet, and a jack rabbit races across the road. Valaida hasn't been around so much nature since the South of her *Jimtown* days, and she is surprised that it brings her such a sense of well-being. These driving times are hers alone, for Nyas has little use for fresh air and spaces outside watching dogs and horses running circles around suckers' dreams. Valaida hasn't had much use for gambling since her days with Samuel Lanier, but at least Nyas didn't lose too much more than he won; and if it kept him happy that was fine with her. No

360

doubt that's where he was right now, catching the last action at the Culver City dog track, then he'd fall by Goldie's for a couple drinks and some pool before allowing their chauffeur, Mr Evans, to drive him home to change. Thank goodness he was enjoying himself more in Los Angeles than he had London.

'Too many crackers in London,' he'd said. 'They just get up my craw, baby. I ain't never gonna trust a one of them, and neither should you.'

Of course Valaida didn't trust white people. She wasn't a fool; but she had learned in London that not every white man she met wanted to kill, humiliate, or rape her; and she was using that knowledge here in Los Angeles to move herself into this position that she was finding so very pleasing. *Lucky me . . . Can't you see . . .* After two more curves, she takes the turn down towards Beverly Hills.

There are restrictive covenants in Beverly Hills which forbid Negroes living in its streets, but the house Valaida and Nyas are renting belongs to Frank Sebastian; and while Sebastian is a gentleman, some of his powerful friends are not; so the neighbours have learned to avert their eyes politely. This does not bother Valaida. She does not need their friendship, enjoys the property's generous proportions, and has come to appreciate quiet during the months spent living in London. Two neighbourhood boys on bicycles stare as Valaida drives past in her elegant Cord. The younger boy starts to wave, but the older one restrains him. A Negro maid is walking a pampered little dog. She doesn't wave either.

The Rolls is already in the driveway, their chauffeur asleep in the front seat. Valaida taps on the half-open window.

'What're you doing out here, Mr Evans?' Valaida is smiling. She likes this old man. He is proud and true and has no problems doing for coloured. 'You know Esmeralda always has something for you in the kitchen.'

'Evening, Miz Berry. It was just so pleasant out here that I thought I'd catch myself a bit of comfort.' The chauffeur's rheumy eyes are straight into her own, telling her everything she needs to know and yet giving up nothing.

Valaida walks the short path to the house assailed by the scent of gardenia from the pots on both sides of the door, so strong it wants to snatch the breathing right out of her lungs. That was one of the things about California. Exotic flowers just grew like weeds. There's a twitch at the base of her neck as Valaida presses down on the lock lever and pushes open the door.

The first thing she notices is the stillness, before she sees the whiskey bottle on its side, the melting ice cubes outside their bucket, the cute little hat on the sofa where the cushions are no longer plumped. Outside, a mockingbird is rippling through its repertoire. The two neighbourhood boys are arguing over who won their bicycle race – 'I did!' 'Did not!' 'Did, too!' 'Did not!' – but inside, stillness. Valaida picks up the little hat, whispering for the maid. 'Esmeralda?' But she knows Esmeralda is not there, has long since left to attend to her children. Perspiration prickles under Valaida's armpits as she heads down the corridor towards what she senses is in her bedroom. A female shoe lies in the hall. It's not so witty as the hat. The door to the master bedroom is ajar. 'Nyas?' she calls. She receives no reply. It is no longer so still, though the breathing other than her own she senses more than hears. She walks down the corridor, dropping the hat beside its shoe, willing her trembling to cease as she pushes open the bed-room door.

The bedroom is strewn with garments, only a few of them not her own. A new trumpet is out of its case, tangled in turbulent bed-clothes. Its mouthpiece is smeared with lipstick. The room stinks of semen and fear. Now Valaida hears a whimper. She is no longer sweating, but stony cold. Retrieving the trumpet, she approaches the walk-in closet and firmly opens its door. Nyas is naked, but the girl, a dancer in the Cotton Club line, whose attribute has always been more eagerness than skill, is trying to cover her shame. Her camisole is twisted, and one of her breasts is bobbling free. She clutches one of Valaida's skirts before her, and she is speechless

362

with fear. Spittle is trickling down her chin. Valaida takes hold of her skirt, *the brown glen plaid with the apricot lining*, and deliberately cleans the trumpet mouthpiece. The only sound is their breathing, all of it shallow, Valaida's and Nyas' angry, ready for battle, the young girl's terrified. The mouthpiece now free of the lipstick, Valaida feels something explode in her brain. She grabs the girl's wrist, sending her sprawling onto the bedroom floor.

'Don't kill me!' the girl's screaming. *What was her name? Lurene? Damned if she didn't look just like a Lurene, with her big cow eyes and stupid, quivering lips.* 'Please don't kill me!'

Valaida doesn't hear the words. She is grabbing her dresses off of the floor, the bed, the divan, her dressing table, and throwing them onto the moaning girl. 'You like my clothes?' she's saying. 'You like the idea of my French perfume hugging up against your titties? Well, here you are, then! More fucking, beautiful rags than a whore like you could earn in a lifetime!' The girl's fear is now laced with confusion as Valaida yanks her up off the floor. 'You've got ten seconds to get out of here, or this brass will split your skull.' The girl's what-but-butting, when Valaida starts to count. 'One . . . two . . . three . . .' The girl is on her feet and running, cradling as many clothes as she can manage. The front door slams on the count of seven. Tears are now edging down Valaida's cheeks, but Nyas is calm, a sneer on his lips, his eyes obsidian hard.

'How long has this been going on?' Valaida finally manages.

'Use your 'Imagination',' Nyas replies. Emerging from the closet at last, he uses one of Valaida's blouses to wipe dry his penis before selecting a clean pair of shorts from a drawer.

'Not with that little . . . thing.' Valaida's voice is strangled. She doesn't recognize it as her own.

'Lurene? No, she was a last-minute volunteer.' He sniffs at an armpit before selecting a laundered shirt. Parchment, they'd called the colour. She had bought it for him in London. And the tie.

'You hate me so much?'

'No baby. I don't hate you. You just seemed to stay confused on who has the dick in this family. It's me, in case you haven't

363

noticed.' He was standing so she would notice, and there was a good deal to see. In spite of her pain, Valaida remembers herself caressing those shorts, feeling the tumble of testicles across her palm, feeling them tighten, tracing his penis as it engorged.

'I was never confused, Nyas. I always knew you were the man. My man, the sweetest man I've ever known. I love you, you know.' *You're leaving me. You're leaving me?* He selected the pigeon grey suit, the one with wide chalk stripe and the double-breasted jacket that skirted the rise of his behind just snug enough to tantalize them that might be looking.

'I believe you, baby, and what's more, you ought to know that everything I know about love I've learned from you.' He sits on the bed to tie his shoes. He is close enough that she can smell Lurene radiating from his torso. He stands, slips on the jacket, shoots his cuffs. 'I'll be rejoining Warren and Jimmy at the end of the week. We're going out on the Pantages, starting up out of Portland. I've already told Sebastian . . .

Before you told me. He's leaving me. No one has left me since my daddy.

'He didn't think it would be any problem. Said he'd miss me though. Right white of him, don't you think?' He picks up his wallet, his lighter, checks his cigarette case for contents, then puts it into a pocket. 'I'll see you down at the Club. I don't think we need to worry about Lurene. Nobody's going to miss her. Couldn't hold a routine in that little pea-brain to save her life.' Five seconds later the door slams again.

Valaida now realizes she has been gripping the trumpet so tightly her fingers are cramping. They are crooked and throbbing when she lets go the brass. She'll need warm water to coax them back to movement. She zombies into the bathroom, turns on the faucet, glimpses a wild-eyed stranger in the mirror, then falls, sobbing and heaving, to the floor.

But she was immaculate that night. In the two hours between her discovery of Nyas and the eight o'clock dinner show, she had picked herself off of the bathroom floor, cleansed herself of bile and vomit, summoned Esmeralda back to the house to work some special magic with her hair, and sailed into Sebastian's with cleared eyes, a radiant smile, and two new performance gowns over her arm. If there were whispers and averted glances among the girls along the gauntlet to her dressing room, she did not choose to notice. She smiled her greetings, drank her tea, and listened to Les Hite put his band through its paces. Having chosen in those hours not to go on in the revue without Nyas, she would want to fine-tune the show before her departure, but she would start taking her notes during the evening's second show. Now, her concentration was concerned with taming the energy necessary for her upcoming slot with the husband she now knew despised her. She would not allow pique and heartbreak to destroy the best work she had ever done. She would sparkle, she would tease, she would dance, and she would blow. Fingering the small gold vermeil box in her handbag, she decided its contents wouldn't help. At least not just then.

Valaida and Nyas didn't appear together until the end of the revue. Nyas had a featured bit in the picture number, doing a sepia Fred Astaire through the large hats and sweeping skirts, but didn't return until Valaida had lustered through the three numbers that were her platform. This was the only part of the show that really changed from night to night. Valaida had a book of a few dozen numbers from which she would make her selections with Les Hite after closing the night before. The first show was always upbeat. Tonight it would be 'Swing is the Thing', 'Sing You Sinners', and then 'Blow, Gabriel, Blow', a very nice concept if she did say so herself, and she'd take off with 'Gabriel'. By the time she'd finished she'd have the audience eating out of her hand, and she would have prepared herself for Nyas.

She was ready when Les bent the music under the applause and back into the little bubbling riff designed to give her a chance to thank the audience, catch her breath, and give the sweet and sly little intro before starting into the lyrics that invited Nyas to strut

365

on the number that was his trademark. '. . . When you see him, ladies and gentlemen, I'm sure you'll know what I mean.'

Papa de da da. He's a ladies' man,
Papa de da da. Sweetest in the land.
Papa de da da. Watch him plant his hand.
He's nice and soft, never cross,
Red hot mamas, he cools them off.
Papa dee da de da da. He's the hottest man in town . . .

He strutted out from behind the centre curtain with the perfect sky-high kick and twist that always took folks' breath away. Nyas had been dancing 'Papa De Da Da' as long as Valaida had known him, had started before she knew him, and would probably keep on at it until he was crippled or dead. Valaida couldn't imagine what it had to be like doing the same routine show after show, night after night, week after week, year after year. It would have driven her stark, staring mad. Nyas was gifted but he was lazy, and knowing this kept a smile on her lips all through lyrics that might have tugged at her heart while describing him to a tee. *He's a ladies' man.*

His eyes told her that he was surprised she was so steady. Her eyes told him, 'Baby, you've underestimated me.' His eyes told her, 'All right then, let's get it on.' The break when they played off each other was what they were squaring for. Usually it was twenty-four bars of fun and games, but this night it would be forty-eight bars of warcraft. Les Hite was caught out of pocket for a beat, which was when he knew the game was serious. Then he led the band into a vamp with some drum bippity-bops as Valaida and Nyas traded shots back and forth and gave the audience a set to remember. She blew on him; he stepped on her. She arpeggioed up into a laughing call of 'You don't faze me, Mr Man'; he double back-flipped into a split and pimp pull-up of 'Your hold on me is through'. She circled around him with a triple-tongued *Diga-Do*; he broke the circle and wrapped around her like a snake. The number always closed with them forehead to forehead for a smile and a short, sweet kiss, followed by a hug and a holding-hands bow. This night was the same, but everything took longer as the crowd roared its approval. The smiles were at once hard and lingering, as was the kiss. '*The Berrys, ladies and gentlemen! Aren't they wonderful?! Valaida Snow and Ananias Berry! Valaida Snow . . .!*' Their eyes opened, he gripped her arms hard, she did not flinch, and then they turned forward for their bow, her hands cupped around the trumpet she hadn't named out of deference to her husband, his right arm outstretched in the general direction of her back. There would be nine more shows in the days that followed, but no more kisses. The plays on their togetherness went the ways of their affections.

'*So, that was it? One extra-mural piece of pussy and you drum him out of your life?*'

'*It wasn't the first time, and you know it.*'

'*I'd have thought that knowing you had that kind of thing in common would have brought you two closer together.*'

'*I'd kept my word after Earl, Cas. I hadn't played around.*'

'*But you didn't curb yourself, either. How's a man supposed to feel with himself all the time in background and his wife calling the shots? I've heard they find that distressing.*'

'*So what? I shouldn't do what I can do so my husband won't feel that I've cut off his dick? I wasn't wandering around with a knife in my hand. If that thing was loose, it was his own damn fault.*'

'*He needed your understanding.*'

'*He wanted me to be anything but what I was. I wasn't his princess or his mama.*'

'*Or helpmate, or port in the storm.*'

'*I never pretended to be something I wasn't. He can never say that I lied about who I was and what I thought was important. It was because of me that we had the life we were leading He didn't seem to mind the nice clothes and the fancy cars. I didn't need to be in charge. If he'd wanted to work harder it could have been him.*'

'*It's not that easy, and you know it. You cooed and coy-ed Sebastian into everything you wanted. How's a black man going to do that and hold*'

367

onto his balls, assuming that a white man let him get that close in the first place?'

'You're supposed to be my friend, Castor. Whose side are you on?'

'Yours, baby. All the time . . . So, what about you thinking that you had one of your own?'

'What, a dick? It would have ruined the line of my gowns.'

'Besides, you had a trumpet.'

'Yes, I had a trumpet, but if you men want to waste your time believing that I think my horn is some kind of dick, that is your problem, not mine. Besides, those things are vastly over-rated.'

'And you never played on the believing?'

'Their fantasies. Not mine.'

'So no regrets.'

'No regrets.'

'So why the tell-tale moisture? Things got complicated after Los Angeles didn't they, darling? Didn't fall into the positive all the time the way they had been. You'd been pretty lucky up to then for a coloured girl from Chattanooga. Scuffed your knees a couple times, but then, almost like magic, something or someone would help you back onto your toes. You run into Bessie in Atlantic City when you needed the back of Samuel. I show up in New York and wham! you're on your way to Paris. Ethel Waters is worrying your nerves, but Nyas is right there convincing you to leave that show and go out on your own. But it wasn't so smooth after Los Angeles. Do you ever chance to wonder if Nyas might have been your luck?'

'I don't believe in luck. Couldn't nobody have done a thing for me if I hadn't been ready. I believe in work and keeping your head up one day after another. I believe in myself: I don't believe in luck!'

'No need to get upset, my sweet. If that's what you think, fine, I accept it. I'm on your side, remember? Always have been, always will be . . .'

$\mathcal{C}$hapter twelve

Vestre Faengsel Prison, Copenhagen, April 1942

In the dull grey light, the mounds of drab, coarse food look even less appetizing than they would if she could bring herself to taste them. She has tried. No one can accuse her of not trying, for she is hungry and hasn't really eaten for days; but when the mound grabbed her spoon, which stood upright among the grains, when her nose caught the smell of lard, and she saw the fat congealing on her dish, Valaida couldn't help herself. Her stomach began to heave. There was nothing left in her to void, so her eyes streamed tears instead. The old pain has returned to her shoulder, and her fingers are quivering with need. How could it have come to this? How could she have gone from the Grand Terrace and Sebastian's Cotton Club, the high life in London and the rush of Harlem to the concrete confines of this cell? How could she have gone from custom-made silks and furs to the canvas now encapsulating her

369

body, from stylishly arranged coiffeurs to pickaninny braids? How could she have dropped so far, be so forsaken? Just because she wanted to go her own way? Was that really so heinous a crime that as penalty she had to forfeit her liaison with luck? Valaida doesn't understand. She does not understand. For all her talks with Castor, she does not understand.

Could Nyas have been her luck?

Fange Nr. 47, Valaida Snowberry
16 April 1942

My dear Inspector
I wrote to you yesterday asking you to please let me telephone the Politigaarden, and again you did not answer. It is not much trouble for you to pick up the telephone and answer me, or I will come to you. I have not eaten since Sunday. I cannot eat here. I am very sick, and no one comes to see me, only in the night to give me medicine for sleep and one time in the day for nerves. You allow the other people to have the door open in the day, but you give orders for my door to be always locked. When I asked to return here I thought you would be nice. Now I see that your heart is made of prison bars and steel. How can you treat a woman who is alone, as you are treating me, when you have a family? Won't you please be gentleman enough to answer me? I know you'll keep me locked in, but you could allow me to telephone? The prison has made me sick again. I think I shall have to return to hospital. Who gives that order? Please answer quickly.
Yours sincerely,
Valaida

Valaida lifts the lever attached to the flat black circle that will stick diagonally into the corridor and summon a guard to her cell. Cas is wrong. Valaida has not lost track of time, but every moment in this concrete is its own forever. There have been endless eternities between yesterday's note and the one today. The grate slides open, and her sheets of paper are accepted with a grunt that carries with it a marked edge of derision. Valaida doesn't care. The Prison Governor must know her plight. She must write her notes or scream.

Could Nyas have been her luck?

Valaida has never had to believe in luck, or pray for luck or pray to Somebody Else to bring her luck, for luck had always been with her dependably as a shadow. She has never considered her life, she has lived her life, day to day, year to year. There has been no attention or time for contemplation; there has only been time to do, to strive, to achieve, to strut. To be inside the joy. She worked for her joy; she earned it; how does it come to this?

The grate slides open, and Valaida feels stabbings in her heart, a roiling in her stomach. It is not time for an outside half-hour. Perhaps the Governor has taken mercy after all?

'*Du komme, Fru Snowberry.*' You will come, Mrs Snowberry. Valaida is trembling as she stands, her heart beating so loudly she cannot hear the clang of metal keys in metal door. Walking down the corridor, she bites at her lips and smooths her hair. She thinks of where she must pitch her voice. She may literally throw herself at his feet, but she must not be shrill. Screeching is useless in seduction, especially in one that must remain chaste. Her cheek is twitching. Should she will it to stop, or would it strengthen her case for transfer back to the *Rigshospitalet*? She must look vulnerable but somehow appealing, despite the sexless anonymity of her prison garb. She straightens her shoulders and pulls herself up beyond her height in order that she can tread more lightly in the awkward clogs. She innocents her eyes, then notices she is no longer walking in the direction of the Governor's Office. The guard has turned her left instead of right. They have reached another door.

'*Du har besog.*' You have a visitor. A visitor? Who could it be, and was there anyone in this entire country she really wanted to see other than whoever was involved in the process of getting her out of there? But Valaida was not going to reject the chance for some human interaction. There was no question of her not taking a seat in the cubicle she was assigned, but Valaida would never have expected to see the woman who sat on the other side of her bars.

There was never any question from whence Henny had come. She and her mother had shared the same eyes, brow, shape of hands, square, with the middle and ring fingers almost of equal length. The mother's chin was more delicate. Henny would have benefited from inheriting her mother's jaw rather than so obviously her father's blunted line. Valaida had met Mrs Thomsen twice before, first in the summer that both Henny and Valaida had been working the Tivoli Gardens. Valaida had felt the mother's eyes upon her, studying the object of the daughter's adulation. Having shared no sense of complicity, having felt no responsibility for the intensity of Henny's rapture, Valaida had seen no reason to meet the mother's eyes. She'd felt no scandalized indignation in the gaze that might have warranted a returned defiance or studied anger and so had permitted the mother's eyes to roam. Valaida was, after all, quite used to and pleased by being looked at. She remembers giving Henny's shoulders a squeeze as the scrutiny neared its end.

The second meeting had occurred two days after Henny moved into the Hotel Rio. Thirteen days before her death. Secreted in her shopping basket, risking her husband's wrath, the mother had brought a parcel of clothes and a Bible to her daughter. The mother hadn't left after handing over the bundle. There had been no choice other than to invite her up to the room her daughter and the *neger* American woman shared. Mrs Thomsen had meant no offence when she used the word; she was a simple woman who knew no other. Once in the room, the mother had looked around, at the trumpet, the narrow bed, her daughter's faded dance costume, Valaida's silks, a colourful kimono and the lingerie she still possessed. Once again the mother's eyes had rested on Valaida, and once again Valaida had chosen not to connect. She had busied herself with her nails as Henny and her mother had whispered, wept, and embraced. Valaida had said goodbye when Mrs Thomsen had taken her leave, but this time it was the mother who had softened her eyes.

Valaida has no idea how the mother has found her, nor why she would want to see her. How much was there to say, even if

372

they had shared a fluency? But in the prison's visiting room Valaida no longer has a choice but to meet the mother's eyes, and what she finds in their grey and yellow is not what she would have expected. Strain, yes, and grief and loss still after little more than a year, but no hate, no accusation, rather a quiet pleasure in seeing the object of her daughter's love before her. And not for the reasons any person would expect. The eyes held no gloating at Valaida's diminished circumstances. There was no smirk about her lips. Instead, the mother brought with her a serenity, which for a few brief moments embraced Valaida in so unexpected a cloak of warmth that once again the prisoner's eyes were streaming.

After the women had exchanged nodded greetings, Valaida found that she had to know. '*Hvorfor har du her?*' she asked. Why are you here?

'*Fordi hun elskede dig.*' Because she loved you, the mother replied, dropping her look to the battered handbag she carries, withdrawing from the handbag a small oblong packet. '*Der er kun lidt at give.*' There is so little to give. '*Jeg haaber du vil modtage disse.*' I hope these you can accept.

Valaida can see that the packet contains two cigarettes before the guard steps forward to prevent its exchange. Valaida's composure is all but gone; only her eyes can manage a thank you. The mother pushes a hand as far towards the bars as the rules allow, and Valaida finds her own hand moving to the bars as well. The women say nothing, but in the few short moments of their connected gaze, Valaida can feel the mother's warmth mitigating the iron's chill. There is the barest hint of tremble at the corners of the mother's mouth.

'*Gud velsigne og bevare dig, Valeyeda,*' she says. God bless and keep you.

Then she rises, then she is gone.

You! You're driving me crazy
What did I do? What did I do? . . .

The two cigarettes are lying on her table. Valaida does not have any matches, smoking is not allowed in her cell. She could probably convince the guard to give her a light during one of her outside half-hours, but will she? The cigarettes are side by side on her table. Is it easier with or without the memory? Valaida cannot understand the mother. She cannot understand someone capable of moving so far away from such a catastrophic loss to embrace someone who initiated that pain.

'I've been told it can come from a profound belief in the Lord, but then maybe she just wanted more of a connection with her daughter.'

Valaida is fidgeting with one of the cigarettes to the point that its wrapper is fraying, and some of the tobacco is falling loose.

'Hold on there, sister! That's cash money you're toying with. You're in a war, remember? Those things are rare.'

'I can feel her, Cas. Her eyes were just like Henny's, like Henny was talking to me through her mother.'

'I imagine she could have a variety of things to say.'

'But I have nothing to say to her! Nothing! It's over! It's the past. Don't you think I'm paying enough? She needs to leave me alone!'

Valaida rubs open the cigarettes and throws their contents around the room.

'Ingratitude is a most unattractive personality trait, my dear, and in blinkered self-absorption lies a fast road to perdition. You should be cottoning on to that by now, Valaida. You are beginning to disappoint.'

'I'm no kind of cotton nigger, Castor! And don't you laugh at me!'

'I'll stop laughing when you start learning.'

*C*hapter thirteen

Chicago to New York, Spring 1936

Goin' to Chicago, sorry I can't take you . . .
. . . There's nothing in Chicago a monkey man can do . . .

She'd packed up her gowns after the split with Nyas and headed
East to the Windy City, which was how Earl Sutcliffe Jones had
come into her life. She'd met him in Los Angeles. He'd been
hanging around for a while. He'd be at Sebastian's during
rehearsals. You went to a party, and there he'd be again. Small,
chestnut-skinned, always sharp. Called himself a manager. Usually
had some cute little girlie by his side, some would-be dancer or
singer with desperation in her smile. Earl would sidle up to Valaida
wherever it was he found her, always with something flattering to
say, always just this side of respectful. Always smelling of violet.
Usually wanting to introduce her to that day's protegée, but on the

day after Nyas, Earl had had something else to say. Valaida had
called a rehearsal in order to re-work the show for after she and
Nyas were gone, and there was Earl, as predictable as a spinster's
monthly. He'd brought in a couple of comics to be considered for
the show, but it wasn't them he'd wanted to talk about when he'd
appeared at her side, oozing charm from every seam of his carmine
garbardine belt-back jacket.

'I was so sorry to hear about you and Nyas,' he'd said. 'This is
all such a shock.'

Valaida had been in no mood for lies. 'A shock, huh? As much
territory that man was covering through the ponies in this town?
When they're your stock in trade?'

Earl Sutcliffe Jones hadn't looked embarrassed, hadn't missed
a beat. 'I hear you're thinking about heading into Chicago. Would
that be back into the Grand Terrace?'

Valaida didn't bother to sigh. There was too much work to be
done to waste time worrying about how fast your business circu-
lated. 'It won't be the Terrace,' she'd replied. 'Ed Fox and I didn't
part on civil terms, and I'm in no mood to stoop to conversation
with that man.'

Earl's face had taken on a hustler's smile, but if she'd been
looking she'd have noticed that his eyes had been glassy. 'A lady
like you shouldn't be having to deal with a gangster like Ed Fox,
Valaida Snow. That's what managers are for.'

Valaida had kept her attentions on the new material the
Rhythm Pals were wanting to incorporate into their spot. The
Pals always had new ideas, especially the pretty one on the right,
who was always looking, always thinking. Valaida was wishing that
Nyas had had some of that kind of drive, but Nyas was who he
was, and they were two different kinds of people. *Some of you men
sure do make me tired* . . . 'You proposing yourself as my manager, Mr
Jones?'

'I wouldn't expect a star of your magnitude to make that kind of
decision off of words alone, Miss Snow,' Earl had said. 'I'm proposing that I contact Ed Fox, and we see how it goes from there.

They have their new season starting in a couple weeks. Brother Hines will still be out on the road, so they'll be opening up with Fletcher. I'm presuming that could make your decision much easier.'

'It's not your place to presume, Mr Jones,' Valaida had replied. 'That will cost you two per cent right there.' She'd turned to face him then. There'd been perspiration by the sides of his nose. The kind that weak men got when someone stronger had shoes on their backs; but two days later he was back with an offer. It wasn't Cotton Club money, but it was no embarrassment either. So she'd sold her pretty Cord automobile, packed up her gowns and her trumpets, and boarded the Twentieth Century to Chicago. Mr Evans would be meeting her there. Nyas had been the one who had truly loved the Rolls, and she was pleased to keep it from him. Goodbye palm trees, goodbye movie stars, goodbye Ananias Berry. Valaida Snow is headed for the rest of her natural life.

> . . . *If you see me comin', raise your window high*
> *If you see me comin', raise your window high* . . .

She'd been loving Chicago, knocking them dead in a place where people knew their music. The audience at the Terrace wasn't as glamorous as movie stars, but they were there to enjoy the show. They weren't trying to get their photograph in next week's *Photoplay*, worrying about how in the hell were they going to be up for that make-up call at five-thirty in the morning when it was already midnight and the photo man hadn't even made it to their table. And Fletcher Henderson left Les Hite twisting in the dust. Performing on the floor with Fletcher's band behind her, pushed Valaida in the way she liked, pushed her further than Nyas' stepping had ever done. She wasn't missing Nyas, not his laziness nor his childish pouting, not his lack of interest in anything that wasn't smack in front of his face and then only if it had a direct impact on his life. And as for that thing he had, well, that was around for the having. Sizes varied, technique as well, but it wasn't as though it

377

was rare on the ground. Valaida was free, hot and on top of her game. She was packing them in at the Terrace, and columnists were happy to be kind. Life was going to be just fine.

'*And then the wire arrives from Allegretta.*'

'*Yes.*'

'*Your mama's poorly and doesn't have long.*'

'*Yes.*'

'*But by the time you get there, she's already gone.*'

'*Yes. Allegretta said that she had tried to reach me in time—*'

'*You believed her?*'

'*She seemed like a nice enough person. No, that's not right. She was a very good person, a good woman. I knew that as soon as I saw her. She was a warm person, and she was bereft. Why would she lie? But I never got any of the messages.*'

'*And your sisters didn't believe you.*'

Arthur, Jr had stood in the door with no recognition in his eyes.

'I'm Valaida,' she had said, and still he'd stood there, not moving to let her enter, nothing flickering or twitching that might suggest he had a brain.

'My mama's dead,' he said finally.

'I know, baby, I know,' she'd said, pulling him into a hug he'd resisted. 'She was my mama, too. You gonna let me come in and see her?' Hattie had appeared in the hallway then, all big and brown and heaving with rage. 'You dare to come here and show your face? Lavada warned us! She said you'd show up trying to steal this show just like you did her wedding with your fancy fashions and crocodile tears! Well, you can go right back where you came from! Mama doesn't need you any more, and neither do we!'

'*No, they didn't believe me.*'

'*They were grieving, Valaida. Grief doesn't follow any rules.*'

'*Lavada wasn't even there! She was over there in London. So how could she be claiming to know the truth of me? They didn't want me there. Alvada and Hattie. They said I should have stayed my selfish behind in Chicago, but it wasn't about them. She was my mama, too. Telling me that*'

Nyas was right to leave me, that I had no love in me, and he'd finally seen what I was. As though that had anything to do with burying the mother who had borne us all.'

Allegretta had saved her. Allegretta had gentled past Hattie and Arthur to take Valaida by the hand. 'Would you like to see her now?' she'd asked, and Valaida had mutely nodded yes.

The parlour's curtains had been drawn, and the scent of too many flowers had been heavy in the air. Alvada had been sitting by the open coffin, but a look from Allegretta had stilled the tongue in a twisting mouth. Allegretta's arm had been around Valaida's shoulder. 'Do you need some time alone?' she'd asked, and Valaida had nodded again.

Her mama's brow had looked smooth and hard. Like that of a hat mannequin in a Paris shop. Her hair was silvered with grey. There were grooves in her cheeks and under her eyes that Valaida didn't know. Her lips looked crêpey yet serene, but they had been painted a pink that didn't look right. She wore a navy blue suit and a green silk blouse with a cameo brooch Valaida didn't recognize. A small Bible rested beneath her hands. Valaida stretched fingers towards her mama's cheek but found herself afraid to touch. She wanted to kiss her brow, but tasted blood inside her mouth, and wouldn't defile her mama that way. She gazed at this woman and barely knew her and felt herself completely alone. She sensed her sisters in the room behind her, a wall of hostility in the cloying gloom. She gagged on the blood in her mouth. She tasted salt from her tears as well, and fury was chasing after her grief.

'They might have still been thinking about the bigamy time.'

'I told you about that! I only did what I had to do! They didn't want me to be there. They made more fuss about the cable Lavada sent than the blanket of roses I had made for Mama's casket. They should have known that I loved her! They didn't want me there. I'll never forgive them for that.'

'You're carrying a weight of anger in you, Valaida. Ever get the feeling it might be tripping you up?'

'Of course I'm angry! I'm still angry! They were jealous because I'd made a success of myself. I'd gone further than they could even think about going, and instead of being proud of me, they rip at my guts! They're happy that Nyas humiliated me. They accuse me of having no love for the mother who was all I had—'

'How could they know what kind of love you had? They never saw you there. You never visited. You were too busy living the swell life. People stumbling from day to day with cardboard in their shoes while you're swanning around in furs in the back of fancy limousines. How could they know you cared? Were they mind-readers?'

'But you know, don't you, Cas?'

'I know what you tell me, baby. So you're out of there in a temper, women screaming and crying, funeral cakes in a pile on the floor. You're on that train back to Chicago, and you have to calm yourself down.'

'I've got shows to do when I get there. I'm not going to let those chippies put me where they wanted me. I had to get my rest. I needed them out of my mind.'

'So you take out the little gift Earl had given you just in case.'

'Look, Valaida,' he'd said, 'I know you don't like to taste unless it's absolutely necessary, but it doesn't get much harder than the death of your mama. Just put this in that little gold box of yours. You could be thanking me, you know.'

'And you thanked him.'

'Yes, I did.'

It hadn't been the silken carpet on which she'd floated with Karol in Shanghai. It was fog, billowing around her, obscuring sight and sound in soft cushions of grey-tinged vapour. The banshees had drifted away with their jealousies and recriminations. She could see her mama's face. It had been smiling, and she'd known she'd been loved. When the feeling faded she had gone there again, and again.

'You're feeling rested when the train gets back into Chicago, too rested maybe, and there's Earl, right on time, ready and able to quicken your pace.'

'He had his good points.'

'Coyotes help to keep the prairie clean, but they are a low, sneaky beast. Earl provides you with some up-dust and then you're ornery as any viper. Ed Fox comes to offer his condolences—'

'And change the terms of our agreement, and I know he's the one who kept those messages from me!'

'You don't know that. Even Ed Fox had a mother. Why's he going to keep you from saying goodbye to yours? Even gangsters aren't that cold. I'd put my money on Easy Earl. That's just the kind of information that a dope fiend can lose track of. But Ed Fox doesn't like your attitude, and you're out of the Terrace again.'

'Ed Fox had trouble with any Negro who didn't treat him like Ol' Massa. He's calling me a lying nigger bitch, and I'm supposed to take that? I was not in the mood.'

'And besides, you had choices.'

'Earl had me opening at Connie's Inn less than two weeks later. I was doing everything I'd done in Rhapsody and with none of the aggravation. I was conducting, singing, playing my horn, but better than before. I was good, damned good. Clarence Williams called me the most talented coloured girl in show business.'

'And he should know.'

'He'd been writing music, producing shows and records for more than twenty years. He'd seen plenty people come and go. His having that opinion was no small thing, and I can't tell you how good I felt in those lights every night, with all that music responding to what I had in mind. The band was with me. It was mine. We went where I wanted to go, and they could play, do you hear me? And the Immermans weren't like Ed Fox. They had gangsters behind them like everyone else, but they knew how to talk to a person. They were a pleasure to work for. We started talking long-term—'

'Good music, good press. If things were that good, Valaida, what made you want to leave? You're making money. Things couldn't be better, and still you board that boat. How'd you get here, Miss Vee?'

It had been a good night. No, it had been a great night. Saturday. Standing room only once the shows let out. Café society debutantes and their escorts jostling for tables with Broadway personalities on their post-performance highs. Valaida preferred Broadway white folks to their Hollywood cousins. The East Coast variety tended to be smarter and snappier, more animated in their listening, less plagued by the languor fostered by posing on the silver screen. Theatre people were in there with you, and on Saturdays there was a tendency for some of them to jump up and join you. Jimmy Durante, Clifton Webb. If you blinked twice, there they'd be, and the unpredictability agitated all your corpuscles. This had been such a night, and she'd been steaming with the joy of it as the customers stamped and cheered. Earl might have wanted to stoke her fire after closing, but she had no interest in letting him try.

'I want to play some more,' she'd told him. 'Let's go uptown.'

She'd worn the simple bottle-green crêpe, the one with the tucks in the front and buttons on the sleeves because it hadn't been about showing out, only having a good time. The club had been crowded when she and Earl arrived, the atmosphere one of good-natured kickback, laced with the aromas of fried chicken, cheap whiskey, and whatever-might-come. Valaida fell into the arms and exchanged steps with dancers she hadn't seen in years, congratulations were offered on her Connie's Inn success, and no one mentioned Nyas even in jest. Earl ordered a bottle and setups as they settled into their seats. The group around the piano was just finishing a lazy blues. The piano man was an old-timer Valaida had known from her *Bamville* days, Prentice, Prentice Wilson. Prentice had a nose that was pure Cherokee and a touch on the keys that could flit around like quicksilver or pound on your breastbone like a John Henry-ed sledge.

'Is that you, Valaida Snow?' Prentice had called out over the hubbub of plates slapping onto tables and patrons negotiating the businesses of the night.

'It surely is, Mr Wilson,' Valaida had replied.

'Haven't seen you 'round here since Cain took Abel. What's that you got there in that oblong box you carryin'?' Prentice had asked, while teasing the upright with some Ellingtonian chords.

'A friend of mine, Mr Wilson,' Valaida had said, shaking off her half-belted jacket.

'You intendin' to introduce us?' Prentice had asked with a grin.

'With your permission, I thought that I might.'

'OK, gal, come on up here if you dare.'

There'd been a minor stir as Valaida had joined the musicians carrying her brass, but this was the easing-into-the-Lord's-Day time when the knowing folk of Harlem were in the habit of being cool. There'd been five of them up at the band end to start with, besides Prentice and Valaida, a ginger-complected brother on guitar, a guy named Sam on bass, a chubby, chocolate brown named Winston Ferguson on alto.

'"Dinah" OK with you, little lady?' asked Prentice, easing in on a D minor seven. It had been one of Ethel's first hits. Prentice Wilson was a sly old dog.

'Just play, Mr Wilson,' smiled Valaida, 'and I'll see what I can do.'

It all started nice and friendly, with a couple of rhythm tricks to make sure everyone was on their toes. Valaida was in there, all senses at high alert, playing to the song she was singing in her mind, responding to the shapes the other players were putting down, toe to toe with the menfolks in the Apple at long last, holding her own with a professional ease. Feeling very good, enjoying the way her lungs were working beneath her breasts, the movement of her abdomen against her silk-satin undergarments, the warm-blood euphoria washing her skull from the stem of her brain. They had to have been going some twenty minutes in this way before the boys with the pale broad-brimmed hats walked in.

The big one wasted no time at all before opening the case he'd been carrying and assembling his trombone. He was already warming the mouthpiece and working the slide as he walked trance-like towards the band, his head steadily bopping to the beat. He couldn't have been more than twenty, twenty-two years old, his chin as smooth as a baby's behind. As Winston was winding up his chorus, the trombone boy nodded towards Prentice and the bass man, knocked twice and jumped on in. Over Valaida. With neither look nor nod. As though she wasn't there. Valaida's cheeks flushed with anger, but folding wasn't on her mind. She'd known this kind of rudeness for as long as she'd played a horn. She let the boy work his show for a while then punctuated his solo with a blistering triple-tongued accent and pulled the next chorus back her way. The boy's eyes remained placid above the workings of his jaws, like he was a big, mahogany-brown lizard on a tree stump, lying in wait.

Later she realized that she had spent so much attention on repelling the trombone player that her senses hadn't been keyed to the trumpet boy's approach. She heard him first. His tone was burnished, strong and true as it penetrated the end of her chorus, like an ice-pick on direct and lethal course to a heart. She let him in. She had no other choice. Then the boy took off, and Valaida knew she had a problem. He had technique, the kind that came from years of serious, formal study, and he had new ideas of how to use it. Of course Valaida had known that there were other things happening in the music, that folks were beginning to move the horn from the land where Louis lived. Nothing wrong with that. Things had to move if they were going to stay alive; if the world stopped moving, it would probably drop straight down to hell; so it just made sense that the music should be moving too. It had moved from the old, syrupy ballads her mama sometimes played to the syncopations of cakewalking prancers. It had moved from old *Jimtown* okey-dokes to the elegance of Messieurs Sissle and Blake, from the holler of Joe Oliver at Dreamland to the finesse of Earl Hines at the Terrace; so it was bound to change from everyone wanting to play just like Louis Armstrong. Valaida had heard some of the change up close in Chicago with young Roy Eldridge in Fletcher's band. Roy played new, but he'd been backing her up, spurring her on. This copper-red boy with the black velvet lashes was laying full into her forehead with a baseball bat, and not even looking at whom he struck. His eyes were closed as he played, lashes caressing the tops of his cheeks, a vein in his temple pulsing in tempo, paying Valaida no mind at all. So blistering was the intensity of what was being put down that Valaida could do nothing but let the boy have his say. For three choruses she listened while the audience mutated from friendly, wee-hours-of-Saturday lay-back into Sunday-go-to-meeting frenzy. He had them, this boy, and as Valaida listened hard, listening to the patterns of what he was doing and where he might be going, she might have sensed that he had her as well, but she was concentrating on her way back in. Come the middle of the fourth chorus Valaida had a plan and gave her signal that it was time for her return. Prentice's eyes were making no comment as he opened up her door. The boy heard the cues and closed out his moves with reasonable grace, his eyes open but not focused as Valaida jumped in.

Valaida had no intentions of following his youngblood path of high and rapid pyrotechnics. That had never been her way, and now wasn't the time to start, but she'd been talking crowds into purchase when this boy had been toddling around in diapers. She'd work what she knew, and for the first two choruses things were going just fine. She coaxed the listeners back onto her side when she bucked around a bar of 'Royal Garden Blues', then leaped back into 'Dinah' like a cat on its way to dining. As Prentice laid in his accent, she could hear a sister holler, 'That's right, baby! You show him like we do!' It was when she was scampering over the bridge that her lip decided to go.

> *Ev'ry night, Why do I,*
> *Shake with fright,*
> *Because my Dinah might . . .*

Right there, in the middle of playing on a D major added sixth, her lip blew like a tyre on an Okie's Model T Ford, and suddenly her chorus was careening toward a ditch. She tried to save herself by dropping down into middle octave and revitalizing her muscles in the pauses between some toots, but here she found that the trouble was more than a fluke. Her mouth was simply gone, struck dead with fatigue, and there was nothing she could do but shake her head to Prentice in a signal that she had nothing more to give. Before Prentice could make his comment, the trumpet boy smashed into Valaida's ending with nary a fare-thee-well, robbing her of the chance to hand over with a save of face, leaving her with nothing but the professionalism that commanded her mutinous chops into a smile. With his eyes once again shuttered, the trumpet boy glissandoed into a war whoop, hurtling to the top of his formidable range with his trombone companion baying at his heels. The two were bent on distinction this evening. That they were new to New York was obvious in the way they had entered the club, heading straight for the band with no look around the room for familiar or friendly faces. Grabbing it was the way young bloods declared, 'I'm here,' in this town. Having kicked aside the skirted pretender, the boys trained their sights on those they'd come to disquiet. Valaida was forgotten, as Prentice, Winston, and Sam fought for their pride. No one noticed the flush of anger and humiliation that rouged her cheeks as Valaida returned to Earl at their table, packed up her horn, and walked straight-backed into the night.

Her reserve evaporated once they'd reached the sidewalk. She could not see for rage. Within her roiled a cauldron of indignation and despair. She fought the urge to scream and retch, her body shuddering from the effort like a tree withstanding a mighty gale. She hunkered down into herself once inside the car, feeling that otherwise she might shatter into a multitude of ragged shards, a kaleidoscope of wrath and pain. She sensed Earl's mouth moving, but she could hear nothing but the sloshing of blood within her skull. She retreated from the arm he tried to place around her shoulder but not from the powder he was offering on the small mirror below her nose. Words unfurled as the horse galloped triumphantly through her bloodstream, but they brought no comfort. *Too much*, after Nyas and her mother and her sisters. *Never*, would the men in this town allow themselves to respect her. *Never* would she ever have enough to satisfy them. *No matter* what she did. *Nothing and no one* did she have in this world to rely on. *Enough* was the amount of time she had spent trying to prove herself in this place. *None* was the amount of reasons for staying here any longer. Valaida didn't want these words. They hurt too much. Their sounds were hooves on her heart. She gestured Earl for more powder. She sniffed again, and again, and the words dissolved into a placid pool.

The light was grey when Valaida awoke the next afternoon. Her lips were still bruised from the last night's debacle; she'd have to tender them with ice and salve; and indentations in her arms throbbed from Earl's fumbling exertions. Earl had a tendency to grip hard when his member wasn't responding. If she didn't want bruises revealed by the cut of her gowns, Earl was going to have to stop trying so hard. The make-up Valaida hadn't removed sludged her cheeks, seemed to pull down her eyes, and her head echoed with the words she'd tried to banish in the night. *Too much, never, nothing and no one, enough.* Valaida went over in her mind what had happened with the music, and realized that her fall had come from not living for her horn. Versatility was the generator of her star's light, but it diminished rather than energized her horn. Singing and dancing, wittering to the audience, producing confections for their pleasure had all combined to circumscribe the stamina of her chops. Two choruses was the way her mind thought, what her muscles were used to, but two choruses made her an act, not a contender. In New York two choruses would never bring her respect, no matter what their brilliance, and Valaida had no desire to retire into the woodshed at this point in her life. She couldn't have that and, besides, she enjoyed her luxuries far too much. There'd be no satisfaction for those who should have loved her; and she knew that the world was large. By the time Earl managed to stir himself, Valaida had made up her mind.

'You want me happy, baby, don't you?' she said.

'Ain't nothin' in this world more important, darlin'. You know that.' Except money and drugs and never raising a finger in work.

'You know I want you to be my bride.'

Valaida stilled his lips with a hand that was nearly steady. 'I've had it with this game, Earl. Get me back across the water, and then maybe we'll speak of other things.'

The ocean crossing was the first Valaida had ventured alone, and that was just fine with her. She took her meals before and after the bulk of her shipmates had dined, remained in her cabin's dark seclusion save for a daily foray about the deck, during which she ignored the stares of the curious, and spirited discussions of a war in Spain. She watched the clouds and felt the wind and tried to keep her mind free of expectation.

. . . When you see me passing,
Hang your head and cry . . .

*C*hapter fourteen

Vestre Faengsel Prison, Copenhagen, 26 April 1942

Valaida stands with her accompanying guard waiting her turn to walk into the chapel. As with everything else in this place in which she is entombed, the intent is that prisoners should have as little contact as possible with other breathing, speaking organisms. Therefore each worshipper is marched to his or her seat no closer than fifteen metres behind the prisoner proceeding. This is Valaida's first Sunday in the chapel, but she is not surprised. She has lost her susceptibility to surprise. She is working her way slowly back from a week of utter despair, and she is hoping that a change of space and the music that comes from any formal worship of the Lord might assist her along this path. Valaida's tangential relationship to the Lord is being amended by this place. If her conviction is still rather shaky when compared to that of any number of true believers she has known, most particularly that of

her own and Henny's mother, in this last time she has been applying herself to prayer as well as hope; and, eight days ago, when a
guard once again came unexpectedly to her door, she had hoped
against hope that her prayers were being answered.

She had been told to gather up all her belongings. She had
been taken to reception and instructed to change into her own
clothes. Her meagre possessions, including the dice Earl had left
behind and her syringe, were checked against the inventory made
upon her arrival, placed in her suitcase, and the suitcase handed
across the counter. After signing a number of papers she was
escorted to a vehicle less ominous than the truck that had been
used before. She was being transported to the Police Alien
Division for transfer over to Sweden, whence a ship would return
her to America. Her papers had arrived at last. There were no
words to describe her relief. She had heard birdsong as she was
driven into the city. She had imagined herself in new clothes
strolling Lenox Avenue on a Harlem summer Sunday, and she
had taken little notice of Germans.

It had taken three hours to learn that it had all been a mistake.
Her passport had not arrived from the American Embassy in
Sweden after all, and then there had been no words to describe her
despair. She had gone numb. She had neither screamed nor crumpled nor cried. There was nothing to her during the process that
returned her to her cell. She could not be roused for her outside
half-hours, and for a number of days they had left her be; but then
the large guard had come into her cell, the one with the lop-sided
wig, whose huge breasts seemed made of stone. She had set
Valaida on her feet and frog-marched her into an outside sliver,
where it had been pouring down with rain. Valaida had sputtered
and groaned and finally crawled, and then she was taken inside,
stripped, and dumped in a bath. The prison had no hot water. The
bath was icy cold. The guard might have smiled. The shock hadn't
killed her, and so she had become more alive. She was not the self
she recognized as Valaida, but she was vaguely capable of sitting
and eating and reading and thought, and this new thing, prayer.

390

The minister stands behind a long simple table on which there are four candlesticks. Guards stand in rostrums on both sides of the altar, arms folded across their chests, sun glinting off the brass numbers and tags of their tunics, their faces without expression. The chapel's pews continue the prison's philosophy of punishment through isolation. Wooden barricades separate each worshipper from his or her neighbour, but there is space beyond and space above, and so Valaida feels more at ease. From here her prayers just might have room to fly. The minister begins to intone, his attitude solemn and dry. He asks a question, and the congregation responds. There is a drone from the organ. The congregation stands and begins to sing. Their singing drones as well. Valaida has never been in a Caucasian church before. She'd not expected worship identical to what she'd known in Tennessee, but she'd also not expected the styles to be as different as life from death. What was it about white people that compelled them to be so morose? Yes, she was in a prison, but wasn't God supposed to be about redemption? If the lack-lustre man behind the altar was selling the Lord's redemption, it didn't seem like much of an offer. It did not seem like something a body just had to have because what good was redemption if it didn't come along with joy? Valaida finds herself bemused by the complete lack of 'carrying on'. Could one God really appreciate the solemn imprecations of these white folk and the hand-clapping harmonies that came His way from Tennessee? There was little confusion about what style He seemed to favour because white folk stayed on top. Or at least their definition of top. The hymn is praising *det Himmelskong*, the King of Heaven, while Valaida's mind is drifting toward another King, a king who brings along his own sweet, floating version of redemption. She is hungering after that King, whom she thinks of as the Sweet King, even as she knows he curses all whom he redeems. In the prison's chapel, the organ ceases, the congregation sits, and the minister begins his sermon. His tone is severe, but it neither rises nor falls. He makes no gestures. He stands in one place. Valaida is tired of white people.

They've had their purposes. Their appreciation of her music was the reason she'd come so far and stayed so long; but Valaida is missing the sights and sounds of home, the shape and sway of coloured behinds, the drawling rhythms of Negro voices, the show-out style in the day-to-day of Bronzeville, the laughing to keep from crying, the laughing because life is a ball. The pale faces and sombre demeanours of Nordics are boring her now. Valaida is vowing that once she gets back home she will never leave again, that never again will she find herself encased by white people. But where was home exactly? Was it that place she'd had to leave in order to try to find her freedom? Looking for her freedom has landed her in this prison, but would she have traded what she's done when the alternative was getting nowhere? No, she would have gone. Playing safe has never been her game, so, despite this prison and pain, still she would have gone. The minister's drone has increased its intensity. Some prisoner behinds are shifting in their seats while Valaida searches for cracks in the ceiling.

'Your return wasn't all you'd hoped it would be.'

'I didn t have any particular hopes.'

'No?'

'No. I just wanted to be able to do what I could do. Folks on this side of the water seemed more receptive to that notion, so this was where I needed to be.'

'You weren't expecting it to be like it had been during the Blackbirds time? Applause from the pretty people, featured columns, fancy cars, buying shoes and hats from all the high-priced shops?'

'That would have been very nice, but it wasn't the reason I'd come. They respected my music, Cas. They wanted me on record, on national radio.'

'I guess that made up for the all the dark, dank rooming houses, drafty trains, inedible food, sad-looking people. My Alistair always said that the English working classes had faces that looked like their diet, all imploded flour and lard.'

'Alistair was a snob.'

'Aren't we all, darling? Aren't we all.'

392

London, 1936

She could not have envisioned how trying it would be. She had, after all, been on the road for more than twenty years. In southern rooming houses on the Toby-Time, bedbugs had been her intimate friends. On a trip between Shanghai and Hankow she had probably eaten cat. But she had never been so alone before. Six days on an ocean crossing was one thing, but week in and week out, in one ramshackle theatre after another, performing after a fading soprano and before a pair of Lancashire comics, always before a carpet of Caucasian faces, unbroken by any colour, most of them as drab as the dingy brick buildings that lined each city's streets, Valaida was trying to ignore the enormity, the possible rashness, of her decision to leave what she'd known. Until she had what she wanted, *and what was that?* What and where was home, after all, to one who'd spent twenty years on the road? She certainly felt no allegiance to the country whose history was about keeping her on her knees. Some would say that home was family, but with her mama dead, Nyas gone, Lawrence who knew where, and she and her sisters on no kinds of speaking terms, Valaida sometimes termed herself an orphan when the gin was gone from her flask, and the last coal in a room fire had turned to powder.

She'd managed not to feel forsaken when she'd been met at the Glasgow docks not with flowers and a car but by a pimple-faced clerk from the Foster Agency's Scottish office, with nothing at his disposal but a smudged paragraph of instructions. This new direction in her career had been her own choice after all. By virtue of how she meant to wow them, the flowers and cars would come in time. She'd been alone on the train ride south, second rather than first class, alone in dealing with the misdirection of her trunks, alone in coaxing rhythm out of house bands that wouldn't know a beat if it were pounding them in their heads, alone in the dreary hotel rooms that took all of her charm and too much of her pay to hold on to. British racism might not be the same as the home-grown variety, but it was there, it was there. The single spots weren't paying anywhere near the money she'd grown used to; and with one pay packet rather than two, the luxuries of her last English visit were less than memories. And she had no folks. Valaida had never travelled without at least a few of her people near her side, and without the soothing insulation of American Negro laughter, she was colder than she had ever been in her life. The calendar declared it still summer but Valaida's bones just didn't stay warm, not in the timid and pale British excuse for sunlight, not under threadbare hotel blankets. Sometimes not even when she was dancing. There'd be sweat on her belly, while her back was contorting with chill. But she wasn't letting it get to her, or keep her from giving out all that she could. 'The Coloured Queen of Rhythm' sent all her audiences home satisfied, and, when the Parlophone boys came calling, she was ready with new songs of her own.

'*You went into that studio thinking that you knew what to expect. You'd worked with an English studio band last time around—*'

'*They 'd started off stiff but I'd been able to bang them into some kind of shape.*'

'*But these boys were worse.*'

'*Oh, yeah. Not so bad by themselves, at least not the tinkler, but put them in a group? Dear God.*'

'*Plodding?*'

'*Oh, yeah*'

'*Ham-fisted?*'

'*From a starved-to-death hog.*'

'*But you kept smiling?*'

'*Grinning from ear to ear. "Are you pleased, Miss Valaida?" "Oh yes, Mr Culpepper, these boys are sending me straight to the moon." To their Bedlam was a lot more like it, but I got my music out there. That's what I'd come to do, and that's what I did. Those boys might not have been able to get anywhere near what the home folks called music, but their hearts were in the right place.*'

'*Meaning they wanted to please you?*'

'*Anything wrong with that?*'

'*And you never even considered trying to coax one of the Blackbird gang onto your dates? They were in town, thumping up a storm. Never even crossed your mind?*'

Lew Leslie wasn't the kind of man to let go of a successful formula before it had been wrung dry of all its commercial possibilities. The *Blackbirds* hunger may have been sated in the States, but Britain was still poised and ready to take on another helping. Seven months after Valaida and Nyas had returned to America, another edition of the revue was strutting across the boards, this time with Lavaida Carter and the young Nicholas Brothers earning the most favourable reviews.

'*She even changed the spelling of her name, did you see that? Put the "i" in there so there'd be no confusion.*'

'*Could have been Lew Leslie, you know. Could have been the businessman trying to connect the public's mind to a pleasing memory. Besides, she performs under the name of Carter. Not so obvious a link.*'

'*Valaida. Lavaida. With an "i".' Who you trying to kid?*'

'*Blackbirds of '34 and '35. Blackbirds of '36. There were bound to be similarities.*'

'*Do you know she even started trying to conduct "Rhapsody in Blue"? Like she had a notion of how a band worked! Like she had ever been serious about music.*'

'*That was after you'd left the country, and you mean to tell me you never got any satisfaction that she had to walk in your shoes?*'

'*The bitch tried to steal my stuff.*'

'*Am I detecting a smile beneath the invective?*'

'*You can stop with the highfaluting vocabulary, Castor. I am not in the mood. You know she broke my shoulder?*'

'*I know you tripped down some steps. You were a grown woman, in charge of yourself. Your sister did not pour that liquor down your throat, and she wasn't the one who gave you the solution for the pain. Your choice, darling, your choice. Like you always say, following your own road.*'

It had started out innocently enough. Yes, she and the Blackbirds were in the same foreign city, but as they had their performances, so did she. And when her week at the Tottenham Court had ended, there were the recordings to prepare for, the odd gig in Soho. Even if she'd had the inclination, there hadn't been the time; but she wasn't so inclined, or feeling guilty about it either. The scenes at her mama's funeral were still too raw, which might have been the reason she hadn't smelled a rat when she'd run into Edwina Dixon on Piccadilly, and Edwina had acted all gurgly then suggested that they meet. Edwina was a member of the Blackbirds Beauty Chorus, a tall willowy farm girl from Nebraska, who'd one day boarded a train to New York and never looked back. Valaida had always liked Edwina, whose disposition was as sweet as her whippoorwill soprano. She'd looked forward to their tea in a Bloomsbury hotel, looked forward to spending some simple time with someone who knew her and liked her and exuded the warmth she craved. She'd been needy, that was the problem. She'd been needing some home and hadn't thought that Edwina was exactly the type of person who'd think that sisters should be together. Valaida had tasted tears when she'd embraced Edwina in the hotel's foyer. Upon being seated at their table, she'd ordered a good bottle of champagne to wash that trace of salt away.

'And you drank it all.'

'You had taught me well.'

'Those were the days.'

' I was feeling good.'

'I bet you were. And then Lavada walked in.'

There'd been a stir in the tea room, and a glance at the entry revealed an aggressively glamorous, reasonably young Negro woman. Ample reason for a stir in London. Valaida almost hadn't recognized her at first, had been draining the last of the champagne, thinking that the woman's long black mitts and dramatic eyebrows were a bit much for the afternoon, but that her overall style was doing its job. Edwina had raised her arm in a beckoning wave. It had made sense that the two were acquainted. The woman had to be an entertainer, and there weren't but so many of them in this town. Why not make the afternoon into an impromptu celebration and order another bottle of champagne? Looking for a waiter caused Valaida to focus her eyes, and when she did her blood ran cold.

Lavada, too, was unprepared, her pace slowing as she approached the table, her eyes narrowing, her mouth hardening. Edwina was on her feet, and Valaida was ordering a very stiff gin.

'I hope you two don't mind my little secret,' Edwina was saying. 'It's just that we're all so far away from home. We need one another, don't you think?'

The look exchanged between the Snows indicated complete rejection of so simple a sentiment, but in deference to Edwina's intentions, Valaida parted her tightened jaws.

'Hello, sister,' she offered, emphasizing her esses.

'Hello, sister,' Lavada replied, with commensurate edge.

Panicked by the hostility over-hanging their little group, Edwina prattled onwards as chirpily as she dared. 'Come sit, Lavada. Do come sit. I'm sure you two must have so much to catch up on after all this time! Shall we go ahead and order some tea?'

'Tea?' repeated Lavada, her eyes lancets of aggression as she lowered herself onto the delicate chair. 'What are you, crazy? She ordered a gin? Make it two. I'd say three except that we have a show tonight.'

'A show?' sniffed Valaida. 'You're in a show, here in London? I'd heard you were busking for coppers on the streets.'

Lavada would not be drawn. 'I wouldn't want to disappoint my public,' she continues. 'It's so nice that people are seeing a fresh-ness in our shows that was missing in former editions.'

'Your public?' snarled Valaida, her sniff now transformed to a snort. 'The one I left for you, you mean. You think there'd be an audience for *Blackbirds of '36* if it wasn't for the success of Blackbirds of *'34* and *'5?* Your public?'

Edwina has placed a calming hand on Valaida, but Valaida shrugs it away. 'Stay out of this, Edwina. You brought us to the dance floor, now we gonna tango. You, sister, have never gotten one damn thing on your own! Always scraping up after me! Always traipsing down the road that I carved out of nothing! And you'd think you'd be grateful! But, no, it's always, "Valaida's a conniver", "Valaida's a selfish bitch!"'

'You're gonna sit here and tell me that you're not?' hissed Lavada. Their drinks arrive, and both sisters bolt them down, Valaida tapping for another. 'You gonna sit here and swear that you're not a selfish bitch who hates seeing anyone in the light besides yourself?'

'Lavada, please!' pleads Edwina. 'You don't mean that. You can't.'

'Can't I?' Lavada asks. 'You're too nice a person to imagine someone like my big, big sister, Edwina. You believe in love and trust. You can't imagine someone telling tales on her own family because of her troubles with the law or trying to buy herself into her mama's good graces after her mama is dead and gone, or begrudging her own sister a little piece of the sun she wants all to herself, or trying to bed that same sister's fiancé not two weeks before her wedding day.'

'Herman! So this is still about Herman?' Valaida cries with a laugh. 'Looky here, sister, your Herman came onto me on that ship. Sidles up talking about the sea gave him more nature than one woman knew what to do with, like he was all kind of mannish. That was your choice of a no-count husband, missy! You can't put that on me! That is not my load.' Valaida has gulped her second gin and drained the last of Edwina's champagne as well. She's tapping her glass again. Other patrons are staring, and Edwina has buried her face in her hands.

If Valaida had really looked at her sister, she might have seen in Lavada's eyes a flicker of needing to understand. 'We were two weeks from getting married! You were my sister. You should have been looking out for me!' Lavada's saying, but Valaida is sloshing about in an exercised indignation.

'I should have gone ahead and fucked him,' she returns with a sneer.

398

'You telling me you didn't?' Lavada's need has transfigured into fury.

'I'm telling you he wasn't worth the effort.'

Lavada's knuckles pale around her glass before she flings its contents into her sister's face. 'You're no better than one of Daddy's down-at-the-heels whores,' she says as she rises from their table. 'Too bad you weren't more successful with that suicide stunt you pulled back in the *Rhapsody* time. You would have saved us all a whole hell of exasperation.'

Valaida is unsteady on her feet after pushing Edwina's mopping napkin aside in order to follow after Lavada. There'd been no sandwiches to absorb the liquor, and the room is whirling on a wobbling axis. 'Don't you run away from me!' she's crying, and now the tears are back. Lavada has her hand on the outside door by the time Valaida reaches the top of the stairs. 'Don't you dare run away from me! Don't . . .' Her foot misses the first step. She's so numbed by gin that she doesn't really feel her body bouncing down the remaining seven, but she feels the tiles on which she lands. Lavada is stopped short by her sister's scream and drops down to her side to help, but Valaida pushes her sister away. 'Get away from me!' she's sobbing. 'I never want to see you again! Never! I don't need you! I don't need anybody! Nobody, do you hear? Not one goddam person! Not one! Not one!'

'Very impressive.'

'So was the pain.'

'And you had to deal with it somehow.'

'I'm still dealing with it, Castor. It's like a ghost, like some old bayou haint. It's always here. It never goes away, not the pain, not the need.'

'It might not have grabbed you so hard if you hadn't let that man snake his way into your life.'

'You weren't in Paris, Cas. I went to your building when I was there for the couple weeks with Willie Lewis. The concierge showed me those two postcards you'd sent her, one from Italy, the other with the coloured women wearing all the jewellery.'

'Tangiers.'

'She didn't think you were ever coming back. You'd told her to rent the rooms.'

'My life had changed.'

'I got sick of slinging those bags myself.'

'So hire a porter.'

Vestre Faengsel Prison, Copenhagen, 26 April 1942

In the prison chapel, the Sunday service is nearing its end. At the minister's behest, Valaida lowers her head as though in prayer.

'It was about to be Christmas, Cas, the first one without Nyas, or anyone else. Just out there, on my own, in the middle of all those white people. Just like I am now. In the middle of all these white people.'

'You didn't need anyone, Miss Vee. That's what you said. Loudly.'

'Christmas, Castor! You trying to tell me that Christmas far the hell away from home has never made you the least bit wingy? Blackbirds was still playing in London. Lavada was still there, and I'm in between engagements . . . It wasn't all bad, you know, not in the beginning. In the beginning if was almost everything I'd ever hoped for.'

'Hold onto that thought, Miss Vee. It might be helping getting you through.'

The prison's pastor holds up his hands in benediction. The organ drones again, and the guards take their places for the prisoners' filing out. Valaida has found the service superfluous to her spiritual needs, but she will return to her seat next week. With more space and better light, she finds it easier to see. The prisoners' shuffle is a mournful one-two beat, but Valaida's aspect has been improved by this bit of light. She superimposes a beat of her own.

   . . . Ma savane est belle
   Mais à quoi bon le nier . . .

Chapter fifteen

Paris, London, Vienna, 1937

. . .Ce qui m'ensorcelle
C 'est Paris, Paris tout entier . . .

It was a different Paris from the one she'd known during that last Jazz Age summer of 1929. America's market crash had dealt a body blow to the giddy hedonism that had characterized that season. Her playful children had quickly abandoned their pleasure-ground, sailing home with the dollars that had been life's blood to the Parisian body economic. In Montmartre, Valaida's old pal Brickie, night hostess *extraordinaire* to the moneyed, titled, and sprightly, had been forced to close her nightclub, was now working for someone else whose roots went deeper into the district's underworld. There were fewer of Valaida's home folk in the District now, which was feeling a lot less like Harlem, like it had in 1929, and a lot more like the foreign place it was; but this in itself was no bad thing. Used to be that most any coloured American ready to take hold of an instrument and act a fool could call himself a musician and find himself a job, but not any more. Standards had gotten higher; a body had to know its stuff, and even then there was no guarantee of its wheedling itself a gig. Times were tougher, but audiences were behaving better, listening closer. They didn't have the natural-born appreciations of the folks back home, but they were working on it. One of those wandering Russians by the name of Hugues Panassie had set up the Hot Club over in Montparnasse that had its own band of better French players and its own magazine as well. Updates of the folk that Valaida had seen in the Greenwich Village café with Lawrence way back when, with their earnest aspects and slouchy clothes, were now to be found in every intimate *boîte* where jazz was being played. The music was still about entertainment, but it was serious business, too, and Valaida was liking the feel of it all just fine. She could sense that there was a place for her here and on her own terms, as a respected musician, not prancing and profiling like Josephine, who was still a phenomenon in Paris despite the fact that she had bombed back home in the States, still holding court at the Folies Bergère with her feathers and spangles and quivering naked limbs. Valaida reminded herself not to worry about Josephine, that Josephine's world was not one that she desired, and most times she succeeded.

After the first weeks in Paris, enjoying Earl Sutcliffe's amusements and reacquainting herself with the lay of the land, Valaida returned to London, where a band was formed around her talents, under the lead of a refugee German by the name of Johnny Pillitz, and immediately went out on tour. It was a mixed group in every way, a German Jew named Gus Finley on piano, Belgian Johnny Claes on backup trumpet, a big, young coloured Englishman named Derek Neville on alto, a couple of white Englishmen on bass and drums. Some were better than others, but each of them was ready to play, and with her. After the first swing through Europe, hitting the Hague in Holland, Zurich, and Vienna, they went back to a group of recording sessions in London, heating up the rhythm session with a Spanish African bass player named Louis Barreiro and a coloured American brother, Norman Brown, on guitar. Lavada had left the city finally, and Valaida was feeling good. The sessions were the most successful she had ever done.

'I'm hearing you humming Pleasant memories?'

'The best. Let me tell you,

The whole world is sayin' that swing is the thing.
The jazz bands are playin', 'cause swing is the thing.
The trumpets are blowin'. It's, oh, what a sound!
The music is goin' around and around . . .'

'I heard that one. You were very good. Fine voice, strong on the horn. I tipped my hat.'

'I was feeling good, Castor. After all that belting from vaudeville stages, I was working my show in smaller spaces where folks had come to really listen. You could concentrate on insinuating instead of having to knock fools upside their heads to get atttention. Gave me more stuff for my trumpet playing, as well; and by the time we hit the studio we'd been cooking together for weeks, had our own charts that we had worked on, gotten close with. We were able to serve up something really tasty. How do I explain it to you, Cas? It was . . . it was . . .'

'Almost everything you'd ever hoped for. Not exactly the musicianship of Earl Hines and his gang, but nothing to sniff at, and you on a creative roll. "Valaida Snow, Queen of the Trumpet".'

'Valaida Snow, Queen of the Trumpet. If you wish, you can kiss my hand.'

'If I could, I'd be on my knees.'

'Sitting beside me would be more than enough. Where are you, Cas?'

'Where do you think, Valaida? So, Johnny Pillitz, such a good group, but it fell apart so fast. You get back on the road, go on down to Vienna, the group keeps going, but you're back in Paris. Why so, my Queen?'

403

'Oh, you know, groups can be as skittish as a thoroughbred colt. The least little thing will send folks stomping off in opposite directions, then two beats later you're wondering just what was it that was so impossible to deal with? Could anything have been that bad?'

'Disingenuous, Your Majesty. Damned if I don't detect the malevolent influence of Easy Earl.'

'You'd have me seeing Earl Sutcliffe as the Devil incarnate. Next thing you'll be blaming him for this whole goddam war. It wasn't just Earl. It always takes more than one, that's what you've always told me. It always takes more than one.'

It was Earl. If she wanted to be honest, she would admit that the signs came early on, during that first swing through Holland. The Hague. After a bumpy start that had brought young Derek over to replace a boy on alto who hadn't been up to snuff, Valaida and the band had been finding their rhythm together, feeling good about it, too. Coleman Hawkins had been performing in a town just down the way, and it had just made sense to spend some party time together. Valaida and Bean had never been close back home in the States, but across the water you didn't stand on ceremony. You were just so glad to hear some English that wasn't spoken with the words all tossed together like a salad, that caressed your ears like sorghum syrup did grits, spend time with someone who understood what you were implying when your voice went into a slide. Coleman had already been a couple years across the water, was kicking back just enjoying, while blowing folks continually away.

'How's it feel up there in the clouds, Bean, with all these white folks treating you like a god?'

'Just fine, Val, just fine. Shouldn't beat it with a stick.'

For all his soft-speaking and gentlemanly style, that pinky sticking out straight while he sipped his cups of tea, the perfectly groomed movie-star moustache, old Coleman was a fundamental sort of person, who ran a string of girls to keep himself in silk socks and good humour.

'They were throwin' it at me, Val. Seemed a shame not to put it to good use.'

Coleman told things as he saw them. No spade had a chance as a club in front of Coleman. Put some blackcurrant spirits in Coleman, and the man would speak his mind. Didn't give a damn about what you did or didn't want to hear. Valaida had been musing on bringing her group home to the States. Spirits talk, maybe, but what language was usually spoken at four o'clock in the morning? Most folks would have just nodded in agreement and reached for another drink, but not Coleman. No, Bean had to speak his truth.

'Come on now, Val,' he'd said. 'You know that ain't gonna happen. These boys are passable, but they ain't good enough to cross no water, and what? You think any club's gonna book a coloured girl trumpet-player with a salt-and-pepper band? You ain't been gone from your homeland for that long, sister! You know that ain't gonna fly. Long before the first note you know crackers would be up there showing the unpleasantness of their natures.'

Well, yes, he had a point, but after the experience over here in Europe Valaida was determined to have a group of her own. It was time, and she had earned it.

'Girl, I been playin' with niggas since I was knee-high to a gnat, and ain't none of them never gonna back a honey playin' a horn if she were the Angel Gabriel himself. And baby, you know your way around that piece of brass – I'll give you that –but your name ain't Gabriella. You got a good thing going for yourself here, Val, with your singing and playing and these eager young men. Work with it, baby, and have yourself a decent time.'

Maybe, if Valaida hadn't been studying so hard on maintaining her own good humour, on not smashing Coleman's pretty, arrogant head with the bottle of Bessen, on drowning her hurt and anger in copious quantities of blackcurrant gin, she might have been able to hear the truth of what Coleman went on to speak of with regards to a decent time.

'I hope that Earl of yours has something for you that we don't see,' he had said. 'Far as I can tell, he can't find nothing to do with his time except having white women suck his dick.'

'They suck his. He sucks mine,' she'd replied. 'You see any problem in that?'

'You ain't no parts of a lady, Val, and I mean that as a compliment.'

Valaida had smiled as mysteriously as she could muster, then withdrawn into the gin, and switched her mind off for as long as the Bessen allowed.

The problem was that Earl hadn't had enough with which to occupy his time. Nyas might have been lazy, but come showtime, he was on that stage, taking care of business. Samuel might have been a failure, but he had worked at the gambling. What did Earl have to do except skulk around the sidelines and try to find ways to be essential, when he only spoke English and didn't know the lay of the lands? The low life had always been his element. It only figured that he'd get up to no good; and he'd never had use for Johnny Pillitz.

'Foreign-talkin' mother-fucker. How we know that he's tellin' us straight? I don't trust him, Val, not one iota.'

And, for his part, Johnny Pillitz couldn't stand the sight of Earl.

'This man is always making distasteful friends. These drug people, these procurers, they bring with them nothing but trouble.'

A clash between Johnny and Earl was bound to happen before time.

The weather in London had been damp. Damp weather made Valaida's shoulder ache, and the little pills and powders available from English chemists never delivered what Valaida characterized as relief. The medicines Earl came up with were far more effective, and they had the side benefit of tossing a veil of absurdity over environments with which Valaida preferred not to engage. Staring, gaping white people took on the aspect of animals in a zoo. The words *fascisme, communisme, Nationalsozialismus, Hitler, Franco, Mussolini* were filtered out of surrounding conversations, as well as the odour that pervaded all trips on Continental trains. Without Earl's counter-irritants, Valaida might have recognized

406

around her what she had first encountered in Shanghai with Karol Dimitrivich in 1926. The eyes of the present, huddled, would-be refugees tended to be hollow rather than wild, but the smell on them was the same, filtered through heavier clothing, manky furs, dark felt hats, distilled through different oils by virtue of diet and whatever racial anomalies brought into the mix. Fear was the smell. Anxiety and dread. A sense of foreboding was everywhere in Europe, and train travel presented some of its most concrete manifestations.

'White folks' business,' was how Earl termed it. 'What the hell all this mess got to do with niggers?' And through use of what Earl had to offer, Valaida could agree, not worry about brown-shirted men in train stations, simply admire their shiny boots and the manner in which leather straps traversed their preening chests. Not think of the sentiments behind the shiny red buttons with their crooked black insignia, just appreciate how dramatically they caught the eye. Border crossings under the influence of Earl Sutcliffe's party favours were exercises in hilarity. While some of their companions wrestled with anxieties, Gus Finley, Louis Barreiro, Johnny Pillitz himself, Valaida and Earl continued their card games, stifling laughter.

After returning safely to Vienna, Johnny Pillitz blew his top. 'You think this is all some kind of joke, playing with drugs while dealing with Nazis? This is no joke! People are arrested!. They are beaten! They are killed! You *idiote, verdammte Schwein!* This is no joke!'

Earl pulled out a knife, and things just went downhill from there.

Earl vanished for three days. Valaida saw him talking to a dark-complected man with a gold earring and a startling scar that ran through an eye. She turned to answer a question from Louis, turned back and Earl was gone. Vienna was not Valaida's favourite city. She found the place disconcerting, couldn't get a handle on its citizens at all. For all its plush and stylish modern interior, the Eden Bar where they were performing reminded Valaida of New

York clubs back in the '20s, fat middle-aged men with their brassy concubines, lascivious ogling, limited attentions to the music. Her few hours spent in daylight brought with them little comfort. The cobblestones stank of horse piss, and church bells would not stop ringing. Valaida found no charm in women wearing aprons on city streets. The fact that the fabrics were often extravagant didn't save the habit from smacking of country ignorance. As did the way they stared. The way everyone just kept on staring and looked as if they'd like to stone you if you dared look them in the face. With Earl at her side, Valaida was not alone with all the stares, and so she was missing her Earl Sutcliffe Jones. Valaida's shoulder was no longer hurting, but her head pounded, and her calf muscles twitched. She saw all of this as the fault of Vienna, and Johnny Pillitz for bringing her there. When Earl returned from his idyll, glassy-eyed and belligerent, Valaida took a bit of what he was carrying and agreed with all he said. It stood to reason that Johnny was holding out on their money, and just how the hell did he justify the size of his cut when all he ever played was the kazoo?

Johnny made an ultimatum.

'I will not continue to be insulted by you, *ignorante Schwein*! Enough is enough! Valaida, we make such wonderful music together, you and me, Johnny, Derek, and Louis. We want to continue, but we, all of us, have had enough of this man. You must decide, Valaida. I won't let him destroy us all.'

Valaida had hardly registered Johnny's argument. It felt warm inside Earl's arm. He smelled of violets rather than horse piss. She didn't resist as he led her away.

'Who's ignorant now, you damned cracker? The lady's staying with me.'

They were on the next train back to Paris. Earl's jag kept him running at the mouth.

'Don't worry about a thing, baby. I'm gonna do you. You gonna be bigger than Josephine, no lie. You and me, baby. I'll be taking care of you, no lie . . .'

408

Valaida barely nodded. The twitch in her limbs had been replaced by a not-unfamiliar wrench in her gut. It was easiest to sleep. Outside the carriage windows, the huge red, white, and black flags were too bright for her eyes, and the travellers, with their rope-tied suitcases, too forlorn.

'I just don't understand it, Valaida. The first time in your life that you let a man dictate your behaviour, and you give up yourself to this low-life slime?'

'It wasn't the only time! Back in '29 you weren't telling me what to do?'

'And you fought me tooth and nail. What was it? You trying to catch hold of a piece of your long lost father? From what you've told me I don't think he would have approved.'

'You've spent entirely too much of your life around these white people, Castor. I've got no time for that what's-in-your-mind mumbo jumbo. Johnny Pillitz was not a saint.'

'Johnny Pillitz led you into the most rewarding musical collaboration you had ever had in your life, Valaida. Every night. Not just when Earl Hines decided to give you a shot, and you let Earl Sutcliffe just lead you away. Nyas might not have been your luck, but Earl Sutcliffe Jones was your curse without a doubt. You missed the music, and your gut starts wrenching, just like during the bigamy time, just like now. Which tends to reveal your least salubrious side.'

'I just couldn't face them alone, Castor, all those white people—'

'It wasn't as if you hadn't dealt with them before. So what was calling the tune, darling, all those white people or all those white powders?'

'You should have been some help! I'd missed you so much in Paris. Then you come back, and you're no help at all.'

'How was I supposed to help someone who wanted no parts of civilization?'

Chapter sixteen

Vestre Faengsel Prison, Copenhagen, May 1942

A whistle blows, and Valaida flinches. It doesn't matter how familiar the sound has become; she is never prepared. She puts down her book. Her hands are trembling. This story she is reading is better than others that she's tried: *Jane Eyre* by Charlotte Brontë. Valaida has never been one for books, but during these last interminable weeks, reading has provided occasional respite from fear and pain. Valaida finds herself empathizing with the sweet and unfortunate Jane, near-imprisoned in a far-off manor under the brooding dominion of the distant Mr Rochester. When Valaida had met Vestre Faengsel's Mr Waagensen upon her arrival at the prison an endless eon ago, he had lacked Mr Rochester's dark demeanor, but the distance, the distance they shared. Mr Waagensen has yet to answer even one of Valaida's notes, but she will not let Mr Waagensen's lack of attention deter her from her resolve. She reaches for a request form and her pitiful nub of a pencil. She breathes in to control her hand, applies nub to paper, and begins to write.

Fange Nr. 47 Valaida Snowberry
2 May 1942

My dear Inspector
One more time I am writing you, this time to ask you to please put me back in the hospital. Here I am getting worse each day, here in this part also I am not strong enough to climb the stairs. The wards will tell you I nearly fell down these stairs yesterday. In the hospital I did sleep a little but you can easily find out that I don't sleep at all in this part of the prison, and they have forgotten three times to give me my medicine. They never forgot in the hospital, and my dear Inspector, it is not easy for you to understand, for it has never happened to you, but for a person who has been through what I have, all this noise . . . The professor in the Rigshospitalet *said I should be where it is quiet. These bells ringing and whistles blowing are nearly driving me mad. I can hardly walk, I'm so weak. I suppose you heard on the 19th they took me out to go back to America. At the last hour they said a telegram came saying the ship would go later. That was awful for me, as I thought now I'll go to my man and my little son, three years old, but I had to come back.* Please, please *put me back in the sick house. Some of the wards here told me to ask you.*
Yours with thanks,
Valaida

Valaida walks toward her door and releases the metal rod that will summon a guard to her cell. The guards know that the coloured American prisoner is different from their other charges. She is neither dangerous nor impossible, but demands much of their attentions. She needs another form to write to Mr Waagensen when no prisoner in their memory has ever written to Mr Waagensen. She is pleased to learn that there are English books in

411

the prison library, but in this book the print is too small. There is too little light in her cell to see. In that book the story is so sad, and isn't this place sad enough as it is? She isn't accused of any crime. Yes, there is an on-going trial having to do with obtaining medicine without prescription, but that was the responsibility of the chemist, not the patient. Yes, there is a rumour of her suitcase containing cutlery that was not her own, but there is no mention of this in her incoming inventory. She is in prison for lack of a passport, a woman alone in a time of war. She would like a book that is not so sad, and somehow it doesn't seem too much to bring in a book that had been studied by the daughter of a friend. Inmates' singing in their cells is against prison procedure, but the guards have had done with denying the *neger* American woman what must be a part of her nature. When she doesn't sing she will often cry, and the sound of her songs is so much more pleasant, and the guards are human, after all. They leave their place of work to return to homes that are no longer their own, that are encased in the grey-green vice of the Nazis. The guards need their balms just like everyone else, and a snatch of a song from the *neger* American woman does sometimes provide a shard of relief. It takes no time for the grate to slide open and present a hand to receive Valaida's note. Valaida doesn't think of how the Inspector will react when he receives the note, if indeed he does receive the note.

'Miss Valaida, you, my lady of the Snows, I've always thought of you as magnificent, but this is not magnificent. This whining? This lying? Your man and your little three-year-old son? This note was peevish and small. This from the young girl who saw her destiny in the stars? From the young woman who left all she knew to seek her star in China? This wheedling and begging? I'm ashamed of you. I'm ashamed for you.'

'Don't talk to me about shame, Castor! I am getting out of this place. This place is driving me crazy, and I'll do anything I have to do to get out of here. Anything, do you hear? I can't act like a whore? There are no takers for a whore? Then I'll act like a child. I'll whine like an old maiden aunt until that man will do anything to get rid of me. I want to make him as desperate to get rid of me as I am to leave. I want my freedom. I will

*have me my freedom. I will tell any lie that works. You have your freedom.
What do you know about this pain?'*

'Oh my dear, we mustn't forget Paris. We will always have Paris.'

> *Le voir un jour,*
> *C'est mon rêve joli . . .*

Paris, 1938–9

. . . J'ai deux amours
Mon pays et Paris . . .

'You singing Josephine's song again when you never wanted any parts of
Josephine, never had anything good to say about Josephine, not to mention
that you saw almost nothing of Paris? What was Paris to you that last
time you were there? The inside of hotel rooms, the inside of clubs? You
didn't see Paris, let alone love Paris. You wouldn't see its torment, or anything else for that matter. You and Earl in your opiated fog, only thinking
about where that next ingestion was coming from.'

'What is it that you wanted from me, Cas? I'm not a European white
person, and I'm not a newspaper woman either. This business of war and
Nazis was their business, not mine. My business is music, so I thought
about my music. I thought about my career.'

'Which was why you were two hours late for rehearsal for the Folies
Bergère, and they fired your thoughtless behind!'

'There's no need to get your panties in a twist! OK, I was late. You've
never been late? It wasn't the end of folks wanting me. I appeared in two
films, that were shown in theatres! I played with Django!'

'You were arrested for stealing money and silver from Jimmie's.'

'They released me without a trial!'

'Because I came down to the jail and spoke the French!'

'Which gave you the right to insult my man? You gonna talk to him like
he was some kind of dog in front of his woman and all those white people?'

'Somebody had to try and bring you to some sense.'

'Earl was my man. I thought you were my friend.'

'And I thought you were mine. You'd changed so much.'

'And so had you. Why'd we change so much, Cas?'

'I don't know, darling. Maybe because we'd come to understand that not all things are possible.'

'You're sure about that?'

'So are you.'

They met in a café they'd often haunted in '29, not far from Sacré-Coeur. It was raining and cold, and Earl had complained about the climb. The café had lost much of the charm that had graced it nine years before. As in so many establishments all over the city, refugees were using as near-residences, as offices, reading rooms, oases, as many tables as they dared, nursing their single beverages for hours, unfolding, reviewing, refolding, unfolding once more, their various identity papers and visa forms. They looked lost and unhealthy. They murmured rather than spoke. Sometimes their lips turned up rather than down, but always with sadness, and the fear smell was always there. Valaida no longer savoured the café experience. She'd rather spend off-hours in the privacy of her hotel room, with Earl or without, sleeping, mending her wardrobe, or simply feeling fine. Cas was sitting in the rear of the café not far from the stove. As a regular customer from before the Deluge, he'd been given a table of value. She almost cried when she saw him. His cuffs were fraying, and his skin-tone was grey. Earl reached across to shake Cas' hand, thereby blocking Cas and Valaida's ability to embrace. Maybe that had been the first misstep right there.

'You still prefer the *cidre* to the *vin ordinaire*?' he'd asked, and she had nodded. 'Smart choice. The *vin*'s a hell of a lot more ordinary than it used to be. Everything of a piece. What about you, Earl, was it? Earl?'

'The beer anywhere near cold?'

'About the temperature outside these walls.'

Earl had grunted and pulled out a packet of cigarettes, lit one for himself and replaced the pack without offering anything to

414

his companions, exhaled a nimbus of smoke, and looked away. Suddenly feeling claustrophobic, Valaida had loosened her scarf and unbuttoned her coat. After looking direct into her eyes, Cas had looked down, caressed his still graceful fingertips, and smiled.

'What's so funny?' she'd inquired.

'Everything these days,' he'd replied. She can sense his commentary and doesn't want to know it. Their drinks arrive. Earl tastes his beer with a grimace, but holds his peace. His attention has been attracted by a blonde woman with kohl-rimmed eyes and thin naked legs, whose age could be anywhere between fifteen and forty. The blonde's woe-filled approximation of come-hither is pitiful in the extreme. Valaida sips her *cidre*. Its taste is no longer the delight it used to be.

'You still in the area?' she asks.

'I like the view,' Cas replies. '"*I'm sitting on top of the world . . .*"' His baritone is still rich and sure. She answers him in kind.

'"*Just rolling along*"?'

'Just rolling along.'

'Your music?' she asks. His eyes are still his eyes, but they're carrying a load of the same ubiquitous suffering that Valaida's been working so hard not to see or feel. She's grateful that sipping cider affords her an excuse for lowering her lids. She wishes both to flee, immediately, out the door, into the weather, and to clasp her friend's spindly body to her breast.

'Never came to much,' he replies, smiling because everything is funny these days. He's not grinning though, and Valaida is wondering if his glorious grin is gone for ever. 'The salons weren't eager for a boot-black Negro who wouldn't grin like some Cheshire Cat; but to be fair I wasn't offering easy morsels for their delectation. I was aiming for an amalgam of Hindemith and the twelve-bar blues. Even if I'd hit, it would have taken a rarefied taste.'

The woeful blonde has risen to walk toward the front of the café, her narrow behind sweeping invitingly close to Earl, who gulps a mouthful of tepid beer and licks his lips in response. Valaida knows that Earl will be leaving for a while and tells herself

415

she isn't bothered. 'Nothing common for my Castor,' she says brightly. 'You still at it?'

'I keep noodling as I can,' he replies, caressing fingertips again. 'I miss the piano.'

'Alistair?' There. It was said.

'No, I had to sell it.' True to form, Earl is on his feet, muttering about some smokes. Valaida checks her bag to be sure that she has sufficient francs for a taxi. She has avoided els and subways since the encounter with Lawrence and the cracker drunk in New York way back when everything was anticipation and hope. She can feel Cas' eyes boring into her brain.

'And Alistair?' she asks.

'He's married,' Cas replies, allowing a moment for the incongruity to sink in with yet another one of his smiles. 'His older brother was killed in a fall from a horse two years ago. His father came all the way to Tangiers to say that all was forgiven, and all would be allowed. So long as he managed to propagate the blood. There was no dearth of suitable brides. Interesting folk, the aristocracy. Amazingly sophisticated in their outlook.'

'And that was that?'

'Things weren't going smoothly. He'd become enamoured with Mussolini and his black-shirted bully boys. He found the Duce's rape of Abyssinia amusing. I insisted we leave Italy, and in Tangiers he developed an insatiable taste for Arab boys. Partly to taunt me. They were beautiful, you see. And then his allowance was curtailed in the campaign to coax him home. I worked, but jobs were scarce.'

'And then papa comes to town. Alistair was an asshole. You're better off without him.' Valaida's comment has been flippant, just something to move the evening onward, but her friend's reaction is not. His fingers clench, one about his glass, the other into a fist. His lips have hardened after a soft intake of breath.

'I loved him. And I still miss him.' Cas' words, though steady, ache with an anguish that sends Valaida's attentions flitting about the room. Earl is indeed gone. A small drab woman in an even drabber black dress has begun singing a mournful song to accordion accompaniment. Valaida has never had much use for the accordion, but better its music than what she knows will be coming from Cas, whose words are now sliding between the chords. 'What's your excuse?' he asks.

'My excuse?' she responds. She will attempt to be blasé. 'My excuse for what?'

'Don't get coy with me, darling.' A flick of her eyes reveals that his are red. The woman's song is clawing its way across her heart. 'Your little piece of slick,' Cas continues, 'your Earl Sutcliffe Jones. Of course I remember his name. He of the impeccable demeanor and conversation. You can tell the Negro columns whatever you want, my dearest Valaida with an "i", but not me. I know you, and I know you know that man isn't worth the muck beneath your shoes.'

The cider is nowhere near what Valaida is needing right now. The hurt and disappointment in Cas' eyes are causing her nose to run. They are more invasive than the caustic edge about his words. Valaida doesn't want to be invaded. She hadn't expected invasion. Cas was supposed to have been her ally, her one true friend who understood everything. And forgave everything. The accordion's groans are causing her head to pound. What can the musicians expect to earn from the pathetic assembly in this café? A few centimes? Maybe enough for two bad glasses of wine? Valaida wishes the singer would stop. Her eyes are stinging with salt.

'I don't need to hear this crap from you, Castor McHenry. You leave me alone about Earl. Right now, he's good for me. He's what I need.' She can't find a handkerchief, not in her pockets, not in her bag.

'What he supplies, you mean.' Cas is offering her his handkerchief. It is worn but snowy white. Their fingers touch as she takes it, and she can feel that their love persists. The linen is soft against her nose, and the singer has finished her song. Valaida is relieved.

'What Earl supplies,' she says, 'is satisfaction.'

'And that's enough?'

'It's more than you've got.' It was only the quickest of respites.

417

The accordion is groaning again, with it the abrasions on Valaida's heart, and now she's feeling remorse. 'I'm being awful, Cas, and I don't want to be awful,' she says. 'I'm famished and this place is driving me crazy. Let's go find somewhere to eat.' Cas helps her out of her seat, as has always been his habit. Her shoulder brushes his as she rises. It is bonier than ever. His hand takes her elbow to guide her through the room, then slips down to hold fast her hand as they walk out into the night.

'*That was our high point. It didn't get any better than that.*'

A Metro ride into the bowels of Les Halles. He protesting her misgivings, 'Save your francs, Miss Valaida! I will protect you from all untoward menace!' His delicate fist aloft, his wrist somewhat ashy above his mended cuff, his smile with just enough mischief tinging the sadness, that she could giggle in the way she had done nine years before. When they were young and knew that the world was theirs. The bistro, a veritable cave catering to the market's hod-carriers and merchants, long communal tables, heavy with the smoke of roasting meats and black tobacco, the few other women present as burly-armed as the men. A mountain of food, a whole chicken, a chorus line of crayfish, wine the colour of bloodied piss. Tearing through the carcasses. Sharing memories. Alistair dancing a tarantella, Valaida in a heap at the bottom of Bloomsbury stairs. No longer giggling, laughing now. Feeling almost young again. Playing hide-and-seek amongst the arcades of the Palais Royal. Scuffing patterns in the gravel. Being young again. Trying to convert him with a seduction of vampish kisses. He weighing a breast, deciding it still wasn't to his taste. Watching dawn rouge the gargoyles perched about the roof of Notre Dame, fingertips interlaced. Her calf muscles twitching. Needing to part. Parting without pledges.

'*I remember that night. That was a good night.*'
'*And after that night? One contretemps after another.*'
'*You wouldn't stop criticizing!*'
'*You wouldn't stop compromising*'

* * *

It is not as though she doesn't know what's going on. Records make it across the water in mailbags and tourist luggage. There are places she can go to listen or to buy, which she seldom does because excess francs and guilders are spent on other things; but she knows how far Roy Eldridge has progressed since his Chicago days in the Fletcher Henderson Band. She knows that Roy is still tossing off the dizzying acrobatics but that now he is almost always landing on his feet. She knows Rex Stewart's plotting new paths with Duke. She's heard Buck Clayton behind Billie Holiday and roiling the winds with Basie. She's felt Walter Page, Freddie Green, and Jo Jones driving into her viscera. She knows America's swinging, and not just the coloured bands, the white bands too. There's nothing she can say against the Casa Loma Orchestra, and, with Fletcher arranging for Benny Goodman, the four-eyed Jewboy was taking care of serious business. The King of Swing? Well, maybe not, but on it? Yes, definitely on it. America on it. All sleek cars, exuberant music, and limitless horizons. Even Negroes doing better, the musicians anyway. Her homeland, her music. But not her life.

It is Valaida's choice to be in Europe; and in Europe the greys are getting darker, and the air is thick with war. Even if you read no newspapers and hear no radio, the foreboding is everywhere and impossible to ignore. Street demonstrations can be avoided, but broadsheet posters and handbills cannot. They are always on the walls near streetlights or strewn in gutters before the entrance of anywhere you need to go, and those words which you've been trying to ignore – *fascisme*, *anti-fascisme*, *Hitler*, *Franco*, *communisme*, *la guerre* – are always writ big, black and bold, always jumping up in front of your face. You decide to see an American movie, have a mindless couple of hours from home, even though it will be dubbed in French and you mostly won't understand the words, but it was always about Caucasian fantasies anyway, so the words aren't but so important, and just maybe you can catch a glimpse of one of your old buddies bowing and scraping in the background and be reminded of why you're glad you're not there, that you're

419

here in Europe and not there in Negro-smothering America, in Negro-lynching America, even though here the money's tight, tighter than a whalebone corset or a size two shoe, so tight you're darning stockings for the first time since you left the South; but before you can see Powell flirt with Lombard, you're watching bombers strafing Catalonia and Germans marching under torch-light. Like *Golddiggers of '35*, but without the hooey. You find yourself admiring the precision of the choreography, but then fear sprays the theatre like skunks surprised on a backwoods road on a new moon night. Folks start to cough and mutter, and you remember it's not a gag. This is serious business, when the only businesses about which you care to be serious are music and feeling fine, and then you've got no stomach for Powell and Lombard any more.

You've heard of this thing called 'Munich'. You don't know what it's all about except that some white men got together and did what white men do, talk about how they were going to run the world; but you do know that since 'Munich', menace has been slinking and slithering through the streets. In reaction to 'Munich', many folks with wherewithal loaded up their cars with trunks and children and removed to country houses, while others forgot their time with the dopes of opulent amusements, dressed themselves up in the guises of any era but their own. You could see them in the magazines that were sometimes left on café chairs, rich white people in satin dominoes and powdered wigs, doing their best not to open their eyes, while people on the ground didn't have those kind of choices. Down on Valaida's ground, choices are fewer, and jobs are scarce. Job scarcity means that you can't be choosy about whom you play with, you're just happy that you've got a gig. One evening you might be cooking with Django or Herman Chitterson and the next week struggling with players that were always north or south in pitch and rhythm of wherever it was they needed to be. Making music with some of these boys was like riding in a car that was always wobbling up on two wheels. It was all you could do to maintain your own balance, continue doing what you did, and not end up in the bottom of some ravine.

At least this is what Valaida tells herself, rather than riff on where she might have gone with the Johnny Pillitz Band, or push herself in response to what she hears coming out of the States, because if you don't have someone to push against, someone as strong or stronger than you are yourself, you could easily end up falling flat onto your tits, with no one in the vicinity capable of extending you a hand. So she keeps her chops in reasonable shape, swings as best she can, avoids the pain as best she can. She is the real thing here in Europe; she is Valaida, Queen of the Trumpet, and people are satisfied; but Cas McHenry wasn't people.

'You were supposed to be my friend.'
'I was your friend, Valaida Snow. I'm still your friend.'

January 1939. The Annual Bal des Elèves des Ponts et Chaussées at the Ministère des Travaux Publiques. A welcome gig, after holidays that had been more morose than absolutely necessary with all the constant threat of war. With Arthur Briggs. A good man, Arthur Briggs. Had been this side for ever. Knew the ropes. Dependable as an anchor, sober as a judge. You could mistake Arthur for a man of finance when he wasn't holding onto brass, but he played some solid trumpet, and he gave the folks around him a chance to shine. The Annual Ball of the Students of Bridges and Byways at the Ministry of Public Works. A welcome gig after too many weeks idle in Paris with Earl Sutcliffe Jones. There wasn't but so much stimulation you could get out of Earl. After he'd served his purposes, it was best when he got out the way, but here, idling in Paris, he'd run out of places to go. One cut buddy after another had taken the voyage home. All Earl had now was Valaida, so most hours he was either under the covers or under foot, and he was no longer smelling of violets.

Valaida had tired of violets. They spoke of spring, and in no shape, manner, or form was it any longer springtime in Paris.

The Annual Bal des Elèves des Ponts et Chaussées at the Ministère des Travaux Publiques. Herman Chitterson was supposed

421

to be playing piano, but Herman came down with a stomach complaint. He was entirely too adventurous in his eating was Herman, always ready to put some form of sea animal in his mouth, and what was a Kentucky boy like him doing sliding barnacles down his gut? Looking like a brown metal statue that's been outside in weather for too long a time. Turning the colour of verdigris. Arthur was about to send for a French boy when Valaida had suggested Cas. She'd been missing her friend, despite his aggravations. Cas couldn't swing as hard as Herman, but they'd have a few laughs and push the Paris shadows back if only a tiny touch. That's all she had wanted, to push the shadows back.

The Annual Bal des Elèves des Ponts et Chaussées at the Ministère des Travaux Publiques. It wasn't her best night. It hadn't been her habit to indulge in Earl's recreational compounds prior to working gigs, but on this night, for some reason, her disposition had been particularly unsettled. She wasn't sure why. Maybe because it was a new year and she was sick of wearing the burnt-orange satin dress, the seams of which she was constantly having to patch, maybe because she hadn't seen Cas since another argument over the way she and Earl were living had ended with Cas' announcement that Louis Barreiro had been killed in Spain, that when Louis and Gus Finlay had been caught when the Germans entered Austria, Louis had been sent back to Spain and shot because he had been on the wrong side of their war. It was just after the Germans had spent a night busting Jewish heads and businesses all up and down their country and Austria too. There hadn't been a way to avoid that one. *Kristallnacht*, the Night of Splintered Glass, had produced banner headlines in every piece of newsprint that anybody held, and on that day it seemed that every man, woman, and child had a paper in their hands. The pictures were unsettling, that Valaida could not deny, and she'd been quietly grateful to the Lord that she hadn't been born a Jew; but Cas had kept on going on and on about how there was no way to ignore what was going around them – war was on its way, and it was going to change their world – and Valaida had kept wanting to

422

believe that Earl was right, that this white people's mess had nothing to do with folks. It was too bad about the Jews, but they were not Jews. Valaida had liked and admired Louis, and no, it wasn't right that Louis had been killed; but it also wasn't right for Cas to be flinging Louis' death in her face. Could she have done anything? Did talking and worrying and arguing about white people and their politics change anything for Louis Barreiro or, for that matter, for themselves? All they could do was keep at the music, giving the people things to hear. That's what she was doing. That's what she would keep on doing. Cas had pinned her with a look and then walked off, just turned and walked away with not so much as a grunt. That had been back in November. Making contact over the holidays had been too much to accomplish somehow, so this night on the gig could hold some kind of weight, which was maybe why Valaida's stomach and underarms felt so twitchy and unsettled.

Needing to feel more settled, Valaida had gone ahead and had a taste of what Earl was offering, and it had had the desired effect. She'd twitched no more, but then the numbness had spread across her lips, making the buzz necessary for her trumpet much more difficult to conjure no matter which mouthpiece she tried. Disconcerted by the numbness, Valaida had wanted Earl with her at the gig – he was her 'manager' after all – but Earl had said no. He had said that the next time he laid eyes on that skinny black nigger, Cas McHenry, her so-called friend, who was so full of himself and knew best for the whole fucking world, he, Earl, would slit said friend's throat from ear to ear. He, Earl, had had enough from the big-word-talking, look-down-his-nose-when-he-had-nary-a-pot-to-piss-in, bug-eyed spider mother-fucker. There would be blood on the floor, and who needed the aggravation? Valaida had known that Earl was right to stay away. Having him sulking and skulking around always made her crazy, and yet still she wanted him there. Why? To bring matters with Cas to some kind of head? To bring at least something, somehow, to some kind of head because even red blood on the floor was better than all the endless grey of this Parisian winter they were living, when it was a brand new year, and she was still wearing a burnt-orange dress that had already seen its better days?

It had been raining. The kind of rain that should have been snow, that was wetter and colder than snow and took less time to seep through your soles, that pooled amongst the cobblestones to depths impossible to discern in the inadequate light thrown by Parisian streetlamps, so you didn't know what to avoid when you stepped out of your taxi. Valaida's shoes were wet before she walked through the door of the Ministère's grey hulk of a building, the hem of her gown as well, and there was no heat, as usual. The organizers of the Ball would depend upon the crowd to provide all necessary warmth, which needn't be too much since white people didn't get cold, just one of the reasons they were so strange. Or maybe they just ignored the cold, which made them even stranger. Valaida tried not to think of all the toasty, efficient heat that could be hers back home in America. She'd made her decision about America, and she wasn't about to go back there with her tail between her legs, not for heat or running water or a plate of fried-up catfish. *How long had it been since she'd had a plate of fresh, fried catfish, the crust crisp and crumbly, the flesh sweet as ambrosia? How long had it been since she'd blown her horn in a way that made up for the lack of catfish?* Valaida would spend at least the first set of this evening playing in her fur, which would weigh down her arm and might interfere with her fingering; but the likelihood was that this audience wouldn't know the difference.

Valaida knew very little of students, having never been one herself – a schoolgirl in a two-room, segregated excuse for a coloured schoolhouse, but never a student – nor had she played on the college circuit back home, but she can sense that the motley-dressed crew swarming the Ministry stairs were in their own most particular world that would only tangentially connect with her music. The students ignored the coloured woman climbing the stairs in the wet, almost elegant fur, carrying the instrument case. Their costumes were not the satin dominoes and powdered wigs one saw in the café magazines. These were makeshift affairs of pieced-together painted fabrics, crowns, shields, and masks made of cardboard and branches, faces painted with tempura and blacked with charcoal, rags braided into bewildering fantasias. Someone had plastered handbills on the stairway's marble walls declaring, '*Barcelona Mort!*' 'Barcelona Is Dying!' *and* 'Down with Fascism!' '*Fascisme En Bas!*', but on this night the students seemed intent on paying the state of the world no mind. They were laughing most of them, guzzling wine from unlabelled bottles, intertwining themselves into a variety of knots and couplings.

Arthur Briggs and the other musicians were clustered in a corner of the cavernous ballroom, where a combo of accordion, clarinet, trombone, and violin was serving up a characteristic French mix of melancholy and jaunty distraction. None of the boys made mention of the fact that Valaida was late. It was, 'Hey, Val, what you know?' 'Looking *ravissante comme toujours, cherie.*' 'Yeah, this weather is more than a bitch.' 'Hey *c'est Paris.* What do you expect?' '*Riens à faire.* Nothing to it, but to do it.' Only Cas didn't say a word. While other eyes had contained, 'I wonder what this honey has gotten up to,' or, 'Time to get down to business and earn that money. *J'espère que mamselle est prête à travailler*', Cas' eyes were almost a blank. His tuxedo is the same one worn in the summer of 1929, no longer fitting him so superbly and a bit faded at the lapels. His cufflinks are silver now rather than sapphires and platinum. As Valaida assembles and warms up her horn, Cas is going through arrangements with Arthur, nodding his head, making notes with a tiny shard of a pencil. Finally, he takes leave of Arthur and approaches. 'I should thank you for suggesting to Arthur that he give me a shot,' he says. His voice is distant and almost non committal.

'No should about it. You've done for me in your day,' she replies. She flicks a glance at his face, where there is no trace of a smile.

'Earl didn't care to come?' he ventures.

'He had other things to tend to,' she replies.

Now Cas is looking hard into her eyes. 'How are you doing, Valaida?' he asks, and Valaida feels her blood rise in response to the tone in his voice. Earl is right. Cas goes too far. What right does he have to be examining her eyes, trying to bore his way into her brain? He is not her daddy, and her daddy wouldn't have cared. To give her examiner something to look at, Valaida exaggerates her eyes' diffusion.

'I'm feeling just peachy, Castor,' she purrs. 'Warm and wonderful all up and down my body, and planning on having myself a grand old time this evening. How about you?' She turns on him then, giving his nose a muff of wet fur. 'Sorry to be delayed, Arthur,' she says, continuing on with the kitten riff; it doesn't matter if a man is happily married like Arthur, the kitten always does her job, 'but sometimes the things we girls have to deal with take more than their portion of time. Any changes in what we discussed?' Arthur doesn't chuckle in quite the way she'd expected, but his smile is benign enough.

'We'll start with "Spreading Rhythm Around," then "Mean Dog Blues", and "It Had to Be You". Then it's all yours, Val. You still wanting "Minnie"?'

'You betcha, Arthur. Now more than ever. Tony, your little hip friend got something to say to me?'

'Sure thing, Val,' says the bassman, Tony Rovira, handing across his flask. 'Help yourself.'

Nickel has a more distinctive taste than silver, but Tony's brandy is more about power than taste. It sets a match to the chemicals already sashaying up and down Valaida's highways and byways. She won't be needing the fur for so long after all. The walls' sconce lights shift slightly on their axes. Valaida takes another hit as the French group completes its set and Arthur announces that they are up. It isn't smart. Her lips are tingling and no more mobile, but Valaida is not in the mood for smart. There'll be no more kitten this evening. One of the kitten's wilder cousins is taking pride of place. Tony reclaims his hip friend, and Valaida's feet begin to move. There is a steadying hand under her arm as they mount the bandstand, which could have been Cas'. Or maybe not.

It is not an easy room. The ceiling is so far above them that it cannot even be spotted in the gloom. The walls are marble and distant from the bandstand. Ideal for sound to be swallowed up or echoed back with no kind of predictability. The band's set starts without distinction, the musicians hardly able to hear themselves play, let alone anyone else. Arthur and Alix Combelle, the alto man, have played many times together. They know how to blend what they do to nimble effect, but the life of this room seems independent of the music. Their 'Rhythm' is going nowhere. Almost no one is directing their attention to the bandstand. Some lean against the walls or one another. Some walk around in packs. One pack is dressed in brown shirts similar to what Valaida has seen on puffed-out chests in German railroad stations, patterning their movements on militaristic marionettes but not in time to 'Rhythm'. There is laughter, tinged more with hysteria than joy, and almost nothing that Valaida can contribute. The odd pepper toot, swaying to the rhythm that she's feeling more than hearing. Cas isn't finding it easy to catch a groove. That much she does know. It's been too long since he's played with this kind of combo, if indeed he ever has, but Valaida is in no position to gloat. Her breathing isn't free; her diaphragm is lazy on her gut. Her lips aren't vibrating; she's tried her back-up, left-of-centre lip position with no success. At the end of 'Rhythm', wanting to add her bit to the chord, she bears down hard on her mouthpiece, and it slams onto the red of her gums. Something she hasn't done since she was just beginning in Chattanooga. The pain of it shocks her diaphragm into an uncontrolled spasm, and what comes out of her horn is a violent honk, atonal and rude. Not at one with the 'Rhythm', from out of a place all its own, into which Valaida can feel herself sliding.

The band guys flinch, but then so does the room. If nothing else, at last a flinch in response to the music. As Cas lays down the outline of 'Mean Dog', doing better with 'Mean Dog' because the blues Cas always could handle, student heads are jerking toward the bandstand. Student bodies, some covered in nothing but paint, are now moving because of the music. Their movements are not dancing in the sense that Valaida knows. They are disjointed, off-beat stompings and gyrations, half the time with spouted gibberish besides, as though the Ministère was the set of some kind of Tarzan movie with the students playing the natives. *Ooga-booga, cheri. Diga-diga-doo.* Strange people, white people, very, very strange, not able somehow to simply move in a groove like folks, their bodies always struggling against the tide of the music, never giving over to the in-and-out, the up-and-down. But responding as they can to Valaida's growling honks. She's blowing them purposely now, and every time she does, she's hearing reverberate through this room a great, guttural groan. Feral eyes are gawping in her direction, some of them she sees, more of them she feels. She can smell their pleading. It is acrid and volatile. The pleading in these eyes is stoking the kindling in her blood, Earl Sutcliffe's pleasers, Tony's brandy, her own disassociations from where she is, what she is and isn't doing. She's needing to sate these eyes, herself as well, with what it is she has to offer this night. The fur coat is too hot and heavy on the satin dress; its burnt-orange is beginning to flame. The flame is igniting her flesh, her blood is seething. She's going to have to break free. Valaida doesn't see Arthur's signals to the guys to ditch 'It Had To Be You' and segue directly into 'Minnie', but she's ready for 'Minnie' when she hears its opening bar. Cas' piano chords are hammer blows to the skull. Valaida's mouth splits open, and Minnie slithers up and out from a chasm just north of her crotch.

Now, here is the story of Minnie, the Moocher,
She was a red-hot hoochie-coocher,
She was the roughest, toughest frail,
But Minnie had a heart that was big as a whale . . .

Her voice is breathy, but gravel as well. Her fur coat parts and departs on the 'whale'. There's a convulsion as Valaida purrs into her scat, a couple of yelps as well. The burnt-orange satin is fluid across her hips. Her nipples are standing to attention. The trumpet's caressing her side.

> *. . . She messed around with a cat named Smokey,*
> *She loved him though he was coke-y.*
> *He took her down to Chinatown,*
> *And showed her how to kick the gong around . . .*

She's tripping her voice along with the gong. There are bodies jigging along with her scats. Her brain is humming in tune with the gong, and Alix's sax is urging her on.

> *. . . She had a dream about the King of Sweden,*
> *He gave her things that she was needin' . . .*

Who knew how many of these kids understood her words, but who of them hadn't been dreaming of a better time and place, away from a Paris brought low by the press of impending war? They were here tonight in response to that dream. To go someplace else, just like Valaida. Valaida's scats are splinters of light leading them away from the gloom. They are picking them up, tossing them back. *Ree dah de doo. Bode dah do dah.* Valaida is laughing in her scats. The scats are rippling through her body, the students are following their path, and she wants them there. She can feel them there. Up and down her body. She's going to give them a reason to stay.

> *. . . Now Min' and Smokey, they started jaggin'*
> *They got a free ride in a wagon,*
> *She gave him the money to pay her bail,*
> *But he left her flat in the County Jail.*
> *Poor Min'. Poor, poor Min' . . .*

Valaida's hanging her head and shaking her shoulders in depiction of Minnie's distress, tumbling her breasts within their enclosure of orange satin. A howl is the crowd's rejoinder. Valaida lifts her head with a smile and gestures that they listen.

> . . . *Poor Minnie met old Deacon Low-Down,*
> *He preached to her she ought to slow down . . .*

Valaida's pulse is the pulse of the room. The students are hanging onto her every sound and move, every expansion of her ribs. Her lungs' exhalations fuel their hearts. Their minds are hers. They belong to her. 'What do you think?' Valaida calls out. 'You think Minnie ought to slow down?'

To which Alix helpfully chimes in with the French, '*Pensez-vous que Minnie devrez se calmer?*'

'*Non!*' comes Valaida's answer, and her chuckle is deep.

'No?' she asks again.

'*Non!*' the students roar.

'Well, Minnie didn't think so either!'

'*Minnie a dit, "Tant pis!"*' All eyes on Valaida as she directs attention to her hips, as she commences to languidly rock from side to side.

> . . . *Minnie just wiggled her jelly roll,*
> *Deacon Low-Down hollered, 'Oh save my soul!'*

Valaida is working the pistons of her horn in preparation for her trumpet break. There's a young man dressed as a pirate who is feeling her fingers not on her horn. Valaida laughs at the sight of his anguish. Lifting her horn up to play, she's aware of hot satin sweeping her bush, perspiration under her breasts and, vaguely, the band's music opening up her door, Alix's alto, the Christian boy's clarinet. Nothing but bangs from the piano. *Whomp! Whomp!* She plants her feet, blows her brass – and produces nothing more than a squawk. Her chops are still unresponsive, pillowy and numb. She works the mouthpiece in search of feeling, and some of the boys in the audience commence to scream. She licks her lips

430

and then the mouthpiece, and screams transmute into sobs. She manages a thin couple of triplets, running her left hand from the bell to the valves, swivelling her hips now in suggestion of Minnie's hard-working jelly roll, and again for emphasis. And again. And again. *Slam!!* from the piano, which Cas might be playing with nothing but his fists. Valaida has dropped all pretext of playing the trumpet. She is using it like a megaphone, broadcasting the spell of her scats. *She ho de ho. Bee de doo de dow. Hunh-hunh, hunh ha-hunh.* She's beckoning and teasing, moving close to the edge of the bandstand then rhythmically retreating from frenzied hands grabbing at the sweep of her gown, ready to crawl right up under it. Her head is reeling with the energy that is causing the room to spin. The room is chanting her scats. She is a priestess laying down law as she rocks back for her closing verse. Only she doesn't get to the close. Breaking loose from the arms of his friends, the Student Pirate lunges onto the bandstand, grabbing and ripping Valaida's gown with one hand, groping toward her person with the other, only prevented by Alix and Arthur, while Tony pulls Valaida up next to his bass. Valaida isn't frightened. She's enjoying the wood curves of the bass pressing along her torso. The Pirate's attack is all of the piece with the tempest of the evening and Valaida's pleased that she started the wind. As the Student Pirate is tossed back to his friends, Arthur is tying his jacket around Valaida's waist, covering what little is left of her modesty. A veteran of white people on the warpath both at home and abroad, Arthur is wary of the direction the evening has taken; but Valaida is laughing, and the students are stamping and clapping and yawling for more.

'What you want to do, Val?' Arthur asks. 'These natives are acting mighty restless.'

Valaida is only barely hearing what Arthur is yelling into her ear. Her head is filled with this evening's power, and she is revelling in its effect, which is stronger than liquor and better than any dope. 'I haven't finished my song yet, Arthur,' she says. 'I've got to finish with "Minnie". I've got to give them more "Minnie". I've got to finish my song.

'All right, Val. We'll crank it back to the King.' Cueing the band with a nod, Arthur sets up their re-entry with a trumpet peal of his own. Valaida is smiling broadly with their music at her back. It's missing some piano, but she doesn't pay that any mind. She gives the students some more of 'Minnie' and more of 'Minnie', 'Minnie' with less abandon, more commentary on the lyric, but 'Minnie' just the same. She keeps on Minnie-ing until she has no voice to give. The band 'Minnies' out their set. It makes no sense to try something else without a break. Better to let the French band change the mood. Valaida is exhilarated as their band returns to their corner of the room. She's had her grand old time, and Minnie has cleansed her blood. Her head is clear, and there's sensation in her lips. She'll be offering something else when the group returns for its second set, she has a new idea for the bridge in 'Swing is the Thing'. She's finally got good reason to be done with the burnt-orange satin gown, and in the meantime, Arthur's jacket is a distinctive fashion accessory that will remind the students of where they've been. Valaida looks around for Cas, wanting to gossip about the fun.

'Why did you have to be so hard?'

Cas had been standing apart from the group and apart from its good spirits. It had been too dark to read accurately the expression on his face. If she'd seen, she might have let him be.

'You had demeaned yourself.'

'I'd done my job. I'd given the audience what it wanted.'

'You'd demeaned us all.'

'Nobody else said a word.'

'Nobody else cared enough. Nobody else knew that you knew better. Nobody else knew what you could have been.'

If Cas' words had been harsh, Valaida's retort had been more so. She'd slapped him hard, more than once, and her ring had ripped his cheek. He'd held her wrist then, with a pianist's strength, and as she'd battled to free herself she had declared him a no-luck pathetic faggot, whose personality was as black and skinny and ugly as his body. No wonder neither friend nor lover wanted any parts of him. He had dropped her wrist then, even as Arthur and the band came to break them up. As blood had coursed down the chisel in Cas' cheek onto his frayed but immaculate collar, Valaida had vowed that she would not continue with the evening unless Cas left that very instant. Cas hadn't waited for Arthur to ease the situation. He'd picked up his coat and disappeared into the night.

'I can't be proud of my own behaviour either. I was unprofessional. I should have stayed. Maybe I would have if I'd been playing better.'

'Our second set was a disaster.'

'Did they notice?'

'Not really.'

'It all seemed so important at the time.'

She didn't see him again. Winter ended, and work picked up. In April, Valaida and Earl were back in The Hague again, without Coleman and so without as many shadows. The Hague led them to Scandinavia in June.

'Did things get better?'

'They went as they do.'

'I am so sorry.'

'I accept your apology, but you are not the Wicked Witch of my story. There were larger things at work.'

'Like you keep trying to tell me.'

'Like I'll keep on trying to tell you until you get it through your head.'

'My head's tired now, Castor, and I've got Minnie back in my heart.

'They took her where they put the crazies,
Now poor old Min' is kickin' up daisies – though not quite yet,
thank goodness –
You've heard my story, this ends the song,
She was just a good gal, but they done her wrong.'

'"They done her wrong." "They've done me wrong." You need to stop thinking that way, Miss Valaida. It's doing you no good at all. You need to take a look—'

'What I need from you, Castor, is a little peace and quiet.'

433

III Nocturne

Chapter one

SS Gripsholm, North Sea, May 30, 1942

I'm so weary and all alone
Feel all tired like heavy stone . . .

The sea is bottle-green, with hints of forest and jade, and celadon just before it breaks into foam. The foam's white is ivory and alabaster. The sky is grey, but not the colour of which she'd despaired. It is not the leaden oppression of her European winters and falls. Its variety is infinite and fraught with memory, the soft, warm grey of a Chattanooga field mouse, the dove of her father's spats, the pearl of his foulard back in the days when her daddy and Luck were the most intimate of friends, the pigeon of Nyas' London suit, the slate of a Parisian roof, the silver of her mama's hair. The sky goes on for ever, and Valaida finds beauty in this fact alone. There are things after all that can be said for the far north of

437

this world, counter-balances to the frigid darkness of its winters and the reserve of its inhabitants. It is three weeks before the first day of summer, which means these days are very long, and the sun's presence is strong behind the clouds. The sky is transfused with light, and it brings Valaida peace in this time of war. Valaida has learned more about the war since leaving Copenhagen. She knows that the waters at which she gazes with so much appreciation are under the control of the Nazis, that, in addition to Denmark, the Nazis have conquered Norway, Holland, and Belgium, every country bordering the North Sea but Britain. The Germans continue to bomb Britain and her ships and any vessels that might be heading in her direction.

Many of Valaida's fellow passengers worry about this. They worry that the bright blue and yellow paint job that declares the *Gripsholm* a ship of neutral Sweden will not be enough to deter German bombers hungering for a kill; but Valaida does not worry. She is too grateful for all this space and light to mar its spell with worry.

Valaida's not confining herself to her cabin this time. After so many weeks of confinement, after so many other months of diminutive enclosures, the clubs, her rooms, narrow stairways, and winding side streets, what Valaida is needing, what she is craving, is breadth and shine. There had been open spaces in Copenhagen, but these had been bristling with barricades and tanks and the ever-present Nazi 'grasshoppers' in their grey-green uniforms, bayonet-affixed rifles their malevolent antennae. Self-protective instincts dictated that you avoid them, even if it made your journey twice as long. You cleaved close to shadows, like a criminal, or a slug. And nothing could compare with this sea, so open, so wide. So barren of white people. Which was not to say that there were no Caucasians on this boat. Of course there were white people on the *Gripsholm*, and, as was now usual in her experience, Valaida is the only Negro in their midst; but there could be little more than three hundred souls including crew on a ship designed to accommodate a couple of thousand. There were many places to be where you encountered no people at all, where there was nothing in your view but sky and sea. It is two days since the *Gripsholm* departed from Gothenburg, Sweden en route to New York and these two days Valaida has spent almost entirely out of doors and almost entirely on her own. It is three weeks before the start of summer, but this far north the air is cool and that is good, for Valaida's wardrobe is limited. She has no summer clothes to speak of, no pert little shoes, no witty hats or flowered frocks. No trumpet.

There had been little warning. A guard had taken her to the bathing room although it hadn't been her week to bathe. The water was not clean, but not as cold as it had been. When she'd returned to her cell, the brown paper parcel that she knew contained her clothes was lying on her cot. The guard indicated that she should change. She had asked no questions. Her heart was in her mouth. She'd dressed quickly, gathered up her books, the picture, what was left of her pencil. She'd stripped the cot, folded the sheets and blanket neatly, organized her prison issue, then sat and waited, breath shallow, hands folded in her lap. There had been no ceremony. She could feel that her dress was loose about her body as she followed her keeper to Reception. There were two men in plain clothes standing off to the side. Their aspect had not been forbidding, but they straightened a bit as they saw her approach. She could feel that her skin was ashen. She'd bitten her lips to give them a bit of colour. The older of the men stepped forward. He spoke to her in English. 'Your papers have come through, Mrs Snowberry,' he said. 'My colleague and I will be accompanying you to Sweden where your passage has been secured on the SS *Gripsholm* on the twenty-third of May.' A mere four days away. Four short days between this hell and maybe redemption. The men had stood to the side as Valaida reclaimed her remaining belongings, the battered handbag, her few bits of jewellery, the razor blades, Earl's dice. She didn't want them to see her syringe. She'd hurried it into the handbag without checking its needle's state.

There had been complications in Sweden. The *Gripsholm*'s first commissioned sailing as a neutral 'mercy ship', that would circumnavigate the globe transporting the stranded and exchanging prisoners between hostile, warring nations, was delayed five days until the twenty-eighth of May. This meant five more days of Valaida living as a supervised guest of the Swedish state, which in Gothenburg meant the Spannmalsgatan municipal jail. There were differences, though. This was not Vestre Faengsel. The walls of her cell were open bars rather than concrete; she was allowed to continue wearing her own clothes. If her Danish escorts knew anything of her medical problems, they made no comment about them. When asked why she was under their supervision, they only spoke of her passport difficulties, and these they didn't consider a crime. The talented, vivacious lady in their keeping was a victim of wartime misfortune. There was no reason, therefore, that she should be confined in a cell all day long. They were more than happy to accompany her about the town.

She'd had to do something about her hair. There were people in Gothenburg who had her recordings, who had seen her perform. She couldn't promenade with her hair stuffed up under a rag. The Spannmalsgatan police woman had understood. She'd secured Valaida milder soap, some hairdressing oil, a mirror, and water that wasn't cold. It had taken hours to coax her comb through the months of naps, to slough the itch from her scalp, to oil and coil her locks into femininity. She'd almost felt like herself as she'd swept her hair into a style. Her face was thin, but it looked better when she smiled, so she'd spent some unobserved moments reminding her muscles how to produce a smile, how to flash it, how to maintain it, how to make it mischievous and coy. When her officers came to call, she was back up on her game. Or at least approaching her game.

She charmed them. She knew this because they took her arms to steady her across uneven cobbles in Gothenburg's streets and stood protectively by her side when the *Aftonbladet* reporter came to investigate what had happened to the 'once so popular Queen

440

of the 'Trumpet'. What were the circumstances of her confinement in Copenhagen? What had become of the one hundred-twenty pieces of Swedish railway silverware that had been found in her possession? Later, the Danish officers translated their replies. 'Miss Valaida had done nothing wrong,' they'd said. 'She has been a victim of disgusting circumstances.' The officers swore that Valaida had not stolen the silver in question. What was found in her trunk were the gifts of her many 'dizzy admirers'. Valaida had not been banished from Denmark. She only wanted to return to her own country, something understandable in these perilous times. Valaida did not question whether their chivalry stemmed from magnificence of her allure or the widespread Danish resentment of the easy life in neutral Sweden. She'd held her counsel. Valaida knew that the newspapers would be documenting the *Gripsholm*'s first departure and determined that she would not be the dark little smudge on an image of otherwise white Americans. She asked her officers for one final favour. Could they find her a trumpet, please?

Cas would have been pleased with the manner of her farewell. She had taken care with her appearance, mended her hem, brushed her coat, buffed her shoes. The sympathetic policewoman had brought her a parting gift of dusting powder and lipstick. Her smiles came more easily now, and her posture was erect. She was her best Valaida, chin-up graceful and apparently relaxed, as she stood among her fellow Americans waiting for leave to board the *Gripsholm*, neither inviting nor eschewing her countrymen's regard.

Her Danish officers looked more like her attendants than her keepers, following her up the gangway when her turn came to board the ship, one carrying her suitcase, the other an oblong bag. As expected, there was a gaggle of newshounds at the dock. As expected, an *Aftonbladet* man was among their number and her poise attracted his eye. 'Miss Valaida! Miss Valaida!' he called. 'Have you anything to say as you leave?' Valaida projected a grin from the deck with a precision gleaned from years of treading the

441

boards. She accepted the trumpet from her Dane with a wink, and peeled out a bar of 'Swing is the Thing'.

There had been no time to practise, and she hadn't blown in over a year; but Valaida had determined that she wasn't going to squawk. She'd been buzzing her lips in private moments, and nothing fogged her mind. One good phrase was not beyond her. Her pulse had quickened as her hand wrapped around the brass. It was a fine instrument that wouldn't trip her up. Her sex was tugging as her lips formed around the mouthpiece, as her breath and fingers formed the phrase, as the notes vibrated through the flesh of her lips and hands into her bones. What she had been missing. The stuff that made her whole.

She'd held the trumpet aloft at the end of her flourish, bowed to their applause, called out, 'I'll be back!', thrown out a farewell kiss and waved as cameras flashed. She did not allow the amazed chill of the Americans disturb her. She would not leave these years of living with her tail between her legs. It had not been easy to relinquish the horn, but better to leave it go with the rest of her Nordic life; for her farewell had been for show. She would never return to that place of darkness and pain. West was where she was heading. West was where the light was.

. . . Trav'lin', trav'lin', all alone . . .

SS *Gripsholm, North Atlantic Ocean, June 2, 1942*

For the past two days there has been too much weather to allow out of doors perambulations. Valaida has no cabin mate. The heavy-busted spinster who had been assigned cohabitation had gone agape when she'd stumbled over the threshold and seen Valaida's reflection brushing its hair in the cabin's mirror. There was too much room on the ship to necessitate aggravation. Shortly after the *Gripsholm* set to sea, a steward had appeared and removed the spinster's battered trunk. Valaida was pleased for the extra space, pleased to sleep and wake without the unpredictability of an American Caucasian pressing against her psyche, but out of doors is where she wants to be.

At first she'd spent hours wandering the ship's interior, going from deck to deck, peeking in empty staterooms, exploring what would be steerage, telling herself that she needed the exercise, anything rather than share common spaces with her countrymen. Mealtimes were quite enough, with their averted eyes or aggressive stares. Never a simple glance and back to business. Sometimes the beginning of a smile in response to her own, but then always some form of embarrassment or restraint, a hand on an arm, a whispered comment, a sputtering cough. It has been years since Valaida has had to contend with the idiosyncrasies of white Americans on a daily basis, and she finds herself out of practice. Her carapace is less resilient to their constant affronts. Some of their snubbing has actually produced a stinging in her eyes, something about which she is profoundly ashamed; but in these days Valaida has found that she needs the company of people, even if they are American white people; so, against all that she has learned to hold sacred, she has begun to frequent the second-class lounge. She sits off to the side with a book or some needlework, sipping some tea and wishing it was gin. Wishing it was something more than gin, wishing for that which made everything seem just right, at least for a little while. There are generally spirited discussions in the lounge, and through these discussions Valaida has been learning more about the war.

It's the Germans that are winning. In addition to Denmark, Norway, the Netherlands, France, and Belgium and of course Austria, Poland, and Czechoslovakia, they have conquered Finland, the Baltics, and the Balkans. They were in Greece and Northern Africa. They were pressing the Soviet Union. Italy is their ally, and Spain in all but name. For almost three years only the British have managed some true resistance, but until the Americans finally entered the fray this previous December, reasons for more than despair have been few and far between. There were huge hopes and expectations about what the Yanks would bring to the fight, but the tide hadn't turned as yet. The Jerries still had the upper hand. That was the reason that this crossing was so dangerous. The Germans ruled the North Atlantic, just as they did the North and Baltic Seas. Their destroyers were virtually unstoppable, their submarines more deadly than fighter planes. The U-boats prowled alone or in wolf packs, and woe betide any ship that came into their line of fire. There was some protection for ships in convoy, the safety of numbers if nothing else, but the *Gripsholm* was travelling alone. What kind of chance did it have? Swedish neutrality was no guarantee. Nazis were rapacious. To them 'mercy' did not exist. Valaida was listening now as she never had to Cas. If for no other reason than there was nothing much else for her to do.

Unlike the *Gripsholm*'s first-class passengers, who were generally believed to be businessmen and diplomats, all of the passengers in second class had dramatic stories of how they had come to make this trip, of making their way to Sweden from Finland, Norway, and Denmark after the Germans invaded. Of journeying even further, from Poland, Latvia, and Lithuania. From her little table off to the side, Valaida could observe hierarchies developing. Those who had travelled the furthest had generally suffered more terrors and depravations and so were commanding superior respect. Among those from Scandinavia, coming from Norway and Finland, where the German occupation was more brutal, was worth more than the Danish 'model protectorate'. Travelling after December 7th, when America entered the war and Yanks became official enemies rather than outside-onlooking sympathizers of Britain, was more perilous than leaving before. The deeper into the last terrible winter, generally the better the story. Travelling with children was good for heart-stirring anecdote. Christmas stories were good, but the New Year's hopes and fears were better. Loss or separation from a loved one could bring an end to conversation for as long as twenty, twenty-five minutes. Valaida was glad that nobody asked how she'd

444

happened to be among them, for she hadn't yet worked out what she would say. It was a cinch that it couldn't be the truth, even as she knew it. The people here would be too quick to categorize and condemn, and she wasn't about to give them that pleasure.

All who spoke were happy not to be Jews. Opinion on them was divided. Some spoke with impassioned eloquence about the plight of Jews that they had seen, known, or encountered, how their rights and property were stripped away, of their being rounded up in their thousands and sent off to prison and labour camps. There were rampant rumours of the treatment meted out in these camps, of train cars of Jews being herded like animals that had no value, of starvation, diabolic medical experiments, torture, and even murder. And wasn't it shameful that there seemed to be no place that they could run to, that virtually every so-called civilized country, even their own and Great Britain, were making it well nigh impossible for them to emigrate from this horrible fate? How could Christians and Americans, who believed in freedom and helping those less fortunate than themselves, look at the *Gripsholm*, and not be ashamed that it was practically empty? Others agreed that, yes, the predicament of the Jews was indeed regrettable, but that a country at war had to protect its interests and its citizenry from those who might exploit and betray it; and how could a nation that must direct all its strength to winning a war be expected to feed and clothe an unstemmed flood of the foreign and needy? And still others voiced the opinion that the Jews had brought their fate on themselves, that they were indeed the polluting influence of which the Germans spoke, and besides, they must for ever carry the stigma and pay the consequences of being the murderers of Christ.

The second-class lounge is not without its Jews. Valaida can see this, and she assumes that her white compatriots are aware of this as well. They are not many in number, but they are there. By and large, the Jews in the lounge hold their own counsel like Valaida, ostensibly continuing to sip their beverages and read their books, as though endeavouring to be as unobtrusive as possible. On the

445

first morning of the storm, Valaida saw a distinguished-looking older man shake with fury and start rising to his feet, but he was restrained by his wife. The couple did not return to the lounge after lunch, or indeed ever again for the rest of the trip, but Valaida doubted that the Christians took any notice. The presence of the Jews does not temper the discussions she hears, as though Jews have no feelings or opinions. Which Valaida can't help but notice is surprisingly similar to the way these same white people deal with Negroes. Whatever would Cas make of her noticing what was going on around her? Valaida feels a genuine smile beginning to play about her lips, not a smile to dazzle, disarm, or charm, a smile from the heart, which has a distinctly different and near-forgotten feel.

> . . . *Who will see and who will care*
> *About this load that I must bear?*

SS Gripsholm, Mid-Atlantic Ocean, June 5, 1942

There are no stars, only the faintest hint of moonlight behind the clouds. The ocean's ridges are black against black. There is a smudge of charcoal near the horizon, and the wind is teasingly slight. It is past two in the morning, but Valaida is not alone on the *Gripsholm*'s deck. Sound carries across water with a freakish clarity. There has been some kind of sea battle not too far distant from where they stand, one hundred knots away or less. The Swedish crew has been too busy to be specific. The passengers have heard noises, which crew members have assured them to be thunder. There have been flashes of light, which they have promised themselves to be only lightning while murmuring the instructions for night evacuations and re-tracing the steps of the day's emergency drills. Adrianna and Maxim are not on deck. No children are. Valaida wonders if they are frightened, but suspects that they have already seen so much in their short lives that they could stand as examples of courage to the woman who weeps into her husband's shoulder. To herself as well. Valaida wants a better view of the moon. There is the odd nod of greeting as she heads in the direction of the stern. Even white people can lose some of their arrogance in face of adversity, and because of Maxim and Adrianna, they acknowledge Valaida now because she, by way of the children, has afforded them some joy.

There have been no organized entertainments on this voyage, but a number of pianos are still in place, remnants from more peaceful times. Most evenings, some amateur tinkler would sit at a keyboard and lead off-key sing-alongs to numbers like 'Yessir, That's My Baby' and 'East of the Sun and West of the Moon'. Only the most inclement weather would keep Valaida anywhere near, but one afternoon having left the dining room after only a bowl of soup for lunch, she had heard the most extraordinary torrent of notes rushing out from the second-class lounge. The style was classical and the touch inordinately accomplished. Stepping in, Valaida was surprised to see not an adult on the bench, but a thin wisp of a girl, dark-haired, with an overly-large cardigan sweater over a sashed, faded dress, woollen socks drooping over scuffed, lop-sided shoes. She was playing from memory, and not simply for the sake of being able to do it. Her eyes were closed, and she looked as though she was feeling every phrase, her frail shoulders dipping toward the keyboard with an eloquence equal to the touch of her fingers on the keys. Valaida couldn't help but be mesmerized and was very happy that, after coming to the end of the first piece, the girl commenced on another; but the girl's brother didn't share that opinion. He was smaller than she and equally slight, pale, and shabbily dressed, but there was strength in the fists that banged down on the piano. After a sibling squabble in a language Valaida didn't recognize, the girl gave up her seat on the stool with an overly dramatic sigh. The boy seemed to be as gifted as his sister, if not more so. His piece started off classical as well, but then he threw his sister a grin and launched into what he must have thought was some jazz. Valaida laughed out loud, and the

447

children's heads swivelled in her direction, the boy withdrawing his hands self-consciously onto his lap.

'No, don't stop!' Valaida cried. 'Don't stop. May I listen?' She asked to approach with gestures, and the children solemnly nodded yes, their eyes not leaving her face for a moment, the boy making no move to resume. 'Are you going to play?' Valaida asked. 'I loved hearing you play. Don't go bashful on me now. I can hear you've been playing a lot. Play some more for me?'

The boy finally nodded, and started in again with his piece, the classical first then breaking the rhythm into what he probably wanted to be a swinging rag, but was closer to a double-timed military manoeuvre. 'Jazz,' said the boy, looking at Valaida with a dignity so solemn that she had to bite her lip to suppress a laugh. 'Jazz,' he repeated.

'Almost,' Valaida replied, bringing two fingers almost together. After a high-spirited, whispered exchange with his sister, the boy gestured toward the piano. 'You show,' he said.

'Oh, no,' Valaida replied. 'I can't play anywhere near as well as you do. I'll count. You play; I'll count. Go on, play for me.' His face scrunched into a determined scowl, the boy first deciphered then considered Valaida's words, then shook out his hands and started in once more. He charged through his classical bit, but Valaida raised her hand as he approached his 'jazz'. 'Now, slow it down. Slow it. Slowly, slower. Now, a-one, and two, and dah-duh-da, boom, da-duh-da . . .' As Valaida guided the boy into a swing, his sister's eye remained trained on her face. The boy was a natural. After two goes at half-speed, he started to really swing. It was eccentric, like nothing that Valaida had ever heard, but it was his and it was jazz. The boy's concentration was replaced by an infectious grin, and at the close Valaida was applauding. The boy was virtually dancing on the bench in the excitement of what he'd done. His jutting chin and impish cheekbones were reminding Valaida of someone she hadn't thought kindly of in many a moon, but before she could ponder the where and whats of Ananias Berry, the sister turned to her and spoke.

448

'Now you,' she said.

'Me?' said Valaida. 'No, not me. You both are so much better than I am. I want to listen some more.'

The kids would have nothing of it. The boy took Valaida's arm and pulled her down toward the bench. 'You play. You must play.'

There had been so much time and confusion since she'd been anywhere near a piano, been around anyone who knew anything about music, let alone prodigies like these two children. She didn't know whether her fingers remembered how to make a sound, how much pressure when, where to find the notes, how to work the pedals. Valaida had been performing nearly all her days, but for all her protestations to Cas about music and performing being the be-all, end-all, everythings of her life, that life now felt on the other side of an impermeable iron door, as separate from where she was now, on this boat, as she herself had been from freedom. Possibly lost from her for ever? If so, how would she find this out? Better here with no one around who might make her or break her. Better to know, and now.

The children's eyes were expectant. Better to start wlth something simple, something to make them smile. 'Ants in My Pants'. She almost winced from the unfamiliar pressure of fingers to keys when she went for the opening chord, but there was a flood of pleasure when the sound was true. 'I'd better sing,' she said, 'so I can disguise how much piano I won't be playing.' And so she sang. She was out of the practice of projecting; she'd had to clear her throat, start again; but then she was off, selling the joyous nonsense of the song to an eager audience of two who had no idea what the words meant. When she finished, they'd wanted more, wouldn't take no for an answer, and so she'd kept on singing. The girl wouldn't be drawn, but she got the boy down by her side for a bit of four-handed rhythm until her voice finally succumbed to the unaccustomed strain of singing out loud and she began to cough. Two small, strong hands patting her on the back were no particular help because the incongruity of it all was making her laugh as well. Then the pressure on her back changed. It was a

449

larger hand, a man's hand, and the other was offering her water. Gulping it gratefully, Valaida looked up to see a broad-shouldered man wearing a cassock.

'Better?' he asked.

'Better,' Valaida replied. Her young companions were now tucked up underneath the priest's arms. 'Thank you . . .'

'Pyzo, Stanislaw Pyzo, most often referred to in the States as Father Stan. I see you've met Maxim and Adrianna.'

'We've been having ourselves a very good time,' said Valaida, offering her hand. 'Valaida . . .'

'Valaida Snow,' said the priest, whose air was all benevolence and whose accent was American, Chicago more than like. 'I saw you perform years ago in The Hague. I enjoyed it very much. We'd hoped to meet you days ago, but the children have been sick. It is important that their lungs are clear when they get to New York. An Ellis Island quarantine is the last thing that they'd need after all they've been through already. Today is their first day out.'

Not understanding the English, the children returned to the piano, where Adrianna again began to play. 'And their parents?' Valaida asked.

The priest's eyes were pensive as they considered his charges. 'One can only pray. The children were studying in Vilnius when the Germans marched into Poland back in '39, but their parents had returned home to Lomza. We've heard nothing, and tracing is well nigh impossible. We travelled to Riga when Vilnius became too dangerous, then just in time across to Sweden. It has taken almost two years to get them visas. It seems even the youngest of Jews can arouse suspicion these days; but faith and friends have finally come through. They are very talented, as you can see.'

Lunch was well over by then, and the second-class loungers were returning to their now habitual seats; but, rather than return to their now habitual idle chatter, they listened to the children play; and in the listening they were visibly eased. The listeners

450

applauded the children, and, thinking to give them more of a show and having no inkling of the manner by which the ways of the lounge had affected their new friend, Maxim entreated Valaida to join him and his sister on the bench. Not wanting to disappoint the children, Valaida obliged. This time Adrianna took her by the hand, pulling a thumb furtively across Valaida's skin, then stealing an equally furtive look. The innocence caused Valaida to smile. 'No, sweetheart,' she said softly, duplicating the action and displaying what wasn't there, 'it really doesn't come off.' When Adrianna flushed with embarrassment, Valaida put a hand to the young girl's cheek to let her know that there'd been no offence, the flesh of that hand softening from the first tender exchange of touch she'd experienced in many a year.

The children's impromptu performance with Valaida so improved the spirits of the second-class loungers that Father Stan suggested an expanded version should take place the following afternoon. There was an amateur magician among the diplomats and an accomplished violinist among the second-class passengers as well. The violinist turned out to be the elderly Jew who had been so infuriated by the loungers' idle chatter. He was happy to play with the children in private, but refused to do anything more. The children were disappointed, but Valaida understood how he felt. She, too, had no particular need to please her fellow travellers, but Adrianna and her brother had slipped through a fissure in the husk that had been shielding Valaida from the vagaries of her surrounds for who knew how long a time. Performing was bringing a flush of healthy colour to their cheeks, and she'd found herself caring, happy that she was being of some help; but the performing was for herself as well, getting at least some of what she had back into shape before she was actually judged. The little revue had been a hodge-podge of styles and emotions. Father Stan had a guitar, and a steward a bandoneon. Valaida had sung with and without accompaniment. The diplomat magician had obliged with cards and coins. Some Norwegians had performed a fable in mime. The children had laughed, and so had Valaida, her ribcage aching from lack of custom with the activity.

> *. . . Prayers are sent to heaven above*
> *About our burdens, woe, and love . . .*

The sky is quiet now, no more thunder, no more distant fires. Passengers are returning to their cabins, to rest if not to sleep; but Valaida is not following their lead. Her anxieties would only increase within four walls, for they are not about whether a roving U-boat will launch a torpedo attack, burning in a shipboard fire, or drowning in a frigid sea. Valaida trusts that the *Gripsholm* will reach New York, that she will walk down the gangway and hail a cab to Harlem and the Hotel Theresa, but what and who will be waiting for her there? Valaida fears that the answer to that question is nothing and no one. Unlike in Sweden, no big city dailies will be at dockside ready to catch her every word. She will be invisible, a Negro woman making her way back into the world behind the masque, not worth so much as a sideways glance. Valaida will wire the *Amsterdam News*, Harlem's newspaper of record, and hope that she hasn't been completely forgotten. After so many years of Nordic reserve, Valaida has looked forward to returning to the warmth of her home folk, but will they embrace her or find her even stranger than they did before she left? There has to be some-one to open his or her arms. She's not feeling the energy necessary for the attraction of somebody new. In these last days Maxim has continued to remind her of Nyas. Nyas at his sweetest and most boyish, his naughtiest and most irresistible. She could go looking for Nyas, place her heart in his hands, ask his forgiveness, be his princess again. They were still married after all. Valaida's hands are trembling as she grips her rail near the stern of the ship. There's a wrench in her gut as she tracks the moon between shrouds of cloud. She hungers for an effective salve for these upsets, but the sky will suffice for now.

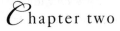

*C*hapter two

Small's Paradise, Harlem, New York, June 13, 1942

Saturday night. Her first Saturday in America. She has been home for five days.

Her heart had been pounding when they entered the harbour. Every able-bodied passenger was already on deck, clinging to rails, straining to see. A cheer had gone up when they'd caught sight of the Statue. There had been hugs and tears, but Valaida had been standing apart, eyes stinging, ears near-deafened by the pounding. She hadn't cheered; she had bitten her lip. The gangway was lowered, the immigration officers came on board, and lines formed in the second-class lounge. She'd seen the tension in Father Stan as a doctor listened to the children's lungs, seen his relief when the doctor nodded, watched them make their way down the gangway to a woman in an elegant hat. Adrianna had looked back before climbing into a limousine. She had spotted

Valaida and waved, then entered the shadowy opulence of the car. Into the parallel world, never to be seen again. What would the doctor have said if he'd had cause to examine Valaida and had heard her pounding heart? For those in the line before her it was, 'Welcome home', 'Good to have you back', 'I know you're glad to be back'. Valaida's processor had peered at her with a sneer. 'We heard about you,' he'd said. 'You caused yourself some trouble.' He'd examined her papers with the utmost of care, then grunted, stamped them, and waved her along.

She has been away for six years. What was that story of the man who fell asleep under a tree for twenty years and woke up to find himself dumbfounded by a world that had passed him by? Most everything around her feels strange, as though her six years away could have been twenty or six hundred. It is not just the being around black folk, being surrounded by English spoken by black folk. It's the happy glory of it all. After so much grey depression, to find herself surrounded by so much laughter, so much music and colour. Shiny cars. Pretty clothes. Yes, there are restrictions on fabrics. Skirts are more narrow and shorter, belts are thin. A lot of women are wearing twisted cloth on their heads instead of proper hats or encasing their hair in decorative nets. Shoulders are straight and hard, but folks are not walking around in dingy tweeds and mouldy worsteds even in warmer weather; and they're not always head down towards the gutter. Their heads are high; their eyes are shining. They're humming, smiling, children are dancing on sidewalks to music pouring out of any number of windows, from radios and phonographs and these new things called juke-boxes. Harlem, New York City, the United States of America are not enemy-occupied. They've been in the war for seven months now, but it all seems more a game than a strain. Save for Pearl Harbor, way the hell off in the middle of the Pacific Ocean, nothing has been bombed. There are no Germans in the streets, no tanks, no curfews, no refugees with their rope-secured suitcases and acrid scent. No sense of pervasive fear.

She had not characterized her pounding heart as fear, but it had continued throughout the cab ride up Riverside Drive, the turn into 125th Street, her entry into the Hotel Theresa. She was not totally destitute. Throughout her time in Denmark, a percentage of her earnings had been held in an account kept by the police. The *Gripsholm* passage had been far less than expected, only a service fee, so she could survive for a little while. A rooming house would have been cheaper, but she was not going to return to Harlem like some unwanted step-child desperate for shelter. Sweating under the weight of her winter coat, she'd walked into the Theresa lobby with her shoulders back, her chin up, with just a bit of swing in her hips. They had not recognized her at reception. They had been solicitous enough, but they hadn't known who she was. The shoeshine man in the corner, he had known. He'd come up and shaken her hand. He'd seen her at the Lafayette that time with Nyas.

'I'd thought you'd passed on or something,' he'd said. 'It would have been too soon, but you never can tell. Where you been keepin' yourself all this time?'

'Over there,' she'd replied. There was no need to get too specific.

'Well, it's good to have you home where you belong. Welcome back, sister. You still killin' 'em with that brass?'

'A girl's got to do whatever she can.' At last, a welcome. Her heart had begun to ease.

It is hot in the club, hot in a manner Valaida feels she hasn't known for years, the warmth of spring cranked up by the exuberance of her home folk. She feels it about her shoulders, up and down her arms, enveloping her like a cloak. The bar is thick with smartly-clad couples folding seductively into one another, rayon-crêpe shoulders under gabardine armpits, drape-covered thighs between naked, burnished knees. Dark heads, no blondes. Dark eyes, no blues. Jewels glinting from ears and bosoms. Doesn't matter if they're real. Lips shining, heads are, too. Ice, ice! clinking into glasses. Amber liquids seen through ebony fingers, through caramel fingers tipped in red. And over all of it, the driving band. A Harlem band, the house band, sporting no players she recognizes, playing more music than Valaida has heard since she'd left in '36. The difference is staggering. She feels herself staggering. She has heard good music. She has played good music. She'd thought that she'd kept up with the music by listening to records from home, but there'd been no more records after the war began; and what she'd heard had been shadows – recordings could only ever be shadows – and what she's hearing now is light, white-hot, like the sun full on you, right up there against your nose. Where would she find herself in a music blazing this bright? Valaida's heart is pounding again, and she is starting to falter when she feels Bessie's hand, a light support against her waist.

'Come on, honey,' says Bessie. It's hard to hear her above the din. 'Roscoe's holdin' us a table.'

The *Amsterdam News* reporter had called the day after her arrival. He had been courteous, save for asking about the weight she'd lost. The boy couldn't have had any sisters or a mama or aunts to think that kind of question was reasonable! But he had been receptive to her story, had listened intently as she'd described valiant Scandinavians preserving their hopes in the face of the Germans. Jerries, she'd called them, like they had on the boat. She'd spoken solemnly of the War, the deprivations she'd suffered along with her hosts. She'd even admitted to the time spent in the Gothenburg jail, while hastening to add that it wasn't a real incarceration, for she was allowed out from seven in the morning until eleven at night. She didn't mention her escorts of course, or the time in Vestre Faengsel. These things were nobody's business but her own. Then she had spoken of her love for Nyas. 'He's the only man in my heart,' she'd said. The only man in her heart.

The waiters are no longer dancing in Small's. There are a few whites sprinkled through the crowd, but they look to be music-lovers. The club's no longer a stop on a tour for slumming downtowners looking for jungle thrills. Harlem has changed. There are still plenty of folks scraping for every last penny, but

456

there are more folks with money as well. These are the patrons of Small's this evening, and Valaida is mesmerized as Bessie guides her to the table. She is back inside the movement of coloured folks, the easy lopes, the graceful arms, the comfort with which folks live inside their bodies, the way bodies have to move with the music because there is no other choice. Valaida's known that she's missed this, but she hasn't realized how much. She is choking on the emotion of being back among her own, as her body starts to ease, unlash the stays on some of her armour, loosen the mask that has ruled her public face these last Nordic years, not completely, never completely, but allowing that much more life into her self.

When the room telephone had rung around midday, she had been hoping against hope that the caller was Nyas. He would have seen the paper if he'd been in town. Everybody did, everyone looking to see if they'd been mentioned in the columns, everyone looking for the home folk take on what was. She'd composed herself before picking up the receiver, pitched her voice low and breathy, but it was not to be. The voice had been female.

'Valaida? Is that you?' it had cried. 'I just can't believe it! I thought you were dead. I thought you were dead!' It had then started to sob, which had made it even harder to identify its source.

'No, they didn't get me,' she'd countered. 'They tried their hardest, but I'm out, and I'm here.'

'I'm so glad!' sobbed the voice. 'I thought I'd never ever see you again!' Then something had clicked.

'Bessie?' she'd asked. 'Is this really you?' Despite what had happened in London in '35, despite the off-handed betrayal. Dearest Bessie, still loving, still loyal. Valaida was glad that she couldn't be seen. She was keening with gratitude.

A vocalist is scatting over a bridge, and they are drinking to her health, Bessie and Roscoe, Roscoe's brother Tyrell, and his wife,

Mary Lou. Bessie isn't dancing in the life any more. 'My knees just gave out, girl. They told me that they were through!'

She and Roscoe are working in his brother's catering business while saving up for a little bar of their own.

'We got our eyes on a swell place on Nicholas Avenue, and we're almost there! Just another couple of months.'

Bessie's filled out a bit – 'You got to try Tyrell's coconut cake!' – and her clothes have been chosen with more care, but otherwise she's just the same, same dip of one eye, the same smile devoid of edges. Roscoe looks solid in body and mind. His arm around Bessie's shoulder is loving and protective. His smile is easy, but his eyes are holding back. With good reason. His Bessie has been burned by this so-called friend before, and he's not about to let it happen again. Valaida is not taking offence. It's a view of the world that is closer than Bessie's to her own. The band has come blaring back under the singer, powering her phrases up to the heavens like Roman candles on the Fourth of July, notes bursting all over the nightclub like prismatic Catherine wheels. Valaida's head is spinning, her breath is coming in gasps. Every player on the stand is as good as the young boys that drove her out of the country in the spring of '36. She wants to tell herself it's not as bad as all that. Maybe once her ears have settled and she's feeling less raw, it won't all seem so forbidding, but right now she's wondering just how she's going to fit, where she's going to place herself in this new world to which she's returned. What she'd hoped for as home has all been remodelled, the old styles swept out, repainted, refurnished, the floor plans all changed. When the band takes its break, she's thankful for the respite. Three young soldiers are shown to a table not far from their own, mahogany and red-brown complexions fetching contrasts to their khakis, high, firm buttocks speaking volumes from inside the regulation slacks. They are a sight for appreciating eyes, and Valaida is thankful for this as well; but Tyrell is not so pleased.

'Damn waste, if you ask me,' he snorts.

'Tyrell, nobody's asking you.' Mary Lou's tone is wary. 'We're here to welcome Bessie's friend home after a long, hard time away.

Folks are here to enjoy themselves. Nobody needs to hear you goin' on in the way you do.'

'I don't mind listening to what Tyrell has to say.' Anything to keep too much thought of the music in her mind. 'You mean to say that you don't think Negroes should be involved in this war against the Germans? You wouldn't if you'd seen what I have, Tyrell. These Nazis are evil people. You can hardly imagine how evil they are. If you saw the devastation! If you saw how people have suffered, how they keep on suffering . . .'

'Who suffering? White folks? Let them suffer! They deserve it! Let them taste a bit of that medicine they been dispensin' all these years! Black folks shouldn't have nothin' to do with this war. We got no quarrel with the Germans. I used to travel, Valaida, just like you did. I was part of a bicycle act and we went all over Europe, Russia, too, ten, fifteen years ago, and those Germans treated us just fine.'

Mary Lou is shaking her head. 'I told you not to get him started. Now, baby . . .' She's putting a hand on her husband's arm, but Tyrell is on a roll.

'Don't be "Now, baby'in" me, woman! The sister's been away for a long time, and she needs to be re-introduced to what is. We Negroes got no quarrel with the Germans! Our quarrel is with these crackers right here, and 99.999% of the folks sitting in this room tonight would agree with me. You think those soldier boys want to be doin' what they doin' when they got as much chance of gettin' lynched down South in those training camps they insist on sending us to as they do gettin' killed overseas? How come they can't be trained up North where these greys ain't so shameless? And it's not as though they get to have some guns. Hell, no! You think them crackers want a bunch of evil niggers with guns runnin' around? No, our boys are out there building roads and shovelling shit and humping supplies they don't get their share of, with no other weapons to hand but their dicks! But their dicks are gonna wreak some havoc, let me tell you. A man's got to use what he has.'

The table has now burst out laughing, and Mary Lou's slapping Tyrell's chest. 'Nigger, I can't take you nowhere, nowhere!' The juke box starts in with a ballad, and Tyrell wants to pull his wife up for a dance. She pouts at first, then concedes, and they join a number of couples intimately shuffling across the floor. Roscoe would like to join them, but Bessie sends him off for more drinks. She wants to stay and talk to her friend.

'Your Roscoe seems like one hell of a guy,' says Valaida, watching him wind his way toward the bar. Another table has exploded into hilarity. The laughter is gravelly and rich. Its tones are particular. Valaida has missed them.

'Yeah, Roscoe's a sure 'nuff sweetie,' Bessie replies with a loving grin. 'I'm forever pinching myself that I could land me a guy like him. He's got ambition, and a job as well. Now, how often is someone like me gonna even run into someone like that? I didn't even get it at first, it was so damn strange!' The friends share a laugh. Valaida is watching the dancing, hips moving gracefully back and forth against one another, a copper hand caressing a black velvet neck, cane-brown fingers working heavy rippling fabric. No silks these days. Silks are for parachutes. Bessie steps into her reverie. 'Is it true what you said in the paper?' she's asking. 'Are you really wanting to get back together with Nyas?'

'Does that surprise you?' Valaida counters. She's liking the purr of the vocalist on the record. Billie Holiday. Valaida hadn't heard enough of Billie during the years she's been away. There was a tear in her voice that a body and heart could fall through.

'Well, I just heard . . .' Bessie continues. 'I mean it sounded pretty final when I heard you guys split up. But that's just what I heard.'

'Do you know where he is?' The force with which Valaida asks her question surprises herself and causes Bessie to look away towards the dancers.

'From what I've heard, he's back out on the Coast,' says Bessie.

'And nothing else?' Valaida knows that there's more Bessie could say, knows as well that she's not going to say it. Valaida, after all, has never been one to ask advice, or to take it.

'Nothing to speak of,' Bessie murmurs, facing Valaida now, 'but you know it's been a while, Valaida, one great big heap of time. The world has a way of turning.'

'So do I, Bessie, so do I, and Nyas always had a thing for the way I turned.' She's not going to be discouraged by Bessie's implications. Better to reek of confidence. Be the Valaida she ever was. Better to wreak than retch. Roscoe is back, he wants to dance, and this time he's not taking no for an answer. Valaida can sense that Bessie is happy to take to the floor. She watches the dancers and remembers Nyas' muscled leg moving rhythmically between her own, remembers the protection she'd felt during their best time.

Thinking of Nyas gives her something to hold onto. Better to think of him than where on earth she's going to be inside this music.

$\mathscr{C}$hapter three

California and New York City, June–July 1942

. . . Give me just another day
There's one thing I want to say . . .

Nyas was in California, so she'd taken the train to Los Angeles. She'd had to travel in a club car because every berth on every train was already booked for days, and she hadn't wanted to wait. The trains were full because wartime rationing on gasoline meant that you couldn't go long distances in buses and cars. The train was full, but its passengers were clean and not slumped over with the fear that had characterized European train travel during her last years abroad. Drinks were served. Decent food was available. Someone had a victrola, and so music was nearly constant. There was lively conversation and a good deal of laughter. Valaida hadn't participated, but it had been heartening to be around. No one acting as though they were worried about a war; it was hard to remember there actually was one. After years of Depression people now had money, much of which was changing hands in card games that went on for days. She was travelling by herself, but she was used to being quiet and alone, so these days were not a problem. The porters and barmen were still paragons of Negro manhood on whom she could depend for countless little favours, a pillow and a blanket, a towel, soap, and a washcloth, the serial use of vacated washrooms, a seat in the dining car whenever she chose, discreet protection from the odd Caucasian tempted to lose his sense of decorum. Valaida tried to imagine what it would be like to see Nyas after all these years, tried to imagine what she would say, tried to imagine his touch, but her mind was strangely blank. She was going to have to improvise with whatever he threw her way, but this notion did not disturb her. Improvisation was something she knew about, both in music and in life; so, in the meantime, she looked out of the club car's windows, drinking in the American spaces. Fields and skies without limit, rivers so wide that they made the Danube look like a stream. Cattle on prairies, too numerous to count, surging waves of cattle. Windmills that were only wooden frames, for drawing water rather than grinding grain. No towns with old stone buildings and narrow winding streets. No domes or gabled roofs. No swarms of grey-green grasshoppers capped with sinister helmets and bristling with guns. This land almost felt like her land and, after so long of having nowhere, the notion of her land was no bad thing.

She had forgotten how bright the light was in California. Without humidity to diffuse it, without tall crowds of buildings to obscure it, the light was a deluge. Holding fingers before her eyes as she disembarked at Union Station, Valaida felt like she might drown in its surging blaze. She was disoriented by its force and so was grateful when a Pullman Porter directed her to a Negro car service at the Station's southern side. It was good to be back amongst coloured folks that did for their own. Another something she hadn't known she had missed in her years of being the only

463

one. Valaida had spent long months in Los Angeles, but she was finding everything she saw during her cab ride surprising: the palm trees, the poinsettia bushes scarlet-bright next to stucco houses and Christmas six months away, the great width of the streets, the heat and the light, the exorbitant light. She had directed the cab to the Dunbar Hotel on Central Avenue but regretted this decision the moment she arrived. Even more so than the Theresa in Harlem, the Dunbar was the centre of what was happening in the Negro life of Los Angeles. All of the race's best bands stayed there. It was the meeting place of choice for those men who had found success in Negro L.A.'s professional and sporting life, and for the women who sought their acquaintance. Even more so than at the Theresa, these women were something to look at. Maybe it was all the sunshine and space. The fabrics of their dresses were more filmy and colourful. Their coiffures were more glossy, rolled on the top, and, for them who could manage, brushing softly towards the shoulders. Their flesh glowed with more health. Valaida caught sight of herself in a mirror and was not pleased with what she saw. She was not at her best. This California sunlight was so bright and so harsh. Staying at the Dunbar, with all its young and desirable women, women who had gone through next to nothing in their lives, Valaida knew that she would not be seen to her advantage.

Rather than check into the hotel, she'd asked for the use of their phone. She'd called Mr Evans, her chauffeur from her days at Sebastian's Cotton Club. She had always been generous to both Mr Evans and his family. When his oldest daughter was admitted to UCLA, the first in her family to go beyond the sixth grade, Valaida had paid Mr Evans a bonus to cover the cost of both a graduation party and the young lady's books. Mr and Mrs Evans invited Valaida to spend her Los Angeles time with them, and Valaida had accepted with gratitude. Mr Evans knew how to track Nyas down. He and Nyas had not stayed close after Valaida and Nyas had parted company, but no one in Los Angeles was more than two hollers away. Valaida's heart began to race as she pondered her direction of improvisation. She wondered if the skin on Nyas' back was still as soft as a child's.

Nyas refused to see her. No matter who Mr Evans used as a go-between, Nyas would not even do Valaida the courtesy of speaking with her on the phone. He sent back word that all the talking had been done. He even had the nerve ask Mrs Evans, 'Valaida who?' but then one day, when Valaida had been in town for nearly a week, a call came through saying that he would be willing to meet that evening at the Last Word Club on Central.

Valaida spent that day piecing her act closely together. Mrs Evans was a beautician who practised out of her home. She dressed and styled Valaida's hair to an elegance Valaida hadn't known since she'd left the States. She treated Valaida's face to creams and massages that she had learned working as a maid at a salon in Beverly Hills. The dressmaker who lived next door loaned Valaida a dress that was altered to enhance the more slender lines of her form. When Valaida arrived at the Last Word, she knew she was looking the best she could be.

The music was mellow and so was the light. It was a challenge for Valaida to keep her smile from running all up and around her face. It was important to appear neither too eager nor too desperate. Sophisticated seduction was still the ticket for her. A cigarette might have helped with this illusion, but her hands had been shaking; better not to show them off. After so long a hard time, to be loved again, protected again. She would work very hard to show love in return. She had done it before. She could do it again. With Nyas at her side, she would quickly find her place in the new world with which she's been confronted since her return from Scandinavia. Though she would be loathe to admit it, there was a weariness about Valaida. She had always known and demonstrated that she could live and thrive without a man, but she had also learned that, with the right man, life and work could be easier. Some time ago, Nyas had been that man. Their life together had been a harmony of musical and sexual good times. Valaida believed that Nyas could be that man again. All she had to do was

465

whatever he required, and she was ready to do whatever needed to be done.

A sax was growling seductively as the slender man approached her table. Valaida was not displeased with the backdrop. She'd taken a breath, shifted her shoulders, arranged her smile, and lifted her chin; but the man wasn't Nyas. It had been his younger brother, James.

'I almost didn't know you, Valaida, after all these years. You're looking . . . lovely. What can I get you to drink?'

'I'm fine, thank you, James.' She'd concentrated hard and maintained the smile. She was a pro, after all. Maintaining a smile she knew how to do.

'Let me buy you another.'

James had never been as handsome as his brother, and now there was a pool of perspiration gathering in the dip above his chin. He was a man who didn't want to be where he was.

'They've got themselves a nice little band here. Hell of a lot more swinging than them clunkers over in Blighty. You have to be glad to be home.'

'Yes, they do a nice job. Yes, it's good to be home. It's good to see you too, James, but why are you here? Has Nyas been delayed?' She'd known that wasn't the reason even as she asked the question. James's eyes had blinked several times before he could release the message he'd been charged to deliver. He could not look at Valaida directly.

'He's filing for an annulment, Val. He'd already done it before you got on your train West. He's saying that you never did get a divorce from Sam Lanier way back when, so your marriage to him was never legal.' The band had switched from fours to sevens, their offbeat right on time with the intake of breath that had stopped Valaida's heart.

'Never got a divorce? But I went through that, ten years ago. We went to court, and the judge found in my favour, and Nyas married me all over again, to prove to everyone that everything was fine! How can he say this? How can anyone listen?' The audience was

466

applauding the band's audacity, but what Valaida heard was muffled, the wing flaps of a thousand ravens.

'It's been a long time, Val, more than six years. There's been a whole heap of living . . .' James had spread his hands. A raven was tearing at Valaida's gut. There was bile on her tongue as she stepped into her space.

'Don't you talk to me about living, James! You can't say a thing to me about living! You know nothing about living! You have no idea all I've been through all these years! I wasn't in "Blighty". I was in Denmark, and in case you didn't know, there's a war going on over there!' Her voice had carried over the band. Folks had turned in her direction, but she paid them no mind. Her improv was composing itself in that place behind the conscious will. This cue James had fed her was not one she had planned on, so Valaida gave herself over to instinct. Technique would take care of itself.

'Of course I know that there's a war going on, Val. Everyone knows that has eyes and ears in their heads . . .' Their drinks had arrived. James gulped his desperately, but Valaida moved hers to the side. Out of the way of her play.

'"Everyone" doesn't know shit, James! Everyone here, listening to their music, drinking their liquor, they don't know a goddam thing! Everyone here laughing and talking trash . . . I was in a concentration camp, James! Do you even know what that is? You folks over here, with all your comfort and cigarettes, you've got no idea about suffering, about fearing for your life, about wondering if a bomb's going to blast you to Kingdom Come as you lie in bed at night, or if someone's gonna pull the nails out of your fingers just because it gives them a thrill. Those Nazis put our southern crackers to shame, James. They arrested me and put me in a concentration camp because they can't stand Negroes any more than they can stand the Jews, and they hate our music. They say it's diseased. They arrested me, the Nazis, because in Denmark I stood for freedom. They took away everything I owned. They threw me in a pen. They starved me, they beat me. Yes, that's why you hardly knew me, James! They beat me and humiliated me,

467

and all that time I was thinking about Nyas. Thinking about your brother kept me alive. I realized what a fool I'd been. I realized how much I loved him, and that love is what kept me strong. Those bastards tried their best to kill me, James. They looked at me and they saw just a little piece of a coloured woman, and they thought they could break me, but they didn't succeed because I had Nyas in my heart. That kind of love has to count for something, James! You tell him. You tell him what I just told you, and then he'll understand. He has to.'

James hadn't known what to say. His lips hadn't known how to lie on his face. They'd moved in and out as though they'd like to form a word but hadn't known which one to choose. He'd looked from one side to another as though hoping someone, somewhere would toss him some kind of a line and haul him out of this mire. Valaida's voice had stayed forceful as her emotions continued to rise. Folks had heard what she'd been saying when she'd gone into her Nazi riff, but no one around them would come to James's aid. They had gone back into their evening because that was the way folks were. Finally, James had drained off his drink and said he'd do what he could. He'd asked if he could drop her somewhere, but Valaida preferred to take a cab.

Sitting in the back of the ramshackle '32 Buick ordered from the neighbourhood livery service, heading west towards the Evans's home at Normandie and 33rd Street, Valaida had marvelled at the direction her improvisation had taken. She'd felt vaguely unsettled knowing that she had traded on those truly suffering in concentration camps, wherever they were, whatever the true dimensions of that suffering was. What, for example, had been the fate of Maxim and Adrianna's parents? But what Valaida claimed or didn't claim wouldn't affect the suffering of those people in one way or another. She had needed an extreme to put her message across to Nyas, and the truth just wouldn't have been appropriate. You had to use what you had, and what Valaida had, in addition to the trials in Copenhagen that she was happiest to forget, was sophistication and a knowledge of the

468

world. Not as broad as some, but certainly wider than that of the average Negro she'd find in Los Angeles, or anywhere else in fact. Why not use it to her advantage? What the hell else was it for? This riff on her Danish reality was the best shot that she had right now. She could only hope that it was true to its mark. She would wait and she would see. She would see and she would wait.

After ten days of waiting James telephoned the Evans's home. 'I'm sorry, Val. I did talk to him, I did, but it's just been too much time.' *Too much time.*

No more time for Los Angeles with its pretty young women and too bright sun. No more time not knowing what to do in Los Angeles. Valaida took the train back East. She got a Pullman berth this time, and she slept most of the way. When she wasn't asleep, she was craving a bit of comfort. More than comfort, oblivion. What she wouldn't have given for a bit of sweet oblivion.

. . . Trav'lin', trav'lin', all alone . . .

She had gone back to New York because she hadn't known where else to go, but she wasn't understanding New York, and she wasn't finding her place there. What she did understand was that her business had changed. There was a new generation, and its style was different. This Lena Horne, this Hazel Scott. So cool and smooth, so serious and hincty. Almost like they thought they were white, but neither of them anywhere near light enough to pass. They weren't like Nina Mae McKinney and the Washington sisters, Freddie and Isabel, who might confuse folk that didn't know what to look for. No, these girls were definitely brown. It was more in their attitudes, the way they held themselves. Maybe it was in the fact that they'd stayed in school for a longer time and all the hard living on the road that they hadn't had to face. This Ella Fitzgerald. Voice as clear as a bell, style as bouncy as a puppy. And Billie Holiday, who was still living a rugged life, but was using it in her songs in the way she turned the words against themselves, in the way it seemed to be inviting you to step inside of her pain, like you had her bleeding heart in your hand. This had not been the way for Valaida and the folks she had come up with. They had gone out and entertained. Their business had been good times, even with the blues. Some blues were sad, but they were always strong. If your heart was quivering and bloody, that was nobody's concern but your own. But both Billie and Ella knew their way through time and notes. You couldn't fault them on how they moved in and out of the music.

With the draft eating away at band line-ups, there were all kinds of girl bands around, and they weren't pathetic. Many of them were swinging hard, but Valaida hadn't changed her attitude towards girl bands. They were not her choice of how she wanted to present herself. When she was ready to present herself. When she had pulled herself and her chops sufficiently together, when she felt herself back in the world to get the process started. Nyas could have been her helpmate, but timing and luck were no longer her companions.

Valaida hadn't gone back to the Theresa. She hadn't had the money or the strength to stand up to its continuous exposure with the necessary air of blasé aplomb. Bessie offered her a bed, and she had quietly accepted. Energy and exuberance seemed to have deserted her as well. She was alone most days with Bessie and Roscoe working for Tyrell. The apartment was small so she took to wandering, just walking in whatever direction her feet decided to point. Morningside Park, Central Park, Strivers Row, Madison Avenue. Just walking, sometimes looking, but never being looked at. For the first time in her memory, never ever attracting attention. It felt as though she were a phantom people looked through, as though she occupied no space, exuded no personality. Then in the heat of one afternoon, she had wandered into a bar near 116th Street.

'Valaida? Valaida Snow? God damn, I heard you were back in town! And it takes you all this time to look up one of the best friends you ever had?'

It was Jack, Jack Carter, her old bandleader in Shanghai. 'Come over here, take a load off, and let the owner buy you a drink.'

He'd been running this bar for a few years now. Business was great. Folks had money with the war. Couldn't beat it with a stick.

'So, what you been doing with yourself since you got back?'

'Just taking it easy, you know, learning the lay of the land.'

'That makes sense. Shit has sure changed since you left, when was it, '37, '38?'

'It was '36.'

'Damn, you never lied! '36?, '36?"

She'd spent the rest of the afternoon there in Jack Carter's bar. They'd shared a bottle of genuine English gin, which didn't get unruly because Jack sent out for barbecue. They'd talked trash and remembered old times, and Valaida had laughed from deep down in her belly for the first time since she could remember, certainly since she'd returned. Which is possibly why she agreed to join Jack that evening.

'You know your boy Earl is up there playin' at the Apollo.' Jack's smile had turned foxy and low.

'You knew about me and Earl Hines?'

'Of course I knew about you and Earl Hines, the whole world knew about you and Earl Hines. It's no wonder that boy husband of yours got peevish. He was gonna have to get mannish on you some way or another even if he did have to wait until he had learned to shave, and what you doing messin' with these children all the time when there's Georgia prime nigger manhood wantin' to show you what it is?'

This was the reason. Knowing that she had no business going anywhere near the Apollo yet, let alone with her pretty-boy former lover Earl Hines on the stage, because her stuff wasn't tight enough, her shit wasn't sure enough, she had agreed to be taken to the Apollo that evening because Jack Carter had talked enough trash to make her believe that she was almost who she'd been.

It had been an old-fashioned good time. The music was balling. The acts were sharp. The comedians had tears running out of her

471

eyes and her belly tied up in knots. For the first time in weeks Valaida hadn't been worrying about how she was going to re-establish herself in her business. She had felt good in her seat in that theatre, surrounded by her people in spirited display of their glory. She'd felt glad to be alive. She'd felt she was home, and she had enjoyed Earl's set. Earl had always assembled musicians who came to play, and his current organization was no exception; it was cooking with serious gas. Valaida was happy for him, happy to hear him, happy to appreciate the drape of his jacket over his attributes when he left the piano to stand and conduct the band. She was looking forward to going backstage to give him a hug, maybe because Jack's party favour had enhanced her mood. '*Got a little present for you, Val, before we hit the Avenue. How long has it been since you had a brightener for the night?*' Jack Carter hadn't changed. He'd always been good for a bit of chemical transgression.

Earl Hines hadn't known her. It had been crowded backstage, but she had been standing right next to Jack when the men had exchanged their greetings. Earl had clapped Jack on the back then turned to embrace a beautiful young girl in a midriff blouse and sarong. As though Valaida was that phantom and wasn't to be seen.

'Don't you remember Valaida, Earl?' Maintaining the smile had worked her cheeks. Muscles in her jaw had wanted to quiver.

'You're kidding! Val, is that really you? You lookin' so fine I didn't even know you! We all need a taste of that cross-the-water you been drinkin'! Come in here to Fatha and let me give you a great big hug.' The embrace had been embarrassed and quick. The three of them had laughed together as though nothing had been amiss, but Jack's arm had been tight around her shoulders when they had walked back out into the night.

'Now, Val, I know you know that Fatha does like his sauce. He's so sloshed sometimes he wouldn't know his mama if she was beatin' him upside his head. It had nothing to do with you, girl. You're looking good enough to eat.'

Jack had always been a buddy, and it was as a buddy he'd offered her a bit of solace. They'd gone back to his room, and he'd stuffed rags under the door to make sure the smoke's odour didn't wander.

'*Not as elegant as we had it in Shanghai, and damn hard to come by with this war goin' on, but I figure you might appreciate some genuine transportation.*'

She had been transported, away from confusion and disappointment into the sweet kingdom of nothing. She'd caught a glimpse of herself in a mirror, hardly recognizing the woman she saw, and she hadn't cared. She'd lain back and closed her eyes.

. . . Friends are well when all is gold
Leave you always when you're old . . .

She needed to get back to herself, but she couldn't find the road. She washed and cleaned for Bessie and Roscoe to earn their patience if not her keep. She occasionally did shopping for the invalid woman two floors below, wrote the odd number for the banker on the corner, spent time with Jack Carter when he had supplies enough to share. It was never enough to keep her even for more than the moment the sharing occurred. She craved, but there was nothing to be done for it. Even if she had been willing to go down other levels of debasement, enough wasn't there to find; so mostly she walked, as though her feet might discern a way to Valaida where her eyes and ears and brain could not. The season changed. The air cooled. Leaves turned orange and vermilion. There were more uniforms in New York. Somewhere there must have been a war on.

. . . Trav'lin', trav'lin' all alone . . .

*C*hapter four

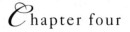

New York City, November 1942

Head bent down in misery . . .

There are voices.

'*I'm afraid she might do something to herself.*'

'*Do something? What you mean, do something?*' The voices are familiar. '*You mean top herself? What kind of foolishness is that?*' The woman's voice is sweet and less forceful than the man's. She is sighing now. Bessie.

'*I told you she's spent too much time around them crackers, picking up them weird cracker ways, that fancy way you hear her talking. Top herself? Niggers got no time to be thinking about such mess. Niggers working too hard just to survive. She needs to come down to the kitchen and spend time cleaning up some greens.*'

Hands are dressing her, putting her arms into a sweater, her feet into shoes. More than two hands. Four hands, all female, but one set firmer than the other.

'*Hush up your mouth, Tyrell, and help us get her into the car.*' A female voice, but lower, firmer. Tender fingers smoothing her hair into a hat, stronger fingers buttoning up her coat. Tyrell's wife, what was her name? Mary Lee? Mary Lou? Mary Lou. A strong arm underneath her armpits, raising her to her feet. Her ankles not holding, folding out towards the floor. Another arm scooping under her legs before she falls. It is cold outside. Her tears are freezing against her face. The car is well-kept. It smells of wax; its seat is firm. The tender hands adjust her coat before drawing her into a fur collar on a narrow shoulder. Not fancy fur. Rabbit or squirrel. A soothing hum into her ear as the car is put into gear. Bessie. Thank goodness for Bessie. The tears not stopping. Her own hands kneading wool.

. . . Nothing now appeals to me . . .

She had been in Morningside Park. *The sky very blue. Bluebird blue. Orange leaves against the blue, vibrating against brown branches. Vibrant against brown branches.* Her eyes had been aching from all the colour. She'd thought they were playing tricks. *Two figures on the path beyond, one slender, one larger, both in long coats, hats and slacks. Slender's skin is ebony. Slender presents a profile. It is familiar. Prominent forehead, chiselled cheekbone, bulging eyes.* She'd gasped, then started to run.

'*Cas! Castor McHenry! Cas! It's me, Valaida!*'

The figures had stiffened and turned. The face had been Cas', but it was female and sad. Dumbstruck, Valaida managed to stammer an apology. The Cas female was clutching another woman's hand. Not one of the three could move.

'*Cas wrote me about you often. I'm his sister, Polly.*' Pollina, his twin, with whom he had shared almost all that was in his heart.

'*Where is he, here in New York?*'

She had known that the answer was no. Polly had bitten a lip that looked so much like her brother's. The lovers' hands had gripped even tighter. Cas had always said that Polly had chosen not to live her nature. What could have occurred to change that? Valaida didn't want to know. The lover's voice was low.

'I'm afraid that Cas is dead.'

A bomb of light had exploded in Valaida's brain. Everything was shards, a kaleidoscope of blue, brown, orange, tan. Green and white. Black. And underneath, the sister's voice, feminine but phrasing like her brother's. Her brother gone now. Cas now gone.

'He was arrested in Paris by the Germans and sent to the internment camp at St Denis. I had pleaded with him to leave. First he wouldn't, then he said he couldn't. He didn't have enough money. There was no way I could get him some. I tried everything I could, and he refused to contact Alistair. Too much pride. A family curse.'

Polly had lost track of her brother for months, and then a letter had arrived by way of Alistair in London, with a note expressing condolences.

'There were blotches in the writing, and sorrow, and probably guilt. Alistair might have really loved him after all, but what good does that do now? What good does anything do?'

The letter had been written by a fellow prisoner in St Denis. Conditions had been grim, and Cas had been very weak. He'd contracted pneumonia. Death had taken him quickly in March, some eight months ago. Polly had come East to try and learn more, but the government knew little and cared less.

'Why should they? They tell me that there's a war on.'

The pain was too raw to share. Cas was expiring right there in the park before them. He was alone. His eyes were hollow with pain. To share would have been like putting him into a pot and stirring him over a fire. The agony was already too much. The women said no more. They parted ways, Polly walking on with her friend, Valaida staying where she was.

She had been lying somewhere hard when hands and arms had helped her to her feet. The faces had been blurs. Lips were moving but she'd heard only buzzing. Buzzing with a steady swing beat underneath. She'd been wet, then warm, then laid out on someplace soft. A warm spoon had touched her lips. Its liquid made her retch. All she wanted now was nothing. Better to accept nothing, when she herself was nothing and nowhere. There was peace in nothing and nowhere. The spoons had kept on coming. Sometimes their liquids slid across her tongue and down her gullet. Her gullet became warm, but she hadn't wanted warm. She wanted nothing.

    . . . Trav'lin', trav' lin' all alone . . .

'*I don't see why we have take her all the way down to 30th Street. We've got a perfectly good hospital right there in Harlem.*'
    The car jolts, and Valaida's head bounces against Bessie's fur-jacketed shoulder. It is frightening. Maybe it hurts. She mewls, and Bessie soothes, while Mary Lou continues to fuss at her husband.
    '*For your information, I spoke to Dr Cassidy at Harlem Hospital, and he said that for whatever it is that's troubling her, Bellevue is the best place for her to be, that they would probably end up trying to get her down there anyway, but since we had a car, it was better to go ahead and take her. So that is what we're doing, and what you have to do is keep your eyes on the road and drive this car, Tyrell.*'

Bellevue Hospital, New York City, November 1942

The car curved slowly, then stopped. The door opened. The wind was cold. More hands about her arms.
    '*That's right. Slide on over to the end. Are you gonna be able to walk? Tyrell's gonna have to park the car. You can lean on me and Bessie.*'
Mary Lou, sounding so clear and sensible, like she could deal with any kind of anything that might come down her way. As Valaida had once felt about herself.
    '*Come on, honey. Try.*' Sweet concern again. Bessie again. Who always came back, who never turned away even from those who

didn't deserve her, as Valaida didn't deserve her. But then, Valaida did not exist, so how could Valaida be deserving?

The room is large. There are many people around. The seat is hard. The ceiling is high. Bessie's hand is warm.

'*The doctor is ready to see her now.*' A white woman's voice. Business-like, but not unkind.

'*Can we come, too?*' Bessie, sounding afraid.

'*Yes, but it's better if it's just one.*'

'*You go, Mary Lou. You're better with this stuff.*' Bessie pulls her hand away. Bessie's lips press against her cheek. Bessie smells like nutmeg. '*You come back, Valaida. You get better, and you come back.*' She's always loved Bessie's scent.

Now she's moving smoothly. She's sitting up but moving smoothly. Into a smaller room. She is so very, very tired. The person across the desk has narrow shoulders. Valaida only wants to sleep.

'*Do you know where you are, Miss Snow?*' Another white woman. She is not old. She speaks through her nose. '*Miss Snow? Valaida? Do you know who's sitting next to you?*'

What kind of question is that? Where do you look for the answer to a question like that? There are murmurs. Salty water is making her nose itch.

Mary Lou's face is in front of her own. '*Valaida?*' Mary Lou's hand is on her cheek. It feels very nice. Not like Bessie's, but very nice all the same. '*Valaida, you're going to stay here with this lady for a while. They're gonna help you to get better. Me and Bessie will visit you whenever we can, and we're going to pray for you real hard.*' Mary Lou's hand squeezes her shoulder and then it is gone.

She is moving smoothly again. Through the big room into an elevator, which climbs very slowly. Out of the elevator into a corridor. Down the corridor towards a wall. There are large knobs and bars on the wall. Something clanks. The wall opens. She is moved forward into a very small space. Something closes behind her.

There are keys and bars. Again. She hears something scream. Something feels caught in her throat. Something keeps screaming.

Where is the sun, oh clouds above me? . . .

There is the sound of grating metal. She recognizes that sound. Not from hearing it just before now. And the time before that. And the time before that. From another place. Like this place. But the walls a different colour. The other place had a cot. And a slip of a window. Here there is just a mattress. On the floor. Without its covers. *What are these covers called?* They call to her. They pronounce her name as she knows it. The blotch on the ceiling resembles a bear. She saw a bear once, performing a dance in a garden at night, with coloured lights. The bear wore a tiny skirt, and a straw hat with flowers. They call out her name, but she doesn't answer. Why should she answer? What do they want? There is nothing to say.

. . . Where are the birds that used to sing?
Everything's wrong . . .

She is on her back. The ceiling is moving above her. The ride is not smooth. She shifts but does not fall. Something restrains her wrists. Her ankles, too. There are noises around her. Like in a zoo. Something warm and wet is pooling beneath her ass. It is pleasing, but then it chills. The ceiling stops. The light changes. This space is smaller. An odour is acrid. Yet another space. Murmuring people. A hand on her forehead. Two on her arm. Thin, wiry snakes. Something like sleep.

Her scalp is itching. A multitude of ants are winding their way through her naps, making far better progress than her fingers. Her hair is as dense as felt. Valaida needs a comb, and some pomade. She sits herself up. The cotton is rough beneath her hands. The sheets on this bed are heavy and slightly grey. She is in a bed and not on the floor. She vaguely remembers that there has been a floor. There are other beds in this room. Valaida is on a ward, but she is not in Copenhagen. She is in New York and she needs a comb. There is a woman bending over another bed, wearing blue chambray and a white starched collar, thick black stockings that are probably warm. The woman's skin is brown. She'll understand the need for a comb.

. . . Oh, where is the sun? . . .

She still has nothing to say to the doctors.
'*How do you feel, Miss Snow?*'
What was the answer to that? If she'd felt well, she'd have been on a stage, blowing her horn. She would not be on this ward, now would she?
'*What brought you here?*'
Probably a car. Her cravings and her pain are not their business. This is America after all, and you watched yourself with American white people. You didn't tell them your secrets. White people are far enough inside your head as it is. You don't give them more weapons against you than they already have. And their food is not for eating. Everything congealed in brown and grey. Vegetables meant to be green and orange, always brown and grey. They should not have tried to force her. The orderly's grip on her arm had started the tears again. Which had gone on for hours. This time she is more aware when they strap her onto the trolley, and she struggles when she is rolled into the room and she sees the box. She doesn't believe the coos of the nurses. She hears a scream and feels grating in her throat, but then she is pricked; and there is something like sleep.

IV *Coda*

The Palace Theatre, New York, May 1956

The notification that there are fifteen minutes before curtain for the United Jewish Appeal's third annual springtime benefit has concentrated the minds of those left in Valaida's dressing room. The Chapman Twins have turned their attentions from annoying Liz LaFontaine to anchoring the tinsel flowers that encircle their ponytails. They stand, stretch, gather their collection of juggling props and leave the room. The Twins are number three in the running order, and Liz LaFontaine is no longer swishing about their brain pans. These they have cleared of everything unnecessary to their performance. The Twins' immediate priority will be finding space in which they can prime their antennae. Neither Liz LaFontaine nor Valaida have noticed the acrobats' departure, nor are they particularly aware of one another. Focus is one of the reasons they have succeeded in their game, and the time for focus has arrived.

Valaida slathers two dollops of cold cream about her face, studying her reflection carefully as she does so. The red threads lacing through her eye have returned with a vengeance despite her recent rest. Is it her imagination, or is the high point of her left cheek sagging more than usual? She will have to follow the cold cream with an application of ice. This was the bother of being almost fifty-two. Valaida has been blessed with the illusion of youth, but these days flesh didn't always stay where you put it. There were good days and not-so-good days. You prayed that the Lord allowed good days when they were needed, but the Lord didn't always see things through your eyes. For which He undoubtedly had His reasons. Reasons you had given Him if you were interested in being honest. But then, what was honesty? What in this ever-changing world was honesty? The Lord probably knew, but He didn't always share His knowledge. Which was where faith came in. Valaida is still working on her relationship with God and faith, but thanks to Earle, it is closer than it was. Valaida's eyes soften as she thinks of her good Earle. After Earl the Feckless and Earl the Foul, her luck had returned with Earle the Good, her Earle with an 'e'.

Love walked in, and drove the shadows away . . .

Earle Edwards's timing could not have been better. Valaida's time in Bellevue had been a step in the direction of health, but her journey towards well-being had been rife with ruts and boulders. Jack Carter had continued being the best friend he knew how to be; but Jack's best wasn't necessarily good. Goodness was not Jack's nature, so how could it have been? Hustling, chasing the good chance, and feeling fine were the keys to Jack's nature, and these were tools he had used for Valaida. Valaida told Jack that she was ready to get back to work.

Bessie and Mary Lou hadn't agreed. They'd said, 'Valaida, please take some more time. You've been through so much. You need to get yourself together. You're welcome to stay with us just as long as you like.' But Valaida had noticed the looks that went between Roscoe and Tyrell, and she knew what they were think-ing; she had been there herself. Why should they be supporting someone grown to sit around on her backside, and she not even family? And Jack had understood.

They had been sitting at his bar during the slow time of his day, listening to Fats on the juke and sipping rye. Jack had studied her face dispassionately. 'I believe you, darlin',' he'd said, 'but let's be real. You know you've looked better, and folks will be wondering about your chops. I can see that you're ready to work but we're going to need us an angle.'

Valaida had wanted to work. She had needed to work, and she knew that many of the folks she'd come up with couldn't find a job. Bricktop had been in New York since before the Germans had invaded Paris, the same time as they did Denmark, in April of 1940, and Bricktop couldn't get arrested, their friend Mabel Mercer neither. So Valaida had told Jack the story of her concen-tration camp stay. She'd heard herself telling the tale as though she was outside of her own body and listening to someone she sort of knew. It wasn't as it had been when she'd blurted it out to James in California. The words hadn't come out of the heat of a moment. They had come out of a hollow, passed up to her lips from a place that was empty and cold, and hollow was how she'd felt when she was through.

Jack had grinned as he'd listened, and then he'd said, 'This is good.' He hadn't offered sympathy. He hadn't asked if it was true. He'd said, 'This is good', then he'd run with Valaida's angle like a backwoods chicken thief with a prize pullet under each arm and buckshot skimming his behind. In next to no time he'd managed her a week at the Apollo with the Sunset Royal Band. To promote the Apollo gig, he'd had drinks with Dan Burley, show business columnist for the *Amsterdam News*, and Burley had lapped up the angle like a cat brought to cream. 'Shaking the Harlem Grapevine violently' Burley had written that week then gone on to relate Valaida's angle, adding a few choice embellishments of his own. It was out there now. What had been a private improvisation on How

Dare He Ignore My Pain? had now been written down. It was her melody now.

Valaida had nerves at the Apollo for the first time in her life. For the first time in her life she had been worrying about how an audience would receive what she was offering instead of giving it no choice but to take what she was serving, with no doubts whatsoever that what they were getting was a feast. Doubts were more present in Valaida's mind at the Apollo than the songs she had come to sing. Was she too old-fashioned? Too thin? Too weak? If she had caught a glimpse of herself she would have wondered who the frightened wraith of a Valaida was hiding behind her eyes.

But the audiences knew. Apollo audiences weren't like the Europeans. They knew what they were looking at, and they knew what was good. They had been kind to her, the audiences, but she hadn't knocked them dead. They had applauded politely, she had bowed, and waved, and made way for the movie. She hadn't known guilt then. She had still been wandering aimless, trying to find her way. It had not been easy doing those five shows every day, knowing that she was nowhere near the Valaida she used to be. After the last show of the evening, what she had craved was peace. Jack had offered what he had, his personal route to feeling fine, and soon Valaida had been dancing with the Sweet King again, waltzing and trucking with the Sweet King, who was about to pull her into a deep and dirty grind just when Earle Edwards took a seat at a table in Jack Carter's bar and entered into her life.

. . . One look, and I'd forgot the gloom of the past . . .

She had been playing the violin because her lips were chapped and the violin was what she could handle when she managed to stay on pitch. She had been singing a ballad because ballads were what she could handle. She never could remember which ballad it had been, but she had seen Earle watching. His shoulders had looked fine in a double-breasted chalk stripe jacket. His tie tack had been pearl, and his eyes had been kind. He'd asked to buy her a drink. He had known her before, known of her at least. He had worked in theatre for a while, played the odd small part. He was a businessman now. He'd always loved her radiant smile.

Earle took it upon himself to help Valaida get her smile back, which was, in essence, to help Valaida get herself back. As alternative to the Sweet King, Earle offered love and faith.

'Give yourself up to God,' Earle said, 'and let Him help you find the way.'

'I've never let God in my life,' she'd replied. 'Why should He help me now? What would He have to gain?'

'What do you have to lose?'

Valaida had taken Earle's love, worked towards his faith, and her road had become less rocky. She backslid from time to time, still did because her nature was her nature, but she stayed the course as best she could, and her road became less rocky. With God and Earle at her side, Valaida got her chops and her style back, found a way to live her life doing what she could do.

. . . One look, and I'd found my future at last . . .

Backstage at the Palace Theatre, the violin prodigy's soprano arpeggios are lingering far too long in Valaida's ears, lending a pinging quality to the headache hammering behind her eyes. Stroking an improvised ice pack about her cheeks, Valaida is wishing that Earle was there to massage her neck in the special style that only he knows. Maybe she should have allowed Earle to come with her this time but, protective as Earle was, he might have wanted her to go home without performing tonight; and no matter how persistent the banging in her brain, Valaida has no intentions of leaving the Palace Theatre without doing what she's come to do. What had started as a work day like countless number of other work days in Valaida's long performing life has developed into something else, thanks to the histrionics of Hannah Eisenberg. Valaida knows that she should not allow her equilibrium to be affected by the hysterics of this little slip of a privileged white girl, so fearful about losing a man who was never hers to begin with that she resorts to accusations of wrong-doing about things that she can never understand. Valaida can tell by looking at Hannah, by smelling Hannah, let alone listening to Hannah, that this cosseted child has no idea about what survival might have been about in a Nazi-occupied country. So why hear this girl and feel stalked by menace? Never having had to fend for herself, Hannah Eisenberg was as unaware of the grey areas of this life as a Shirley Temple heroine. Valaida knows that she should be able to ignore Little Miss Hannah's aggravations, but Valaida's headache has been joined by a roiling stomach. *When you stayed on this road, you had to know that there'd always be menace, laughing in your face, before clamping you in its jaws.* Valaida slows and evens her breathing in an effort towards physical peace.

How could she have known? Nobody knew until the pictures came out, the newsreels and the photographs of American soldiers liberating a place called Buchenwald. The stacks of bodies. The piles of shoes and eyeglasses and tooth-shaped gold. The walking skeletons with their sunken, uncomprehending, gaping eyes. And this was not the only place. There had been many of them, many of them. Auschwitz. Dachau. Bergen-Belsen. What all those refugees had been running from. Which could have been something of what Cas had known. She'd felt herself shattering. Again she'd wanted nothingness, complete this time though and never-ending, but Earle had been there, holding her, protecting her. At first, Earle hadn't understood.

'But, baby,' he'd pleaded, 'now folks will understand what it is you went through.'

Until she'd confessed that this was not what she had known, that her camp had been a spur-of-the-moment fugue on a theme that had become her melody, that she had been hobbled by the Nazis, thrown off her track, absolutely; but it hadn't been this way.

'We must pray,' Earle had said, bowing his head and closing his eyes, to which she had wondered, What will God think of me now?

Valaida blots her face dry after the ice pack and is satisfied to see that the sag in her cheek is less prominent than it was. She removes the lids of the three colours of pancake make-up necessary to obtain the one colour she needs for her complexion and blends them with a sponge in the palm of her hand. She hopes that more Coca-Cola will soothe her stomach upset.

How could she have expected that one riff played in haste would acquire so much momentum? Negro soldiers had been among the Americans who liberated the European camps, so naturally the sepia-tinted world wanted to know more about these places, particularly as they had been experienced by one of their own. Valaida had been asked questions, invited to write articles. Most of the time she'd demurred, saying she was just so happy that she'd been able to get on with her life; but exactly what was it that she was supposed to do? Say, 'Gee, I'm sorry. I lied?' What kind of person would lie about experiencing this kind of horror? Should she have admitted that she had embellished her truth, when self-creation and self-definition were the only constants in the world in which she lived? What after all was the Greatest Show on Earth, or the Cleanest Clean You've Ever Seen, or a man in a satin cape cutting a woman in half? What about the European royalty given to tailoring establishments and marrying movie stars who were neither more nor less than suave and ambitious peasants? If no harm had been intended and no harm had been done? Could anyone claim that she'd done them harm? Earle had counseled that God was a source of infinite mercy. 'And besides, you have something that you can offer Him in return.'

Valaida knows that she has put in her time offering what she had to give in return for God's mercy. In addition to the benefit concerts, she has worked at settlement houses with the children of refugees. She has brought joy into young lives that have seen too much, far from the eyes of those who might find her jobs. And why shouldn't she have worked in the Jewish Catskills resorts? Better there than in the still-cracker South. And didn't she always more than justify her bookings by giving her audiences the times of their lives? Valaida knows that her ability to get good work despite the changes in times and tastes has been cause for jealousy among some she's known, but she is a child of the Lord now, so she doesn't toss her head in defiance, but neither does she feel guilt. Valaida's life has always been about work, and in the work is where she plans to stay, no matter what the Hannah Eisenbergs of this world might say.

The opening bars of 'There's No Business Like Show Business' can be heard through the dressing room walls as Valaida completes her make-up base. The evening's entertainment has begun. Valaida can see that she is looking paler than normal. She will have to apply more rouge.

Paul Goldman knows the song the band is playing, but aside from the refrain, he doesn't know the words, even though he was taken to see *Annie, Get Your Gun* when it opened on Broadway – What had he been? Twelve? Fourteen? – even though his sister Dolores had played the Original Cast record album until there was no music left in the grooves. Paul had blocked the show out of his mind because of Ethel Merman. Paul never could understand the appeal of Ethel Merman. You couldn't take your eyes off her, that was true, but that was because everything about her was loud, not just her voice. Ethel Merman was too brassy, too vulgar, a prime example of old-time, razzle-dazzle entertainment. As he buttons up the fresh shirt that Hannah went out of her way to bring him from his family's apartment on Central Park West, what Paul sees reflected in the men's room mirror is someone modern and new.

This has been an extraordinary day for Paul. What had started, as so many of his days have, with his fumbling with some task, in this case the transportation of Valaida Snow, and his characteristic attendant feelings of inadequacy and fear, his father Manny's son the *nudnik*, his mother's too precious boy had turned into something else. Valaida Snow had not hung him out to dry. She could have, not because Paul had done her a particular wrong, but only because it was in her power to do so. Paul has been accustomed to a world, his father's world, where people exercised their power merely because they had it. 'It's about business, Paulie boy.' That was Manny's motto. 'It's always about business.'

But Valaida had spared him for some reason, and then Paul had been able to find some ice, no big deal, but essential enough in that moment that opinions about him changed. Suddenly he was clever. Suddenly beautiful dancers were seductively batting their eyes in his direction; but for much of this day, Paul's attentions have stayed with Valaida Snow. He has been captivated by the heart-wrenching energy of her performance in rehearsal, as well as a sensuality that he had felt reeling him into her net, he a perfectly willing victim, and this taking place against a backdrop of Hannah's strange behaviour and tears.

Hannah needn't have been so frantic. Paul's watching over Valaida Snow while she slept in that bar had loosened the hold she'd had on her net. Asleep, with all guards down, the woman's age and vulnerabilities were easier to discern. Paul felt himself protective of Valaida, but no longer so mesmerized. So many experiences, such a wide range of emotions, in so short a time. Paul is loving the exhilaration of this show business world, this feeling of vividly living every moment, and he thinks that this is where he needs to be, but not in the old-fashioned Ethel Merman way, in a direction that was modern and new. At the moment, the only show business contact Paul has to his name is Mel Blumberg, this benefit's producer, and Paul knows that Mel won't be enough. The plans beginning to swirl about Paul's brain are going to require strong support, both in terms of contacts and finance.

Looking over who and what he has at his disposal, Paul suspects that he has been too harsh in his treatment of Hannah. It was, after all, very sweet of her to bring him the shirt. He wouldn't even have thought of it himself. He would have just soldiered on, guaranteed to end the evening looking and smelling like some lowly *schlemiel*, some unimpressive dogbody. True, Hannah had acted wildly erratic this afternoon, but, Paul realizes that her behaviour arose out of her affection for himself. While Hannah is not the wife Paul envisions for himself, there being no clear picture of whom he envisions for himself, that is not to say that they shouldn't be friends or some other form of partner. Hannah does, after all, have at least initial access to much of what Paul will need. Her family has influence in a variety of New York circles. Yes, Paul has been too harsh with Hannah. As he flicks his hair into place and dries his hands, Paul determines that he will be making some amends to Hannah, but first he ought to make himself useful in a way that Mel Blumberg will see.

Hannah Eisenberg stands in a wing of the Palace Theatre stage as the Benefit's singing, dancing chorus high-step and grin through their opening number, 'There's No Business like Show Business'. The air backstage is over-heated and close, but Hannah has chosen to be here, ready to hand out water and towels to sweat-drenched entertainers, rather than sit with her cousins in one of the top price orchestra seats they purchased from her last month. After the debacle caused by Valaida Snow during the pre-Benefit break Hannah's make-up and her silk shantung dress had become bedraggled with tears, and she'd had neither the strength nor the wherewithal to resurrect her appearance.

The Negro woman had been impassive, sitting across from Hannah in the diner booth as though she had no knowledge that she was turning Hannah's dreams into dust. She'd then left the diner without warning, with barely a word; and then Paul had turned on her, Hannah, as though she were the cause of the unpleasantness when it was that Negro Lilith who had caused everything with her lying about experiences in Denmark, with her systematic enchantment of Paul. Paul hadn't listened to Hannah. He'd called her a spoiled brat then left her alone with the embarrassment of a table full of food. After her tears had subsided, Hannah hadn't known what to do or where to go. Not home, certainly. Not all the way up to Morningside Heights and her mother's questioning eyes. Given her ultra-liberal opinions, Serah Eisenberg might have sided with the Negro woman, counselling Hannah to take the woman's under-privileged and persecuted past into consideration when looking at her behaviour. Valaida Snow looked neither under-privileged nor persecuted to Hannah, but she hadn't any more strength for that subject this day. Hannah had had her suspicions, gotten her evidence, and then been repudiated by the person most important to her life. She wasn't going to risk rejection by the next in line. No, Hannah Eisenberg would not be heading home. Instead she'd returned to the Palace Theatre's backstage area, she'd sought out the Lucy girl and asked if there was more she could do. Lucy had asked no questions; she'd just put Hannah to work at a plethora of stupid little chores, beneath what Hannah might have considered her dignity before this day, but more than welcome now.

Banishing headache pain to the furthest reaches of consciousness, Valaida is giving Eugene his once-over before putting on her gown, removing, wiping and oiling each of his valves, then putting them back again. Making sure that the valves are in alignment, tightening their tops. Removing and shaking dry his slides, applying a small amount of grease, working them back and forth, making sure that their action is smooth. Eugene was the first of her trumpets that she had named in quite a while.

It had been right after the war had ended, after the success with Fletcher, but before she'd scored with Basie. She'd been back in Los Angeles again, but in happiness this time. She and Earle had been married two years, and he was making everything right. Earle had said there was cause for celebration. She decided it should be with another horn. New. The best they could find. Eugene had sung to her just lying in his case. They'd toasted their good fortune that evening, the three of them, watching the sun set on the Santa Monica beach. Valaida had blown a paean to love, luck, and the mercy of God, and there had been no disapproving white folks around wanting them to move on. Eugene was Earle's middle name. It had just seemed right.

Other trumpets have come and gone in the eleven years since the war but Eugene has remained, just as Earle has remained. On a day like this, such consistency is reassuring. Valaida had never been someone with needs for reassurance. She'd just done what she'd wanted to do and the consequences be damned. How bad could any

493

consequences be when you were moving too fast to absorb a hit? But after Earle, her old style had changed. Maybe that's what came from allowing your heart into another person's care; you were no longer so self-sufficient. Maybe that's what came when you couldn't move as fast as you had in the past. Maybe that's what came from being on this earth a while. Valaida wasn't going to spend much time thinking about this set of affairs, just as she wasn't going to spend too much time wondering if the strength of this headache has been made worse by the foolishness of Little Miss Hannah's aggravations. Valaida has made her peace with her God about her time in Copenhagen. If He was satisfied, what had anyone else to say?

Valaida can hear the Benefit's chorus clattering up and down backstage stairs. The opening number is done. She herself is fifth in the line-up between the dachshunds and the violin girl, as expected. Figuring another ten to fifteen minutes of Henny Youngman's borscht-belt one-liners, she has a good twenty minutes before needing to climb into her gown, enough time for drops to clear her eyes as well as a brief, upright-in-the-chair form of rest. The drops' cool is a delicious pleasure.

Convulsions of laughter greet the witticisms of Henny Youngman, while, behind stage, Paul Goldman and Mel Blumberg share a laugh of their own, the older man chortling so enthusiastically behind his cigar that he begins to cough, the younger man slapping him on the back; and still they laugh. From her post in the stage left wing, Hannah Eisenberg is wondering what the two men are finding so funny, wondering as well about the new Paul Goldman who has emerged this day. This new Paul stands at once straighter and more relaxed, hips looser above his legs, hands more knowledgeable of how to position themselves. He looks fine in the shirt she brought him, smooth and cool despite the day's exertions. He's wearing a tie, but his top button is undone. Rather like Frank Sinatra. His eyes seem more focused, but what lies behind them is less clear. This new Paul's reactions cannot be predicted. Hannah watches from afar, as though at the behaviour of some exotic, magnificent bird, profiling, preening, astonishing her with the breadth and power of its wings.

Stepping away to give Mel Blumberg space to flirt with a chorus dancer, Paul spots Hannah fiddling with her towels and cups. Her hair is less ordered than usual, her mouth softer, and there are smudges under her eyes. She seems different, not the harridan of the afternoon's unpleasantness, and it is easier than he expected to direct a smile her way as he walks in her direction. 'I didn't know you were here,' he stage whispers towards her ear. 'I thought you'd be out in the audience with your cousins enjoying the show.'

'Yes, well, I changed my mind,' Hannah manages. 'The way things were . . . I just thought it would be better.'

In the theatre beyond, Henny Youngman completes his opening *schtick* to waves of applause and laughter. He grabs one of Hannah's towels as he barrels past, but guffaws at her offer of water. 'You gotta be fucking joking,' he yells, wandering off into the gloom. 'Mel! Mel Blumberg, this *meydele*'s trying to poison me! Mel Blumberg, where's my stash?' The orchestra is playing something that is probably Khatchaturian as the curtains part to reveal the Chapman Twins in an absurdity of convolution. Hannah suppresses an instinct to sneer because the eyes of the man beside her are shimmering with excitement. 'I can understand why you're attracted, Paul,' she ventures. 'This has to be more exciting than sitting by a phone in Manny's office.'

Paul's smile is easy on his lips. 'Look, Hannah, about before—'

The Lucy girl has appeared from out of nowhere. 'There you are, Clever Boy,' she rasps in Paul's direction. 'I need you to help wrangle those sausages on legs, and notify Miss Snow that she'll be on in fifteen.' On stage, the Chapman Twins are juggling flaming stakes. Paul squeezes Hannah's hand as he leaves. Lucy notices and suppresses a smile, for there is truly no business like show business.

Noting a flaw in her costume, Liz LaFontaine has abandoned the dressing room for emergency repairs in the Wardrobe Department. Valaida is alone, elbows on the arms of her chair, head bowed, breath even, eyes closed but not at rest, twitching intermittently as she wrestles her way towards the peace she needs.

The white girl's face is contorted in outrage. She is speaking, possibly screaming, but her oaths cannot be heard over the beating of the drum. Valaida cannot see the drum, but it has to be immense. Her bones throb with its pounding, its sound more felt than heard. Lights are flashing with the pounding, their flare blinding, overwhelming. In the flares, shards of memory. Mama saying goodbye in the Chattanooga dawn. Floyd bleeding to death on an Alabama creek bed. The disapproving eyes of all of her sisters. Frightened Jews on an Austrian train. Nyas pulling back in their final duet. Intercut with the white girl's anger that cannot be heard. Valaida hears a voice say, 'No'. She knows this voice. It may be her own. There is a door that vibrates with the drum. This door must be closed. It is heavy, intricate with detail. Valaida pushes against its weight. Her once-broken shoulder screams from the effort. The door moves. As it always must. Once the door is closed, the place can be pushed away. As it always is. But the drum still pounds. The trick is to counter-point a 'Sentimental Journey' to its beat.

'That's how you do it?'

'I haven't heard from you for a while.'

'I tend to be drawn when there's a particular need.'

'According to whom? I'm doing just fine.'

'So, maybe I was wrong And that's how you do it?'

'That's how I do it.'

Valaida's eyes have opened. She notes with satisfaction that her eyes are cleared of much of their scarlet webbing and that her left cheek no longer sags. Her hands are cool, but that is not unusual.

'You are indeed cause for admiration.'

'That, my friend, is what I've been waiting for you to admit.'

There is a light knock on the dressing-room door. 'Fifteen minutes, Miss Snow. Or maybe less. I'm not sure how these things are figured.' The young man's voice has transmuted yet again, still pleasant but ever less tentative.

'Open the door, Mr Goldman.'

And let me see you. Yes, this boy has changed. He'd be more amusing now than earlier in the day when Valaida's mind first toyed with his seduction, but her attentions now hardly flit in that direction. She is, almost, all preparation for her 'Sentimental Journey'.

Gonna make a sentimental journey . . .

Paul is amazed by the woman he sees in the mirror. She is not the vulnerable, diminished form over which he'd sat vigil in the bar. Her cheek no longer sags; it is buoyant. Her lips are full and coralled now, like her fingertips. Paul's adrenaline spurts as Valaida abandons the distance of reflection to face him more directly, whether from fear or desire he does not know. Paul's earlier instinct would have been to avert or drop his eyes, but he has learned today that he has his own resources. If Paul intends to travel this show business road, he will have to contend with powers like this one, capable of transformation, enchantment, and destruction all at once; and so again he smiles, having learned today that this smile has some effect. 'You know that I'm kind of new at this,' he grins. 'Lucy told me to tell you fifteen minutes, but I had to deal with those little hotdogs first. They took more time than I'd expected.'

'Are they on now?' Valaida asks.

'Just on,' Paul replies.

'Then I'm in the wings just about ten minutes from now.' Yes, there has been a strengthening along the young man's jawline. It might be interesting to keep a connection to his life. 'Tell me, Mr Goldman, did they pee all over the floor?'

Paul laughs and shakes his head. 'We're working on it, Miss Snow.'

'I'd be much obliged, Mr Goldman.' Valaida smiles as well, with perhaps less mystery than had been the case before. Detecting a niche of opportunity in the older woman's smile, Paul has not yet closed the door.

'You know, Miss Snow, when I came to pick you up in Brooklyn, I had no idea how important a day this was going to be for me,' he begins. Valaida does not encourage, but she does not turn away. 'I was just glad to get away from my father's office.' A bit of flush rising now. The earlier young man is not yet gone completely.

'And now?' Valaida asks. The young man's hand tenses on the door's knob and then relaxes. He may be on his way.

'And now, well, I've had a few ideas. They're not all formed yet, and maybe I'm crazy, but working with you today has set me to thinking that maybe there need to be more opportunities for white artists and Negro artists to, I don't know, work together, I guess.' Paul is liking the feel of hearing himself play with an idea out loud and in company. He is warming to the pitch. His teeth feel smooth against the inside of his mouth. 'I'm brand new at all this, of course,' he continues, 'and probably naïve. But that may not be such a bad thing, and anyway—'

'Mr Goldman, did you just give me my fifteen minutes?'

'I did, Miss Snow. I'm sorry.'

'No need to be sorry, Mr Goldman. I'd love to hear more about what you have in mind. Will you be driving me home?'

'Yes, I will.'

'Then there will be ample opportunity for you to tell me what you have in mind.'

'I'll look forward to that, Miss Snow.'

'As will I, Mr Goldman.' The dressing room door closes, and Valaida is back into the mirror. Good that she had already applied her lipstick. Amazing how colour lifted cheeks that have seen some miles.

'So the old girl ain't done yet.'

'Not until she's cold and mouldering in the grave. The kid could have something.'

'And if it's nothing but a pipe dream?'

'Dreams are what put us together in the first place, what keep us going, what we deal in.'

'The lodestar.'

'I've always loved your way with words, Castor, but you'll have to excuse me, unless you can help me into this dress.'

498

. . . Got my bag, I got my reservation
Spent each dime I could afford . . .

She is grateful for her Arpege as she stands waiting in the wings. Its cloud of scent is just enough to mask the ammonia of dachshund piss. Henny Youngman is on stage before the curtain, but she doesn't follow the words of his entr'acte *schtick*. The rhythm of Youngman's delivery tells her all that she needs to know. As he approaches the close of his bit, there will be a double bark at the end of a line of rapid joke delivery. The capping words pronounced between gaps in convulsive audience laughter will demand contributions as well as tie the jokes into a whole. As the laughter ebbs and the audience finds its breath, the comic's voice will turn conversational. Then he'll announce Valaida's name forcefully while gesturing towards the wings, and the band will hit the chord which greets the next entertainer while saying at the same time, 'So long, Henny.' Valaida buzzes her lips while looking into the band's pit to gauge their disposition. The contrast of the light of their music stands against the ink of the pit is causing her eyes to blur. Possibly more than during rehearsal. Possibly not. No time for that now; Youngman has entered his double bark.

'*So, you're ready, Valaida?*'

. . . Like a child in wild anticipation . . .

'*Go out there, darling. Tell the truth as you know it.*'
Youngman's money demands bullet between audience guffaws. 'You're going to put a Shaeffer to your checkbook. You're gonna give until it smarts . . .'

. . . I long to hear that 'All aboard'.

Youngman has moved to conversational, and Valaida onto another plane.
'*Show me that you care, Valaida. I'm pushing you now.*'

'When have you not been pushing me, Castor?'

Youngman has spoken Valaida's name and extended his arm. Valaida breathes deep as she walks into the music, now blending the welcome with a hint of her 'Journey'. The weight of topaz satin is pleasurable swivelling about her legs. Valaida does not care that Youngman's eyes do not follow his arm. He is not her audience.

'I push because you've always been my heart. Work your show, Valaida.'

'That's the only thing I know how to do.'

The welcome chord ends as Valaida reaches her position on the stage, the theatre's lamps adjusting their focus as she bends towards the microphone for her introductory patter.

'Thank you, ladies and gentlemen! It gives me great pleasure to join you once more this evening in support of this worthy cause . . .'

The speaking part of Valaida's mind has shifted to automatic. She hardly hears the words that she speaks with so easy a smile. Her eyes appear to look from this audience member to that audience member, but Valaida herself sees no details of their expression, nor does she need or care to. Her concentration is given to cueing the band for the opening chord of her 'Journey'. The spotlight intensifies as the band responds to her nod. The lamps have not been scrimmed in the manner she had requested. Their heat is intense, their colour harsh; but Valaida's eyes are shaded now with lids and lashes. The light of the Palace stage is not the light of which Valaida is thinking as she raises Eugene to her lips. It's that other light, the comet's light, up a flight of stairs, on the other side of a door, in that place her mama called joy. When things go well the steps are washed in the comet's tail. Its light floods from around the door. The Palace band lays down a carpet at the foot of the stairs to the light. Eugene's mouthpiece is warm, firm to her chops, but somehow flexible as well as Valaida steps on the carpet. The 'Journey's lyric is in her mind as Valaida fills her horn with sound. *Gotta take this sentimental journey . . .* Its notes are the words to her story as Valaida blows her way towards the light.

On the night of May 8, 1956, following a performance at New York City's Palace Theatre, Valaida Snow suffered a massive cerebral hemorrhage at her home in Brooklyn, New York. After lingering in a coma for three weeks, she died without regaining consciousness on the 30th of May. She was buried in Brooklyn's Evergreen Cemetery on June 2, 1956, her fifty-second birthday.

$\mathscr{A}$fterword and acknowledgements

Though I have spent a good deal of time and effort in the research of Valaida Snow, Her Life and Times, I emphasize that my *Valaida* is first and foremost a work of fiction, my own speculation on how this most extraordinary woman might have evolved to what she became.

Very little is known about Valaida's early years. Save for her birthdate and place and the names of the immediate members of her family, everything that takes place between 1898 and 1919 is the work of my imagination. From 1920 onward, I follow closely the path of her life to be gleaned from contemporary newspaper columns and articles as well as the work of a number of jazz archivists and historians. The clubs, shows, and cities in which she appeared, the known entertainers with whom she performed, the men whom she married, are all presented when they occurred but the personal and contextual are my invention.

When I began my journey to Valaida, I believed the commonly held myth of her incarceration by the Germans in a Danish concentration camp. I learned differently during the course of three research trips to Denmark, and the outline of her years in that country from 1939–42 follows closely this new information.

For their generous assistance in my Danish search for Valaida, my most heartfelt thanks go to Anita Hugau and Knud Ploughmann of the Royal Danish Embassy in London; to Jens Rossel of the Danish Music Information Centre in Copenhagen who organized my first research trip to Denmark, including a newspaper campaign that drew responses from Danes who had seen Valaida perform; to jazz violinist Svend Asmussen, radio journalist Mogens Landsvig, and to Mogens Skjoth, who shared their memories of Valaida in venues organized by Mr Rossel; to Arnvid Meyer of the Danish Jazz Centre; to Esben Kjeldbaek of the Danish Resistance Museum; and to jazz historian Morten Clausen for his unhesitant sharing of hard-gleaned specifics of Valaida's time in Scandinavia over the many years of this project.

For helping me get to the bottom of what can be known of Valaida's incarceration, my special thanks to Jens Tolstrup, Director of the State Prison Nyborg, to Ole Hansen, Director Copenhagen Prisons (Vestre Faengsel), and to Dr Peter Kramp, Head of the Clinic of Forensic Psychiatry, Copenhagen.

The community of jazz archivists and historians has been generous in their embrace of *Valaida*. I am most indebted to Dan Morgenstern, Director of the Institute of Jazz Studies at Rutgers University, for his translation of Scandinavian news articles and being the point of first resort for any number of connections. My thanks to Herman Openeer and Chris Ellis of the Netherlands Jazz Archive, Amsterdam, to Laurie Wright, Editor of *Storyville* magazine, to Richard Newman of W.E.B. Dubois Institute at Harvard University, to Bruce Lundvall of EMI-Angel Records, to Howard Rye, whose detailed research of Valaida's time in Britain and analysis of her Parlophone recordings was of immense import, to Jayna Brown for her work on Valaida in Sweden, and to Norma Jean Darden for sharing the fruits of oral history accounts garnered in her own search for Valaida.

Immense gratitude to Carol Criswell of Chattanooga, Tennessee for digging through the Hall of Records in that city and coming up with Valaida's birthdate, to Dr June Christmas and Eleanor Albert for information on the workings of Bellevue Hospital, to John Wallace on the workings of the trumpet, and to Trevor Battersby for additional Danish translation. For their personal memories of Valaida, my thanks to Evelyn Cunningham, to musicians Sarah McLawler, Harry Hayes, and Eugene Cairns, choreographer Cholly Atkins, and to Bobby Short, the first volume of whose autobiography, *Black and White Baby*, contained my first introduction to Valaida.

Any historical novelist consults a plethora of sources during the course of his or her work, but I would like to make particular mention of *Josephine: The Josephine Baker Story* by Jean-Claude Baker and Chris Chase for its insight into the lives of chorus girls during the early years of the twentieth century, *Thinking in Jazz* by Paul F. Berliner, and to thank Zora Neale Hurston for her wisdom on love, upon which I could find no way to improve before placing it in the mouth of Ruby Jones.

And lastly, my personal thanks to Diane Skene-Catling, to my editor Lennie Goodings for her encouraging support and infinite patience, and to my late and profoundly missed agent James Hale for his inspiring confidence and giddying championship of my idiosyncratic search for Valaida. James, you are in my heart.